"With each of the books in this series, Ms. Hunter's skill shines like a beacon."—*Rendezvous*

"Ms. Hunter has raised the bar, adding depth and texture to the medieval setting. With well-crafted characters and a delightful love story BY DESIGN is well-plotted and well-timed without the contrived plot twists so often used in romances. I highly recommend BY DESIGN to not only lovers of medieval romance but to all readers." —*Romance Reviews Today*

BY POSSESSION

"With the release of this new volume . . . [Madeline Hunter] cements her position as one of the brightest new writers in the genre. Brimming with intelligent writing, historical detail and passionate, complex protagonists. . . . Hunter makes 14th-century England come alive—from the details of its sights, sounds and smells to the political context of this rebellious and dangerous time, when alliances and treason went hand in hand. For all the historical richness of the story, the romantic aspect is never lost, and the poignancy of the characters' seemingly untenable love is truly touching."
—*Publishers Weekly*

"Madeline Hunter's tale is a pleasant read with scenes that show the writer's brillance. *By Possession* is . . . rich in description and details that readers of romance will savor." —*The Oakland Press*

"Ms. Hunter skillfully weaves historical details into a captivating love story that resounds with the sights, sounds, and mores of the middle ages. This is another breathtaking romance from a talented storyteller."
—*Romantic Times*

Also by Madeline Hunter

BY ARRANGEMENT

BY POSSESSION

BY DESIGN

THE PROTECTOR

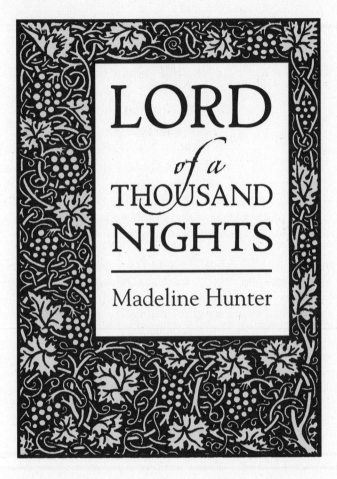

LORD
of a
THOUSAND
NIGHTS

Madeline Hunter

BANTAM BOOKS

LORD OF A THOUSAND NIGHTS
A Bantam Book
PUBLISHING HISTORY
A Bantam Book / January 2002
All rights reserved.
Copyright © 2002 by Madeline Hunter.
Cover art copyright © 2002 by Alan Ayers.
Insert art copyright © 2002 by Franco Accornero.

ISBN 0-7394-2216-2

Bantam Books are published by Bantam Books, a division of Random
House, Inc. Its trademark, consisting of the words "Bantam Books"
and the portrayal of a rooster, is Registered in U.S. Patent and
Trademark Office and in other countries. Marca Registrada. Bantam
Books, 1540 Broadway, New York, New York 10036.

PRINTED IN THE UNITED STATES OF AMERICA

THOMAS AND JOSEPH,
WHOSE SMILES MEAN MORE TO ME
THAN ANY WORDS.

MAIN CHARACTERS

❧ SCOTTISH

Maccus Armstrong: *Scottish Lord of Clivedale; he took Harclow from Morvan Fitzwaryn's father*

James Armstrong: *Maccus's dead son*

Thomas Armstrong: *Maccus's nephew*

Margery: *Thomas's wife*

Andrew Armstrong: *Kinsman to Maccus, and the steward of Black Lyne Keep*

Robert of Kelso: *A knight in service to Maccus, and the lord of Black Lyne Keep*

Reyna Graham: *Robert of Kelso's widow*

Duncan Graham: *Reyna's father*

Aymer Graham: *Reyna's half-brother*

Alice: *The cook at Black Lyne Keep*

Sir Reginald: *One of Robert of Kelso's knights*

Sir Edmund: *Reginald's brother, and a Hospitallar*

ENGLISH

Morvan Fitzwaryn: *English knight and dispossessed heir of Harclow*

Ian of Guilford: *A knight in Morvan's service*

Anna de Leon: *Morvan's wife*

Christiana Fitzwaryn: *Morvan's sister*

David de Abyndon: *Christiana's husband*

Gregory: *An archer in Morvan's service*

John: *Ian's squire*

chapter
ONE

B e sure he drinks the wine before he gets your clothes off."

The instruction was merely the last in a litany of warnings that Reyna had heard as she sightlessly felt her way along the cavernous tunnel.

She squeezed the thick hand of the motherly woman who accompanied her. "I will be sure to do it as planned, Alice. They appear a coarse lot, and this siege must be boring. He should be glad for the diversion."

"There's only one diversion most men are interested in, child. That is the danger, isn't it?"

"Do not worry so."

The total darkness in the tunnel terrified Reyna, so she moved quickly, one hand securely in Alice's and the other on the wall.

Sounds resonated through the stone beneath her palm. Sappers dug their own tunnel not far from this one. Over the months, she had come to this hidden exit, torch in hand, and listened, judging their progress. She hadn't worried at first, because surely help must come before they completed their work. It wasn't a large army that surrounded the tower house, and a small force from either Harclow or Clivedale could easily lift the siege. But no relief had arrived, and now the sappers were within days of reaching the surrounding wall. Even more worrisome had been the second excavation progressing on the southern side of the fortress.

They reached a sharp jog to the right. A sliver of light flooded through the narrow entrance carved behind an obscuring rock formation. Thick brush further hid the entrance from view, and only someone carefully examining the entire terrain had any chance of finding it. This army had not done so thus far, and Reyna smiled at the irony of all of that digging when the postern entrance stood just feet away.

"You will know by morning if I have succeeded, Alice. Watch from the tower and alert Sir Thomas and Reginald." Reyna took the basket that Alice carried, and tried to sound brave and calm. "I will go to my mother first, and then to Edinburgh. I will let you know when I am safe there, and you can join me."

Alice hugged her. "It is a brave but rash plan that you have, child. Sir Robert would not have approved if he were alive."

"If Robert were alive, I would not have to do it."

The older woman nodded in resignation. "God go with you, then."

Reyna pushed through the entrance and stood within the obscuring brush. Fifty yards away lay the camps that ringed the tower house. It was not a big army, but large enough to ensure that no one left and no provisions arrived. There had been no assaults, no wall scaling, no war machines hurling fire and stones. Nor had there been any negotiations. Just two months of relentless siege.

Men moved around the camp, their motions lazy in the summer heat. They didn't wear many clothes, and their bodies had browned in the sun. A few had adopted the cooler kilts of the Scots. But these men were not Scots.

English, she thought with disgust, and the notion gave her renewed resolve. The English had been the monsters of her childhood and the enemies of her youth. Their Scottish king may have accepted defeat by King Edward of England ten years ago, but no Scot, especially those on the borders of Cumbria and Northumberland, readily submitted to the authority that the English claimed.

She knew all about English soldiers, and what would happen if their sappers succeeded in breaching the walls. Descriptions of English atrocities had been repeated for generations. She forced herself to picture people she knew being butchered and tortured, and she sought strength in those horrible images. It was not in her nature to do what she planned now, but she saw no alternative. Hopefully God would aid her, and then forgive her.

She darted out of the brush and walked at an angle until she would appear to have arrived off one of the northern paths.

The men examined her, assessing the meaning of her unbound hair and silk gown. She marched on, circling around to the western camp and the large tent in its center. When it came in sight, she slowed. Once she entered, there would be no turning back.

A lewd whistle caught her attention. Two knights grinned at each other and began walking toward her, making obscene sounds with their mouths, taunting her.

Her skin prickled, and she ran the last few yards to the large tent with green-and-white pennants.

A squire sat by the entrance cleaning weapons. He looked up, startled, as she bore down on him, swept past, and plunged through the flap. She prayed that the man she sought was within, and that these others would not follow. Then again, for all she knew, he might simply shrug and let them carry her away.

The white canvas created a diffused, soft light, and it took her a moment to adjust her eyes. She looked around at the simple cot and table and chest that the tent contained. Polished armor glowed on the ground a few steps from her. Not a sound filled the space.

And then a shadow moved. A man rose from the stool where he had been sitting with his back propped against the tent's central supporting pole.

"What are you doing here?" he asked sharply.

She just stared.

She had watched this man from the top reaches of the tower house. He was taller than most, but when everyone is just a speck that doesn't count for much. However, she was shorter than most, and the marked difference in their sizes suddenly made her acutely aware of her vulnerability.

What she hadn't seen from the tower was just how handsome he was. Thick lashes softened and framed dark, brooding eyes that looked like liquid smudges in this light. Sharp bones defined his cheeks and jaw. A wide, straight, slightly full mouth compelled her attention. Dark hair hung to his shoulders, bound by a sweat cloth twisted and tied around his forehead.

He wore only a pair of loose peasant chausses, cut off above the knees. Those legs were well formed, all slender muscles and tight lines. The same athletic leanness shaped his broad shoulders and sculpted chest. With his primitive garment, he reminded her of the ancient warriors she had read about in Robert's books. He was the enemy, but her breath caught all the same.

Magnificent. Stunning.

Too bad she had to kill him.

He walked toward her. He gave her gown and hair and tinted cheeks a cool appraisal while he pulled the sweat band from his forehead and ran a strong hand through his hair. She hoped that he couldn't see her blush, because the woman she was today would never be disconcerted by a man's examination, no matter how handsome he might be.

His expression lightened, and he raised one speculative eyebrow. He had figured out the only part he needed to know.

He smiled.

Dear lord, what a smile. Close-lipped, straight, the edges barely lifting at the corners. Utterly charming, subtly suggestive, vaguely sardonic. It formed alluring little creases on either side of his mouth. It transformed the handsome face and fathomless eyes from distant and brooding to sensual and friendly.

But she saw something else as he looked down at her. She saw it in the casual stance of his body and the glint in his eyes and even in the smile itself. Conceit. Arrogance. Pride. Insufferable self-confidence. She read his awareness of the effect his face and body had on her. On all women.

She had met such men before. Her father's household had been full of them. Perhaps she wouldn't mind killing him so much after all.

"What are you doing here?" he repeated.

She gathered her wits. "I was called by the town of

Bewton. The town sent to Glasgow to hire me. The townspeople wanted to be sure that their gift would please you, Sir Morvan."

"Gift? Are you saying that the town bought a whore—"

"I am Melissa, a courtesan," she said peevishly. "I assure you I am no whore. That is why I am here. The town did not trust their bawds with such a duty."

"And what is the purpose of this gift?"

"They hope that, if you are well pleased, you will spare the town and restrain your army."

"And you have come to persuade me of this?" He stepped around her, examining her like an animal for purchase. She half expected him to yawn and announce that she wouldn't do at all. "The knight who gives such an order to his men would have to be very pleased indeed. What is the good of conquering if there are no spoils?"

"The town will pay tribute. There will be spoils enough. It is the barbaric looting and rape that they wish to avoid."

He reached out and stroked her hair, lifting a section, letting his gaze and fingers run along its considerable length. "What did you say your name is?"

"Melissa. You may not have heard of me, but I was trained by the famous Dionysia."

"You don't look like a courtesan to me, Melissa. I had always assumed that they were voluptuous women. You appear too puny and scrawny for it. Lovely hair, though. An unusual color. Very pale, like spun moonlight." He still held the end of the long strand of hair, and it hung between them like a strip of silk.

"What you call puny and scrawny, great lords consider diminutive and delicate, Sir Morvan. Besides, a courtesan's skills make such details insignificant. However, it is clear that you are base in your preferences. I will return and tell the town elders that they miscalculated."

"Nay. It was a brilliant strategy. There is just one problem with it, and it is not your size." He still fingered her hair. "I am not Sir Morvan."

"But this is the largest tent, in the center of the camp. I was told that this army belongs to Morvan Fitzwaryn."

"It does at that, but I command here. Morvan is occupied elsewhere. The main army is at Harclow."

No wonder help had not come. Everyone in the tower had assumed that Morvan Fitzwaryn had first besieged this outlying fief in order to have a foothold before he tried to take the more formidable Harclow, but the man had attacked both strongholds at once. And Clivedale, too? How big was this army?

She rapidly recalculated. If this man commanded here, the plan should work as well with him as with his lord.

"If you are not Morvan Fitzwaryn, who are you?"

"Ian of Guilford."

"And you truly command here?"

"Aye. The fate of this tower and the nearby town are in my hands. If the town sent you to negotiate, you have the wrong name, but the right man. Their gift was intended for me."

He regarded her in a frank way that thoroughly unsettled her. His gaze contained the consequences of failure that she had carefully avoided thinking about.

Her courage disappeared in a blink. "It is unfortunate, then, that you do not find me to your taste. I will leave now."

"I insist that you stay. You will lose your pay otherwise, and you traveled a long distance. It was churlish of me to criticize such a gift. Besides, if you were trained by the famous Dionysia, I doubt that there will be disappointment."

He stepped yet closer, and his dominating size and masculinity assaulted her. She groped for excuses to leave. "These men appear to be mercenaries. Will they obey you on this? No doubt they are to be paid with spoils."

"They are mercenaries, but they are my mercenaries, and will obey me. Morvan Fitzwaryn pays with silver, not the promise of looting. They probably hoped for some, but it was not part of their bargain."

"What if something happens to you?"

"I did not realize that the townspeople had sent a lawyer as well as a courtesan. Do your favors first require a contract with all eventualities covered?"

His words and look reminded her of who she was supposed to be, and why she was here. She thought of the danger to the innocents in the tower house if the fortress fell, and of the horrible death awaiting her if it did not. Her plan was the only way to solve both those problems.

"Let us get undressed, Melissa, so that you can show me this great art of yours." He coolly regarded the cot. "Hardly fitting for a courtesan. Would you prefer some furs on the ground? More room, then." He strode to the other side of the tent and scattered several large furs. "Aye, that will be better."

He began unlacing the tie on his chausses. "On your hands and knees the first time, I think."

She watched with horror this too rapid development of events. "Sir Ian, you do not understand. As I told you, I am not a whore. I am a courtesan. We do things differently."

"Really? And here I had made it a point to try it every

way there was. I look forward to learning something new."

Aye, killing him was not going to be hard at all. "That is not what I meant. Courtesans do not just couple like beasts. We create a whole mood and experience. There is much preparation and relaxation first."

His hands left his garment. "You will have to instruct me, madam. I am just a simple knight. I am accustomed to whores who do a man's bidding. I see that with courtesans it is the other way around."

"You will get all that you desire, and more. But I have been trained in many arts besides those. Music, conversation—Surely after living little better than an animal in these tents, a courtly evening must appeal to you. Here, let me show you." She marched to the furs, retrieved some nearby bags, and used them to create a bolster at one end. "Now, rest yourself. There. Isn't that better?"

He stretched out on the furs, his head and shoulders propped against the bags. She knelt beside him and lifted the cloth from the basket. She laid out the meat pies and wine cup, and then poured the good Bordeaux wine. She offered him the cup.

He sipped and looked over at her. "You will not have any?"

"Nay. It makes me less skilled. We wouldn't want that, would we?"

He nibbled at a meat pie and raised his eyebrows appreciatively. "Whether you surpass the camp whores remains to be seen, but your food definitely surpasses the camp cooking."

She beamed foolishly, and almost launched into an explanation of the herbs she had used before she caught herself. "Shall I play the flute for you while you eat?"

"Absolutely. This is a rare experience for a poor

knight like myself. I don't want to miss a single part." He rested on an elbow. She tried not to watch the cup moving toward his lips. *More. A deep swallow.*

She started a slow melody on the instrument. While she played she thought about the next few minutes, and what she would have to do. She prayed that she would find the courage to complete her mission. Success would lift this siege for a few days at least, until Morvan Fitzwaryn discovered what had happened and sent more men here. In that time, the others could go north to Clivedale.

Out of the corner of her eye, she saw Ian set down the wine cup. It was empty. She sighed in relief and missed a note. She missed another one when two fingers touched her arm and drifted lazily up its length to her shoulder.

Movement behind her. Hands pushing her hair over one shoulder. A face nuzzling her neck and hot breath on her skin. A kiss on her shoulder and teeth grazing her ear.

She stared at the white canvas, appalled that this stranger's attentions were unsettling her and making her breathless. The melody dissolved into a disaster of fits and starts.

She lowered the flute and glanced at him skeptically. His face was inches from hers, all smoldering eyes and sensual mouth. She looked frantically at the empty wine cup. *Go to sleep.* Unfortunately, Sir Ian did not seem drowsy at all.

"That was lovely," he said softly, kissing her neck again. "The little pauses gave the melody a poignant touch." He turned so that his torso faced hers. "You are lovely," he murmured, easing her head toward his.

He kissed her almost languidly. It was more a lover's kiss than a ravishment, and it deepened slowly, summon-

ing something inside her that she didn't control, something made expectant from long abstinence. A delicious
anticipation awoke and stretched and scampered
through her limbs in a scandalous way. Reyna should
push him away, but the courtesan Melissa certainly
would not and so she suffered it, painfully aware that she
wasn't suffering nearly as much as she should be. She
tried to block out her shocking response, and her befud-
dled mind silently chanted a command for him to sleep,
damn it, sleep.

He separated from her. His expression was indescrib-
able. Warmth. Desire. The promise of untold pleasure. He
rested on one arm and his naked torso hovered, almost
touching her shoulder. That forbidden something inside
her thrilled in response against her will. She couldn't take
her eyes off his incredible face. She couldn't move.

"Do not be embarrassed," he said. "Surely enjoying
yourself on occasion is permitted." He looked down and
ran his fingers along the edge of her gown where it
plunged to the top of her breasts. He leaned forward and
kissed the skin exposed by the low-cut garment. The
strangest thrill crawled through her whole body. She
watched, mesmerized, as that hand eased the fabric off
her shoulder.

Be sure he drinks the wine before he gets your clothes off.

She found her senses. She leaned away and forced a
little laugh. She tried to look like the practiced courtesan determined to play out the game a certain way. "You
have finished your wine," she said, reaching for the flask
and cup. "Let me pour you some more." *Lots more.*

He gave her a look that said he would do it her way
for a while, but not much longer. He moved back to the
bolster and stretched out. She turned in time to see the
cup at his lips.

She forced control on the unsettled blood in her veins. "Now we talk," she said firmly. "Finish your wine and tell me how you came here."

"I do the talking? You are the one trained in the art of conversation."

"I am trained to listen. Men enjoy talking about themselves, and we listen."

"I do not enjoy talking about myself. You talk."

"Me? About what?"

"You can talk about me. You can tell me how handsome I am and admire my face and body. Women always do that."

"Do they indeed?" How convenient of him to remind her of his conceit just when she needed help in disliking him. If this preening stallion expected her to sigh over his beauty, he had another thought . . . She did sigh, but at the pointlessness of her rancor. The wine should take effect very soon now. Lord knew he had drunk enough.

She grimaced and turned toward him. His eyes looked closed.

He took her hand and laid it on his chest. It pulled her forward a little, and she noticed that his lids were open a slit and that he watched her. Nay, she might not mind killing him one bit after this humiliation.

She pasted a smile on her face and began tracing the lines of his shoulders and the muscles of his chest. Her mind scrambled for appropriate phrases. "You are certainly a very handsome man. Very beautiful eyes and a charming smile. And your body is strong and lean." Dear saints, courtesans and whores definitely earned every penny. *Go to sleep, you conceited idiot.* "Not bulky and hairy like some fighting men."

"What do you like best?" His voice sounded drowsy and slow.

"Uh . . . well, these hollows along your collar line are very alluring . . ."

His hand rose languidly and wrapped in the lengths of her hair. He pulled gently, guiding her head down. "Then kiss them, madam. And then the rest of me. Isn't a courtesan's greatest talent in her mouth?"

She found her face inches from his and those smoldering eyes regarding her from beneath their lowered lids. Her breasts hovered over him, grazing him a little, and her ridiculous, traitorous body tingled. Gritting her teeth, she bent her neck and pressed her lips to the hollow above his collarbone.

Skin. Warmth. That intoxicating male scent. A gentle but controlling hand on her head guided her lower, to his chest.

Sleep, damn you. She kissed his chest and tried to disregard the stunning, frightening intimacy the action evoked. He was the enemy, a stranger, and she hated him, but something inside her ignored that.

He guided her lower, to his torso and stomach . . .

Suddenly, the hand at her head went slack. She held her breath, and waited for the utter stillness that said he slept.

Cautiously, she slipped away from his body. His arm fell limply to his side.

She pulled the basket over and dumped out the rest of the pies. She pulled aside the loosely stitched cloth that made a fake bottom, and stared at the steel dagger hiding below it.

For Alice and the other women. Aye, even for Margery. For Reginald, and even for Thomas for that matter.

She lifted the dagger. She looked regretfully at the beautiful man laid out like a drugged sacrificial victim.

He appeared helpless all of a sudden, sleeping like a child, and she suddenly imagined him as such, innocent and fresh. Her heart twisted in rebellion at this course she had set for herself.

She raised the dagger, clasping it with both hands, its lethal point aimed at his heart. Her arms shook, her body shook, the knife itself wavered in the air.

She tried again to summon courage from her fear for her friends. When that didn't work, she turned to her fear for herself. The suspicious looks and accusations. The bishop's letter. The books and herbs and potions.

She had ceased to see the dagger, but suddenly it loomed in front of her, very real, very sharply. She looked to her clenched knuckles around the hilt and then to the point and then to the hard chest. Finally, she glanced at the handsome face.

He looked back. Dark eyes glared dangerously from beneath feathering lashes.

Panic gripped her. Knowing that now it was kill or be killed, she rose up on her knees and brought the dagger down.

Strong arms flashed up, and iron fingers gripped her wrists. He thrust her to her side and she fell. In the scuffle that followed, the blade connected and a line of red oozed out across his upper arm.

She found herself pinned on her back. Fury hardened the face above her. "Did you really think I would play Holofernes to your Judith?" he snarled. "That was the plan, wasn't it? Like the Bible story. You kill the general and the leaderless army dissolves in confusion."

"Apocrypha," she corrected absurdly, her voice sounding very far away. "It isn't from the standard Bible. It is Apocryphal."

"I don't give a damn if God gave the story to Moses

himself, you bitch." He grabbed her hair and stood, dragging her to her knees. He pulled her over to the central pole, and tied her to it with her arms stretched above her.

He went to the furs. She was sure he would fetch the dagger and slit her throat. Her heart pounded like a lead pulse in her chest.

He returned with the flask and held it to her lips.

"Drink," he ordered.

chapter
TWO

S he groaned and stirred. Ian looked over from the stool where he sat eating one of the meat pies. She lay stretched out on the cot, arms and legs spread and tied to the corners. He had considered stripping off her clothes, but had decided that might be overdoing it. He wanted her scared and vulnerable, not paralyzed by terror.

Their struggle had torn her gown, almost exposing one small, pretty breast. The skirt hitched high on her shapely legs. She had a very nice body, even if it was a little too thin. Small and curved and compact and neat like Elizabeth's had been, only younger.

When he first saw her standing in the dim light, formidable and determined, that pale straight hair hanging to her hips, he had thought for one instant that she was Elizabeth. But the face, while pretty enough, had none of Elizabeth's precise perfection, and much more warmth and expression. And the hair was not white like Elizabeth's, but the palest blond shot through with silver highlights, and her skin possessed a pleasant pink glow. Elizabeth had been a snow queen. This woman looked like the first sun of dawn.

In her middle twenties, he guessed. Lovely and brave. Too bad he had to destroy her.

His squire John entered through the tent flap, carrying a plate of stew. The youth had been slow delivering the supper, bringing one item at a time to have an excuse to ogle the woman. His hot eyes scanned the naked legs.

Best to clarify things now. "Keep your hose laced, boy. She is not for you."

John flushed and set down the stew. Ian made a face at the tasteless mass. Fortunately, he had filled himself on Melissa's delicious meat pies. Picking up the last one, he tossed it to his squire as he left. "A consolation. The pleasure from all women is much alike. The same can not be said for food."

She stirred again. Her lids slowly rose. Alertness spread as she comprehended her position. She yanked at her bindings, and the movement made her groan again.

"How is it?" he asked. "I've never heard of a sleeping potion that doesn't split your head later."

Her lidded gaze slid over to where he sat. For an instant, before she composed herself, panic flickered.

Good.

"Lucky for you it wasn't poison," he added.

"I didn't have a recipe for poison."

He resisted the urge to laugh. Feisty little thing. "Too bad."

She managed the slightest shrug. "Since it is obvious that you never drank any, it wouldn't have mattered." She looked down at her vulnerable body again. "What are you going to do?"

She tried to sound brave and cool. He felt a little sorry for her. "I have been considering that these last few hours. I was all set to hang you when you woke."

"Hang me!"

"Aye. For murder."

"But I did not—"

"You tried."

"I didn't really. I lost my courage."

"I have a cut on my arm that says that you did."

"Only because you attacked me. If you had been asleep as you were supposed to be—"

"I would be dead now. Don't get all pleading and innocent on me, Melissa. Your plan was bold and brave, and I respect that. But you failed, and that makes your life mine to dispose of. I considered hanging, but my squire convinced me that would be a waste. So I have devised a plan for your redemption."

He walked over and sat beside her on the cot. "As you pointed out, this has been a long, hot siege. There are many bored men here, and the camp whores . . . well, they are not the same as having a courtesan."

Her eyes went wide. "Are you saying that you will give me to your army? That you expect me to—"

"Not the whole army. Just the knights."

"That is disgusting."

"So is hanging."

Her expression hardened in fury. He had expected tears. She had spirit, he had to give her that.

"I can not believe that your lord, Sir Morvan, would approve of what you plan. He is rumored to be an honorable man."

"He won't give a damn. Soon, I will have taken this tower for him and half this army can join him at

Harclow. That is all that will matter. Also, I saved his life once, so he is at a disadvantage with me."

Her jaw tightened with wavering control and her eyes glistened before she closed her lids. "I would rather hang. There are at least twenty knights here. They will probably kill me, anyway."

"Not if they are pleased. In a way, you will be fulfilling your mission. Tomorrow at dawn we will fire one of the tunnels. By midday, I expect the tower will fall or yield. Your favors will reward my knights, and perhaps salve their annoyance that they can not pillage what they have conquered."

Her gaze locked on him. "You fire the tunnel at dawn?"

"I expect so. We are digging two. The one to the south has reached the wall."

His gaze drifted to the dewy skin of her face and shoulders and exposed swell of breast. No longer a girl, but then he had never much cared for girls. The urge to lick her glowing paleness, and the knowledge that she could not prevent him from doing so, tightened his body. Melissa the courtesan had been right about one thing. He had grown tired of camp life, and he did desire the illusions of some courtly lovemaking. He had been sorely tempted to play her game to the end, but then he might have lost the heart to use her the way he planned now.

He could not help himself. He reached out and stroked her cheek. Soft. Warm. He leaned forward and brushed it with his lips. "For a courtesan, this should be an easy punishment. The way I see it, there is just one problem." He smiled down at her. "You, Melissa, are no courtesan."

"I certainly am."

"You surely are not. I have met virgins who kiss with

more skill than you. Who are you? Are you from the town?"

She nodded.

"So a young matron decides to be a heroine for her people. Very brave and impressive. Does your husband know that you tried this mad scheme?"

"I am a widow."

"Ah. Still, your man didn't teach you much, did he? And that is the problem. My squire has spread the word that I have a courtesan here. Some of these knights might think that you are insulting them, or saving your best for others. They could get ugly. I could explain the mistake, but then they may think that I lie and am the one for whom you save the real thing."

He twisted and looked down her half-exposed body. She glared apprehensively at him.

"Well, since the goal is to keep you alive, there is nothing for it but to have you first," he said. "I will teach you, and perhaps you will be able to fool them."

"There is no need. I will take my chances."

"I don't think so." He slid his hand down her body. It tightened to his touch. She was not immune, but then he had known that when he kissed her. She possessed needs that she did not control, and it appalled her that he could tap them. If she was the sort of woman he thought, this was the most frightening thing he could do to her. Even more frightening than the twenty knights that he threatened her with.

A tremor shook through her and into him, and he gritted his teeth against it. The temptation to keep her and wait out the summer with her on this cot and those furs almost won out.

He pulled away. "I must leave now. The work at the tunnel requires me. We will finish well before dawn, however. Since I command, I can permit myself an early celebration." He rose and stood over her. "A pity to share you with the others, Melissa, but they know that you are here and it would be unwise not to. Besides, you are mine before and after, anyway."

"After! Surely you must let me leave after."

"Eventually. When I no longer have use of you."

As he turned to go her body collapsed in a disheartened way, as if this latest detail had finally undone her.

I an waited with John and five men near the base of the low hill on which the tower house rose. The camps were quiet, all of their occupants carefully positioned within quick access of the gatehouse. Above him, Black Lyne Keep rose like an impenetrable shaft of stone surrounded by a skirt of thick battlements.

The campfires burned low, giving off little light. His captive should not be surprised by the silence and emptiness. She would surmise that everyone worked on the tunnel this night.

It had been easy to lure her with subtleties. In some ways, a clever woman was the simplest to dupe. Unless, of course, she duped you first. That had occurred once in his life with catastrophic results, and he had sworn it would never happen again.

"You are sure?" the archer Gregory whispered. He was Morvan's man, thick and gray, sent to sit out the summer with Ian's company in order to keep an eye on things.

"I am sure," Ian said. "She knew too much. She had counted the knights. She did not know that Morvan is at Harclow, nor that we had settled with the town a month ago. Furthermore, she is a lady, not a courtesan or a merchant's widow, and could have come from only one place."

And if she got out, she could get back in.

He felt no impatience. Even after she realized that the rope binding one hand was not totally secure, it would take her a while to free herself.

The only question was whether she would choose the wise course and try to escape completely, or risk herself by going back to warn the others. He was relying on the lady who had posed as a courtesan in order to kill him to choose the latter, reckless option.

"If you are right, it will be quick and clean. Morvan will appreciate that," Gregory said.

Ian was counting on that. Counting on putting Morvan Fitzwaryn yet more in his debt. Despite certain old tensions between them, he respected Morvan and was willing to fight this war on his peculiar terms, knowing that Morvan would reward him generously. Rich payment in the least, but Ian was playing for higher stakes. Once Morvan retook Harclow, once he reclaimed the ancestral lands wrenched from his grasp when a boy, he would return to his estates in Brittany and his family there. Then Harclow would need a seneschal to manage and protect her.

Ian planned to be that man. Not the same as holding one's own lands, of course. But far better than the freebooting life of a camp rat that fate had ordained for him these last four years.

A shadow moved near one of the camps. The fires picked up the silver lights of Melissa's hair as she darted from tent to tent. She paused at the one closest to the path leading to the northern road.

Come, little one. Ian silently coaxed. *Do not lose your courage now. Show the stuff you are made of.*

She took a few quick steps away from the hill, and he cursed under his breath. But she halted abruptly, paused a moment, and then turned resolutely and headed toward the tower.

Ian glided after her.

chapter
THREE

Reyna pushed through the brush and found the postern entrance. She stared at the gaping black slit.

No Alice to help her this time.

One hundred and fifty yards of underground tomb awaited her. Five hundred steps of utter blackness and enclosing rock.

The old childhood panic tried to grip her, and she fought it desperately.

She had never planned to go back. She had expected to have stolen a horse and been on the northeast road by now. By morning she should have been in her mother's arms, and planning her journey to Edinburgh.

The entrance beckoned like a stretched mouth wanting to swallow her.

It was just the dark. There was nothing to fear.

Summoning every bit of courage, she stepped in.

Her heart immediately began a slow, horrible pounding. Running would make it go more quickly, but she

could not will her legs to more than halting, hesitant
progress. Feeling along the wall, she fought the old memories that urged her toward hysteria.

Terror. Cold. Desolate loneliness. Invisible claws reaching to grab her.

But then, thank God, another memory. A warm light
and a kind face and a hand reaching through the blackness. *Come with me, girl. You will be safe, and will never be
frightened like this again.* She fixed her mind on the image
of that hand and the care and security and love that it
offered. She walked a little more quickly, absorbed by it.

Suddenly, the ghostly hands snatched her. She
screamed and the sound bounced off the stone walls and
echoed back at her. She kicked and pummeled until
strong arms pinned her against a tall body and warm
breath flowed over her face. In a daze she emerged out of
the nightmare and found herself surrounded by the
strength and scent of Ian of Guilford.

"Quiet, now." He soothed her the way one does a
horse.

For a disoriented moment she almost collapsed
against him, grateful and relieved. Then the memories
completely faded, and she realized what his presence
meant. She struggled again.

"Don't make me have to hurt you, Melissa," he said,
pulling her back to the entrance. He held her there and
stuck his head out and whistled.

"You bastard. You whoreson," she hissed. "How did
you know?"

"The town came to terms with me long ago. And you
can not pass as an artisan's wife any better than you do as
a courtesan." His arms still wrapped her from behind.
"Do not feel bad or blame yourself. It is better this way
for those within."

She seriously doubted that. A horrible guilt filled her. Instead of saving them, she had hastened their suffering. She wished that she had that dagger now. There would be no hesitation this time.

A cluster of shadows blocked the dim light at the entrance. "I'll be damned. You were right," an older voice said.

Ian pushed her up against the rock wall, keeping a firm grip on her shoulders "It is over. Do not try anything stupid," he warned.

She glared at the vague shadow of his head. Damn the man. *Damn him.* Carefully, deliberately, she pulled herself to her full height, tipped back her head, and spit.

The others must have heard, because a motionless silence fell over the little group. Ian took her face in a tight grip. "Watch yourself, Melissa, or I will treat you like the whore you pretended to be."

He stepped away. "Guard her with your sword, John. Do not let her leave here until I come back for her."

"You mean that I have to stay here?" a squire's young voice complained.

"Do it. And, John, remember what I said earlier. She is mine. You would not ride my horse without permission, so do not take liberties with her either."

John cursed and unsheathed his sword. The other men began groping away into the blackness.

Reyna rested against the rock wall, facing the squire John. As the minutes passed and she offered no challenge, vague relaxation claimed him. Finally the sword point fell from her chest and he sidled over and leaned against the rock too.

She strained to hear sounds from the tower, but the

night remained silent. She pictured Ian and the others slipping out of the tunnel into the passage in the northern wall, gliding through the shadows to the gatehouse, picking off the guards one by one.

"Your lord seems to be a great warrior."

"He is at that," John agreed proudly. "Few can match his sword arm, and he is the champion of many jousts and tournaments." He launched into a description of one particular joust in Brittany, and Reyna prompted him with questions, encouraging him to become comfortable with her.

Still no sounds from the tower. "He must be very famous in England."

John chuckled. "He is to be sure, but not in the way you think. Most of his fighting has been in France, with this free company he brought here when Sir Morvan hired them. He became their leader several years ago."

Reyna knew something of free companies, the bands of independent soldiers and landless knights who hired out to barons and kings for pay. When not professionally engaged they continued their conquests independently, laying sieges that they would lift if ransom was paid. They had become a serious problem in France, harassing towns and farms. If Morvan Fitzwaryn had hired such brigands for this siege, it did not speak well for the future of her people.

"He fought at Poitiers last year with the Black Prince," John added defensively, as if he sensed her disapproval. "Saved Sir Morvan's life there. Morvan has an old feud with the Beaumanoir family of Brittany, and on the field they went after him. Ian didn't even know who he was aiding, just saw those knights trying to cut Morvan down and jumped in for the fun of it."

"Such heroism would indeed make him famous."

"Oh, it isn't that. Not in England. Here I think he is best known for his way with women."

"Sir Ian is an attractive man, I can not deny it."

"That is calling a sea a puddle. My lord has to fight women off with his sword. Great ladies and scullery maids alike throw themselves at him." He sighed with admiration, then leaned toward her conspiratorially. "When we came back here, I learned that the court at Windsor had given him a special name, like a title."

"A special name? An honorific?"

"Aye." She could almost hear him smirk. "In Windsor and London he is known as the Lord of a Thousand Nights."

Reyna burst out laughing, and John irreverently joined in. Now this was rich. Other men received names based on their daring deeds. The Hero of thus and such. Ian of Guilford had been immortalized for the number of times he had fornicated.

All the while she talked with John, Reyna gently felt the ground with her foot. As their laughter degenerated into giggles, she found what she had been searching for. "That was a mistake," she said.

"Nay, my lady. Sir Ian finds it amusing himself."

"I did not mean that. I was stuck a long time in that tent, and laughing . . . that is to say, I need to . . ."

"Need to? . . . Oh."

"Perhaps you would wait at the entrance for a moment," she suggested. "I certainly could not leave then."

He pondered that, then walked the few feet and positioned himself, back turned, at the entrance.

Reyna stooped and found the small boulder that her foot had touched. Lifting it with both hands, she cautiously moved in on the unsuspecting John. Raising it

above her head, she crashed it down. The youth sagged
to the ground.

Filling her mind with fear for her people in order to
hold off the childhood horrors, she hurried down the
stone tunnel. Mixed emotions overwhelmed her. Lethal
determination. Numb resignation. Consuming worry.

And through them all, the whole time, the tentacles
of terror stretched through the relentless darkness to en-
snare her.

Fifty feet from the end, her hand found the gap that
she sought. Another tunnel turned off here, cut at an
odd angle to the main one, almost invisible even with a
torch. This one continued under the yard to the tower
itself.

She ducked into it, running faster, for surely Ian
would have reached the gatehouse by now. Finally she
came to the stairs and, pausing only a moment to catch
her breath, she began the long climb through the tower
walls.

Stone steps, scores of them, rose in blackness. She
could barely breathe when she finally struggled her way
to the top. Exhausted, and with legs like water, she
pushed against the stone wall. A low section gave way
and she fell into the lord's solar.

She lay on the floor sucking in breath, reveling in the
light that bathed her. At first she assumed that the solar
was empty, so complete was the silence. Then strong
arms reached down and lifted her up. She looked into
the kind, worried face of Sir Reginald.

"The gatehouse," she gasped. "They are inside and
will open it to the others."

"What?" a deep voice behind her boomed.

She turned to face Sir Thomas Armstrong and five

other knights. She had intruded on a council. "They have breached the wall and are inside." She ignored the suspicious way Thomas surveyed her torn gown and unbound hair. "A small band came in through the tunnel. They will take the gatehouse and raise the portcullis. You must hurry."

"And how did they find the tunnel?" Thomas snarled.

"There is no time for this. Make your interrogations tomorrow."

Thomas closed in on her with several strides and stuck his darkly bearded face down at hers. "As if your last crime were not bad enough, now you have handed over the tower? Did you seek your own safety by selling us all out? I told Robert and Maccus they could never trust a Graham."

"While you stand here accusing me, this tower will fall. Get to the gatehouse. If it has fallen, fire the stairs to the tower."

Even as she yelled, the door of the solar flew open and a guard ran in. "The gate is open," he reported. "Some are already in the hall below."

Thomas looked around at the other knights with panicked, wild eyes. None of them were armored, and two did not even wear their swords.

Reyna doubted that these men would live long if they fought against such odds. "Use the postern tunnel," she urged. "Save yourselves and get help from Clivedale."

Thomas and the other knights hustled over to the section of wall pivoted open on its internal heavy hinges. As they disappeared into the stairway, Thomas turned his red face on her. "Do not think this betrayal will change things. You will answer for this, and for Robert."

Reginald hung back. He drew his sword, walked over and closed the chamber door, and positioned himself in front of it.

Dear Reginald. Sweet, honorable, simple Reginald. She touched his arm. "You must go too."

"I swore to Sir Robert that I would protect you, and I will." His craggy face showed blank determination beneath his straight blond hair.

She could hear the raucous activity in the hall below. Shouts and noise echoed in from the yard as well. Ian's whole army had entered. Thanks to her, this tower had fallen into Ian's hand like an overripe apple.

"Go, Reginald, while you still can. I command it. You can not protect me if dead. Go with the others and get help."

He wavered. "Come with us."

She shook her head. "The first thing Thomas will do when he gets me to Clivedale is judge me. You know his mind on this, and I will not win. I am a Graham, and old feuds die hard. No one will believe me."

"I will take you elsewhere."

"We have no horses. Nay, Reginald. In a strange way, I am safer here with the enemy than with the people of my husband. For a while, anyway."

Closer sounds now. No time to lose. "Go," she ordered.

He strode to the open wall. "I will stay nearby and find horses. Look for my signal, my lady. I will get you away from here as Robert would have wanted me to."

She watched him disappear, and then leaned her weight against the stones and pushed them back into place. She hurried over to the hearth where Robert's sword lay. Unsheathing it, she placed it against the wall beside the door. Then she darted to the bookshelves by the writing table and retrieved the biggest bound folio. Heavy and solid, it bore a silver cover.

Positioning herself beside the door, she waited. Soon someone would come to investigate this solar. She knew who it would most likely be.

It didn't take long. Steps sounded in the passageway and paused outside. The door slowly opened and the glint of candlelight sparked off steel. She held her breath, the open door obscuring her presence. When he stood in full view with his back to her, she stepped forward, raised the tome, and brought it down.

With a shorter man she might have inflicted serious damage, but Sir Ian only staggered from the blow, for a moment off balance. In that instant Reyna grabbed Robert's sword, stepped around, and put the blade to his neck.

He still gripped his own weapon and he glared at her, first in surprise and then in fury.

"Drop it or I will slit your throat," she said. "Do not doubt my will this time, you son of the devil, for you have made it clear that I have nothing to lose."

Muttering a curse, he let the sword slide to the floor.

"Now close and bar the door."

He did as she ordered and she kept her blade on him the whole time. "Now on the floor, on your back."

Teeth clenched, he stretched out at her feet. She stood over him and rested the point of the sword on his neck.

He glared up at her. "Who the hell are you?"

"Reyna, wife of Robert of Kelso."

Surprise briefly replaced his anger. "I expected someone older. I heard that Sir Robert died not long before we came here. Do you command in his place?"

"Nay. Maccus Armstrong, our liege lord, sent his nephew Thomas to hold the lands after Robert died."

"And where are Sir Thomas and the other knights?"

"Gone."

"No doubt they left the same way you entered. If John has been harmed, it will go badly for you."

"At the moment, it is going badly for you."

They stayed in silence a moment, Reyna's sword at his throat, the deep pools of his eyes looking up at her. "If you kill me, there will be no controlling these men," he said.

"And if I do not kill you?"

"Name your terms. I have no choice but to listen."

"The tenant farmers are to be left in peace. Your men are not to molest or steal."

"We have not harmed them these last months. We will not start now."

"There are to be no rapes or tortures or executions."

He smiled faintly. "It will be so."

"The children are to be fed well, and not harmed."

"Aye, and furthermore I promise that we will not spit and roast any babies. I lost the taste for such things several years ago."

His mocking tone infuriated her. She pricked the sword tip against his skin and a little blood flowed. He went very still.

"There is one more thing. You are to give me a horse and an escort to take me where I choose."

His gaze slid up the sword and then up her body until he looked her in the eyes. "That I can not do."

"Of course you can. Your victory, and the way you achieved it, mean that I can not stay here now."

His expression softened a little. "I understand your position, but I can not let you leave. When I came here, Morvan gave me very few orders, leaving things to my judgment. But one of those orders was very clear. If by some means I took this tower, I was to see to the safety of Lady Reyna. Since you are she, I can not let you leave."

"My safety? Sir Morvan bothered with an order regarding me? Why?"

"I believe it was at the request of your father."

"Duncan! Duncan Graham's request? What has Sir Morvan to do with Duncan and the Grahams?"

"He has an alliance with them to ensure their neutrality in this conflict. Your safety was a condition of that agreement."

"I will be perfectly safe if I leave. Safer, in fact. You must permit it."

"Nay. Other than that, I accept your terms. I will treat the people here like my own so long as they obey me, and the men will be restrained. Is there anything else?"

Her confused mind could think of nothing else.

"Then remove your weapon and place it on the floor. The tower is taken and the lands long secured. You have tried your best for your people, and negotiated well. It is time to yield."

She stepped back and did as she was told. He rose, walked the few paces to her, and hovered, his contained anger leaking out in dangerous ways.

"Now, my lady, listen carefully, for I will tell you this only one time. Twice now you have raised a weapon on me. The next time, be prepared to use it." He grabbed her arm and pulled her to the chamber door. "You will come to the hall and hear me give the orders so that you know that I keep my word."

The castle folk packed the hall. As she and Ian entered, her eyes quickly found Alice. The plump old cook shrugged sympathetically.

Ian pulled her with him to the front of the crowd,

onto the dais with the high table. She surveyed the sea of faces. Some grimaced sadly at her predicament, but most eyed her suspiciously. She guessed that word of her presence in the enemy camp had spread, and they were drawing conclusions according to their prejudices.

Ian gestured for attention, and a hush fell. "I claim these lands in the name of Morvan Fitzwaryn," he began. "Some of you are old enough to remember his father, from whom Maccus Armstrong took Harclow many years ago. Sir Morvan comes to reclaim what is rightfully his, and which King Edward has returned to him by decree. This is no conquering army, but the return of your true lord. Obey and you will be well treated. Any man who swears his parole may move about freely."

The tension in the chamber cracked, and relief flowed. Ian dragged Reyna outside to the top of the tower stairs and spoke with the army gathered below. There the mercenaries learned that there would be no raping or looting or killing.

"Are you satisfied, my lady?" he asked when he had finished.

"If they obey, I am satisfied. I assume that your orders extend to me, and that you no longer expect me to entertain your knights."

The torchlight played over his handsome face, making his beauty appear mysterious. He wore a sleeveless tunic, and the binding on his arm where she had cut him glowed like a banner.

"They extend to you. But I will not try to create a monastery here. I do not interfere with willing adults. You should tell the women to avoid misunderstandings."

"So your men may bed any woman who is willing. Does that extend to me, too? May I take a man who pleases me to my bed if I am willing?"

He smiled his disarming, devastating smile. "Aye."

He reached out and lightly stroked her cheek, then tilted her chin up. It was a gesture that spoke familiarity, even affection. She realized in that instant that he did not simply assume that she found him attractive because all woman did, but knew it for a fact because he had sensed her reactions to his kiss and caress.

She resented the little shiver that defeated her efforts to remain indifferent to his touch. It was distressing that he could evoke this. Her responses, and his knowledge of them, filled her with anger.

"Any man who pleases me?"

He shook his head. "Just this one."

She stepped away from his touch and laid her finger thoughtfully on her lips. Very slowly, she walked around him, examining him just as he had done her earlier in the day. She barely resisted the urge to prod at his muscles and tell him to lift his hoof. When she had completed her circuit, she saw the combination of amusement and annoyance in his eyes. She had laid a trap for this conceited Englishman, and he knew it.

"Well, Sir Ian, if it is your goal to become known as the Lord of One Thousand and *One* Nights, you had better look elsewhere." Feeling the only satisfaction she had earned on this dreadful day, she turned primly on her heel and walked away.

"Reyna," he called after her softly. "I think that I just heard the sound of a gauntlet being thrown."

chapter

FOUR

T he next morning, Ian sent half of the company
to Harclow with news of the capture of the
tower house. He then began assigning the re-
maining men to chambers and barracks and deciding
who would remain outside in the camp. All the while
that he established his command of the tower, he kept
looking for the slender body and silver-blond hair of
Robert of Kelso's widow.

She never appeared. If he had not been sure that no
one had slipped past the guards he had posted at the end
of the postern tunnel, he might have suspected that she
had escaped. Succumbing to curiosity and concern, he
ventured into her room next to the solar. Parchments
spilled off a table in the spartan chamber, but the lady remained invisible.

He attended the midday meal tired, hungry, and in a
mild state of anticipation. His stomach remembered the
taste of Reyna's meat pies as surely as his lips remembered the dew of her skin. He looked forward to feasting

on the tower cook's delicious food and sparring with the spirited little Reyna.

Taking the lord's chair at the high table, he was annoyed to find the place beside him quickly claimed not by Reyna, but by Margery, Thomas Armstrong's wife, one of the ladies left behind when the knights fled.

Margery was an attractive, sharp-featured woman in her early thirties. She wore her red hair in an intricate coif and possessed a lush figure well displayed by her tight cote-hardie. She smiled very warmly and Ian, feeling an uncharacteristic lack of confidence regarding his odds of success with Lady Reyna, smiled back.

He let the effect sink in, then turned his attention to the arriving food. He was cursed with a stomach totally unsuitable for a soldier. Eating his company cook's food had been the greatest torture of camp life these last years. Knowing those pies had come from the tower would have almost been incentive enough to storm the walls if his deception of Lady Reyna had failed.

As the cauldron approached, he eyed its contents suspiciously. The spoonfuls of glop that landed on his plate looked depressingly familiar. He dipped some bread and tasted. The bland flavor killed his appetite at once.

Andrew, the keep's steward, moved about the hall, and Ian called him over. "Who prepared this?"

"The cook."

"Your cook or my cook?"

"Our cook, but your cook supervised. Nothing went into that pot that he did not see. You can eat it with complete confidence."

Andrew spoke in reassuring tones. The man was in his late fifties, rather short and small-framed, with meticulously groomed gray hair and beard. He bore a courtly, restrained manner marked by an elegant impassivity.

"Why wouldn't I have confidence in it?"

Lady Margery leaned close. "Under the circumstances, you would not want to eat just anything here, would you? I certainly would not," she said.

"What are you suggesting, my lady?"

"Well, consider that Robert was poisoned, and that Alice the cook has always been practically a mother to Reyna, and came with her from the Grahams. Reyna sometimes helps Alice, and personally prepared her husband's food those last days . . ." Margery raised her eyebrows meaningfully. "My husband always demanded that a man watch the food preparation after we came. No substance entered the food served in this hall that was not recognized by the watcher."

Ian stared down at his plate. If his own cook supervised now, that meant that no herbs, fruits, roots, or anything else that imparted flavor would find its way into the pot.

"I assumed that you would want to continue the practice," the steward said coolly. "Seeing as how you are the enemy."

Ian dismissed Andrew and decided to give Lady Margery more attention. "What do you mean, Sir Robert was poisoned?"

"He was hale and fit one day, and vomiting and in pain the next. Three days later he was dead."

"He was over sixty, I have heard. Old men die."

"Aye, and at first most were inclined to think thus, except a few of us who wondered from the start. After all, Reyna nursed him, and had often cooked for him in the evenings if he came in late from the demesne. It is a quaint interest of hers. Not becoming to a lady, but then neither are those books and letters. The servants report that she fed him potions while sick that seemed to make it worse, too. But what really pointed the finger was the bishop's letter."

Despite himself, she had his interest. "What of this letter?"

"Soon after Maccus sent my husband here, a letter came for Robert from the bishop in Glasgow. It seems that Robert had written to him on a matter of great importance seeking his advice. The letter referred to this matter, and said that the bishop would investigate the proper disposition of the matter, but could not visit himself until summer's end."

"What matter was this?"

"The letter did not say, but it is clear, is it not? Robert planned to put Reyna aside, and sought the bishop's advice on how to proceed. Maccus enfiefed these lands to Robert and his descendants, but there are no heirs. They had been married twelve years and she is barren. As you said, Robert's time was limited."

"And so it is thought that the lady, knowing her husband planned this, killed him?" He put more sarcasm into his voice than he truly felt. Husbands had been disposed of for less. "Not much proof."

"Along with her attempt to escape judgment by helping you last night, the proof seems very clear to me."

Ian almost explained that Lady Reyna had not come to him to betray her people but to save them, and had tried to kill him in the process. Even as the words formed, he bit them back. Reyna had not given any story about last night in her defense, and now he understood why. Her attempted murder of him would only support this other accusation against her.

Had she done it? He bore a cut in his arm that proved her capable of such things. She had planned to run away, a usual sign of guilt, and had tried to negotiate her departure even as the tower fell. And yet, while he had learned a healthy skepticism regarding the honesty and constancy of women, he hadn't sensed evil in this one. Quite the opposite.

With the intimacy of gossip now binding them, Lady Margery chattered on through the meal. Ian didn't pay much attention to her tales of the old feud between the Armstrongs and Reyna's family, the Grahams, which in Margery's opinion only supported Reyna's guilt. He didn't bother to point out that Sir Robert had not been an Armstrong, because his fealty to Maccus had essentially made him one.

The whole time he kept his eyes on the various entrances to the hall, looking for Reyna. This tower's five levels were connected by two sets of stairs, not to mention the secret ones he had discovered in the walls. That made it difficult to keep track of anyone who did not want to be found.

He gazed around the hall which filled the second level and took a rough measurement. He mentally compared it with his memory of the building's exterior. The walls must be almost fifteen feet thick. They would need to be at the base to support the weight, but up above, some of those walls had probably been hollowed out for chambers.

Lady Reyna could probably live to old age here without his ever seeing her again.

"Lady Reyna has not attended the meals," he observed to Margery, interrupting an unfortunate turn in the conversation where she probed about his past. He wondered what had given women the notion that men liked to talk about such things.

"She never does. At least not since Thomas and I arrived. She eats in the kitchen with Alice. A few others do too."

Ian pushed away from the table. He had not visited the kitchens yet. This seemed a good time.

As he descended the stone stairs, sounds of conversation and laughter drifted to him. So did the aroma of very good food.

All talk ceased when he appeared in the threshold. Two plank tables seating twenty-five people cramped the center of the chamber, and a servant girl stirred a pot hanging in the large hearth. Andrew Armstrong ate here, and some serving women and two men he recognized as grooms. An old, thickset woman he guessed was Alice sat between two boys about ten and eight years old. Other children peered around their mothers and fathers at him. He didn't see Reyna.

At the far end of one table he spied Morvan's man, Gregory, and he walked to him with fifty eyes watching his progress. Gregory grinned up sheepishly. "I happened to walk by, and it seemed a merry group," he explained.

Ian looked down at Gregory's plate. A moist slice of duck and a colorful mix of roots lay in a pool of brown sauce. The scent made his mouth water. Evidently Alice the cook did her duty for the diners in the hall, and then practiced her art for this little group.

He broke off a piece of Gregory's bread and dipped it in the sauce. It had almost reached his mouth when a wooden spoon flashed by his face like a catapult. It smashed into his hand, and the morsel flew across the room onto the floor.

"Don't you dare, you English whoreson," a familiar voice warned.

He turned in surprise to the servant girl who had been stirring at the hearth, only it wasn't a servant but Lady

Reyna, dressed in a loose, simple gown with a kerchief tied around her head.

She shook the spoon at him. "Not one bite, you devil. If you get sick, I'll not have people pointing at Alice or myself." She took her place on the bench. "Besides, there isn't enough for you, and because of your damn siege this is the first fowl or meat these women and children have had in over a month."

Ian made a mental reminder to speak with the lady sometime about her cursing. "Was the tower so badly provisioned as that? There should have been dried fish and meat to last this long."

From the other end of the table Andrew Armstrong coughed for attention. "Sir Thomas ordered only the men to have such things. They might have had to fight, and there was no telling how long the siege would last. It is customary, of course."

Aye, it was customary, and Ian had seen and caused it before, but he felt an unusual guilt all the same.

"Who cooked this food?" he asked, taking more bread, dipping it, and popping it into his mouth before Reyna could attack. Delicious.

"Alice and myself," Reyna said, eyeing his throat, daring him to swallow.

These then were the castle folk who did not think her a poisoner. Very deliberately, he dipped again, popped, and chewed at length.

"You all will no longer eat here, but join the others in the hall," he ordered. "Alice, cook as you see fit, with such assistance as you choose. No one will watch. Gregory, organize some hunts so there is plenty of fresh meat." He turned to Reyna. "You, my lady, will attend all meals. When the food is brought in, you will eat first."

The kerchief, dipping low over her brow and tied behind her neck, completely hid her bound hair. He thought that she looked fresh and charming all the same. He wondered if he had passed her numerous times today and simply not recognized her.

Her sensual lips pursed. "What makes you so sure that I will not kill myself to get the chance to do away with you and this army?"

"You might if it were just you, but you will not risk your people, that much I know," Ian said as he retreated to the stairs. "Besides, my lady, if you knew a recipe for poison, you would be dead already."

L ater that afternoon, Andrew Armstrong approached while Ian directed the walling up of the postern tunnel. The steward looked unruffled and courtly in the heat despite his wool pourpoint. Ian himself was sweating like a plow horse.

"There is a small problem, sir," Andrew said mildly.

"What kind of problem?"

"It is the well. It seems to have run dry. It was fine this morning, but just now some servants went to draw water and . . . nothing." Andrew spread his hands and smiled blandly.

Ian sighed at Andrew's mastery of understatement. The well running dry was hardly a small problem. "Show me."

He trailed Andrew up the forty steps to the keep's only entrance off the hall, and down the forty steps to the kitchen. Damn border tower houses. In one day he had grown to hate the eternal stairs.

In a small cellar chamber off the kitchen, Andrew presented the errant well with a small flourish. Ian lifted the bucket and let it drop on its rope until he heard a thump instead of a splash. He brought it back up even though he knew it would be empty. "Has this ever happened before?"

"I have been here over twenty years, since Maccus took the lands. Once before, during a drought, it happened."

"It has been hotter and drier than normal, but not a drought."

"Well, with water, one can never tell, can one?"

Ian began pacing off the chamber in methodical rows. "Did Robert Kelso hold these lands all those years?"

"Not until his marriage to Lady Reyna. It was an arrangement to end a blood feud between the Armstrongs and the Grahams that had started eight years earlier. Maccus had no unmarried sons or nephews to represent the Armstrongs, and everyone in these parts knew his knight Sir Robert to be an honorable man. Even Duncan Graham respected him. When the match was made, Sir Robert received these lands. He held them through Maccus, but it was understood that they formed a buffer between the Armstrongs to the north and south and the Grahams to the east. A neutral area, so to speak."

Ian fingered the joints in the rock wall. "The lady must have been very young at this marriage. A child."

"She was twelve. The church permits it at that age."

Ian found some loose mortar and pulled out his dagger and probed. "Presumably Sir Robert waited to take her to his bed."

"I wouldn't know."

Aye, he would. He was the sort of steward who knew everything. Ian pulled at the stones he had been probing. They didn't budge. Once more he began a careful pacing of the floor. "What sort of a man was Sir Robert?"

"He was a good man. A brave knight, highly honorable, and something of a scholar."

"Do you think she killed him?"

Andrew deliberated before responding. "She came here a frightened mouse. There had been no love in her home, and much strife. Robert gave her freedom, wings, care. Nay, I do not think she killed him."

Ian turned his attention back to the well. "You know, of course, that it is not dry."

"Really?"

"The bucket did not hit mud, or even dry dirt. It came up as clean as it went down. Someone has covered the water with something. A door or plank. How do you think she did it?"

"She? I'm sure that I don't understand you, Sir Ian."

"Lady Reyna. I see her hand in this. How did she get down there? I can find no hidden doors in the floors or walls."

Andrew shrugged. Ian knew that, short of torture, he would not get the man to speak. "Well, steward, what do you suggest?"

Andrew appeared to ponder the matter. Ian wasn't fooled in the least. "We will have to do as your army did. There is the river for bathing, and a spring near it has good water for cooking. The latter could be carted in every day and the women sent to the river as needed with laundry. Under guard, if you prefer."

Ian had been wondering about the point of this sabotage, but Andrew's solution provided the explanation. In order to provision the tower with water, in order to bathe in this summer heat, the gate would have to be opened frequently. The tower would become significantly more vulnerable.

He glared at the well that had suddenly made his work here much more difficult.

He should have let Reyna take a horse and run away to hell itself if she wanted.

T hat evening, the hall filled for supper. Lady Margery sat to Ian's right again, but he saw to it that the place on his left remained empty for Reyna. The only other spot available at the high table was near the end amidst six of his knights.

Venison in a savory sauce had been prepared. The castle folk knew that Alice and Reyna had cooked it unsupervised, and they munched only on bread in a dejected way. The aroma from the plates permeated the hall and one could hear stomachs growl. Finally, Ian's men bravely picked at their portions and a few others dared to follow.

Reyna suddenly appeared on the steps, and every eye turned to her. She wore a pretty blue cote-hardie that hung more loosely than it should. Her blond hair was bound into a thick plait that dangled down her back. With a determined expression, she strode across the hall to the high table. She moved up behind Ian, and he waited for her to take the place beside him.

Instead, she reached over his shoulder and plucked a chunk of meat from his plate.

She dramatically held it up high and examined it. Glaring a challenge around the assembly, she placed the meat in her mouth, chewed broadly, and gave a solid swallow. She looked up to heaven, as if awaiting divine judgment. Silence claimed the hall while everyone watched and waited for the food to hit her stomach.

Ian smiled at her performance, and turned to eat himself.

A violent gesture beside him stopped the action. Reyna

suddenly gagged. Her face turned red. She bent over, her arm clutching her stomach. She fell to the floor.

Pandemonium broke loose. Men shouted and women screamed. Those who had eaten stared aghast at their plates. A few rose and stuck fingers down their throats.

Ian threw aside his chair and dropped down on his knee beside Reyna. Christ, he had killed her. With all of the rumors about a poisoner, he should have considered that it might be true, but be someone besides Reyna.

He felt incredibly vacant and helpless while he watched the poison do its work. A crowd gathered around with silent, morbid fascination. Finally, desperate to attempt something to save her, he reached to turn her over and try to force the meat back up.

While his hands closed on her body, a relaxed repose spread over her face and limbs. Ian's chest clenched at the image of death's peace. He felt an overwhelming urge to embrace the last warmth of her life, and began to do so.

Her lashes fluttered open. Those lovely lips moved. "Take your hands off of me, Englishman."

A tight moment of shocked silence greeted her miraculous resurrection, and then laughter broke throughout the hall. Reyna threw off his hands and scrambled to rise.

Fury at the scare she had given clapped through him like thunder. He hauled her up after him. "Do anything like that again and I'll—"

"You'll what?" she hissed while she righted her garments and jerked her arm free. "Trick me into betraying my people and returning to this place that holds only danger for me? Keep me here to await the trial which must eventually come? Force me to perform a ritual at every meal that confirms their suspicions?"

Ian looked her in the eyes and she looked right back, bravely and belligerently. "Seat yourself," he ordered, retaking his chair.

To his further annoyance, she walked away and plunked herself down in the free space among the knights.

Still livid at the way Reyna had made a fool of him, still confused by the hollow despair he had felt when he thought her dying, Ian pointedly looked away from the little blond woman and turned his most charming smile on Lady Margery.

He held his own with Margery throughout the meal, but a part of his awareness remained solidly fixed on the end of the table. He heard the light conversation while Reyna bantered with the knights. He heard Sir Lionel's florid flattery. He noted Sir George's suggestive innuendoes. Finally, someone told a quiet joke and their laughter broke out in peals.

His gaze drifted to Reyna. She smiled brightly, and delightful little swells formed over her high cheekbones. He realized that he had never seen her really smile before. It transformed her face, making her appear very youthful and sweet.

Sir Lionel and Sir Matthew beamed at her in a besotted way. They would probably begin writing poems for her by nightfall. Sir George, however, watched her with a hooded, predatory expression.

Ian thought about the lady's artless kisses. A widow and not a virgin, and for all he knew not even virtuous, but not what George assumed, either.

Morvan had said to see to her safety. Well, there was only one way to do that.

chapter

FIVE

Reyna watched with misgivings the reactions of the men around her. She had provoked such attention before from visiting knights or lords, but her status as Robert's wife had protected her from unwelcome complications.

She debated how to handle any advances, should they come. Maybe such men got dangerous if a woman didn't reject them in the appropriate way.

The chatter around her abruptly stopped. The men looked past her, through her. She startled when hands came to rest possessively on her shoulders. Twisting her head, she looked up into brooding eyes beneath feathery lashes.

"Your meal is finished?" Ian asked.

"Aye."

"Then let us retire, my lady."

The insinuation shocked her speechless. The men around her scooted aside. Ian took her hand and lifted her up to step over the bench. He drew her toward the stairs.

It was either follow, or create a spectacle that would garner the attention of the whole hall and not alter by one whit the conclusions that Ian intended these men to draw. Still, she wanted to pummel and kick and make a clear statement that repudiated his gesture.

She glanced at his calm profile. "You are despicable. Is it your intention to see that I have nothing left here?"

"It is my intention to see to your safety as I was ordered. In the opinion of those men whom you enjoyed beguiling this evening, you are a loose woman at best and a harlot at worst. To your mind you may be the persecuted widow, and to many of these people you may be a murderess, but to my knights you are only the woman who came to my tent and offered herself to me."

"Not really, and only in good cause."

"To a man at war looking for some warmth and pleasure, such details hold little consequence."

They had reached the stairs. He ushered her up, his hand still resting on the back of her waist. She ascended until they were out of sight, then turned to him. "You need come no further. I think that you made your point to your knights. Now they are certain that I am a loose woman."

"Aye, but *my* woman, and none of them will touch you now." He gestured upward. "I will escort you to your chamber. I want to check its walls."

He followed silently, an unsettling presence behind her. Up past the third-level chapel, then past the fourth-level chambers for knights and servants, and finally into the passage flanked by the solar and the small rooms claimed by Margery and the other women. She quickened her step and put some distance between them. She wanted to run in and bar her door.

She walked to her desk and began folding and rolling

parchments with shaking hands. Even though she knew he was coming, his slightly delayed arrival startled her and she jumped back from the desk.

He entered casually. His gaze quickly took in the narrow bed and the three tall night candles, already lit by the servants. She moved away from the desk, over to the wall beside the door, and pressed herself against the cool stones.

"A small chamber. The one Lady Margery uses is larger. Did she displace you when Thomas and she came?"

"Nay. I have always been here. I chose this chamber. It has three window slits, and the others have only one."

He glanced to the table strewn with parchments. "Better for your reading?"

"Aye. And at night, if the candles gut or blow out, there is still some light."

"You fear night demons?"

"In a way."

He began pacing around the narrow room, examining the walls, occasionally feeling at the mortared joints between the stones.

"What are you looking for?"

"Chambers, carved into the thick walls. Do you have one?"

"If I did, what would you expect to find there? Hemlock?"

He ignored her and continued his search.

It unsettled her to have him in this space. His size and energy and lithe movements filled the chamber like a mild invasion and put her on her guard. She pressed closer to the stones, feeling their rough edges on her back. He didn't speak for some time, just methodically continued his search, pushing aside her clothing chests to check behind them.

"Were you faithful to him?" he asked while he crouched near the floor. He spoke as if it were the most natural question in the world, and not an intrusive query.

She hesitated, and he glanced over at her, his dark eyes seeking hers. "Aye," she said.

Aye, she had been faithful. With her heart and her body. Only once had there been a misunderstanding, not on Robert's part, but on hers and, more disastrously, on the squire who fell in love with her. They had grown up to-gether, and she saw him as a brother. In her ignorance, she had not recognized the signs that his affection had changed. When she was seventeen and he a year older, Robert had abruptly sent him away. She had been angry and confused by Robert's gentle explanation until, at his parting, that sweet friend had kissed her in a most unbrotherly way.

Her hand went to her lips at the memory. She noticed Sir Ian standing now, looking at her. "Aye," she repeated more firmly.

He sauntered over to the table. He moved like a lean, strong, coordinated animal. A big cat or a young horse. He was a man with total confidence in the strength and beauty of his body. He fingered the parchments. "What are these?"

He was the conqueror, she reminded herself. He had the right to question anything he chose. "Letters. I corre-spond with several people. Robert encouraged me to write to men of letters with questions I might have on my readings."

"So your husband was a scholar, and taught his young wife to be one. It must have been a consolation to you."

She heard the pity and criticism. *Kind of your husband to find some occupation for you under the circumstances. After all, you had no children to busy yourself with, did you?*

"Robert taught me to read English and Gaelic and

Latin and Greek, and encouraged me to use his books. He himself was both brilliant and chivalrous, both strong and kind. Like King Alfred." She let the last words drip with their own criticism. *Unlike you.*

He raised his eyebrows at this reference to the great English king of antiquity. "King Alfred, no less. Your husband was an impressive man indeed. To whom do you write?"

She wished he would leave it alone. "I have written to many men, but only a few have responded. They might not receive the missives, of course, but I suspect they do not bother with a woman's query. One philosopher, Thomas of Chartres, did respond most kindly, and informed me of several women on the Continent with similar interests. Over the last few years these women and I have corresponded."

"I have heard of Thomas of Chartres. In fact, I met him once. Do not put it about that you correspond with him, my lady. Last year he had to answer a charge of heresy." Before she had a chance to absorb this startling information, he added, "Do you mourn him still? Your King Alfred?"

He stunned her with the impertinent question, and with the confused responses it summoned in her. Did she still mourn him? Certainly at first she had, deeply, almost dreadfully. Now she had moved to acceptance and warm memories, and to resentments that provoked guilt. Resentment that he hadn't prepared her better for the old hatreds from which his presence had shielded her. Resentment that protecting his memory placed such burdens on her. Resentment that he had died at all, leaving her horribly, vulnerably, alone.

"Nay, I no longer mourn him in the way you mean."

"Did you kill him?"

Finally, the question hanging between them since he began down this path. "Do you think I did? Most everyone else does."

"Nay, I do not."

He hadn't hesitated. Poignant gratitude squeezed her heart. "Why don't you think so?"

"One does not become known as the Lord of a Thousand Nights without learning something about women."

"Aye, I suppose not. Well, I did not kill him, but I think that perhaps someone did. His illness had all the signs. But my denial will not matter. I had the chance to do it, and the knowledge, they think, and I am a Graham. It was only this siege that saved me. Maccus Armstrong was visiting Harclow before coming here for my trial when your company arrived." She did not have to add what would have happened if Maccus had come and judged her and found her guilty.

A dangling image from her dreams, of herself limp and blue, flashed through her mind. It had been a sporadic premonition her whole life, but recently the nightmare had become sharper and more frequent. She laid her head against the stones and fought back the panic that always threatened when she considered that possibility.

Ian walked over to her. "Your being a Graham will not work against you anymore. No Armstrong will sit in judgment of you. Morvan Fitzwaryn will be the lord soon, and if anyone demands a reckoning, it will be him. He is a fair man."

Perhaps it was the flickering candlelight, but she thought that she detected concern and sympathy in those fathomless eyes. She saw so little of either any more. Her spirit lurched hungrily at the notion that someone believed her.

He just stood there, a hand span away, completely comfortable with the silence between them. His expression did not change, he did not move, but suddenly, clearly, the mood between them altered as if a different air had been let into the chamber. His long gaze unsettled her, and the wariness she had first felt when he entered returned. His presence here, his personal questions, his belief in her innocence, had produced a strange intimacy.

"Let me leave," she said. "I have a friend in Edinburgh who will help me. I will be safe."

He reached out and stroked her jaw and chin in that affectionate gesture he had used two nights before. "I can not."

Her skin prickled where he touched her. The room held an unnatural stillness. Candles flickered behind him, casting his face in shadow, but still she could see the firm jaw, the straight mouth, the eyes looking down intently. She could hear herself breathe, could feel the aura of his power and maleness, could smell his compelling, faint scent. She thought his gaze would absorb her.

"You can. If my father demanded my safety, it was merely a gesture on his part. He does not care about me."

He slowly shook his head. "It is not just that."

What, then? She almost asked, but she didn't have to. The answer throbbed between them, frightening her, finally splitting through her ignorance with its intensity.

His hand took her long plait and eased it up from her back until he held its length. He slid off the ribbon that secured its end and began letting the thick tresses unwind, combing them out with his fingers. "You have been avoiding me, Reyna," he said, watching his hands. "Hiding from me."

She glanced down at that hand stroking higher and higher, working out the plait, occasionally grazing her through its thickness. A shaky, weakening, delicious fear spread all through her. "Not hiding," she lied, trying to sink back into the stone wall. "I have been evading all the men. You warned the women were to avoid misunderstandings."

"It is a little late for that with me." He slid his fingers under her hair until they rested behind her ears and he cradled her face in his palms. "And I misunderstood nothing."

"That is not fair." She tried not to look at his wonderful face, vainly seeking some safety from the uncontrollable and unnameable feelings. A demanding expectation swirled through her, pulling apart her secure sense of purpose. His rough hands felt so warm, so welcome on her skin. The contact soothed and terrified her. "What happened in your tent was not my intention. You took advantage of me."

He smiled. Dear lord, what a smile. "A very small advantage, considering your vulnerability. I could not help myself. Just as you could not help that you enjoyed it."

He stepped closer. *Do not do this*, she cried. *It is cruel and dishonorable of you.* But her trembling mouth would not speak. *Stop him, fight him*, her mind urged desperately. *For your sake and your pride. For Robert.* But his closeness and gentle touch summoned that irrational yearning so long denied, so overpowering, and she could only hold her breath and watch the face bending down to hers.

Warm lips on hers, gentle, soothing, luring. Kisses brushing her cheek, shocking her ear. A dangerous swell in that sensual power streaking out of him, into her, and arms pulling her into a tight embrace.

Her mind clouded with a confusion of horror and de-nial and desire and relief. For a moment she became rigid. But his hands moved over her back, and the com-forting touch defeated her. Her mind lost its battle against her senses. Duty succumbed to need.

She knew that he knew, but suddenly she didn't care. He raised his head and looked down at her before claim-ing her with a more demanding kiss. She lost all thought, and let herself submerge beneath the aching desire.

His kiss grew more intimate, probing slowly inside her mouth, and shivering sensations spilled through her limbs and body, finding a destination deep and low inside her. Her arms rose of their own accord and embraced him, bringing her closer yet. Her breasts hardened at the pres-sure of his chest, and she gasped at the pleasure the contact gave. She turned her head to accept the hot, impatient kisses exploring her neck. She was lost now, utterly lost.

Tight, thrilling pleasure spun through her, building quickly to something excruciating and insistent. He leashed whatever drove him but she could not do the same. More calmly, he caressed the length of her body, and she sighed at this intimacy that both brought relief and made it worse. His firm touch rose and cupped her breast and the sensation, more wonderful than the memories of her dreams, made her cry out. He swallowed the sound with his kiss. His arm arched her up to his seductive hand and he circled and stroked the nipple, driving her to delirium.

He half carried, half guided her over to the bed. He sat on its edge and pulled her between his thighs.

She gazed down at those smoldering eyes and tight jaw and parted straight lips. She had never known that a man could look so beautiful and strong in his passion. She could have looked at him forever. His hands stroked down her hair, following its path over breasts and stomach and hips. His fingers found the lacing on the side of her gown and untied it.

She couldn't move. She could barely stand. Without his embrace she felt vulnerable and bereft and hungry for contact. She closed her eyes in relief at the faint touch when he slid the gown and shift off her shoulders and arms. The garments fell down low on her hips.

Through lowered lids she watched him look at her nakedness and push her hair aside and trace her breasts with a light touch. He gently caressed and rubbed the hard, begging peaks, and looked up with hot, knowing eyes. She tensed her body for some vague control and pressed her thighs together to relieve that lower, throbbing awareness.

He had driven her mad even before he pulled her closer and teased with his tongue, first at one nipple, then the other. She stroked her hands into his hair and leaned into his tantalizing torture. Her hips squirmed in a shocking way, and he embraced them and took her breast in his mouth. She held his head to her and gave herself over to wonderful, mindless bliss.

He pulled her further, easing back, making to recline. "Come and lie with me, Reyna."

She looked down at his beautiful face and felt the dream crack. A strange sorrow flooded her. Better for him to have never spoken. Words were rational things and encouraged rational thought. His summoned back her mind, her awareness, her restrictive sense of duty and virtue.

She pressed lightly, stopping him. "I can not. Must not."

Anger flashed as he realized that she meant it, that she would go no further. Anger and amazement. He pulled her down on his knee and took her face in his hand. "Is this a challenge, my lady? To see if I spoke the truth when I said there would be no rapes here?"

"Nay," she said, knowing she was very vulnerable and that no one would ever call it rape now.

He pushed her off his lap onto the bed. She almost fell to the floor. Feeling very ashamed, she scrambled to cover herself with the gown.

He rose. "You have certainly taught this English whoreson a lesson." He strode to the door. "Do not think to do it again."

Reyna sat forlornly on the bed after he left, trying to subject what had just occurred to some logic. Her mind felt too scrambled. She only knew that she had betrayed herself in a disgraceful way, and almost betrayed Robert as well.

She wanted to blame Sir Ian, but knew it was pointless to do so. What did it matter to him that old loyalties and hard needs battled inside her? She doubted that this was a man who reflected much on consequences, or thought twice about his women after he left them. He was a brigand who laid siege to her castle, and once she yielded he would exact his tribute and move on.

Aye, his actions had been understandable and predictable.

The real blame lay with her.

She went to one of the windows and climbed into its deep niche, sitting near the slit, letting the air flow over her face to cool her humiliation. Her chamber faced east, and from here she could look out over the final mile of moss to the abrupt rising of the waste and the subsequent mounds of the Cheviot Hills.

Her gaze fell on the old motte-and-bailey castle that had stood sentinel for centuries by the first crag of the waste, near the source of the Black Lyne river. It was an ancient fortress, used before Black Lyne Keep had been built. It was no more than a jumble of rocks falling over cavernous foundations now.

Something flickered amidst the ruins, like a yellow star glittering at the base of the distant structure. She squinted and saw it again.

Reginald's signal. He had found some horses.

I an felt almost in control by the time he reentered the torchlit hall. Forcing himself not to think about the woman who had just made a fool of him, biting back the fury that she had found the strength to deny him in a way few women ever had, he scanned the large chamber until he found Gregory.

Striding over, he pulled the man aside. "Tomorrow morning, take ten men and go to Harclow. Tell Morvan that Maccus Armstrong is within the fortress."

Gregory whistled lowly. "A shrewd move, their hiding that fact even during the parlays. No wonder Maccus has led no force down from his stronghold at Clivedale."

"Aye. The seneschal at Clivedale would not risk it, but Thomas Armstrong will be there now, and perhaps he will. Tell Morvan that we will increase the patrols and keep watch on the north, but that he should be alert too."

Gregory left the hall to choose the men whom he would bring. Still fuming about the woman upstairs, Ian threw himself into the lord's chair at the high table.

Had she planned it? Deliberately enticed him toward the garden so that she could close the gate at the most effective moment? Had she resorted to fighting this war with a woman's weapon, when the daggers and swords had failed her? Had her soft yielding been no more than another ploy by the actress who had first posed as a whore?

He didn't believe it. He had known women highly adept at deception but had been taken in only once, when he was little more than a youth. He had learned his lesson well, and his instincts in these things had become well honed over the years. It would take more skill than she possessed to fool him.

He considered the other possibilities and finally forced himself to face the most obvious. She had claimed to be faithful to her old husband. A virtuous woman, then, and by his own code he should be leaving her alone.

So, why hadn't he walked out of that chamber as he had intended?

He resisted the reflection that the question demanded. She was in his head, that was certain, and he wanted her, that was more certain. Wanted her more than he had wanted a woman in a very long time. Not since Elizabeth, but this was different from that too. He had gone to Elizabeth a scarred, vengeful boy, and left as a man. It was the man who wanted Reyna now.

He glanced down the table's length from his dominating position in the lord's chair. It was the closest he would ever get, but it was still better than most younger sons saw. Tonight, however, that thought gave him little comfort. He was, in the end, only a paid sword, and had been little more than a thief these last years. At least one person in this conquered tower would always see him so, no matter where he sat.

What role had that played in her denial? Why should he give a damn?

He shouldn't give a damn but, unaccountably, he found that he did.

At the end of the hall, a servant girl scrubbed the tables, her long dark hair draping from beneath her kerchief. She glanced at him and continued her work. He watched her move to her labors, her breasts and buttocks swelling against the fabric of her homespun gown.

She noticed his attention, and approached. He recognized her. She had sought his eye several times during the last two days and given him warm, shy smiles. She smiled less shyly now. "My name is Eva. Would you like me to fetch you some ale, my lord?"

My lord. Not really accurate, but a minor point to the servants under the circumstances. One person in this keep would never call him that, even if it were accurate, even at the point of a sword. Despicable whoreson, dishonorable bastard, aye, but never my lord.

Ian looked across the table at Eva. He smiled.

chapter SIX

Throughout the next day, Reyna made very sure to avoid Sir Ian. If she heard his step coming up one stairway, she darted down the other.

In the late afternoon, a commotion in the passageway drew her out of her chamber to see Margery and the other ladies conversing with excitement.

Margery's gaze raked over the simple gown that Reyna had put on after dinner. "Go and make yourself presentable," she ordered. "We are expecting a visitor. The rider just came announcing him. It is a French noble, the Comte de Senlis."

"Why would a French comte visit here? This keep is held by an English army, and the French are their enemies."

"Whatever his reasons, we must greet him properly. I have instructed Alice to do her best for the evening meal. We don't want this man to think he is amongst barbarians. Make yourself decent or hide in the kitchen. He arrives soon."

Reyna returned to her chamber, slipped on her blue cote-hardie, and descended to the yard, where the women waited to greet this luminary from France. Ian was there, and he hadn't done anything to avoid looking like a barbarian.

He was completing a pulley that he had devised to bring water to the upper levels of the tower. A large beam jutted out from the top-level garderobe, and ropes dangled down from its wheel.

Alice's grandsons, Adam and Peter, hung in the shadows. Ian noticed and called them over. Grinning with delight, they helped him run a test of the pulley. They fitted a water-filled bucket into the sling at the bottom of the rope, and Ian began hauling it upward.

He wore a sleeveless tunic and the cut chausses, and his body stretched against the fabric. The taut muscles of his arms made powerful lines as he reached hand over hand. Reyna realized that this was the first time she had seen him in full daylight. The sun picked up red lights in his dark brown hair. The feather-edged pools of his eyes looked deeper and more compelling out here.

He finished his test and stood back with a satisfied expression. She walked over and studied the mechanism. "If you fit a crank to the rope, even women could do it," she said.

"A good idea. Of course, in time of war the pulley makes the keep vulnerable. Whoever commands here will have to destroy it then." He finally noticed the line of women in their finery standing by the tower stairs. "What is this? Are we expecting the pope?"

"Margery said that a visitor is on his way here."

"All of this is for David? He should find that amusing."

"David?"

"David de Abyndon, Morvan's brother through marriage."

"Margery misunderstood. She thinks the Comte de Senlis arrives."

"David is the Comte de Senlis. But before he received Senlis he was a London merchant, and I knew him as such. In England he is still known as Master David the mercer. He never renounced his citizenship, and keeps his place in the trading company. He and Christiana, Morvan's sister, spend some of their time in London."

"An unusual story."

"An unusual man." He turned his attention to the rising portcullis and the sounds of approaching horses.

Six riders trotted into the yard. Reyna identified the comte immediately. He was a very handsome man with golden-brown hair. He swung off his horse and walked toward the keep with a vague smile on his lips and intelligent scrutiny in his deep blue eyes.

Ian strode forward and the two men greeted warmly. They spoke only a few words before David turned to the women. Margery stood forward in the position of prominence, and the comte accepted her proffered hand in a courtly gesture of greeting. "Lady Reyna, I assume."

Margery flustered.

"Nay, this is Lady Margery, Thomas Armstrong's wife," Ian explained. "That woman there is Robert Kelso's widow." He crooked his finger at Reyna.

She walked over, knowing that she looked very poor compared to Margery and the others. She wore no jewels and had refused to don heavy velvets. She wondered if this comte was the sort of man to be insulted by her lack of effort.

Beautiful hands took her own graciously. Intense blue eyes ignored her gown and looked only at her face. She experienced the uncomfortable feeling that another mind had just invaded her own and instantly learned all that it needed to know.

She was struck by the unaccountable fear that her situation had just become much more precarious.

W hat are these other chambers?" David asked as Ian led him to the solar door.

"Lady Margery has one, and the other ladies have moved up here for seclusion. Lady Reyna's nun's cell is down there."

"Nun's cell? And here I thought that you had created a harem for yourself. Protected by and accessible only to the sultan."

David walked around the solar, and his attention quickly lit on the shelves with their books. He became absorbed, handling them carefully while he examined bindings and flipped pages. "This is an excellent library, better than most bishops own. Aquinas and Augustine. Penitential tracts, but also part of the *Roman de la Rose*. An Ovid." He opened a cover. "Several of these came from the same source. They bear a device with the initials of a previous owner. J.M."

Ian lifted a tattered quarter folio from the shelf. "You should find this interesting. Bernard of Clairveaux, with a gloss commentary in the margins in French."

Ian watched David peruse the volumes and considered what he knew about this merchant-turned-comte. David had been one of the first English merchants to travel south and east and establish a trading network. That network had made him wealthy before he turned twenty-five. An enigmatic man, easy to know superficially but almost impossible to know well.

"What brings you here?" Ian finally asked.

David turned his attention away from the books. "I was at Carlisle awaiting the ship from London, but it has been delayed and I grew bored. I went to Harclow, and Morvan asked me to come here before I returned to the port."

Morvan had asked him to come and check on Ian of Guilford, was what Ian knew he meant. Morvan owed Ian the debt of his life, and had agreed to repay it with this chance of redemption, but Fitzwaryn was not entirely comfortable using a free company in his private war.

"As you can see, all is in order and the people are well cared for. This tower would have fallen sooner if Morvan had told me about the postern tunnel."

"He did not know about it. It wasn't here when he was a youth, or at least his father never mentioned it to him. Most likely Sir Robert built it. Morvan is very pleased with your success here."

"How goes the siege at Harclow?"

"The hunger finally forced them to send out the nonessential people. The women, children, and some servants. Morvan was waiting for it. Now he will attack. The machines are built and ready. Once the ship arrives with the men King Edward promised, it will be done." He paused. "It will be bloody."

"Does he want me there? Anyone could hold this tower now."

"When it is time, he may call for you. Now, however, he wants you here, keeping an eye on the roads down from the Armstrong manor at Clivedale. We expect Thomas Armstrong to attempt a relief action. Your news that Maccus is inside Harclow explained much, by the way. How did you learn that?"

"Lady Reyna let it slip."

"We learned from the men whom you sent that she led you to the tunnel. Did you seduce her into it?"

"Is that what the men said? Aye, I did, but not in the way that they mean." Ian described the events of that day.

"Shrewd of you to see through her plan. A vainer man might have decided she had fallen in love watching from the tower, and used the ruse to fulfill her desire."

"No such good fortune. She came to kill me."

"A brave woman. Quite lovely. When I first saw her, she reminded me of Elizabeth at first. Much younger, of course."

Ian flinched at this casual mention of the widow with whom he had spent two years of his life.

"She sends you her affection," David added. "She was wounded that you did not visit her when you passed near London."

Aye, she had sent her affection. But she had sent Morvan Fitzwaryn her love. One of the old tensions between them.

"Tell me about Lady Reyna," David said.

"She is bold and willful and nothing but trouble. A little hellcat. She has caused the well to go dry, I am sure, and never speaks to me without cursing me."

"Your men also brought the story of Sir Robert's death."

"I do not believe that of her."

"Still, strife which you do not need."

"Strife or not, she will be safe here, as Morvan ordered."

"The men who came with Gregory also say that she has become your lover." David spoke with the tone of a man being casual but wanting information nonetheless.

"I let them think it to protect her from them. I understand Morvan's goals here, David, but these men have lived a rough life a long while now—"

"I am not here to criticize, Ian. But I am glad to hear you have not taken up with her, because it will be best if the lady leaves."

So that was why David had come. To remove Reyna. The realization that she would disappear soon, that he would not even have her company at meals, numbed him in a strange way.

"As you know, Ian, Morvan has promised her safety to her father. Duncan Graham's neutrality is important." David explained as if he sensed that Ian needed convincing. "Morvan can not be fighting the Grahams while he also deals with the Armstrongs. With the accusations against Lady Reyna, the issue of her safety takes on new meaning. If the Armstrongs abduct her from here to judge her, the Grahams will interfere."

Ian listened to the relentless logic that would remove Reyna from Black Lyne Keep. "Where will you take her?"

"To her father, Duncan Graham. The colors of Senlis are permitted to cross his border."

"She may not want to go back there. She has asked to leave, but not to go to her father."

"She will be safe there. Call the lady, Ian."

His squire John waited outside the door, and Ian sent him to fetch Reyna. While they waited he asked David about Christiana and their children. David's normally inscrutable face lit when he talked about his family, and a warm expression suffused his eyes at the mention of Christiana in particular. Ian had seen that look on young men newly enraptured, but rarely in a man married for years. He glanced away, because the emotions that he saw left him a little hollow.

Reyna arrived, looking like a servant in the simple gown she wore in the kitchen. At least she had removed the kerchief.

David invited Reyna to sit in the chair, and then perched himself on the stool behind the desk. "I met with your father before this war began," he said. "He was concerned for your safety once the fighting started."

"I find that peculiar . . . er . . . How am I to address you, my lord?"

My lord. Ian's teeth gritted.

"David would be fine."

"I will not be comfortable addressing you thus."

"Then, if you prefer, Sir David. I finally allowed Morvan to knight me some years back. Since he once threatened to kill me with his sword, I thought this other use of it wonderfully ironic."

She laughed, lyrically. "That will suit me better, Sir David. Anyway, I have not seen my father since I left his household twelve years ago. Nor have I heard from him. His sudden interest makes little sense."

"You are his daughter."

A silence ensued. Ian watched Reyna. She was acting like a demure, sweet woman. Submissive. Not one whoreson or bastard out of her yet.

David absently pulled a book toward him. A little frown puckered Reyna's brow. "Do be careful, Sir David," she blurted. "They are very rare."

"I know their value, my lady. This is a large library for a minor Scottish lord. Some of these are quite old. How did your husband come by them?"

"He had some when he came back to Scotland. Over the years he purchased more. Some of them are mine."

"Back to Scotland from where?"

"He had traveled widely. Constantinople and Greece,

I think. Then the Continent. France. It was long ago. Upon returning he met Maccus Armstrong and entered his service, and had been here ever since."

"I am sorry that I never met him. We would have had much to discuss. You say some of these are yours?"

"A few. I keep them here with the others. I trust that when I am allowed to leave that I will be permitted to take them."

"The laws of chivalry say a noblewoman should be allowed to take her clothing and jewels. They do not mention books."

For the first time since she had entered, Ian saw a flash of the Reyna he knew. "I own no jewels, Sir David. These books are all I possess. I chose them instead of fine garments and pearls," she said pointedly.

"It will be for Morvan to decide their disposition. It would help if your ownership were documented. Perhaps your husband's accounts made note of it. Have you found the papers related to this estate, Ian? The ledgers and charters and whatnot?"

"The ledgers, but nothing else. I assume that Thomas took the rest when he escaped." Actually, he *had* found something else: the ambiguous letter from the bishop. It was now tucked among his own belongings.

David abruptly lost interest in the books. "Your father has made your safety an important matter, Lady Reyna, whether you accept the sense of it or not. Considering the accusations made against you in your husband's death, it would be best to remove you from here. Tomorrow I will bring you to your family."

His announcement stripped Reyna of her demure demeanor. She shot to her feet. "The hell you will."

"The charges against you promise to complicate things in ways we do not need. You will return to your father."

"My father has no authority over me." She raised her chin obstinately. "He handed that over when he gave me to Robert. He has no rights to me, and I will not return there."

"Would you return to those who *do* have authority over you?"

"And who would that be? My husband had no family. His liege lord, Maccus Armstrong, is besieged in Harclow. Does he want me so badly that he will open Harclow's gate to let me enter?"

Ian watched their exchange with delight. *That's my girl.*

"There is the option of sending you to Clivedale," David said.

"If you do, Thomas Armstrong will execute me in violation of all laws and his authority. Would Morvan Fitzwaryn send me to my death, and an unjust one at that?" Reyna spoke defiantly, but the threat had some effect, because her body shook as though a chill had slid through it.

David studied her. "Why do you refuse to return to your father? It is the safest place for you."

"Have you visited my father's household, Sir David? Surely you noticed the fear in the servants. You saw the way the women were treated and used. It has been thus since he put my mother away."

"I saw what you describe. But you are his daughter. Surely—"

"It was no different for me as a child, and it will be worse now. Duncan Graham holds no love for me. I will not go back there."

The air pulsed with the force of emotion echoing off her words.

"Ian said that you have asked to leave, however."

"Aye, but not to go to Duncan. I wish to go to Edinburgh. I have a friend there who will help me."

"Who is this friend?"

"His name is Edmund."

Edmund? "Edmund!" Ian shouted.

"He is the brother of one of my husband's knights. He is a cleric," she said, keeping her eyes on David. "A Hospitaller, with the knightly Order of Saint John. He is attached to their prefectory near Edinburgh. He knows of a widow who will give me a home."

"You mean he knows of a knightly monk who will give you a bed," Ian said.

"He is avowed to celibacy, damn you," Reyna shot back.

"*Jesus.* Are you that ignorant? A lot of good your books have done you, woman, if you think the Hospitaller's livery changes a man that much."

"Just like you to impugn a good man's intentions. What would you know of a man's chivalric concern for a woman in trouble? You prey on such as me. It is your life."

"What do you know of this honorable cleric?" Ian demanded.

"We have corresponded at length for five years."

"You write a few letters to a man about philosophy and you think that you know him? *Christ.*"

"I have met him, you idiot. He visited his brother Reginald here five years ago. Robert was much taken with him, and he visited again last year. He and Robert became good friends."

"And you and he became better friends."

"Just like you to think such a friendship could never be virtuous. What good is a woman, after all, unless she is on her back."

"Enough." David's quiet voice interrupted firmly.

Ian bit back the ribald retort that had formed in response to her last statement. Edmund the Hospitaller, for heaven's sake. "She obviously can not go to Edinburgh, David," he said. "If she has misjudged this man, she will be helpless."

"I am not such a poor judge of men. I had your measure in two blinks, you conceited, ignominious, hedonistic, English whore—"

"Enough, my lady," David warned. "Leave us now. You will not be going to Edinburgh, for we can not ensure your safety there. As for returning to your father, I will decide by morning, but you should prepare yourself."

Reyna marched out of the chamber with a determined gait that did not bode well for the next few days. Ian wondered if he should put a guard on the grain supply.

"A hellcat to be sure," David said.

"Hell. If I had not seen through her plan that night, she would be at that man's mercy by week's end."

"He might be as she claims."

Ian gave David a man-to-man look of supreme skepticism.

"She seems quite taken with you," David said dryly.

"Aye, I have clearly impressed the lady."

David sat behind the desk again. "Her father's home is as she described. With the concern he expressed for her, I thought, however . . ." He frowned as he flipped through the open folio. "I wonder why he wants her back."

"Does he? You said he sought only her safety. If he wants her, why not let him come and get her. Perhaps they will reconcile upon meeting here."

"I will think about that. Right now, help me to go through these books. I often place important documents in mine. Personal things. Perhaps he did too."

"What do we seek?"

"Anything. His testament. The marriage contract. His entitlement. It is odd that you did not find them. Why would Thomas Armstrong take them?"

They spent the hours until supper working their way through the tomes. Ian found a few private letters of no consequence, and a short poem of a religious nature.

Some of the volumes distracted Ian. One was a small Book of Hours with lovely illustrations showing the labors of the months. Toward the end he found a small scrap of parchment with a crude drawing. Just some circles and a square and some curving lines. It appeared that, among his other interests, Robert of Kelso toyed with astronomy.

Toward the end of their search, David discovered a large parchment inside a folio of the Gospels.

"Here is something."

"What is it?" Ian asked.

"The testament of Sir Robert of Kelso. However, it is also a motive for the lady to murder her husband." He handed the parchment over. "He left her everything. Not just some dower lands. Everything."

chapter
SEVEN

Ian stayed up most of the night thinking about Robert's death. He kept weighing the evidence against Reyna.

The discovery of the testament had certainly tipped the scales against her. He suspected that she knew that the document lay within that book, and had perhaps even placed it there herself. She would not destroy it, for it might still prove valuable, but she didn't want it found. It was an effective hiding place, since no one but Reyna and her husband read those tomes. That was why David's handling of the books had distressed her, and not concern that he might do damage.

So, she had known that Sir Robert had left Black Lyne Keep and all of its lands to her, making her a wealthy widow. Even if Maccus sought to depose her, that testament would have given Reyna a powerful weapon in any negotiations. At the least she would have probably been spared the fate of most childless widows, left with a small dower property and condemned to an impecunious existence.

Worse, if Sir Robert had sought to find a way to put her aside and annul the marriage because she was barren, she had good motive to hasten the man's death to get this inheritance before it slipped from her grasp.

Finally, if all that were not bad enough, there was Edmund. She had been corresponding with this man for over five years. Philosophy and theology and the great questions regarding the human condition, no doubt. Hell's teeth.

Dawn broke. He rose and pulled on some clothes. As he headed down to the hall, he finally let his mind follow the obvious path that he had been avoiding all night.

She and Edmund had fallen in love when he visited. They had continued their friendship with their letters, and he had come again to see her last year. Slowly, subtly, Edmund had begun to lament that they would forever be separated. She regretted this, but she had put off contemplation of any solution until Robert began the moves to put her aside. Suddenly her future was at risk, and that alluring life with the other man not only seemed attainable but necessary. Robert dies, she inherits, Edmund arrives first to console her and then to stay, and eventually he finds a way to be relieved of his vows.

But the suspicions against her had fouled her plans, and suddenly the testament became a piece of damning evidence to be hidden. Then, with the arrival of Morvan's army, these lands were no longer Robert's to bequeath and hers to inherit. She still sought to join her love, but now it was to escape the consequences of her action.

Aye, with the discovery of the testament and her relationship with Edmund, the thin evidence against Lady Reyna had gotten much thicker. It was neat, plausible, and convincing enough to send her to her death.

And what could be placed on her side of the scales? All he could summon in her defense was his own sense that she would not do such things. It didn't amount to much.

David sat at a table with his bread and ale. Ian slid onto the bench across from him. "She will not be going with you," he said.

Defying David was the same as defying Morvan. He was risking the future he had planned in the cause of a woman who could well be a poisoner, whom he may have misjudged, and to whom he owed nothing. It annoyed him to admit that he wasn't even sure why he had spoken.

David placidly ate his food. "Nay, she will not. I would probably have to tie her to the saddle, and even then she would bolt and we'd be searching the Cheviot Hills for days. I will go back to Harclow on my way to Carlisle and tell Morvan, and suggest that Duncan come for her. If he does, however, you must let her go."

"I will let her go, but I will not force her to."

"Whatever waits for her in Duncan's household, it is better than a noose or the stake. Have no expectations that Morvan will ignore this crime."

"She does not know a recipe for poison. If she did, she would have tried to use it on me. Much easier than a dagger."

"If she knows about poisons, she knows that their properties are changeable and unstable. A dagger is harder to use, but it is also surer."

"You have already decided her guilt."

"I only point out the damning evidence. Actually, I do not think she did it. She is very intelligent. If she had wanted to kill Robert of Kelso, I think that she would have found a way to do so that would have never brought suspicion on her. All the same, keep a close eye on her. She will try to escape. Behind her brave pose she is very frightened, as well she should be." He brushed his hands and rose. "The men and horses await. Hopefully I will make Harclow by sunset."

Ian accompanied David out to the yard. Lady Reyna stood at the bottom of the steps, arms crossed over her breast, her foot tapping impatiently.

"I am not going," she announced. "Furthermore, I have a message for you to bring to Sir Morvan. I have learned something of the fall of Harclow when he was a boy. Remind him that Maccus Armstrong allowed his mother and her children to depart, and to go where she wished. I demand the same chivalry of him."

"I will give Morvan your message, but I will soften the tone. He has small tolerance for women who presume to lecture him. Until your disposition is decided, you will remain here and obey Sir Ian."

Ian accompanied David across the yard to the horses.

"Nothing but trouble there, Ian."

"Aye."

"Don't lose her. I don't want to have to explain to Duncan that we don't know where his girl is."

"I won't."

David swung up on his horse. He looked again to Lady Reyna. She stood straight and determined and not one bit cowed. He clamped his hand on Ian's shoulder. "I will pray for you."

T he next day, a tenant farmer arrived at the gate to make a complaint about thievery. It had taken all of his courage to come, since the thieves had threatened to kill him if he did. Not much had been stolen, for these farmers did not own much, but that only made such losses more severe on them.

Ian had the man identify the culprits, and then searched their camp outside the wall. When the stolen items were found, the thieves' fate was sealed.

He had the thieves brought to a large tree near the river. He could have hanged them within the walls, but he took this action as leader of the company and not lord of the manor. He required forty of his men to attend, and included the ones he most expected trouble from. He made it clear that the punishment was not for the thievery, since that would be hypocritical, but instead for disobeying his order.

When it was done, one of his youngest knights walked forward and unsheathed his sword. It was the most direct of challenges, a blatant bid to replace him. Like two animals, they would fight for supremacy of the herd. Ian had not won his own authority in this manner, but had been elected by the other knights three years earlier, when the last captain died.

The other men formed a circle, and Ian turned to the challenger. It took him very little time to defeat the man.

The two experiences left him feeling sour and dark the rest of the day, and in no mood to brook any defiance. And so when Lady Reyna did not show for the evening meal, he stormed out of the hall in search of her.

He found her in her chamber, lying on her bed with a blanket up around her neck. The parchments and papers on her desk had been neatly stacked, and he wondered if the letters from Edmund were among them. The notion did not improve his humor any.

"Do not glare at me like that," she said. "I am ill."

"The hell you are. This is nothing but another rebellion to annoy me. Come down to the hall at once."

"You flatter yourself that I starve myself in order to vex you. I assure you that I am not well at all."

"Women like you do not get ill. You are too willful."

"That is the most stupid thing I have ever heard. I often get ill. As I am now."

He felt her brow. She did seem a little warm. "What ails you?"

"It is nothing serious. It will pass in a few days."

Concern made his voice harsher yet. "Lady, I will ask one more time. What illness is this?"

She heaved a breath. "It is a female malady, if you must know. Monthly pain. If a woman does not have children, it can be worse."

He instantly felt awkward and abashed. "Do you need a servant to attend you?"

"Nay. I simply endure. Have someone tell Alice that I will not be there for a while."

"I will send her to you. Don't you know any potions or whatnot to deal with such things?"

She rolled her eyes. "If I did, do you think that I would suffer? Really, Sir Ian, this is most embarrassing."

"How long will you be ill?"

"At least two days," she snapped. "Perhaps as many as four. Now get out of here, you English barbarian, and permit me some delicacy on this."

"That is more like it," he said, turning to leave. "If you hadn't cursed me, I would have sent to Carlisle for a physician."

Two mornings later Ian sat in the yard on the horses' water trough with a huge leather bladder on his lap. He pricked small holes in its bottom with his dagger.

"Like this, Sir Ian?" a young voice called.

He looked over to the wall where Alice's grandsons, Adam and Peter, had built a stockade enclosure the height of a man's shoulders. His men could have done the job in one third the time and with better results, but these were good lads and had taken to following him around, so he had let them participate on this project.

"Aye. Just big enough for one man is plenty," he said. The enclosure hugged the stairs leading to the battlement, and he had already attached a beam and hook above it.

"Let us see how it works." He walked up the stairs and hung the bladder from the hook. Adam hauled a bucket of water to him and Ian poured it into the leather holder. Sprays immediately sprung from the holes.

"It will be like being out in the rain," Adam said. "I wouldn't mind washing if I could do it in the rain."

"This afternoon you can go first, then. I'll use you to test how much water is needed for one man."

"I would think a lot. A bath takes many buckets."

"This will use less. Maybe only half a bucket, if you wash quickly."

"Have you had one of these before?"

"Nay, I just thought of it." Necessity had made him think of it. He didn't want to send the men to the river to bathe in great numbers, with trouble from Clivedale expected. Using tubs was out of the question, since they would have to haul nonstop from the river in order to service everyone here. Bodies were getting ripe, and he hoped that he had found a solution. If it worked, he would build a few others.

He jumped down and examined the security of the rough-hewn logs in the ground. While he pushed and tested, he heard the sounds of the laundry women leaving for the river. He wished that there were some device

to solve that problem as well. Reyna's sabotage had created a whole series of irritations.

Thinking of the lady turned his mind to Robert
Kelso's death again. The issue of the poison had caused
him much thought recently. If she did know a recipe,
where would she have found the ingredients, and where
did she keep them? For that matter, where did she keep
all of her herbs?

He gave the boys some praise and instructions, and
walked around the tower to the south yard. It held a garden enclosed by a low wall, and he strolled into the neat
plantings of flowers and toward the cool arbor of apple
trees. He came here sometimes to think, and found its
solitude restful.

Unfortunately, he was not going to find solitude now.
Lady Margery sat under one of the trees plying embroidery. She called to him with a delighted smile.

He did not find Margery unattractive or undesirable.
She was just the sort of willing woman whom he would
normally take up with in these circumstances. But her
blatant availability struck him as cloying and irritating
for some reason. It didn't help, of course, that she had a
husband who would undoubtedly issue a challenge if he
learned Ian had bedded his wife, and he would certainly
learn it, probably from Margery herself. Ian didn't fear
Thomas Armstrong. He just tried to avoid killing men
over women whom he didn't want all that much.

Edmund the Hospitaller, on the other hand, he would
gladly hack to pieces.

*I only want her because I can't have her. Like some
green boy.*

He sat beside Margery and spoke a few flatteries and
admired her embroidery and did all of the things that a
chivalrous knight was expected to do. She blushed like a

virgin and kept turning her face up to his as she spoke. He knew she expected him to kiss her. Instead he rose and offered his hand. "Perhaps you will show me the garden. I have never seen all of it."

Margery flashed a look that suggested this bench and tree were all the garden they needed, but she set her embroidery aside and joined him.

They strolled past some roses and other flowers that he recognized, and a few beds of vegetables. Margery moved relentlessly closer and he moved implacably forward. Finally, up against the back wall, in a patch of sunlight beyond the last of the trees, he found what he sought.

"What is this bed?" he asked.

"Those are Reyna's herbs. Ugly things, aren't they? I hear that she collected some in the hills, but Robert used to bring her seeds and plants sometimes. Herbs and books. What kinds of gifts are those for a lady?"

Gifts that would please her more than silks. King Alfred had known his young wife well. "Do you know what grows here?"

"I know nothing about such things. Only Reyna does."

"How did she learn, do you think?"

"Probably from that herbal she has. Robert gave it to her."

"You mean a book about herbs and their properties?"

"Aye. It even has little pictures. It is up with the others in the solar."

Nay, it was not. Neither he nor David had examined an herbal that day. Nor were there any books in Reyna's chamber. Had someone taken it? Did this herbal include plants with poisonous properties? He would have to find out the answers to those questions.

It was time to have a frank talk with Reyna.

He brought Lady Margery back to the stone bench, and politely but emphatically took his leave of her.

As he climbed the interminable steps, he scowled at their inconvenience once more. Too bad he couldn't hook up a pulley to carry people up here as well as water. The notion struck him as not nearly so outlandish on second thought, and he spent the time reaching the fifth level toying with the idea. Mental pictures were still occupying him when he scratched on Lady Reyna's chamber door.

No response came. Foreboding pricked at him. She might be asleep, of course. He pounded with his fist and the door swung open under its force.

He looked around the chamber, and then turned on his heel and flew down the stairs, level after level, until he landed on the threshold of the kitchen where Alice was cutting some meat.

"Where is she?"

"She?"

"Lady Reyna. She is not in her chamber."

"Ain't she? Well, she said last night that she was feeling better, so I guess she be up and about."

"She is not here, though."

"She doesn't spend all of her time here, Sir Ian. She has other interests. Did you check the solar? She reads there at times. And the garden, aye, she likes the garden. Or perhaps she is with the other ladies, doing needlework and such."

Fuming, Ian stomped back up to check the other chambers, barging through door after door. The foreboding didn't abate one whit, and by the time he returned to the hall's threshold it had turned into a furious certainty.

The hellcat had bolted. He knew it as surely as he felt bloody anger begin to split his mind apart.

His gaze rested on the gate. In his mind's eye he saw a bevy of women following a laundry cart through the wall.

Damn. She had walked out right under his nose, and he hadn't even been looking because he thought she was abed. Monthly pains, hell.

He shouted down to a groom to saddle a horse, and then went and harassed the man when he didn't work fast enough. Seething with silent threats of the things he would do when he got his hands on her, he kicked his horse to a gallop once he passed through the gate.

He should have let David take her away. Nay, he should have *insisted* that David do so. She was a demon from hell, disrupting peace, deliberately trying to drive him mad. Worse, she had become an invisible presence that he couldn't get out of his head. He spent his days in ridiculous anticipation of her presence, and his nights in tortured dreams of her yielding. And now, after he had been stupid enough to defend her, had assured David of her safety in Black Lyne Keep, she had walked away in a fashion sure to make him look like a fool. How could Morvan trust him to hold onto an entire estate as seneschal if he couldn't even hold onto one puny woman?

He found three guards lounging in the grass a hundred yards from the river's edge. Feminine laughter and chatter drifted in the breeze. "You are supposed to be guarding the women," he snarled, pulling up his horse. "How can you guard them if you are so far away?"

They shot cautious, confused glances at each other. "If we were any closer, we could see them," one offered helpfully. "You ordered we weren't to watch. We can hear if there is any trouble."

She knew that. She had learned the routine by

questioning the women who came. "How do you ensure that no one escapes?"

Another man lifted his hands and gestured to the surrounding moss. "Escape to where? We can see for miles, and there's barely brush to hide behind between here and the farms. Besides, we count them coming and going."

"How many today?"

"Twelve."

Ian rode down to the river's edge. The women noticed him and began squealing. He saw a melange of breasts and hips and thighs. He quickly counted the shocked, embarrassed, or inviting faces. Eleven.

He surveyed the surrounding terrain. If she headed toward the farms, she would be easily visible.

Suppose she expected help. Suppose someone waited for her with a horse. Where? His gaze swept the deserted countryside and came to rest on the ancient motte-and-bailey fortification upriver. It was the only landmark in sight, and the growth along the river would hide her.

Searching the water's edge, he began trotting in its direction.

chapter
EIGHT

R eyna shifted the cloth sack slung over her shoulder and quickly moved through the brush and trees. She had seen Ian ride up to the river and had surmised from his speed that he had discovered her escape.

Damn the man. He shouldn't have suspected for another day or so. Alice had promised to continue bringing food to her chamber to further the deception. She should have been well away before he noticed her absence.

Her plan had gone so well too. So easy to slip out among the other women. Her poor garments didn't surprise them, because she often dressed thus, and her willingness to help with the laundry had not raised eyebrows, since she helped with cooking. Once at the river, it had been simple enough to drift away while the women undressed.

She had walked a good ways upriver before she noticed Ian, but now her progress slowed because she needed to stay hidden in the growth. Sticking her head out a bit, she looked back and saw that he followed in her direction.

The sound of horse hooves became audible. She looked at the river. It was now or never. She would never get another chance.

She picked her way to the water's edge. She quickly stuck her shoes into her hemp sack and hid it beneath a fallen tree. She removed her kerchief and laid it open on the ground, then slipped off her gown, folded it, and tied it and the kerchief into a little bundle. Dressed only in her shift, she waded into the cold water. She would cross to the other side, and later she could retrieve the other things in the hemp sack.

A few yards from shore the water got much deeper. She took the kerchief bundle between her teeth so both arms would be free. It wasn't a wide river this close to its source, and she began swimming across.

"Damnation, woman, you are going to drown yourself."

She had reached the middle of the river when the furious voice boomed. She turned to see Ian glaring at her. His horse stood in the water's edge, the flow halfway up its legs.

She took the bundle from her mouth and treaded a moment. Ian stretched, looking in both directions.

"The only bridge is downriver, past the keep," she called.

"Get back here *now*."

"I would be a fool to do so, and you know it."

"I am going to kill you."

"In that case, let me drown. No blood on your soul, then."

Ian swung off the horse and walked forward until the water was up to his hips. He went no farther.

Reyna grinned. "You can not swim, can you? I thought

not. Most English can't. You should have read the ancient Romans on warfare, Sir Ian. All of their soldiers could swim."

His pose and expression were a picture of fury. Reyna laughed and his eyes only grew darker. Grabbing his horse's reins, he swung into his saddle and began sloshing away through the shallow pools near the bank, twisting to keep an eye on her.

She bit her bundle again and swam. It would take him at least half an hour to gallop down to the bridge and back up the other side. Much longer if he stayed alongside the river itself. By then she could make it to the ruins, or find a place to hide along the way.

A strong current grabbed her. She fought hard to escape it. She gasped for breath from the effort, and the bundle slipped from her teeth. The current bore it away.

She noticed to her horror that Ian had found a spot where the water ran shallow. He was already halfway across, pushing his mount through the chest-high flow. Her gown and kerchief floated right to him. He pulled an arrow from a quiver on the saddle, leaned over, and plucked it up.

They faced each other over the expanse of water. She turned to the eastern bank, but swam backward. Ian fell for the ruse. He kicked his horse forward and disappeared up the bank and into its thick growth.

Desperately, Reyna struck out for the side from which she had started. As she dragged herself out of the water, she could hear the loud curses that said Ian had discovered her deception.

Heaving from her exertions, she sought a place to hide. The brush and reeds looked very thin to her all of a sudden. Close to despair, she leaned against a tree. She looked up.

It was not very thick, but it appeared strong enough. Some of its branches were low, and perhaps the leaves would help hide her. Mumbling profanities at Ian of Guilford for forcing her to go to all of this trouble, she managed to lever herself up to the lowest branch. She climbed until the slender arms looked too weak to hold her weight. Straddling a branch where it met the trunk, she tried to get comfortable.

Her bottom rebelled against sitting with only a wet shift between it and the rough bark. She looked down at her almost naked condition. The shift reached only to mid-thigh. She pulled the wet clinging fabric away from her body. If there truly were a God, he would never let Ian of Guilford discover her in this condition. Since she was quite sure that God existed, the thought gave her renewed confidence.

The horse sounds said that Ian had tied up his mount. Soon she heard thrashing near the river while he sought the spot where she had left the water. He walked into the space below her. She held her breath and didn't move a hair.

He searched around. When he moved away through the growth, she permitted herself a small exhale. Eventually he would decide that while he searched she had swum the river yet again. She rested against the tree trunk and tried to ignore her discomfort.

Movement in the brush snapped her alert. Ian came back. He looked all around. He leaned against her tree trunk while he contemplated.

What was wrong with the man? She could be halfway to Edinburgh before he continued his search. She glared down at him, feeling very uncomfortable now and blaming him for it.

Suddenly his hand went to his head. He brushed his

hair and looked at his hand. She swallowed a cry as she realized that a drop of water from her soaked shift had landed on him. Another one now worked its lazy way down her leg. She twisted her foot to try and catch it.

It didn't work. She practically heard the plop on his head.

Ian stepped away from the tree and looked up at her. When she saw his expression she was very glad that she was out of reach.

"Come down from there, my lady." He spoke in the careful tone a person uses when struggling not to become a madman.

"I do not think that would be a good idea. You appear very annoyed."

"Annoyed doesn't begin to describe it. Down. Now."

"I think it would be best if you calmed yourself first."

"I am quite calm. I will be even calmer after I get my hands on you."

"You are most distressed. We will wait a while. Otherwise you may do something that you will regret."

"I will not regret one whit what I will do, Reyna. King Alfred indulged and spoiled you and you think that you needn't obey anyone. I am going to give your rump the punishment that your husband should have dealt you years ago. After that I will be calmer than I have been in days. Get down here quickly and it may not go too badly for you."

The discomfort of her perch suddenly didn't seem so bad. "You have no right or authority to abuse me thus."

"My lady, you forget your situation. You are a war captive. I am the man who commands the army that captured you. I have all the rights and authority to do whatever I wish with you. Now, for the last time, *climb down that tree.*"

She glared at him. Her situation was ridiculous, but his threats were intolerable. "Fine. Turn away. I won't have you watching me and looking up my shift."

With an expression of profound exasperation, he turned away. She waited a short while before saying, "I can not."

He turned and narrowed his eyes dangerously. "What do you mean?"

"I am stuck. I can not get down."

"Of course you can, you little witch. You got up there, you can get down."

"Don't be stupid. It doesn't always work that way and you know it. Even animals get stuck. In fact, I can not even get myself off this branch."

"Like hell. I've wasted enough time, you half-sized bitch. Climb out of that damn tree or I will come up and get you."

"Really, Sir Ian. War captive or not, I am a gentle-born lady. Your language—"

"My *language?*"

"See? You are not the least bit calm. And you should not come up to help me, gallant though the offer is. Look at this tree. It is not very strong. It barely took my weight."

He studied the limbs with grudging recognition that she was right. "I think that you should go and get help," she suggested. "I might be able to manage if I had a rope to hold on to."

"You insult me, Reyna. I do not have to be a philosopher to see what you are up to. When I leave here, it will be with you slung over my saddle, woman."

"If you are going to be unreasonable and stubborn, we have a serious problem, Sir Ian. I suppose we are going to stay here until we starve? That is a very clever solution."

He glared up at her. She half expected his fury to give him wings so that he could fly up and get her. He stomped over to a nearby tree and sank down to sit in its shade. He stretched out and made himself comfortable.

He planned to wait her out. Well, she had a very strong incentive to beat him at that game. They stayed thus a long, silent while, Reyna dangling on her high branch while her shift dried, Ian sitting below and glowering up at her.

"Who was going to help you?" he finally asked. He sounded a tiny bit less furious. "You came to meet someone. Who? Edmund?"

"Edmund is in Edinburgh. I planned to meet no one."

"That is a lie. The last in a whole series. You are well practiced in deception. I will have to remember that in the future."

She began to refute him, but stopped herself. For one thing, there was no point in arguing. For another, it *was* a lie, and in some ways she *was* well practiced in deception.

"You look quite lovely up there. Like some wood nymph. But it must be uncomfortable, since you are practically naked. . . ."

She really could do without his noticing that. "Aye, it is not pleasant. It is unkind of you not to get help or a rope."

He didn't answer. He simply rested his head against the tree and closed his eyes.

Taking a nap was out of the question for Reyna, and she was left to wait out the long minutes shifting and trying to find some relief.

Every moment felt like an hour. The sun had moved quite a bit when he looked up at her again. His expression seemed calmer, even normal. "Are you ready to come down now?"

"If I could do it, I would have long ago. While you slept, if I sought to escape. I truly can not move from here."

He rose and walked around, studying her predicament. "Perhaps you speak the truth. The closest branch is some distance away, and turning on that one could be treacherous."

"That is what I have been trying to tell you."

"You seem well treed. I don't think that you will be going anywhere. I will ride back and fetch some help and a rope."

"I suggested that over an hour ago."

"Don't move too much. That branch is bending in a dangerous way from your weight."

"Your concern touches me."

"I will be back shortly. Do not fall."

She followed the sounds of his departure through the brush, and then the movements of his horse trotting away. She forced herself to count to one hundred before raising one stiff leg and swinging it over the perch. Just moving felt wonderful. She rolled carefully onto her stomach and lowered herself while her feet flailed to find the next branch. When she connected with it, she let out a little laugh of triumph and quickly eased her way back down the tree.

Except for some small game moving in the distant brush, silence greeted her. Quickly, she picked her way upriver to the spot where she had hid her hemp sack. She knelt beside the fallen tree and felt beneath it.

Nothing. She pushed her arm in farther, and then leaned low to look.

"Searching for this?"

She froze for one despairing moment, then straightened up on her knees. Ian stood twenty feet away holding her hemp sack in one hand and her sodden bundle of gown and kerchief in the other. He let the sack drop to his feet and threw the wet lump toward her.

He leaned casually against a tree and folded his arms over his chest. He had seemed unfazed by her state of undress while she sat in the tree, but now his gaze blatantly drifted down her body, and her skin prickled in a hundred places.

"You said you were leaving," she mumbled accusingly. She jumped up and picked up the tied kerchief and fussed nervously at the knot. The water had tightened it into a nub of stone.

He didn't respond. He just stood there watching her in that silent, dangerous way. There wasn't much anger in his expression, but she decided that she would prefer fury to what else she saw. Her fingers clawed desperately at the kerchief to get at the dress, and she blinked hard against the expectant fear suddenly pulsing through her.

"You are really very beautiful," he said, as if he had just discovered something that explained a conundrum.

She sucked in her breath and kept her eyes safely on the knot. Her heart pounded a little harder. "For one so puny and scrawny, I am passable."

"Not so scrawny, now that you've eaten for a few days. Diminutive and delicate, as the great lords prefer." She glanced over and saw his vague smile as he threw her own words back at her, just as she had done to him.

The air between them was getting very heavy, and despite his relaxed and distant stance, something predatory emanated from him. That dark gaze did not move from her.

She turned her attention back to the knot and sought some distraction in her efforts with it. The silence pulsed with his awareness of her. She sensed that he knew that he was frightening her. It appalled her that the fear possessed an exciting quality that hummed with a quiet thrill.

"I want you," he said, calmly giving a name to the terrifying power invisibly reaching toward her.

"Am I supposed to be flattered? Am I supposed to swoon with delight that the handsome brigand favors me? Your attention has been spread so wide and thin that it has become much devalued to my mind, you devil's spawn."

"Considering your situation, my lady, it would be unwise to provoke me right now."

The threat stunned her. She became acutely aware of their isolation, of their distance from the keep and the motte, from everyone and everything. A silent, slow, primitive rhythm beat between them.

"You look perfect out here, with the flowers and grass around your legs," he said. "Much more becoming than surrounded by books and parchments. For all of your learning and logic, this suits you. Your mind may have been trained into neat garden beds, but your core spirit is still as wild as the growth here."

"You are wrong," she said, as horrible, wonderful tremors screamed silently through her body. Her skin felt unnaturally alert to the sun, the breeze, his gaze. Strange and amazing that he could do this to her while he stood twenty feet away. Frightening that just his presence could be so confusing and make her helpless.

"I do not think I am wrong. After all, I have tasted your passion." He tilted his head back a bit, examining her. It was a small movement, but it made the rhythm quicken.

"Take off your shift, Reyna."

Her breathing stopped. She stood motionless, mesmerized. She grasped the little bundle as though it were all that stood between her and perdition.

Mottled blotches of sunlight fell through the trees, picking out the dark lights of his hair. His face held a serious expression, and those eyes looked out from beneath their long lashes. He was so beautiful. This wasn't fair at all.

"Remove your shift," he repeated. "Let down your hair and come here and kiss me."

His command sent sharp, twisting sensations through her belly. She almost obeyed. "Do not do this," she said.

"It is inevitable. You know that."

"It is not. You do not even really want me. You are just annoyed that I deny you. We will go back to the keep and you will find someone else and all will be well." She kept throwing more words at him. Wonderful, rational words.

He smiled in his devastating way. It softened his expression, but not the intensity of his attention. "It is not that simple. I do not know why I want you so much. It is rare. So is the restraint that I have shown with you. I believed that you still held your husband in your heart, but now that I have learned about Edmund . . ." He pushed off from the tree and took a step toward her.

"I did not lie about Edmund. Don't you dare use that as an excuse."

He continued toward her. Lithe. Strong. Confident. Nothing really existed anymore but him and her and the aching pull between them. "Looking at you and feeling what is between us, I need no excuse. Do you? Then tell yourself later that you hate me and did not want this, even though neither will be true."

Damn him. He had no conscience. No shame or

mercy. She turned away from him and his beauty, but mostly she tried to turn away from the horrible knowledge he had of her, and from the old, treacherous yearnings that he played with now.

It was a hopeless gesture. Even as her mind rejected him, her spirit waited, urged, savored the male power approaching. Her body tingled the way it did in her dreams and had from his touch. That yearning already pulsed deep inside her.

Run, her mind yelled. *You are nothing to him.* But the voice was drowned out by that rhythmic beat, submerged in the scent of grass and flowers and river, overwhelmed by the hidden, buried something inside her that didn't care about anything but being released.

I an looked at her standing with her back to him, trying to pretend that she didn't notice the invisible tie twisting tighter and tighter between them. Her erotically charged fear sharpened his desire. He let the tie wind tighter as he approached, enjoying its delicious tug.

He pictured her removing her shift, unveiling the body that he already half knew. Memories of that evening in her chamber flew at him. Her tremulous, frightened passion . . . Her helpless yielding . . . High, round breasts leaning into his touch and mouth . . . Her waist, so narrow that his hands almost met when he held it, curving down to the garments falling around her hips.

Violent desire ripped through him. A few paces away, standing in the wildflowers, Reyna startled as if his hunger had jumped through the air and struck her.

She quickly plied at the knot on her bundle. He walked over, drawing out his dagger, and she visibly shook as he neared. He stood behind her and reached around and cut through the knot, his hands covering hers for a moment, the brief contact a tease to his senses. His surrounding arms dominated her small form, and he caught the faint scent of female arousal.

The kerchief opened and the gown fell out. "It is wet," he said, looking at the lovely nape of her neck.

"It will have to do," she muttered, snatching it up and shaking it out.

"You will not put it on, Reyna. And you will remove your shift."

She clutched the garment to her body. He touched her hair, his fingers gently prying for the pins that bound it. Her whole body trembled and a blush ran up her neck. The gorgeous, bright tresses spilled down her back. He stepped closer and ran his hands lightly up her arms and pressed his mouth against the silken fall.

"I want you," he said again.

"Do you always take what you want?"

"Usually. Eventually. I am not well practiced in denial." He bent to press a kiss on her shoulder, still stroking the length of her arms. Little paths of heat rose beneath his touch. He could not see her face but he knew that she had closed her eyes in resistance. Hopeless, of course, but he admired the strength that made her worth pursuing.

"You think Edmund and I were lovers, and so I am of loose morals and free to be used," she said.

"Nay. You are in my head all the time and I can not fight that forever."

"So you seek to get rid of that inconvenience."

He nuzzled the side of her neck and took her waist in his hands. So small, almost breakable. But a spirit that would never break. Still, he would bend it to his will, in this if nothing else. "I want to give you pleasure. It fills my dreams." He kissed her ear. "You want this, Reyna. If not, you can run away. But you haven't yet, and I do not think that you will. Something tells me that you feel as I do, and that you know this will be good between us."

His arms moved to embrace her. He heard her sharp intake of breath. The wet gown fell from her clutch. He felt her expectant wariness, sensed her amazed surprise, almost smelled the sensual fear mixing with the subtle scent coming from her thighs. All of it stirred primitive, dominating reactions in him.

He caressed her, pulling her closer until her hips pressed against him. She grabbed his arms as if to wrench them off her body, but she did not. For one tense moment she hovered on indecision. He could almost hear the clash of steel as rational thought battled sensual need. Then breathing deeply, trembling gently, she sank into his embrace and yielded.

Elated triumph flooded him. He caressed down her slender curves, reveling in the frail feel of her, his senses clouding to everything except her slow, audible sighs and her clean, cool scent and the dewy taste of her skin beneath his lips and teeth as he found the places on her neck that made her gasp. And so he barely heard the words carried on her low exhales.

"If I do this, will you let me go?"

His hands halted. He raised his head. Sympathy twisted in his chest for the mortal fear that made her offer such a trade. "Nay, but only in part because of my duty to Morvan."

"Later, when you tire of me?"

"You do not leave now or later."

She twisted her neck so she could see him. "They will kill me."

"They will not. I will not let them."

"You are only one man."

"I will not let them. Even if you deny me now or later, it is so. You do not have to whore for me to have that protection."

A pitiful hope flashed in her eyes. Then she closed them and laid her cheek against him. He took her closer and she did not resist, but instead tilted her head back to accept his kiss.

He cupped her breasts and teased her until she arched into his touch and her bottom pressed against his body. He lowered them both so she knelt between his spread thighs, sitting back into him, grasping him above the knees.

He played at her until she was whimpering and caressing his thighs. The aimless progress of her small hands and the rhythm of her bottom against his lap drove him mad. He separated from her a little and pushed her hair over her shoulder. "Take off your shift."

She hesitated and glanced back at him. Then rising slowly to her knees, she slid the hem of the thin garment up. His gaze and hands followed its progress as it unveiled creamy thighs and round buttocks and thin back. Her delicate muscles stretched elegantly while she pulled it over her head and dropped it beside them.

He traced the beautiful curve from her waist to her hips and pressed kisses onto the small of her back and up her spine. Her head lolled back with her sighs. When he rose on his knees and embraced her naked warmth, she moved into him with a sinuous, pliant stretch.

He laid her in the flowers and grass and swung to straddle her legs. He knelt tall and looked down at her parted lips and passion-blurred eyes.

His heart thought that he had never seen a woman more beautiful. He bent down and kissed her slender thighs and blond mound, her curved hips and flat stomach, the perfect round swells of her breasts, smiling at the sounds and flexes each contact summoned from her. Leaning forward, hovering over her on his extended arms, he sought her mouth and kissed her deeply, biting, probing, savoring the taste and warmth of the intimacy, feeling her whole being rise into it. She tentatively touched her tongue to his. He suspected she had never done that before, and he encouraged her, withdrawing, parting his lips until she ventured her own kiss and her delicate, innocent tongue flickered.

He turned his kisses to her neck and she groaned when he pressed the sensitive places he had discovered. Putting his weight on one arm he traced along her shoulder and chest to her breasts with the other hand. The lighter his touch the more she cried out. He moistened her taut nipples with his tongue and teased with his lips and teeth for a long while before he drew more demandingly. Her body was out of control beneath him and her hips rocked in that begging way of women, but he would not be denied this slow love-play.

Kneeling up, he unbuckled his belt and drew off his shirt. She looked up at him, her eyes wild, her breath coming in short, deep sighs, her silver-shot hair spread out around her. He lowered himself until he felt her breasts against his chest and her leg between his and closed his eyes so as to know only this perfection of her welcome embrace. He caressed down her body and her soft groan of pleasure undid him.

A storm of desire and sensation clapped through him. Leveraging his weight on one forearm, he kissed her again and again, devouring her mouth and neck and breasts, claiming her whole body with his hand, reveling in her sharp responses, relishing her submission and his complete control of her. The scent of grass and flowers and sweat and her need filled his head, intoxicating him.

He slid his hand between her thighs and stroked. She gasped with startled pleasure and clawed at his shoulders. He looked down at her shocked expression. He gently touched her again and again, finding the spots that made her cry, and she accepted it, closing her eyes in ecstasy. Her stunned abandon pushed his body to its limits.

He slid his hand down her thighs and spread them and settled over her.

"Oh, my God," she cried, looking up at him, terrified alertness suddenly in her eyes. "Oh, my God. Nay. *Nay.*" Her body thrashed beneath his and she pushed frantically at his shoulders and weight. "Nay, I can not," she yelled, squirming and pushing. Over and over she yelled her denial. Her face held a despairing panic.

Anger was his initial response, but the force of her reaction stunned him. Concern pierced his single-minded desire. He pushed off of her and wrapped her in his arms. "I will not take you. I will not," he reassured again and again.

Finally her body calmed. She lay there with that sad expression he had seen when she pushed him away in her chamber. *I can not.* She had said the same thing then. *I can not. I must not.*

She turned her face away with a devastated expression. "I am sorry," she whispered. "I did not mean to do this to you."

"I will live. I think."

That made her laugh in an embarrassed, painful way. "You must think I am either a madwoman or truly a half-sized bitch. It was not intentional, last time or this."

"I know."

She glanced down, suddenly aware of her nakedness,

and blushed. She turned her head to find the shift and reached for it.

"Nay," he said. "Not yet. Lie here with me a while longer."

She raised an eyebrow. "If you think to seduce me past my resolve, it is not possible."

"As I have learned to my pain." He touched one finger to her brow and traced down her nose and across her lips. Slowly he continued the line lower. Her pink nipples hardened as his hand neared. "I think to give you pleasure. I will not enter you in any way, I promise."

She began shaking her head in wary denial, but he kissed her objections away. He would bet a year's plunder that she didn't know what he referred to.

She was helpless against his touch. Her passion climbed again with stunning quickness, refiring his own desire. He spread her legs wide so he could caress her freely. Burying her face in his shoulder, she accepted the pleasure.

He thrust his leg across hers and pressed himself against her rocking hip and watched her half-hidden face tense as the sensations became excruciating for them both. Then she was crying out lowly, grabbing him frantically, raising her hips to demand more. Her end was beautiful and violent. He kissed her and swallowed her scream and let her tremor carry him with her.

She lay in his arms gasping and spent. He did not have to look at her face to know her surprise. He experienced a boyish pleasure in having brought her to this before any other man.

"There are many ways to give and take pleasure without joining, Reyna. Lie with me at night. I will show you."

That sad look returned and she slowly shook her

head. "I am weak with you, Ian. Eventually . . . Nay, I can not."

He did not coax her. There would be time enough for that. And she was right. Eventually he would find the pleasure that obliterated her resolve or fear. He wasn't known as the Lord of a Thousand Nights for nothing.

He bent to kiss her sweet lips.

Quick movements in the brush stopped him. Close. Clumsy. A new scent, sharp and human, drifted on the breeze.

Danger shouted through him. He quickly covered her body with his and stretched for his dagger in the grass. And then, in one broken instant, his head split open and oblivion swallowed him.

N ay! Do not kill him!"
Her cry caught Reginald as the blade began
its downward stroke. He paused, the sword
hovering.

She frantically pulled on her shift and gown. "Those
are his men in the keep. If you kill him, they will come
with vengeance, and may rampage in the tower and
town before they do."

Reginald glared at his victim. Blood oozed through
Ian's hair and glistened on the discarded tree branch lying by his side. "Did he have you?"

"Nay. I fought him off. Surely you heard me."

"Aye, I heard your screams. It is how I found you. I
had seen you in the river from the ruins and came
down."

She bent and felt Ian's neck. Her horror retreated
when she found a pulse. "We should leave at once. He
has been gone overlong, and others will come to find
him."

Reginald's knuckles whitened as he gripped his sword tighter. "Damn English bastards. Think Scotswomen were born for their use."

"Did you find horses?" she asked, trying to distract him.

"Aye. They are nearby." He looked up to the sky. "We will wait at the ruins tonight and go north in the morning."

"Nay, we must be away now. It will not take them long to think about the old castle. We can be in my father's lands shortly. They will not cross the border."

"I smell rain, my lady. We will be safe at the motte, and can see if any approach. I'll not spend the night in Graham lands, getting lost on those paths in the dark. If we leave at dawn, we will get through by nightfall. You must follow me on this. I know what I am about."

Reyna shot a worried glance back at Ian. He had not moved, had not made a sound. She said a prayer that someone would search for him soon.

The horses were a half-mile upriver, hiding in the growth. Reginald lifted her onto hers and swung up on the other.

She noted his frown and thin lips. Straight blond hair hung down to his chin, and broad flat cheekbones defined his craggy face. His blue eyes held a dangerous glint. He looked like a man determined to complete a mission, and prepared to fight demons from hell if they interfered.

They rode up the ruins, and Reyna was relieved to see that Reginald had made his camp behind some stones and not in the donjon's cavernous foundations. For a man who had escaped from Black Lyne Keep only days ago, he had managed to provision himself very well. Blankets and a pot and a water bladder sat to one side of the cold hearth circle. He had somehow procured a bow.

She had never minded Reginald's taciturn nature be-fore, because he was always just a silent shadow in Robert's presence. Now that she was alone with him, she found it a little unsettling. She realized that while Reginald had been a part of her life for twelve years, she really didn't know him. Certainly not as well as she had known his brother Edmund after one month.

"It is my plan to go north to Edinburgh," she ex-plained.

He nodded. "Edmund told me. Said he had made the offer long ago, should Robert die and you want to leave here."

"He said I could stay with a widow there who teaches some girls. I sent a letter to Edmund before the siege and told him that I would be coming if I could. The notion has appeal. Robert taught me, and now I will teach oth-ers. It has a certain rightness to it."

"It is not a fitting life. Two women living alone in the city? No man protecting you? Robert would not ap-prove."

"Robert is dead, Reginald."

"Aye. He is dead, but I am not."

The rain that Reginald had expected rolled into the sky, and they sought shelter under the entrance to the ruin's foundations. Reyna nested amidst some blankets and fell asleep with the cool rain dripping all around her.

When she woke, the setting sun had turned the moist air sultry. Reginald had left, and the bow was missing.

She thought about the life waiting for her. It had al-ways sounded very alluring, and then, after the accusa-tions began, had turned into a dream. Now that she was on the road there, however, her enthusiasm had failed her. A lump of melancholy had lodged under her heart instead.

She decided it was because she was leaving her home. Still, something else tinged the sadness. Something inexplicable and poignant.

She wondered for the hundredth time if anyone had found Ian. It would be better not to think about him, she decided. Wonderful to never remember what had happened a few hours ago. Dear saints, she hadn't even resisted much, hadn't run away, hadn't told him to stop once he touched her. She not only had succumbed to his practiced seduction like so many other women, but had probably done so more readily than most.

That notion humiliated her. And yet those lush sensations had been glorious, obscuring thought and duty, rolling her along to that special ecstasy. She had been both removed from the world and also more essentially in it than ever before. Oblivious to her surroundings, but absorbed into their natural rhythms. Close to the man in her arms in a way she had never been close to anyone before.

It amazed her that she had found her mind at the last minute, but that memory only humiliated her more. She should be grateful for his understanding about that. Most men would have just forced her if she did that to them.

A strange man, Ian of Guilford. Proud and arrogant and conceited to be sure, and an opportunist no doubt. But kind in his own way. And very clever. She had rather enjoyed matching wits with him these last few days. She admitted with amazement that she would miss him, and that part of her sadness came from her loss of him.

She needed to get her mind off him. She reached inside her sack for the one volume she had brought, a small Book of Hours.

It was the first one she had ever owned. Robert had given it to her as a wedding gift because it had lovely pictures. While he had lain ill and dying, she had read it to him bit by bit, even though he knew the words by heart. It had stayed on the table beside his bed amidst the potions and parchments and quills, a reminder of their love and promises.

She smiled at the detailed illuminations of peasants and townspeople showing the labors of the months. She never tired of looking at them. When she turned to the month of August, a little slip of parchment fluttered to her feet.

She picked it up curiously, concerned that a page had torn. But the scrap did not come from the book. It bore no words, only a square and circles and curving lines. This scrap must belong to Thomas. He didn't read much, but he would have enjoyed looking at these pictures while he lived in the solar. She slipped it back in the book and continued reading.

Reginald returned at twilight with two rabbits. He built a low fire in the stone circle and set about skinning them. The fire would be hidden here, and Reyna guessed that he had used torches to signal her these last nights. When the meat was cooked, they ate in silence.

Twilight was dimming when Reginald abruptly spoke. "Before Edinburgh, we will stop in Hawick for a few days."

"That is too close, Reginald. Let us make our way to Edinburgh quickly."

"Nay. It will be Hawick. I have been thinking about what Robert said to me, about his request that I protect you. I am convinced that he wanted us to marry."

Reyna went very still. She prayed that she had misheard.

"It is the only way to protect you," he went on. "Elsewise, on what authority do I do so?"

"Chivalry gives you the authority. My late husband gave you the authority. If that is not sufficient, I will give it to you."

He shook his head. "It will not be fitting for us to travel together otherwise, and Robert would not want you living alone without protection. We will marry and go to Edinburgh and I will find service there. Edmund will know of lords who need a sword."

"I go to Edinburgh only because of Edmund's suggestion that I teach there and live with this widow. I do not wish to go there to be the wife of a knight in service."

"It is well away from here, and apart from the jurisdiction of the bishop of Glasgow. It is still the best place to go."

He had missed the point completely. "Reginald, I am sure that you misunderstood Robert's intentions. If he wanted us to marry, he would have said so to me, and he did not."

Reginald looked over in a way that was not nearly so simple as normal. "I am convinced that he did so intend. You have no kinsmen to protect you except the Grahams, and you will not be wanting to go back to them. This oath creates a duty that I'll not be handing off to another. If you are unmarried, men will be preying on you like that English bastard back there, and I'll be killing them. Nay, my lady, if we are to be bound for life, then properly bound we will be."

"I will not let you sacrifice yourself thus."

"Marrying you will suit me." He gazed up with a very different expression. Reyna looked into his eyes, and saw what was there.

Oh, dear. Oh, hell.

"Robert is barely cold. To force a marriage, and on a newly bereaved widow at that—"

"From what I could tell this afternoon, your bereavement is well over, my lady."

So. He had seen or heard enough to reconsider his opinion of her.

The lord's wife and widow had suddenly become available. Not a slut, though, if he was considering marriage. He had probably rationalized her behavior in the way of the church. A woman, being of base nature like all women, would obviously go astray if there were not some man keeping a firm leash on her.

His decision took care of all that. He would fulfill his oath to protect her, save her from the damnation inherent in her femininity, and have his lord's lady whom he had desired as well. No doubt very neat to his mind. Since her first marriage had shown her to be barren, he probably felt incredibly chivalrous.

"I will refuse, and the priest will not wed us."

"I will explain the situation, and he will. If need be, I will pay him."

She rose and glared at him. "This is intolerable, Reginald. I always thought you an honorable and decent man, as Robert did, but I see that we both misjudged you."

"And I always thought you an honorable and virtuous woman, as Robert did, but perhaps we both misjudged you as well. A decent woman would be glad of a husband to protect her. Perhaps today was not the first time with that Englishman. Perhaps Thomas was right, and you handed him the tower after he had had you." He paused. "Perhaps you even tired of your old lord and sought to be free of him."

She sucked in her breath with dismay. An unspoken ultimatum hung in the air. If she had loved Robert and had not killed him, if she was virtuous, she would marry

Reginald. If she refused, she was a whore and had probably killed her husband.

Sickening fear seeped through her, announcing her
danger. For if she were a whore and murderer, if she declared herself one by refusing his protection in this marriage, she felt convinced that Reginald would take her
not to Edinburgh, but to Clivedale.

Well, damn him. There was a third choice. Not much
of one, and only a brief reprieve, but better than his.

"I relieve you of your oath." She snatched up her sack
and walked away from the fire. "I never thought I'd see
the day when being a captive of an English army was the
safest place for me."

He was upon her in an instant, his iron grip clamped
on her arm. "You will not go back there to him."

"I do not go to anyone, madman." She stretched to be
free of him. "I go *home*."

He pulled her back toward the fire. "Tomorrow we ride
to Hawick. By morning, you will see the rightness of it."

"Tomorrow we ride through my father's lands. I will
scream until we are found by Grahams, and it will go
badly for you."

"Then I will see that you make no sound, my lady."

Her eyes widened in horror as she realized where he
was dragging her. "Nay, Reginald. Do not."

He bent to scoop up a rope. He forced her into the ruined donjon. She grabbed at a stone and dug in her
heels, and he pried her free and lifted her into his arms.

"Not in here, Reginald," she pleaded, as the black
cavern of the foundation vaults closed around them. "Tie
me outside."

"If the gag comes loose, you will scream," he said,
dumping her on the ground and quickly binding her
hands together. "I do this for your sake, my lady. You will

see that soon enough." He drew the rope down and circled her ankles. "All will be well. I will take care of you."

Already the darkness was working its terror. Defeating
her. Making her a child. "Then stay here with me," she
whimpered.

"I must keep watch outside," he said, striding away.

Oh, God. Oh, God. She closed her eyes, trying to ignore the silent darkness by pretending she only slept.
But it pushed on her as it always did, the void growing
fingers to prod and poke at her, the silence beginning to
echo with cruel laughs.

She desperately squirmed around until she could see
the way from which they had come. The vaguest flicker
of the dying campfire was visible between the stone sen-
tinels of the threshold. She pulled over her sack and
clawed inside until she found the book. Holding it to her
breast like a talisman of rationality, she huddled against
her knees and kept her eyes on that small orange glow.

She watched a long time, waiting for the dreadful moment when the coals would die.

Cold. Chilling cold. Desolate loneliness. Sounds to
the left and right, and beneath her in the stone itself.
Faint sounds. Scurrying and footsteps.

She noticed every spark extinguish. Finally she faced
nothing but eternal blackness. The terror seeped into
her slowly, insidiously.

She clutched the book and began reciting every
prayer she had ever learned, every passage she had ever
read.

I an slapped Margery's hand away from his head and
bent to pull on his boots. Margery reached over with
some more salve, making irritating little cooing sounds.

"Away with you," he snapped. She moved away with a pouting expression. Then she glanced back, with a look that said he was a fool who couldn't take care of himself if he planned to ride in his condition.

It was all so predictable that Ian barely kept his temper.

He turned to Gregory. "It is done?"

"Aye. Twenty men to go check the farms. Another ten to the town. A patrol will leave at daybreak to look for signs on the moss." His skeptical tone indicated he doubted they would find anything. Ian doubted it too.

"You should eat something," Margery ventured. "I will bring up—"

"Leave now, woman," Ian ordered dangerously. She drifted away shaking her head. She was acting like his worst nightmare of a wife.

"Who do you think it was? How many?" Gregory asked.

"I saw nothing," Ian said. He saw nothing because he was lying on top of a naked woman, damn it.

"It could be Thomas Armstrong who took the chance to grab her. Or even Grahams for that matter. You weren't all that far from their border. Of the two, most likely Grahams, since they didn't kill you."

Nay, they hadn't killed him, although he had lain unconscious a very long while, until the rain had brought him to. Had she argued against his death? A part of him wanted to think so. The weak part.

"Not Armstrongs or Grahams, I think. Someone she knew and trusted is more likely. I do not think she intended to walk to Edinburgh alone." He strapped on his sword. "I think she was heading to the old castle. I will ride there and see if they left that way."

"How many men will you be wanting?"

"None."

"Sir Ian, I know that you are angry, what with the lady snatched from your hands. No doubt you want to even the score. But who knows what awaits? There are myself and six others ready to ride."

"*None.*"

"That is unwise, sir, and you know it."

It *was* unwise. And stubborn and prideful. He had lost her, so he wanted to get her back by himself. But mostly he didn't want anyone around when he killed these men and then dealt with the deceptive little bitch who had played him as if he were some green squire.

Only once before in his life had he so completely misjudged a woman. While he had made his way back to the keep, his head splitting with pain, he had finally seen this one for what she was. She had been manipulating his interest to create an ally and protector, encouraging him to argue away the clear evidence of her guilt in Robert's death.

Her performance today had been masterful. Jesus, but she had shown him for a besotted idiot. Drawing out the time, dangling in that tree, trying to get away, prolonging his seduction. All the while she was waiting for her rescuers to find her. She hadn't yelled her denials at the beginning, but waited until the end when he would be most vulnerable to attack. She had pretended innocence and ignorance and virtue from the start to beguile him.

I can not. Like hell she couldn't.

"You will be wanting me with you, I think," Gregory said meaningfully. "Morvan insists she is not to be harmed."

"Then come, damn it. And bring the others. You are right, there is no telling what awaits."

Taking no torches, they rode quickly upriver toward

the dark shadow of the ruins. A quarter-mile from the motte, Ian called a halt. Gregory drew up alongside him.

"Well positioned," Ian said. "If anyone is there, they can see in all directions, and watch the river too."

"Do you think they would be so foolish as to stay this close?"

"Why not? It would take a whole army to surround that hill. We go up one side and they slip down another, and by the time the search is done they are well gone, up the waste and into the hills." He swung off his horse. "Give me time to circle around and go up the south side. Then move forward none too quietly, pretending to search in the growth by the river. If they are there, maybe it will distract them while I get a look. If there are too many, I will come back. Otherwise, listen for my signal."

Ian began running south. His head throbbed from his jostling gait, but a different pulse in his blood drove him on. He angled over to the hill, slid down the ditch where the old wooden bailey wall had once stood, and scrambled up the other side. Moving more slowly, he climbed toward the dim ragged shape of the ruined circular donjon. As he neared the stones, he paused.

No sounds greeted him except the vague snort of horses. He waited in the darkness until he heard Gregory calling orders to the other men, telling them to check along the river.

Ian squinted in the night. A man stood facing away, peering around some stones. The clouds shifted, and moonlight vaguely reflected off his blond hair and the steel sword in his hand. No one else seemed about.

Ian circled around the back of the structure to where two horses stood. He'd be damned if he'd have Reyna riding off into the night. He untied the reins and sharply smacked both rumps with one hand while he unsheathed his sword with the other.

The scurrying of hooves and the sound of steel on scabbard jerked the man around. Ian stepped into the clearing and faced him across the cold fire circle. "I think that you have something that is mine."

"I have nothing that is yours, English pig."

"All that was within Black Lyne Keep when I took it is mine, including the lady. Where is she?"

"Well away with the others. I stayed to cover their escape."

"You are lying. There were two horses."

Ian couldn't see the man's face in the night. He could barely see his form. Down the hill, Gregory and the others continued searching. He called out to them.

His mouth had barely closed when the dark form charged. Ian caught the sword on his own, and the harsh sound of connecting steel rang out through the night.

The man fought with the desperation of a crusader battling for Jerusalem. The dark only made the contest more perilous. Ian relied on sheer instinct and subtle senses, listening for the whistling air that told him how the weapon arched, feeling the other's movements more than seeing them.

He knew when the man twisted in a vulnerable way, and brought his own sword down at an angle, connecting invisibly with hip and leg. A guttural cry accompanied the sounds of a body and weapon falling to the ground.

It hadn't been a death blow, because he wanted the man alive. He grabbed for hair and jerked the head up. Gregory and the others were riding up the hill. "Where is she?"

The man didn't speak, but just angled his head back, exposing his neck for the coup de grâce. Snarling with irritation, Ian flung him to the ground.

"The lady?" Gregory asked, jumping down from his horse.

"She is here. Probably hiding in the ruins." He had visions of spending the night playing children's games as Reyna slipped around these rocks, always out of grasp. "Position the men at points around the motte, Gregory. Tell them to let nothing pass, not even a mouse."

Head throbbing and mind cursing, he strode toward the tumbling building.

T he only thing keeping Reyna sane was the beat of her own heart.

She concentrated on the quick, heavy pulse. It seemed so real, almost tangible, and it reminded her that she had not fallen into a black eternity, but that she was alive and that time passed in the normal way. Even so, a part of her, a growing part, had long ago abandoned itself to the terror.

Those invisible hands reached out for her again. Not startling her with prods and pokes now, but sliding along her arm and hip. The laugh was different—lower, dangerous, taking cruel pleasure in her fear. She grasped her knees tighter, and willed those demons away. Only this time, they would not leave.

Panic began rising, spreading, determined to defeat her. She had fought it so long that her spirit was exhausted, and succumbing held a seductive lure. *Robert,* she screamed silently.

Steps in the dark. Not faint scurries, but the steps of a

man. She waited, breathing heavily. She squinted into the blackness, looking for the light and hand of salvation even though her soul knew it could not be there.

Closer now, pacing slowly. Stumbling into her. Screams of terror came from somewhere, echoing off the stones, as her tired spirit collapsed.

"*Jesus.*" A loud voice. A real one. Angry, but she didn't care. Firm hands grabbed her shoulders, shaking her.

The voice again, still angry but softer now. "I will not hurt you. You do not have to be frightened. Now come with me out of this place."

Her own voice, separate from her body. "I can not."

"My lady, I do not *ever* want to hear you say that again."

A tiny corner of sense cleared in her clouded mind. "The rope."

"Hell. Do not move." Sharp movements made the bindings fall free. "It seems your scheme did not end as you had planned, Reyna."

The dark space slowly took normal shape around her. The scent and presence looming over her shrieked with new reality. Her whole body shook with relief.

Ian lifted her to her feet. She clutched the little book still pressed against her breast. His strong arm circled her shoulders. "Come with me, Reyna. You will be safe."

He guided her out of the blackness. Only the faintest moonlight awaited, but it was something. Ian called out and men came running.

"We caught one of the horses," Gregory said.

"Put the man on it. I will take the lady," Ian said. He was still angry, but in her gratitude that she would not have to ride alone through the night, she didn't care.

"Who is he?" he asked as he lifted her onto his horse.

"Sir Reginald."

He swung up behind. His arms circled her as he took the reins. "Your husband's knight? Edmund's brother? Hell. Still, it makes more sense than the Hospitaller." He began leading the little troop back to Black Lyne Keep. "Why did he tie you up? Didn't he trust his lover to complete the bargain she had struck before the murder of her husband? I must congratulate him on seeing more clearly than I did."

His words barely penetrated. She felt as if her spirit had been wrung dry of all emotion and caring. It hung inside her like a damp cloth impervious to any wind, even that of Ian's anger.

She huddled against him all the way back to the keep, knowing only relief that he had come, had found her, had saved her from the terror. *Come with me, girl. You will be safe and will never be frightened like this again.*

chapter

TEN

I an barged into Reyna's chamber early the next morning, waking her. She blinked the sleep away and sat up in her bed, pulling the sheets around her.

"You are recovered?" he asked. "Sir Reginald has been cared for. He is not maimed. You can see him if you wish, but only if Gregory or I accompany you."

"I do not wish to see him."

His expression darkened. "You are a cold one."

"He was supposed to help me, not threaten me."

"You must think all men great fools if you expect their aid to never have a price. A man does not help a woman kill his liege lord and then let her walk away from her debt."

"Is that what you think? That Reginald aided me in murdering Robert?"

"The prize might tempt any man. You, and the lands you would inherit."

"The lands . . . What are you talking about?"

"Your husband's testament. David and I found it."

"I know nothing of my husband's testament. We spoke of such things only once, seven years ago. He assured me that he had provided for me, that is all. The lands to the east."

"Do not waste your time with me anymore, Reyna. I tire of your deceptions. You will dress now and come with me. You will stay near, so I know where you are. I don't want you out of my sight."

True to his word, he made her follow him everywhere during the day. When he left one part of the yard to work in another, he looked for her and gestured. In the evening, while he perused the estate ledger, he made her sit in the solar with him, and she read to pass the time. When she rose to retire, he accompanied her to her chamber and, after she crawled into bed, came in and tied one hand to the low headboard.

"This is excessive," she said.

"These stones have absorbed you before. I'll not risk it again."

"You are treating me like a prisoner."

"I am treating you like a liar who can not be trusted."

"You bastard. I outsmart you and you blame me for it. I never lied to you. You knew I intended to leave if I could."

"Aye, you outsmarted me in many ways. For all I know, even the fall of the tower was intended, to get you away from the Armstrongs' justice. But I do not play the fool for any woman twice."

It continued like that for two days. He rarely spoke to her and barely looked at her. She became an errant puppy trailed along by an invisible leash.

On the third day, he was collecting some weapons from the solar when a commotion in the yard drew him to the window. "What is it?" he yelled down.

"Trouble on the moss," Gregory called up. "Riders on the west road. Fifty, maybe, the patrol said."

"Have fifty ready to go, Gregory. Twenty archers. Call in the men from the camps and then close the gate."

He turned, ready to run, and saw her standing there.

"Am I to follow you into battle too?" she asked.

He glanced around, anxious to be off. "Sit on the bed," he ordered, reaching for a belt on top of a chest.

"Do you expect me to sprout wings and fly over the wall?" she asked while he wrapped the belt around her wrists and tied it to the bedboard.

"Nay. I expect you to slip out through the gate during the confusion of men leaving and returning."

"And then what? I walk to Edinburgh through Armstrong lands?"

"Maybe you have lovers in their army who will help you. Maybe Edmund waits in Bewton to take his brother's place in your bed."

"Those are the irrational ramblings of a stubborn man."

"Nay, they are the sensible thoughts of a man who has had a veil lifted from his eyes."

He strode out of the chamber to a litany of colorful curses. Putting Reyna out of his mind, he ran down the stairs and into the yard. John held his destrier and outside the gate his riders waited. "No armor?" John asked.

"No time, John." He reached for his shield. The prospect of the upcoming action filled him with joy. It would be good to use his body and mind for what they were trained, instead of debating the character and fate of the woman upstairs.

Five miles from the keep, Ian heard the sounds of shouting and battle. He spurred his horse over and down

a low rise. Ahead he could see three long wagons, surrounded by swords and archers, holding off the circling,
riding Armstrongs.

He unsheathed his sword and led his men into the
fray. The arrows stopped their flights as he and the other
horsemen clashed with the enemy. Vastly outnumbered
now, the Armstrongs began to stream away over the
northern moss. Ian gestured for Gregory to take the
archers and go after them.

Flushed with excitement from the brief action, Ian
headed back to the road.

David of Abyndon sat on a horse near the front
wagon, sheathing a sword. "I welcome your aid, Ian. This
could have taken all day otherwise."

"What are you doing here?"

"Looking to become ransom bait for the Armstrongs,
it seems." He gestured to the wagons and the archers.
"The ship came. I was bringing some of its cargo to your
keep."

"Why not just go to Harclow? It is closer."

"Morvan may not want all of it there. I kept King
Edward's archers for protection. Good thing. Has
Morvan arrived yet? He was planning to visit you."

"Nay, he has not come." Ian glanced at the wagon and
raised his eyebrows in question. David paced to its back
and lifted the canvas. The round bottom of a long metal
cylinder gleamed.

"Guns," Ian exclaimed.

"Aye. Also from Edward. The question is whether
Morvan will use them."

Ian understood the comment. Morvan could be old-
fashioned in his sense of honor. The capricious destruction of these new war machines struck him and others as

unchivalrous. Ian had seen them used at Poitiers and found them fascinating. "You still could have brought them to Harclow. He wouldn't have to use them."

"Ah. Well, that is true, but there was other cargo that he most definitely would not have wanted at the siege." David walked back to the second wagon and tapped a small lump under its canvas. "You can come out now, darling."

The canvas flew back, and a black-haired, bright-eyed woman rose up, grasping a jeweled dagger. "Ian!" she cried.

Ian bent over to kiss Christiana Fitzwaryn, David's wife. As he did so he raised one eyebrow at David.

Some of the men were checking the fallen bodies. One called out that he had found an Armstrong who still breathed. Ian and David walked over to the man.

Ian crouched down. "Who led you? Thomas Armstrong?"

The man nodded. "He sought captives. To exchange for the women."

"If Thomas wants his wife and the other ladies, he has only to ask for them. We will give you a horse so you can bring him that message."

He looked to the fair Christiana sitting elegantly in the wagon. "You are going to ask me to keep her at Black Lyne Keep so that you can have your wife nearby, aren't you, David?"

"I knew that she was coming, but it was my full intention to leave her in Carlisle. However, under the circumstances, I could hardly demand it."

"What circumstances?"

"The ones riding up behind you."

Ian turned. Three archers approached. The center hooded one trotted forward, tall and straight, slinging a bow over one shoulder.

The horse pranced closer and he noticed the slender

body, the long booted legs, the slight bulges beneath the tunic. A sick foreboding spread through him.

"You didn't," he muttered.

"Aye, I did, although there will be hell to pay with Morvan. Her arrival was a complete surprise. She obeys no one, and once she insisted on coming here, I had no legs left with Christiana."

The archer came up and faced Ian. A slender hand went to the hood and pushed it off. Unruly blond curls, acres of them, poured down the very tall body. Blue almond-shaped eyes regarded him.

"Ian, you remember Anna, don't you?" Christiana called happily from the wagon.

Aye, he remembered Anna de Leon, Morvan's wife. He hadn't seen her in eight years, since before she married. From the way she looked at him, he suspected that she hadn't forgotten their meeting. Not one detail of it.

"Ian of Guilford," she said in a low, velvet voice. "Morvan told me that he had hired you and your thieves."

Nay, she had not forgotten.

He tried his most charming smile.

It had no effect whatsoever.

Hell. He may as well pack his weapons and head back to France today.

As soon as they entered the gate of Black Lyne Keep, it became clear that if there would be hell to pay with Morvan, it would be paid at once. Horses and men crowded the yard. High on the steps leading to the hall the towering, dark-haired figure of Morvan Fitzwaryn stood with several other new men.

Anna had pulled her hood back up and rode a bit to

the rear. Morvan did not notice her, but he did see his sister. Annoyance flashed in his sparkling black eyes and he descended the stairs.

"Have you gone mad, David? You bring my sister into a war?"

Ian decided this was not his argument. He handed his horse to John and went over to the stairs to find a spot with a good view. He settled himself against the railing in front of two of the men who had come with Morvan. One was a red-haired knight and the other was an older man with white hair and beard who appeared to find the public display in the yard distasteful.

Andrew Armstrong eased over until he stood beside Ian. Ian quietly explained the relationships of the people playing out this strange welcome.

"You are being too protective, Morvan," Christiana said, jumping out of the wagon and embracing her brother. "David said Ian has secured this keep, so it isn't as if we will have to stay at the siege camp."

Morvan scowled down at his sister and glared at her husband.

"She has survived the fall of Caen and crossed the Alps twice, Morvan. All will be well," David said.

"And this way, we can be near David and you," Christiana said.

"We?" Morvan repeated suspiciously. He turned on the mounted men. His arms fell from Christiana when he saw the tall, thin, hooded one. "Hell's teeth. What are you doing here?"

Anna calmly removed her bow and hooked it to her saddle. "A fine welcome to give your wife after five months."

Morvan went to her, but the yard had gone quiet and everyone could hear. "You are supposed to be in Brittany."

"It appears that I am here." She dismounted with a lithe movement.

"We agreed that you would remain at La Roche de Roald."

"We agreed no such thing. You decreed it. But I grew bored and remembered our marriage agreement. You promised that if you ever came back here, it would be my choice whether to accompany you or not."

"My concession was that you would not have to do so if you chose not to."

"Then you should have picked your words more carefully when we negotiated our bargain."

"Damnation. Did you bring the children too?"

Anna pushed off her hood and ran her fingers through her curls. "Only Roald, but I left him in Hampstead with Christiana's children." She turned with hands on hips, a tall amazon facing down an opponent. "I can see that I have displeased you. I will return to Carlisle at once and find passage to London and Brittany." She made to remount her horse.

"The hell you will." Morvan grabbed her before she could swing her leg. He pulled her into a fierce embrace and kiss.

A ripple of laughter flowed through the yard. Anna returned the greeting with equal passion.

"A handsome couple," Andrew said. "Will they be staying here? Should I see to chambers?"

"Most likely," Ian said. "The ladies to be sure, for a while. Morvan and David for at least a night or two, I would guess."

Morvan's hands had begun to travel intimately over his wife's back and hips.

"Perhaps I should show them to the solar before he ravishes her right here in the yard," Andrew suggested.

Ian began to laugh, but the sound choked in his throat. Hell. The solar . . .

"Better not. She is there."

"She? Are you referring to Lady Reyna?"

"Aye."

"I am sure the lady will remove herself. Besides, her father will be wanting to speak with her."

"Her father?"

Andrew gestured over his shoulder with his thumb. "The old man behind us is Duncan Graham. The one with the red hair is his son Aymer. They showed up at the gate soon after you left, but refused to enter until Morvan arrived. Seems Morvan asked Duncan to meet here today about Lady Reyna. I expect the Grahams will be staying tonight as well. I will have to remove myself and some others to pallets in the hall to accommodate them, and I suppose I can ask the Armstrong ladies to all share a chamber . . ."

Ian ceased to hear Andrew's contemplations of sleeping arrangements. He snuck a glance at the two men behind him, and thought about Reyna tied up in the solar. This, he suspected, was part of the wages of sin. Fate had no mercy for the wicked.

He debated if he could slip up very quickly and . . . But David was interrupting Morvan and saying something while he gestured to the stairs. Morvan turned with Anna under his arm. "Ian, where is Lady Reyna?" he asked, walking over.

Andrew answered for him. "She is in the solar, Sir Morvan."

Ian gave Andrew a subtle but vicious nudge. "I will fetch her," he said, turning to go.

"We will go to her," Anna said. "I look forward to meeting the lady. David has regaled us with stories of her spirit. I think we will be great friends."

"There are many steps, my lady, and you have traveled a long distance. My steward will bring you refreshment in the hall while I go call the lady."

"Nonsense. I want to examine the keep. I have never seen one this tall, and am curious. It reminds me of a cathedral tower," Anna said, narrowing her eyes in a way that indicated her insistence had nothing to do with keeps or spirited women, but with contradicting a man she disliked.

All the same, he tried again. "Some ale first, perhaps—"

"Hell, I didn't come here for ale and revelry, but to see my daughter," a voice boomed from behind him. Duncan Graham's heavy hand appeared to grasp Andrew's shoulder. "You, show us this solar."

Andrew cringed beneath the grip and obediently turned to lead the way. Duncan and Aymer followed. Ian tried to catch Morvan's eye as he passed to communicate that this was unwise, but Morvan and Anna had become reabsorbed in each other. With a martyr's sigh, Ian fell in step with the little procession heading up the stairs.

Through the hall they stomped. Up the stairs, not nearly as numerous now as Ian would have liked. Down the passageway to the solar door.

In they filed, Morvan and Anna, David and Christiana, Duncan and Aymer, with Ian bringing up the rear. Even as he passed the threshold he could see their surprised faces as they lined up and stared at the bed. He walked forward, opening his mouth to explain.

And then he saw her. It was worse than he expected. Reyna had maneuvered herself onto the bed so that she could lie comfortably. Her hands were still bound by a belt, *his* belt, to the bedboard, her arms stretched up over her head. Her movements had scrunched her skirt high up her thighs. Her position bore an unfortunate resemblance to the one in which he had tied her in his tent, and it conveyed the same vulnerable, sexual message.

Reyna looked back at the assemblage in surprise. "Father!" she cried. "Aymer!"

David sighed audibly. Morvan shot Ian a look that could kill. Lady Anna pursed her lips. "I see that you are still wooing women with your old subtlety, Ian," she said.

Duncan Graham stood over his daughter, his body tight with fury. "Damnation, Fitzwaryn," he boomed, turning furious eyes on them all.

Ian opened his mouth to attempt an explanation. Before he had the chance, Aymer Graham strode over to him. "You dare to use my sister as if she were some common war prize, English bastard?" With one quick jerk, Aymer pulled off his gauntlet and flung it to the floor at Ian's feet.

Total silence fell in the chamber. Ian looked up from the gauntlet into Aymer's gray eyes. "Total combat?"

"Aye. On the morrow," Aymer snarled.

"Nay, Aymer, you will not do this," Reyna cried.

"Silence, woman," Duncan yelled.

"I'll not be silent. This is not as it seems—" She didn't have a chance to finish. Duncan's hand swung back and hit her sharply across the face.

Outrage split Ian's head. He started forward, but Morvan's firm hand on his arm stopped him.

"You are the witch's spawn to be sure, daughter, and no doubt as bad as your mother," Duncan said. "Your brother will avenge the family honor, even if your own can not be saved."

Ian shook off Morvan's hand and placed his own on his sword hilt. If Duncan hit her again, he would cut the man down and damn the consequences.

Christiana glided over to the bed and untied Reyna's hands. "Since the time and terms of the challenge have been settled, perhaps *now* you would like to refresh yourself in the hall," she said to Duncan. She spoke with a gracious calm that seemed out of place, as if Duncan had indeed arrived for ale and revelry.

It disarmed the old man as a sword never could. Duncan stared at her a moment, then nodded with a growl. He yanked Reyna to her feet and pushed her toward her brother. Fear and anger lit Reyna's eyes as the two men pulled her to the door. Her body tensed in resistance and she jerked free of Aymer's hold as if it revolted her. Andrew Armstrong went over to escort them.

"Lady Reyna, may I join you?" Christiana asked, still soothing the mood with noble grace. "I am told that you read Greek. I never learned, and had hoped you might instruct me while I visited here."

"She will not be here after tomorrow," Aymer hissed.

"All the same, I'm sure we have much to discuss," Christiana said firmly, falling into step beside Reyna as they passed through the doorway.

Morvan, Anna, David, and Ian stood silently. Aymer's gauntlet still rested on the floor.

"Hell, Ian. Didn't Elizabeth teach you anything?" Morvan finally muttered.

"As the lady said, it was not as it seemed." He described her escape and the events that had led to her being tied to his bed.

"Even if it is as you say, they will not believe her denials," Anna said. "Women used thus will lie about it, because they are scorned afterward even though the fault was not their own. When she returns to her father's house, it will be in shame now."

The last thing Ian wanted was this woman participating in the council that needed to be held, especially since her willfulness had forced this little drama. Unfortunately, Morvan looked unlikely to order her dismissal, and she didn't seem to accept that she should retire on her own.

Anna perched herself on the edge of the bed. David calmly took the chair. Morvan paced over to the window and stared out. "So, tomorrow you will kill Aymer Graham," he mused bitterly.

"I trust we are all praying it turns out that way."

"We will have that family on our backs for generations."

"Are you suggesting that I sacrifice myself to avoid that complication?"

"No doubt that is too much to hope for," Anna said. "Harclow is retaken now or never. If the Grahams come down out of those hills, it could all unravel."

"I did not make the challenge, my lady."

"It does not look or sound as if you treated Reyna with chivalry."

"She was not harmed and if she had obeyed and stayed put—"

"Why would such a woman obey such as you?"

Morvan glanced from his wife to Ian and back again. "Leave us, my love," he said. "Join my sister and help blunt Duncan's anger. If we find a solution, we will need him amenable."

A challenge flickered for an instant in Anna's eyes. Ian felt both surprise and relief when she rose and left.

Morvan turned to Ian. "You think that I should stop my wife from speaking to you thus."

Ian shrugged. "It is clear that she strongly dislikes me and is prone to think the worst."

Morvan turned back to the window. His body became

immobile, and an aura emanated from him, as if a fierce power were being contained. "I could bid her hold her tongue, Ian. But then, perhaps it is not in my interest to do so," he said. "After all, you are the only living man beside myself who has ever touched her."

Ian noted an unfortunate emphasis on the word "living." He also recognized the tone, and the undercurrent of danger flowing through it. Over on the chair, David went very still.

During the months since Ian had saved Morvan's life, they had never before referred to that night eight years ago in that Windsor garden.

"It was long ago, Morvan, and I was little more than a boy," Ian said, while he calculated his odds of surviving if he and Morvan met with swords. About even, he guessed. If Morvan killed him first over this old insult, it would certainly settle things nicely with the Grahams. He wondered if Morvan were weighing that possibility.

"Aye. Long ago," Morvan said, turning with a vague smile. "Well, David, we have one hell of a problem here, don't we?"

"We do at that. Short of Ian conveniently falling to Aymer's sword or ax, it will not end tomorrow, and I do not think Aymer will best him."

"I thank you for the confidence," Ian said.

"I have no doubt that Reyna is trying to convince her kinsmen that they have misunderstood, but it will not be accepted as truth. As Anna pointed out, women who are raped will often deny it to avoid the shame and scorn," David said. "So let us assume that convincing the Grahams of their error is unlikely. We must then deal with the insult itself." He looked not to Ian, but to Morvan.

"Aye," Morvan said. "And there is an easy solution to that insult."

"An old solution. Time-honored," David agreed.

"With no real cost, and a certain usefulness in other matters," Morvan added thoughtfully.

"Duncan will have no choice but to agree. Aymer too. And if they had hoped to plot some future mischief, it will neatly corral them there," David continued.

Both men simultaneously shifted their gazes to Ian. They smiled.

Ian looked at Morvan and then at David, and then at Morvan again. Revelation struck. "Oh, hell. Nay."

"At least consider it," David said.

"*Nay.* Better if you asked me to fall to Aymer's sword, Morvan."

"Nonsense. She is a lovely woman."

"She is disobedient and troublesome and manipulative. She may well be a murderess."

"Just days ago you were convinced she was not," David reminded him.

"I have reconsidered the evidence."

Morvan leaned against the edge of the window niche. "I'm sure that you have guessed that it has been my intention to give you land when this was over."

Ian hadn't guessed that at all. Most men would consider helping him return to England sufficient payment for the debt of their life.

"I had been thinking of lands to the southeast, but perhaps this makes more sense. You took this keep. You are known, and the strategic location will require a strong vassal. Graham lands begin a mere half-mile east, and the Armstrong holdings of Clivedale start five miles north. This keep was built to guard those borders."

"Is there no family to whom these lands must be returned?" Ian asked. What Morvan had said pricked at his memory in a provocative way.

"Black Lyne Keep and the surrounding farms were never enfiefed. A castellan held them."

"I had assumed that you would give the free lands to your younger sons."

"There are properties enough here and in Brittany. Nay, perhaps there is gold in this problem, Ian. Sir Robert of Kelso's testament can present difficulties even after I retake Harclow. Lady Reyna's father or future husband may make claims in her name. If they petition through the courts it could drag on for years, and if they use an army, that is just more opportunity for long conflict. If I give you the lands and you marry the lady, the title is clear and secure. Are you willing?"

"If I refuse?"

"The lands are still yours if you swear fealty to me. We will do it as soon as I have Harclow again."

"And if you do not retake Harclow?"

"Then they are still yours through the lady, if you wed her."

Ian considered this astonishing offer. Land. His. Not extensive or rich, but his to hold. And Reyna. The notion of being tied to her filled him with a strange joy and a peculiar dread.

"Are you willing?" Morvan asked again.

"I am willing. The lady may not be."

chapter

ELEVEN

Reyna entered the solar where Ian, David, and Morvan waited for her. She was glad for the excuse to escape her father and brother.

Twelve years had not blunted the fear she felt of Duncan and the darker emotions that Aymer evoked, but she had not let them see it. It had infuriated them to realize that they no longer dealt with a cowering, biddable girl. She felt sure that if Christiana and Anna had not been present, Aymer would have struck her at several points in the heated conversation.

Morvan Fitzwaryn greeted her courteously. "We did not meet properly, my lady. As a boy, I knew of your late husband. He was respected throughout the region as an honorable knight."

She studied this new man. He was in his early thirties, with sparkling black eyes like his sister Christiana's. It occurred to her that she was surrounded by three different but equally compelling examples of male beauty.

"Is it a particular conceit of yours, Sir Morvan, that

only handsome men serve you? An identifying mark for your retinue, rather like the colors of a lord's livery?"

He didn't even blink. "Aye, my lady. And I insist that all the archers be blond and the foot soldiers dark-haired. Ian's company didn't match, which is why I sent them here."

She laughed and he smiled back. Despite their humorous banter, she felt a dark mood in the room. It emanated from Ian, out of view behind her at the hearth.

"Lady Reyna, I'm sure you will agree that it would be best if the duel between your brother and Ian were stopped," Morvan said.

"I do agree. I just spent an hour trying to convince Aymer of his error. However, my father and brother do not take any woman's counsel, least of all mine."

"Since you are a widow, there is, of course, no way to prove that you were not misused. However, if Ian meets your brother, he will kill him. I know Ian's skill, and the duel will end with Aymer's death. We would like to avoid that. Wouldn't you?"

"Of course. But as I said, they will not hear me when I explain."

"There is another alternative that will satisfy them."

"I do not think there is."

"Of course there is. If a man seduces or rapes a woman, her honor and that of her family are regained if he marries her."

She suddenly felt small and vulnerable and outnumbered in a way that Duncan and Aymer could never equal.

"I do not wish to marry Sir Ian. I am sorry if that unhinges your plans." She sensed Ian's spirit quake behind her in reaction to her announcement. "You men make your wars and feuds, and we women become pawns to resolve them. I have already been used once in such a game, which is quite enough for any life."

"It is the lot of women not to control their fates. My own wife and sister can tell you that."

"I need no woman to instruct me in one of life's great truths, but I remind you that I am a widow. We have more control than most. Besides, Sir Ian and I are not suited. Surely he does not welcome this either."

"He is willing."

"I find that odd. Two days ago he was convinced I had contrived with a lover to murder my husband. Just this morning he suggested that I had whored for half the Armstrong army. Why would he agree to marry such a wicked woman? Surely not to avoid Aymer's challenge. Ian is many things, but a coward is not one of them."

She studied Morvan's face when he did not answer. "You have bribed him," she said, analyzing aloud. "Money or land? Land, I think." The pieces fell into place. "*This* land."

"You are most clever, Lady Reyna," Morvan conceded.

"Aye, this marriage is most convenient for your purposes, but I do not see how it benefits me. Ian is not very promising husband material, and there has been little but strife between us from our first meeting. Nor does he trust me. Marriage to him will condemn me to a lifetime of hell."

"You insult Ian and do him a disservice," Morvan said. "His birth is better than yours, and his family a good one."

"Well, he is far from home, in many ways. He is a brigand, with many ignoble deeds on his soul. And his appetite for women is notorious. In fact, I think that you make a mistake giving him these lands. It will not work out mathematically."

"Mathematically?"

"Consider his reputation. A thousand nights, it is said. I calculate that he has required at least three women a week. Counting this keep and the surrounding farms, and assuming that a few of the wives will resist his seduction, these lands will not keep him contented long. No doubt with such a man repetition breeds boredom. He will be howling to get out of here in a year."

Morvan's mouth twitched. David coughed lightly. Something like a hiss seethed out of the man at the hearth.

"So you see, Sir Morvan, this marriage will prove a disaster all around."

"Still, I require it."

"You can not require me to agree to it."

"Nay. So I give you a choice. You can either marry Ian, or he will kill your brother tomorrow, after which your father will take you back to his household. You did not want that before and I do not think your situation will be any improved after this. Aside from the shame attached to what they think happened here, you are known to be barren and thus of little value to them for future marriage alliances. Being in your father's authority will probably not even relieve you of the judgment regarding your husband's death, since your father does not strike me as nearly so interested in protecting you as I had thought."

He had summed up the situation neatly and cruelly, but had told her nothing she did not know. However, he had touched on a subject that opened a fear far bigger than the harsh life in Duncan's home. It was a fear that threatened to overwhelm notions of duty and promises whenever it surfaced.

"If I wed Ian and help you in this way, will *you* still see me judged in Robert's death?"

She held her breath during the pause that followed. When he finally spoke, it was with resignation. "It is best if that question is settled."

"Then this marriage does not benefit me at all. Do not think to bully me, Sir Morvan. I learned as a child how to survive that. If the alternative is to go to my father, I will do so, and I will survive again. Better this time, for Robert of Kelso taught me how to be strong."

Turning calmly, and deliberately not looking at Ian standing near the hearth wall, she swept away.

T hat one is no fool," David said.
   Ian cursed vividly in response. To have to listen as the little thing piled insults on him had been intolerable. He wanted to chase her down and . . . He realized that he wanted to chase her down and caress her body until she was begging for him.

"I can not believe she is willing to go back to Duncan," Ian said. "If that man abuses her in front of us, who knows what he will do when he has her." That Duncan's harsh treatment was preferable to marrying *him* only added to the insults.

"She does not wish to go there, but she is holding out for terms that benefit her," David said. "Morvan, you will have to guarantee her life in the matter of her husband's death."

"I can not ignore such a crime if I am lord, just as you could not at Senlis."

"Some compromise, perhaps."

Morvan pondered the suggestion. "If she is guilty, she need not die. She can go to a convent."

"That might be enough."

Ian suddenly saw other terms that had not been offered but which might sway the woman.

He strode to the door, seething with determination.

"Where are you going?" Morvan asked.

"To trap a hellcat. Tell the priest and steward to expect a wedding tomorrow."

R eyna crouched on a path beside a bed of flowers and pointed out the medicinal plants, explaining their uses. On a nearby bench, Christiana listened with interest, but Anna, who had asked for the instruction, kept glancing up the length of the keep.

"They are up to something. I can just feel it," Anna muttered, her brow furrowing. "What solution did they propose?"

Reyna gave a little shrug. The last thing she wanted was these women making further arguments on their husbands' behalf.

"Oh, dear saints. They want you to marry that thief, don't they?"

"Is she right, Reyna? Is that what they asked?" Christiana said.

"Of course it is," Anna snapped. "Just like men. Ian behaves like a knave and his victim pays the price. I trust you refused."

"Aye."

"Good for you. The very notion of being tied to such a man is horrible."

"I have always thought Ian was very nice," Christiana said.

"You have only known him while you were married to someone who could hit his mark with a dagger from forty paces," Anna said. "You are too kind to everyone."

"I remind you that he saved Morvan's life. For that reason alone, I think you would be kinder in your opinions. David said that he asked only for the chance to return to England and honorable service in return for his bravery."

"He probably calculated that he would get more if he did not grasp. He did not have to go to France and join a free company in the first place. Morvan didn't, and he possessed no more than Ian as a young knight."

"Morvan at least had the dream of reclaiming these lands, and the friendship of a king," Christiana pointed out. "And then he had you and your estates. What was Ian to do when he left court?"

"He could have returned to his family. He did not have to become a criminal."

"He could not return, although I know not why. And many respected knights join and lead those companies. I have seen a city plundered by knights led by a king. The victims of war do not debate the relative honor of being sacked by a royal army or besieged by a free company."

Reyna was fascinated by this argument between two women who knew Ian better than herself. She wondered why Ian could not return to his family.

"Speak of the devil," Anna said, staring at the garden portal where Ian had just entered. "What do you want?" she demanded.

Ian approached with a flinty spark in his dark eyes. "I would speak with Lady Reyna. It is in her interest to hear what I say. I ask that you and Christiana leave us."

"I do not think—"

"I will speak with Sir Ian," Reyna interrupted.

Christiana began pulling a reluctant Anna down the path.

"He has a weakness below the right ribs if you need to hit him," Anna called before she was dragged out of the garden.

Ian faced Reyna in the sudden silence of the garden. She could tell that he was angry. She couldn't really blame him.

"What did she mean by that?" Reyna asked.

Ian began walking her back toward the shaded apple orchard. "It is an old story."

Reyna looked up at his profile. His expression was enigmatic, but for some reason she had no trouble reading it.

"You *didn't*. Morvan's wife? Really, Ian, this is too much. Does he know?"

"He knows. That was the whole idea. He had been gone from England for several years, and brought Anna to court to meet with he king regarding her family's estates. He was only a knight in her service, but I could tell how he felt about her. I sought to make him jealous, so I wooed her."

"Wooed hardly describes it, if she knows you have a weakness beneath your right ribs."

"There was a woman at court who had been Morvan's lover before he left England. She was the one I was really interested in, but with his return it looked as if she would take up with him again. So I pursued the lady *he* really wanted instead."

"Did it work?"

"Aye. He found us just after she had used her fist to fight me off. He almost killed me. But I chased the woman he wanted, and the one I wanted had become distracted by him, so I pointed out the obvious solution."

"Which was?"

He shrugged. "We traded."

Reyna pictured him and Morvan, years younger, Ian probably a new knight. Two men sure of their success if they exerted their considerable skills with women, dividing up how they would exert those charms.

Ian leaned against a tree trunk and folded his arms over his chest. He regarded her in a frank way that uncomfortably reminded her of that day by the river.

"You have no real choice," he said.

"I most certainly do."

"I will kill him tomorrow. Do not doubt that victory will be mine. Would you send him to his death over this misunderstanding? And later, when Duncan moves against Morvan, how many will suffer? This keep will be in the thick of it. Fitzwaryn people and Armstrong people, but your people nonetheless. How will the farmers fare when this region erupts with war amongst three families?"

"You are despicable. How dare you play on my sense of duty for your own ends."

"Morvan has not bribed me with these lands, Reyna. They are mine with or without you. But if our marriage will avoid the bloodshed I describe, we will wed."

"Very neat for everyone but me, you rogue. Do not presume to tell me how it will be, as if your will is law with me."

He grabbed her arm and swung her around, up against the tree where he had been standing. He rested his hand above her head on the trunk and arched his body over hers. "It will be the law with you soon, and you will accept it. You are no more the perfect wife than I am the ideal husband, but still it will be so. What waits for you if you return home? The blows and neglect you may survive, Reyna, but what of the rest?"

She looked up into his face. His expression was thoughtful and determined and hard. Not a stupid man. How much had he guessed?

"What of it?" she asked.

"Your fear of darkness, Reyna. It surpasses the normal.

What did they do, lock you away at times when you were a child? In a dungeon? As a punishment?"

"A crypt. It was a crypt, below the chapel." Even as she said it, she could smell that small, black space's dampness, hear the eternal silence, feel the hands of the dead reaching for her.

"Do you think your fear of it has been forgotten by Duncan? By Aymer?"

"I was a child then, and it is a child's fear. I am older now."

"It may be a child's fear, but it still lives in you. Aye, you will be strong with them, until the first time they put you there again. And then you will break, as you almost did the other night at the old keep."

She glanced away from his relentless gaze. "You are cruel. I hate you."

He cupped her chin. "Nay, you do not hate me. You are afraid of yourself with me, but that is another thing entirely from hate."

The memory of the passion they had shared flickered in his eyes. Her breath caught as she became horribly aware of the warmth of his hand on her face and the closeness of his body. Suddenly she felt cornered, and weak against the power of that attraction that he could summon in her at his will. The danger in him, and the way he could so easily burn away her knowledge of duty, of responsibility, of what was good and necessary, frightened her.

"I will take my chances with Duncan and Aymer," she managed to say. "Even broken, I will at least be alive, and I may in time be able to leave them."

He smiled. Her heart heaved. Dear lord, what a smile. It sent an unwelcome thrill to the core of her body. "Nay. You will stay and we will wed. Morvan has guaranteed your life no matter what the judgment in your husband's death. A convent instead, he says, but it will not come to that. As your husband, I will demand trial by combat. I will not lose."

A pitiful hope jumped in her heart. "You would fight for me? Have you changed your mind again and now think me innocent?"

"God does not truly involve himself in such trials, Reyna. I will not lose because I am skilled."

His lack of belief in her innocence angered her, especially since he had once pretended to be her ally. But he had sought to seduce her then.

"What kind of man are you, Ian of Guilford, that you would agree to marry a murderess? And one childless after twelve years of marriage at that."

"I am a practical man who offers you a bargain you can not resist. You do not want this marriage? Fine. In three or four years, it will be annulled. Because these lands will be English again, it will be the bishop in Carlisle whom we petition, and he does not want strife in this region either. He will accept your childless state all these years as reason, or help us find another excuse. Morvan will give you some lands, with a decent income, and there will be a house in London for you. Christiana will introduce you to the court. You can discuss philosophy to your heart's content with the learned men who follow in the King's wake. Better than Edinburgh, and more secure for you."

He was indeed offering her a bargain it would be hard to resist. To live in that great city, independent, free to study or do whatever she wanted . . . the prospect instantly excited her. Vistas and possibilities jumbled in her mind. She had never been away from this region in her entire life. And his offer to fight as her champion in a trial held far more security than counting on Duncan's protection.

There were promises that might be compromised if she agreed, but if he said the marriage would be annulled, that meant there would never really be a marriage at all.

"You promise it will be so?" she asked warily.

"Aye. In a few years you will be free of this English whoreson, and I will be able to marry an obedient, biddable woman who can give me sons. Not a real marriage, but a temporary convenience."

"A marriage of convenience," she mused. "That should not be too hard. I have had one of those before."

"You agree, then?"

"I agree."

Triumph briefly lit his hard expression. Her heart began beating harder, because she suspected that he was going to kiss her.

Instead, with a restraint appropriate under the circumstances, he pushed away from the tree and held out his hand. "Then let us go and tell the others. Your father and brother must believe you accept this of your own will. It may anger them, since for some reason they want you back. I will stay with you, however, or the ladies will. You are not to be alone with them again."

Reyna hesitated, and then accepted his hand. If they were to wed on the morrow, the gesture was the closest they would get to a betrothal.

chapter

TWELVE

T he wedding dinner was festive and lively. Alice outdid herself with the abundant and varied food, and Andrew produced some special Gascon wine. The hall rang with the sounds of merry company. Reyna tried not to feel guilty about all of this fuss and expense over a marriage that was not a marriage and that would last only a few years.

Ian's presence by her side only made it worse. On occasion she would find him regarding her with a hooded expression, as if he were weighing her blame in the events that put him in this situation.

He appeared more handsome than ever this day. She had seen him in the rough garments of camp life and in the armor of a warrior, but never like this. He wore a soft gray pourpoint with black embroidery and darker gray hose. The belted garment fitted his tall body beautifully and fell to mid-thigh above high black boots. Ian the courtier, she thought, glimpsing for a moment his life before France. Lean and strong and beautiful. Small wonder that he had cut a wide swath through the ladies of Windsor and Westminster.

As the afternoon leached into evening, and the wine and ale flowed, the reason for the festivity began making couples amorous. Christiana perched affectionately on David's lap, wrapped in his arms. Morvan fed Anna a savory as though they were holding a silent, erotic conversation. The obvious love that her new friends shared with their husbands gnawed at Reyna. It caused an aching awareness of what had been lost to her own life.

She looked down her body at the rose surcoat and gown she wore. She could smell the flowers bedecking her head. She remembered another day long ago, and another wedding. The gown had not been so grand nor the dinner so lively. The men crowding that keep had been more interested in the truce being negotiated than in the child being traded. She had anticipated the wedding with soul-wrenching fear, but on that day she had waited for it impatiently, because she had met her fatherly husband and had seen the kindness and salvation he offered.

Memories and regrets overwhelmed her with a renewal of grief for Robert more intense than she had felt for a month.

A hand touched her shoulder, and Christiana spoke low in her ear. "One never knows how these things will work out. There are no footprints yet on the snow covering the field that you will cross."

Reyna smiled at her new friend's optimism. But of course there *were* footprints, many of them, put there by people living and dead, and the freshest ones had been made by Ian and herself in the garden yesterday.

She decided it was a good time to visit with Alice and the servants outside. She extricated herself from the unsettling company of the man she had ostensibly wed, and spent the next few hours among her old friends.

The sun was setting when a commotion stirred at the gate. Gregory hustled up into the hall and returned with Ian. They disappeared through the gate. Awhile later they returned, and the word spread that a messenger had come from Thomas Armstrong requesting the return of the ladies of Black Lyne Keep. Reyna heard Ian instruct Gregory to have one hundred men ready to ride to the border in the early morning. When he had finished he walked over to her.

"Christiana was looking for you. It is time to retire, madam."

Reyna looked to the growing twilight. Aye, time to play out the next part of the farce. "Tell Christiana that Alice will assist me."

He gave her a peculiar look before walking away. Alice had overheard and came huffing to her side. "Can you make all the steps, Alice?" she asked.

"Of course. You think I would let anyone else do this?"

Reyna helped Alice up the stairs. On the fifth level, Alice made to enter the solar, but Reyna guided her away.

Alice followed her into her own chamber. "Ah. You not be wanting to share the same bed that you used with Sir Robert."

Reyna didn't answer. Alice reached for the shoulders of her surcoat and lowered them. "You are not feeling guilty or anything, are you? Some widows do when they wed again, if they had affection for their first husbands, but Robert wouldn't want you living alone."

Together they unplied the wilting buds from her hair and removed the crown of roses. Alice combed the long silken strands, then unlaced and removed the lovely gown.

The cook went over to prepare the bed.

"Leave me now, Alice," Reyna said.

Alice eyed her suspiciously. "What are you up to, child?"

"I would just like some time alone, that is all."

"I can see your unhappiness. Feel it. You've been odd all day. Had you planned to remain faithful to him, even in death?"

"If I have been odd, it is because this has happened so fast and unexpectedly. Should I be dancing with delight?"

"Perhaps not, but it might help with this knight if you didn't look as if you were facing the gallows."

It was an unfortunate choice of words, but not entirely an accident. Alice was reminding her of the protection Ian afforded, and of what she owed him in return. "Leave me now," Reyna repeated.

Alice grunted and shook her head. She patted Reyna's cheek and left.

Reyna exhaled deeply. She went to her trunks and pulled out one of her simple gowns and drew it on. Then she quickly plied her hair into a long braid. Throwing it over her back, she moved the three night candles close to her writing table. She felt too restless to sleep yet. She would begin her letter to the Lady Hildegard in Sweden.

She carefully composed the first Latin line to the learned abbess with whom she corresponded. The abbess had last sent her a detailed argument carefully proving that women had souls, a point on which theologians sometimes debated. Reyna had found a few flaws in the logic, which she wanted to point out so that Hildegard could correct them before circulating her thesis.

She was preparing to dig into the body of her analysis when her chamber door opened. Ian walked in and closed the door behind him.

"What are you doing?" he asked.

"Writing a letter." She scratched another word onto the paper.

She tried to concentrate on a difficult Latin construction that she needed to form. It wasn't easy to do so. Ian had a way of distracting her whenever he was near. She really wished he would leave.

"You have a peculiar attitude toward weddings, Reyna. You spend the day ignoring your husband, and retire to write philosophy."

She grimaced at his tone but did not look at him. She *had* ignored him. She hadn't expected him to notice, or to care much if he did. Being a proud and vain man, he probably thought that she should have played her role better and fawned a bit and pretended some interest.

She returned her thoughts to her Latin.

A movement and sound broke into her attention. She lifted her eyes a fraction. Ian's knight belt lay on the floor near his booted legs.

She stared at that belt and a thud of alert foreboding pounded once inside her.

Her gaze rose up his length. He was unfastening the front of his pourpoint.

"What are you doing?" she asked cautiously.

"Undressing. A dutiful wife would help me."

The foreboding thudded again.

"You forget that I am not a dutiful wife. I am a temporary convenience."

"It is temporarily convenient for you to be my wife. As such you will perform any duties that I command." He looked at her, his eyes large and black in the candle glow. "Why are you still gowned? Why didn't Alice prepare you?"

"Prepare me?"

"Prepare you. For bed. For me."

She set down her pen. Appalled astonishment twisted inside her. "You can not think . . . you can not intend to sleep here."

"It was my intention to sleep in the solar, but since you were not there, I assumed that you did not want to share the bed used by your late husband. I will indulge you on that, for a while."

"It would be unfitting for us to share any bed."

His hands froze on the garment. "It would be most fitting. We are married."

"Not a real marriage, you said. A temporary convenience." She felt real desperation now, mixed with growing anger. He knew the implications of their agreement. It was incredibly dishonorable of him to pretend that he didn't.

Ian rested his hands on the writing table. Dark pools glinting with anger looked down at her. "Aye, convenient all around. It is convenient for Morvan to maintain the neutrality of your father. It is convenient for your protection. Since this land would have been mine anyway, the only convenience I see for myself is having a woman available when I want one."

She summoned every speck of courage to meet his hovering fury. "If you want a woman, go find another. There are at least a dozen here who would welcome you."

"But I do not welcome them, Reyna, not on my wedding night." His voice was very low and level. "Besides, as I see it, we have some unfinished matters to attend."

Her breath caught. "You churl, you deliberately deceived

me." She stood to face him. "You said a marriage of convenience. Temporary. Not real."

"Real enough until it is annulled."

"Do you expect me later to lie to a bishop in order to procure that annulment?"

"I expect your barren state to speak eloquently for you on our behalf. I said that would be the grounds for annulment, Reyna, not lack of consummation."

Her mind scrambled for a solution to this horrendous misunderstanding. This was terrible. Dreadful.

Perhaps logic would help. "Ian, the goal of marriage is to produce children. We entered this arrangement with no intention of doing so. Therefore, we are not married."

"An elegant, if flawed, syllogism. Try this one instead. Vows make marriages, and only bishops can undo them. We just exchanged vows. Therefore, until a bishop ends it, we are married. If you sought a marriage in name only, you should have said so."

She noted with dismay that *his* logic had been completely flawless.

He began coming around the table toward her. She scurried away and kept the desk between them. Her heart pulsed like a drum, and she tried to find some explanation that would end this nightmare. There was none. Nothing that she could say would make any sense.

Looking at him beseechingly, as if the silent words in her head could travel like an underflow on her voice, she whispered, "I can not."

The dark glare he shot at her almost knocked her over. "Can you not?"

"Nay."

"You actually thought to live as brother and sister? You do not know men well, do you?"

"Well enough, but this is impossible."

"Then you can not live here. Nor will we disrupt Morvan's plans because of your capriciousness. I offer you now another bargain, and the only one that matters this night. I have never forced a woman, and I'll be damned if I will let you drive me to it. If you can not be a wife to me, you will go to a convent. One in Brittany, I think, where you will not create future trouble. Annulment or not, you can rot there."

His anger rippled through the air. His expression looked dangerous and determined. He meant it. He would do it.

He walked to the door. "Make your decision, Reyna. Subject it to all the philosophy you want."

Reyna sank down in the chair and gazed blankly at the candles glimmering in front of her. She dully relived the day and admitted that, if she had been paying attention, she might have been forewarned about this. The long looks. The tension twisting around them that made her so unsettled. Her smug contentment that she had managed things so well had blinded her to Ian's assumptions.

She looked down at the ring on her finger. Dear saints, what had she done?

He hadn't really given her much choice. His bed on occasion for several years, or immured forever in some Breton convent. No one had a right to ask that latter sacrifice of her.

She thought about the kind old man who had showed her that some men could be good and generous. She reviewed the promises she had made. She would not betray them. Could not. But if she did this, he would be betrayed as surely as if she had deliberately planned it. Still, she would let the circumstances do it, and not her words, and try to salvage something, somehow. She owed Robert that much, even if he had insisted that she did not.

She walked to the door, picturing the proud, insulted knight waiting for her. She doubted that Ian would be much inclined to either goodness or generosity tonight.

This was going to be horrible. Completely horrible.

S he opened the solar door and silently stepped inside. The night had turned cool, and the servants had prepared this chamber, lighting a low fire in the hearth. Three candles glowed on their tall holders by the bed, and she wondered if, remembering her fear of night, Ian had ordered the extra ones.

He sat against one of the window niches, one leg raised and crooked inside and the other foot resting on the floor. He didn't notice her at first while he looked out into the night.

He was still angry. She could feel it. She stayed by the door. All of her, even her limbs, filled with a fear that eddied like water.

He became aware of her. His head turned. She could not see his face clearly in the shadows.

"Come here."

She took a deep breath and walked over. She couldn't look at him, but she felt him watching her. She stood silently for a terrible eternity, with his hot gaze on her and his power shaking the space around her.

His fingers slid down the length of her braid. Her lowered eyes saw him grasp the end. His hand began twisting slowly, and the braid wound around it. She felt the pull on her scalp and lowered her head, but still the hand circled.

Aye, angry, and not generous at all.

Closing her eyes in humiliation, she had no choice but to bend her knees as the braid pulled her down. Lower. Lower still, until finally she knelt on the floor beside him, her plait wound like a snake around his lower arm. He straightened his arm, moving her head down until she was bowed. Her heart pounded with indignation, but she held her tongue.

"It seems that you can after all, Reyna."

"Aye," she whispered.

"Aye, my lord," he corrected.

She gritted her teeth. "Aye, my lord."

She thought that he would release her then, but he did not.

"Did you love him?"

She startled at the unexpected question. "Love who, Ian? Robert? Reginald? Edmund? You have made me out to be the lover of several."

His hand tightened in warning. "Your husband. Did you love him?"

He was offering her an excuse, an explanation for her repeated rejections. She suspected that the answer would not change anything, and so she spoke honestly. "Robert was everything to me. I built my life around him, and his death has left me without a center. He was my savior, my teacher, my father." She paused. "He was my friend."

Ian glared down at her, stunned by the irrational emotion her answer evoked. An avowal of undying passion would have been easier to hear. Passion he could compete with, but her words made clear that, whatever happened this night, the old man had possessed a part of her that he would never have.

He was jealous of a dead man, he thought with rueful anger. Her King Alfred.

He had developed a picture of Robert of Kelso in his

mind, based on the little she and others had said. Not a tall or powerfully built man, but strong in a lean, wiry way. A fine warrior, but his intelligence probably counted as much as his skill at arms there. Light gray hair at his death, and probably a beard. Not a handsome man, but kind, intelligent eyes, especially when he looked at her.

She had come to Robert while still a child, and had lived as one in his household for several years. What had gone through his head when he finally took her to his bed? He had cared for her and loved her like a daughter. Had helped her conquer her fears and given her spirit the freedom to stretch. He had recognized her sharp mind and gently guided its development.

He probably put off taking her a long time, and then that bed had been full of warmth and caring, but not great passion. The closeness probably counted for more than the pleasure. Their real joinings had taken place in other ways, across the fire as they discussed those books, across the table as he ate her food, across the yard as he watched her youthful play.

Ian looked at her silent body bent in submission beneath him. She didn't move or speak, but he could feel the complex fear pouring off her. Images of her naked beneath him by the river, of her startled pleasure and wary resistance, jumbled in his mind. A strange notion prodded at him, and more words and images attached themselves to it. *He was my savior, my teacher, my father, my friend.*

Ungrasping her hair, he unwound the braid. "Get undressed and get into bed, Reyna."

She rose to her feet and walked over to the bed, breathing to control the panic. Turning away so that she would not have to see him watch her, she unfastened the braid, hoping the fall of hair would cover her a little. She began removing her gown, and felt his relentless gaze on her the whole time.

Slipping off the shift, she quickly climbed into the bed and pulled the sheet over her. Shutting her eyes tightly, she lay on her back and waited.

Time pulsed past. Lots of it. She began to actually get drowsy. Opening one eye a slit, she saw Ian still sitting on the niche, looking at her. His head was cocked to one side, as if he were considering whether she was worth the trouble.

He slid off the niche and she closed her eyes again. No longer drowsy, she listened to the sounds of his movements. Boots dropping to the floor. Cloth against cloth. A heavy weight depressed the mattress beside her. His scent and warmth assaulted her senses and her heart began pounding.

His hand took her chin and turned her face toward him. She sensed him bend close. Lips brushed hers, and then he leaned away.

"Don't you think that you should tell me now?"

She opened her eyes in surprise. His naked torso hovered up on one arm. The sheet covered him to his waist.

"I will learn the truth soon enough," he added.

He knew. A variety of reactions collided inside her. She said nothing. There was nothing she could say.

"Nay, if you did not speak to save your neck or your brother's life, you would not now to spare yourself from my angry pride." His hand thoughtfully traced the top of the sheet along her shoulders. She sucked in her breath at the sensations that slow touch stirred. Perhaps that was how he knew. Perhaps he finally saw her shameless hunger for what it was.

"I sat over there thinking about what you said about

Robert," he said. "And then I thought about this misunderstanding, and what you said in the garden yesterday, about having a marriage of convenience before. Other things occurred to me. The courtesan Melissa's ignorance, for one thing. I told myself later that you had faked your lack of experience when I made love to you by the river, but that night in my tent it was not yet in your interest to do so."

He looked her right in the eyes. "Robert of Kelso was indeed many things to you, Reyna. All that you mentioned. But I do not think that he was truly your husband. You are still a virgin, aren't you?"

She turned her head away. He forced it back. "You can not speak of it, even now that I know? If you promised silence, you have not broken that with me. Did he make you swear an oath?"

She desperately examined the emotions flooding her. She debated the value of continued silence and found none. Sighing deeply, exhaling a breath held for too many years, she shook her head. "He did not make me swear. He only asked me to keep my silence while he lived. He did not know that I swore to do so after he died."

"Then why did you?"

"I would not have people talking about him. Ridiculing him. Guessing the reasons for it. He was a good man, respected and honored. If this were known, they would make him into a fool, or worse."

"He is dead."

"Aye, he is dead, and all he left is his memory. I will not have it destroyed."

She wondered if he thought her a complete fool. Perhaps to such a man, no one was worth the risks she had taken.

"Was he incapable?" he asked. "Did he prefer other men?"

"That is the sort of speculation I wanted to avoid, Ian. The answer is, I do not know. We spoke of it only once, when I was seventeen. I had realized by then that our marriage was not normal."

She blinked at the memory of that night seven years ago, when Robert returned from a visit to Clivedale. She had decided that perhaps the problem was that he still saw her as a child, and so she had decided to greet him this time as a woman. How carefully she had tended her hair and gown. How boldly she had tried to kiss him upon his arrival. It had worked. She had seen the stunned realization in his eyes and noticed the way he looked at her during their meal. But that night, he had left her at the solar door as he always did.

"He did not explain the reasons. He asked me not to seek an annulment, because it would undo both the marriage and the truce. Of course I agreed. I had no desire to find myself back with Duncan, and I loved Robert and wanted to stay with him."

"Does anyone else know?"

Another memory came, of a voice in the solar that night, berating Robert. *She thinks it is her. She has a right to know.* "Andrew, I think. If there are others, I do not know about them." She rose up on her elbow, clutching the sheet around her. "You must promise not to tell anyone."

"I promise nothing. This changes everything."

She sank back onto the pillow and covered her face with her arm. Aye, it changed everything. Too much to ask Ian to continue this marriage on the terms she had assumed, to let the world still think her barren, to get the annulment. Why should he wait and go through all that trouble? If she had admitted the truth, there would have never been a marriage in the first place. The proof that she had not been misused lay inside her, and a simple examination would reveal it. No challenge from Aymer then, and no need to avoid the consequences of one with this arrangement.

She knew that Ian would not be touching her again tonight. He would not destroy the evidence that would set him free of the murderess he had been forced to wed. Immediately, at that, since she guessed that once he betrayed her deception everyone, even the priest, would just agree to tear up the contract and declare the vows invalid.

I tried, Robert. If you had not died when you did, if Morvan Fitzwaryn had not chosen this year to return, if Reginald had proven true and taken me away to Edinburgh . . . She sighed at the pointlessness of all those "ifs."

She threw back the sheet and sat up, reaching for her shift, indifferent to her nakedness now.

"Where are you going, Reyna?"

"To my own chamber."

"The night is chilled and there is no fire lit there. You will stay here."

"I will hardly freeze to death."

"You will stay here. The servants will talk otherwise." He lifted the sheet for her.

The servants and everyone else would be talking plenty in a day or two. She lay back down and pulled the sheet around her.

Ian settled on his back beside her. His eyes were closed, but a thoughtful frown vaguely creased his brow. She felt the warmth of his skin alongside hers. The intimacy of lying naked like this beside his strength and beauty swept her. She wondered if he had done this so often that he was immune to the disturbing, alluring mood it created.

If she knew anything at all about seduction, she could solve this dilemma right now. Of course, she would have to spend her life with a man who neither trusted nor wanted her, who hated her because she had trapped him. And he might be angry enough to still tell the world about Robert. Yet . . .

"It will not work, Reyna," he said. "Despite what you think, I am not a slave to my senses when the circumstances warrant."

chapter

THIRTEEN

I an slipped from the bed before dawn and pulled on
his clothes. His grand statement last night to Reyna
had been brave talk indeed. Most of the night he
had just looked at her, fighting the temptation to wake
her with his mouth and hands, silently urging her to turn
to him and reach out with the touch that would shatter
his resolve.

He laughed to himself at the irony. He had spent days
dreaming of getting her into bed, and when she was finally
there because he had *married* her, he couldn't touch her.

He looked down at her again now. He had said that
last night changed everything, and indeed it did. While
he watched Reyna's sleeping face during the night, he
had been able to set aside his pride and see her love for
Robert for the pure thing it had been. She had not betrayed him with lovers in life and had not intended to do
so in death, and she certainly did not kill him. There was
no reason to, for one thing. Robert surely had not
planned to set her aside, least of all for being barren. But

also, as she said, she had built her life around him, and she would not have destroyed that.

Would she have maintained her silence even as they fitted the noose around her neck, or finally forsworn her reckless oath and revealed the evidence in her defense? Ian gazed at her fragile, helpless body, awed by the strength and devotion that had carried her through the last few months. Despite what she said, Robert of Kelso had not left her without a center. He had helped her build a core of honesty and goodness that supported her soul like a rod of steel. An admirable woman, strong and clever and true. He had met few men with the mind and spirit to match her.

One course of action was clear. There really wasn't any choice, but she would hardly thank him for it.

He left the chamber and walked down to the shadowy hall. Servants were already putting out bread and ale. He spied the figure of Andrew Armstrong at one of the tables and slid onto the bench across from him. The gray-haired steward stopped chewing for one moment, and then impassively continued. Resignation passed in Andrew's eyes during that brief pause, and Ian saw that Reyna was right, and that Andrew knew and assumed that Ian now did as well.

"Was Sir Robert already married when he wed Reyna?" Ian asked while he poured himself some ale.

Andrew set down his own cup. "Not to my knowledge."

"He had traveled widely. He could have been."

"Possibly. But from what I knew of the man, he would not abuse a sacrament in that way, taking one wife while he already had another."

"Was the man impotent?"

Andrew's lids flickered low on his eyes. "I do not think so."

"Did you ever know him to take a woman to his bed?"

"Nay." Andrew looked at him in a frank way, as if challenging him to continue.

Ian looked back, just as frankly. "Did he prefer men and boys?"

"Nay. Such men can perform their marriage duties when they are obliged to, for one thing. Plenty of your English kings have proven that."

"This obligation was not so great."

"Whatever story you give out about this, that is the wrong one." He paused and added quietly, "Such men know each other when they meet."

"Perhaps. Perhaps not." Ian waited for the steward to offer an alternate explanation. The man's placid silence annoyed him. "You are not going to tell me the real reason, are you? Did you also swear an oath to protect his memory?"

The steward didn't respond and Ian's anger spiked. "You would have let them judge her and would not have spoken? Let them kill her? The honorable Sir Robert expected much of his friends."

"She intended to go north. I would have helped her do so. But if it came to it, I would have spoken enough to require someone to seek the evidence that she was not barren."

Ian knew that he would get nothing more definite out of the steward, and he rose and walked through the hall. He needed to talk with Christiana Fitzwaryn before he led his men to the border to exchange the Armstrong women.

A cluster of thirty Armstrongs waited atop a hill. Halting his troop, Ian gestured for David to bring the horses bearing the women forward.

Thomas Armstrong and ten men rode down the hill. Ian and David moved forward, with the women straggling along with them. They stopped fifty paces away from Thomas, and the women began crossing the divide.

Thomas eyed the approaching women. "Where is Lady Reyna?" he called.

"She does not choose to come," Ian replied.

"I demand—"

"You have no right to demand anything. These ladies are here through my generosity, but the other stays with me."

The ladies reached their rescuers. Margery rode up to her husband. Thomas barely nodded his acknowledgment. And then, in a gesture lacking any subtlety, Margery twisted on her horse and cast Ian a poignant look of farewell.

Thomas frowned at his wife and then at Ian. His face turned red. A sharp exchange with Margery ensued.

"Hell, Ian," David muttered. "No wonder you brought one hundred with you."

"She kept throwing herself at me. I assure you that my restraint was impressive."

"Eventually one of these husbands or brothers will kill you."

"Probably."

"Here he comes."

Thomas trotted toward them. "I do not think that you have returned my wife as I left her," he snarled.

"Is that what she says?"

"It will be my pleasure to kill you when we drive Fitzwaryn from these lands."

"There is no need to wait. If you wish to try it now, I am agreeable."

Thomas sputtered angrily. "She says that you have wed Robert's widow."

"Aye, it is true."

"She killed a good man!"

"If so, she will answer for it, but not to you."

"Is Duncan Graham behind this?"

"If he were, he would be cutting you to pieces right now."

Thomas sneered and jerked his horse around. "If you survive this summer, we will meet. In the meantime, be careful what you eat."

C hristiana emerged from the hall to greet David and Ian upon their return. Ian looked meaningfully at her. Christiana gave the smallest nod.

"Where is she?" he asked.

"In the garden."

"I am sorry to have involved you in this, my lady."

"Better me than Duncan and Aymer, Ian, although she is distraught because she does not think they will accept my word and will demand . . ." Her words drifted off and she grimaced. "I could not promise to spare her that ordeal."

He left her, but did not go to seek Reyna in the garden. He needed to check something first. Asking David to accompany him, he took a torch from a wall sconce and mounted the steps to the solar.

"What are we doing?" David asked when Ian stood in the chamber and eyed the walls thoughtfully.

"These walls are thick, David. It is common for them to be hollowed out for chambers and such in keeps like this. There is one off Lady Margery's chamber, for example, which she used as a wardrobe. It has a door and is obvious. I find it odd that this solar does not have one too."

"You think it is hidden?"

"Aye. A safe place for coin and such." He moved the torch carefully over the eastern wall without any luck, but then he had done this before and not found anything. He turned thoughtfully to the south.

"The stairs leading to the postern tunnel come up this way," he explained. He handed David the torch and bent to pull the stones. The low entrance swung open.

David examined the internal hinges and iron bar that held the stones together. "Ingenious."

"Aye. Almost impossible to notice if you do not know it is there. I think Robert of Kelso built this. It bears the mark of his intelligence. But this is the only other external wall, and with these stairs here . . ." Ian crouched low and slipped into the wall. The vaulted ceiling above him was too low for him to stand upright. Walking down a few steps, he turned and pretended he mounted the stairs, seeking the entrance.

"Hand me the torch."

David passed the flame to him. The stairs and vaults became illuminated. Straightening, he looked at the wall facing the top of the stairs. It was hollow at the top. Not a chamber, but more of a deep niche. The average-sized man, coming up these steps, would see only a shadow in the torchlight, if he noticed it at all.

Holding the torch close, he peered inside. Metal gleamed at the back of the space. He recognized old armor and the edge of some cloth. Closer, within arm's reach, were two smaller objects.

He picked up the first. A book. He flipped some pages with one hand. The missing herbal. He put it back and pulled the other object toward him. A coin chest, but he guessed that it did not contain coin.

Tucking it under his arm, he returned to the solar. David raised his eyebrows when he saw the box.

"It had to be somewhere," Ian said. He carried it to the desk and set it atop the books. He flipped it open. Parchments lay within.

"The documents," David said.

"I decided that Thomas Armstrong would not have taken them, even if he knew where they were. He had to leave fast when the keep fell."

David began unfolding the parchments.

"Find the marriage contract," Ian said.

"Here it is."

"Find the description of her dowry. Lands to the east? Secured to her as dower property when he died?"

"Aye. How did you know?"

"She mentioned the lands once, but Morvan spoke of his property ending just a half mile east, even before the waste begins. That old motte-and-bailey castle was originally on Graham lands then, but given to Robert as part of her dowry."

David found a small piece of parchment and some ink and a quill. He began to draw. "Here is Clivedale to the north and Harclow to the south, with Black Lyne Keep between them. Graham lands lie east." He drew three stacked horizontal rectangles on one side of the paper, and a long one vertically along their right side. "From what I can make out, Reyna's dowry transferred these lands here." He sliced off a thin swath from Graham lands.

Ian studied the new configuration. The dowry land did not simply extend Black Lyne Keep's holding a few miles to the east. It thrust up and down, thin arms separating the borders of the Grahams and Armstrongs both north and south. That was how the marriage created a neutral area.

"No wonder Duncan wants her back," David mused. "The dower lands alone put the Grahams on the Armstrongs' back again. Since it was not originally part of Harclow, Morvan would let him have it."

"Look again, David. If the final testament is known, and Black Lyne Keep and its lands go with her, Duncan Graham surrounds the Armstrongs at Clivedale on two sides."

David's expression turned hard. "He also surrounds Harclow on two sides. Maccus Armstrong put a lot of faith in Robert of Kelso to let the man have such strategic property. If either the Grahams or Armstrongs claim Black Lyne Keep or even the dower lands through her, it is not good news for Morvan, and does not bode well for any future peace."

Ian studied David's drawing, but its strategic implications really would not make any difference. In the dark hours of the morning, he had already decided the fate of Robert of Kelso's widow.

chapter
FOURTEEN

Reyna heard the footsteps coming down the path through the orchard. She knew who this would be. She continued digging in the garden soil until the steps stopped behind her.

"You bastard," she said without turning. She inched her knees toward the chamomile, pushing along the box of dirt into which she transplanted the herbs. "You might have warned me."

"Would that have made it easier?" Ian asked.

In truth, Christiana had made the examination as easy as one could hope for, distracting them both from what was happening with humorous tales from the English court. "Nay. You might have taken my word, though."

"I needed no proof, but others will. Your word and mine would count for little."

"Why should they believe Christiana, either?"

"Morvan and David will never doubt her, and she is the Comtesse de Senlis, so no priest will call her a liar."

Morvan and David and the priest. Fewer men attending the next time, at least.

She stood and brushed the soil from her hands. The transplanted herbs looked pitiful in their box of dirt. This was a waste of time. Duncan would never let her bring them with her. Everything about her life here would end in a few hours, when she left with her father to return to her childhood home.

She turned to Ian. He had removed the armor that he had worn to the border and had on a blue pourpoint. He looked so handsome, his expression serious, those thick lashes lowered to shield the dark pools from the sun.

"I have only two requests," she said. "Duncan and Aymer probably will not accept Christiana's word. If I must suffer that with them, I want to get it done with at once. I also ask that you find out from Morvan if I may take my books. If I could just have the ones given to me by Robert—"

"The books will stay here, Reyna."

"They are all I have, Ian. Let me keep something of this life."

"The books will stay. And so will you."

Her shock was so staggering that she thought at first she had heard him wrong. "I don't understand."

"We are married. We will stay married. No annulment now or later. When you get with child, we will attribute it to God's grace."

"Then why . . . Christiana . . ."

"Not proof for Duncan. As you say, he wouldn't believe her. But your virginity supports your innocence in Robert's death, since it removes the motive everyone attributed to you. Only Morvan need hear about it when the time comes, and he will not doubt his sister."

She looked at her herb garden. It was full of plants

found on rides with Robert, or brought to her by him after he visited distant markets. The circle of small beds had spread over the years, as new plants were added. In a way, these herbs represented the history of her life with him.

Tenderness for Ian washed through her. He was giving her this. Offering her the protection of Robert's memory. No one but Christiana and Morvan need ever find out. It was an incredibly noble gesture on his part, for the reputation of a man he had never known.

"You do not have to do this. Robert is dead. People will talk, but then they will forget, especially if I am not here."

He stepped close, and ran his fingers along her jaw and chin and tilted her face up to his. "I choose to do it."

"Why?"

"I could say that I fulfill the promise of protection that I made to you at the river. I could say it is because our marriage secures this property to me more completely. But the truth is neither so noble nor practical." He brushed her lips with his. "I have not allowed you to leave from the start, and I do not now."

He kissed her. A sweet kiss, but luring and seductive. It made her feel weightless and airy, as if he were casting a spell on her.

"I want you. It is that simple," he said. "You do not go."

She gazed into his perfect face. She saw none of the anger from the last few days, but instead a tight and determined expression, as if he expected an argument. She wondered if he thought she would repeat the insults she had heaped on him, and declare she would rather go with Duncan than be his wife, no matter what it meant about Robert's name. He could not know that she had taken refuge in that animosity to protect herself from these other feelings that he evoked.

Then again, maybe he suspected as much. *You are afraid of yourself with me, and that is another thing entirely from hatred.*

He kissed her again, and her whole body tingled. It was a wonderful sensation. She did not fight it, because she no longer had to. "I thought that had changed," she said.

"Nay. Wanting you never changed." His hands caressed down her face to rest possessively on her shoulders. His thumb stroked up and down her neck, creating a little line of pulsing, warm contact.

"You make a bad bargain, Ian. After that hunger is satisfied, you will still be stuck with me. Forever."

"Aye."

"I am hardly the biddable woman you planned to marry after we parted."

"True. But I expect you will be less ill-tempered after you are well bedded."

"Is that what you think? That I—"

"I think that Robert asked you to live an unnatural life. Some women are suited to it and it does not matter, but not you."

"And you think to show me my true nature?"

"If ever I met a woman who was too long a maid, it is you."

It might be the truth, but it sounded like an insult. Her anger flared. "My life was happy and content and full."

"For a long while, but not for some years now, I think. Not since the virginal girl became the virginal woman. Do you deny your resentment that the savior and teacher could not be a man with you?"

Pulling away, she glared at him. "Do not mock him. Do not ever. If you prove to be half the man Robert was, I may not regret this marriage too much."

He pulled her back, into his arms, against his taut body. "And if you show me one tenth the loyalty you showed that old man, I may not either," he said tightly, claiming her mouth with a consuming kiss.

He took her lips fully in his. A gasp of surprise died in her throat and the desire he had been toying with rushed, stunning her. His own passion waited for her, pulling hers with it as it climbed, awing her with its force and danger. There was nothing gentle about the way his tongue grazed her teeth and palate before thrusting in a savage, insistent way. Her whole body responded to that command with a frantic immediacy.

He gentled the kiss, replacing ravishment with seduction. It was just as devastating in its own way, as he teased at her mouth almost delicately and caressed her body almost chastely. He played at the hunger he had awoken, and marvelous chills of pleasure spread through her until she nearly cried for him to give her more.

He wrapped his arms around her. "I want to claim you now, here, at once, but I will wait for tonight. A virgin deserves a little wooing."

She leaned against his strength, her ear against his chest, the need he could so easily provoke racking her with frustration. It had been an eloquent demonstration of his knowledge of this hidden part of her, and of what he expected in this marriage.

"You like that, don't you? That I am an overaged maid."

"I find that I am glad for it."

"Why? Because it is a prize taken only once?"

"Perhaps. Or a gift given only once."

She made a face at him. "I don't think it will be as nice as your kisses suggest."

"Don't tell me that you still have a young girl's fear."

"I have had more time than most to worry about it."

"You are in luck, Reyna," he said softly. "After all, you give yourself to the Lord of a Thousand Nights. I will show you such pleasure that you will not be worrying about such things at all."

She gazed into his eyes. She really had little choice in this. The decision had been his, not hers. She wondered if his temporary lust didn't lead them into a grievous error, and if this life might not be the hell she had declared it would be two days ago. He was no Robert of Kelso, she thought, and realized with shock that she was glad for it. Tonight would have been somehow obscene with Robert.

"What are you looking at?" Ian asked.

"You."

"And what do you see?" He asked a little stiffly, as if he anticipated an offensive response.

"I am not sure. Odd contrasts. A man who can be both kind and cruel."

"Do not read complexity where none exists, Reyna. I am very simple. When I am pleased, I am kind. When I am angered, I am cruel." He guided her toward the orchard path. "Now I will give you some advice to avoid the latter. You may call me Ian, or husband, or your lord, or any endearment you may want. But no more whoresons, bastards, churls, or spawns of the devil."

He smiled when he said it, but she knew it had been no jest.

H e had lied. He did not woo her during the day. He seduced her.

Reyna suspected that with Ian of Guilford it had always amounted to much the same thing.

No pretty words and flatteries. No poetry and chivalrous

gestures. Just a constant presence, and considerate attention full of the unspoken reminder that he wanted her and
would have her soon.

A blur of festivities created a colorful setting to the
anticipation drumming between them. Throughout the
tournament and dinner and hunt, even during Duncan's
leave-taking, each warm look and casual touch and oc-
casional kiss he gave her increased the cadence of excitement to a more expectant pace than before.

She was helpless against it. Her spirit had already
yielded, and it knew no resistance to his practiced talent.
Her body knew even less. Her arousal in the garden
never completely quelled, and her condition made her
very alert to him, very conscious of the arm on her
shoulder or waist, of the lips brushing her cheek, of the
hand taking hers. His possessive touches became little
plucks on the strings of desire. Delicious. Devastating.

By the evening meal an odd tightness had lodged low
in her belly, and her whole body felt taut and strangely
alive. Her excitement, and his subtle awareness of it,
made her unsettled and silent. He, on the other hand, appeared completely at ease. As if he had done this, well, a
thousand times before.

Morvan and David planned to depart for Harclow
in the morning, and so the evening meal lasted longer
than normal. Everyone seemed prepared to sit at the
table talking over wine, even after the food was gone.
And so it startled Reyna when Ian's hand slid up her
back.

"We will take our leave now," he said.

She glanced up and down the long table. "Everyone
will know."

"They already know, Reyna. We are newly married. In
fact, Morvan has given me several peculiar looks, as if he

finds it extremely odd that we left the bedchamber at all today."

"I'm sure he does, considering how little he has been out of his since he came."

He rose and took her hand and led her toward the stairs. Reyna tried to retreat like a worldly widow.

As soon as they were out of sight, the hand resting on her waist suddenly pulled her close and a scorching mouth found her neck. With a gasp she found herself pressed against the stairwell wall, looking up into a severe face and fiery eyes. He held her head and claimed her mouth with a searing kiss that made the earlier one in the garden seem tame. It was wonderful. And terrifying.

"I thought the day would never end," he muttered, pressing a possessive caress down her back and hips. "I should be canonized for the restraint I have shown with you."

He grabbed her hand and pulled her up the stairs, taking them two at a time. She scampered to keep from being dragged, worrying that his impatience meant he would just throw her on the bed and do this thing. She had rather counted on things building more slowly, as at the river.

He pulled her into the solar, kicked the door shut behind him, and turned her into his arms. She was awestruck by how dangerous he looked. She instinctively pushed against him a little.

He noticed. "I have frightened you."

"A little," she mumbled, feeling absurdly foolish. "Not much."

"Too much."

He walked away, toward the table. Some wine had been placed there, and he poured a cup. It took him too long to do so, and she wondered if her failure to match his passion annoyed him. He came back looking much less threatening, and offered the wine to her. She shook her head.

"I think maybe you should." He drew her to the chair, onto his lap, and offered her the cup again. She took dutiful little sips. He watched her while he stroked her back in a comforting way.

"How do you feel now?" he asked.

"Stupid."

He laughed. "Stupid? So much for my reputation."

She bit her lower lip. "Nay, not just stupid, as you well know, but stupid enough. I am twenty-four years old, Ian, and here we sit with you calming me as though I were some girl."

He took the cup and set it on the floor. "I should have been more careful with you. You did say that you had worried about it more than most."

"Aye. When I was younger I convinced myself that I was very fortunate to have a husband like Robert, and to have never had a proper wedding night."

He stroked her arm. "And when you were older?"

She looked at the fingers caressing her through the silk sleeve of her cote-hardie. The warm, light lines of pressure felt incredibly soothing and compelling.

"And when you were older?" he asked again.

She was embarrassed that he had guessed about that. But then he understood the world of the senses far better than she.

"And when I was older my mind held to that notion. But sometimes . . . at night . . ."

"Who was in your dreams at night? Robert? One of his knights?" he asked softly, moving his hand to her hair and face. Gentle touches. Subtle and exciting.

"No one I knew. A presence more than a person." She

had become very conscious of sitting on his lap, of his arm around her and that other hand lightly stroking her cheek and shoulders, artfully summoning again the anticipation of the day, which her fear had temporarily suppressed. Sparkling sensations dripped through her. Talking about those nights of dreaded, compelling discomfort only made the titillating expectation worse.

"And did you prefer that phantom's kiss to mine, Reyna?"

"Will you be jealous of a specter now?"

"Perhaps."

The mood had subtly changed. She sat in a heavy silence, watching his hand caress her arm more firmly and then move to her thigh and leg. That sensual power flowed from him, surrounding her, invisibly reminding her of the pleasure she had felt with him before.

"I almost went mad with you lying beside me last night," he said, kissing her cheek, keeping his face next to hers, inhaling and closing his eyes as if to savor what he smelled and felt.

"You should have let me leave."

"I could not. I could tell from the way you undressed that you had never done that before. You lay so rigidly I knew you had never shared a bed with a man. That is how I knew your secret for sure. It should not matter that I am the first with you in all these things, but it does, and I kept you with me so I could savor my pleasure in it. You looked so beautiful while you slept, I could not take my eyes off you."

His soft words pulled at her heart. They vaguely alluded to emotions other than lust. She straightened and looked at him.

Eyes full of warmth met hers. His hand stroked into her hair and cradled her head. "Kiss me, Reyna."

She leaned forward hesitantly and pressed her mouth to his, awkwardly aware that her lips trembled. He responded gently, carefully drawing her into it. When his tongue joined them together her own met it, the touch a poignant connection.

He embraced her tighter, making her feel very small within his enclosing strength. No longer impatient, he led her slowly into her passion this time, seducing her toward the yearning pleasure with languid kisses on her mouth and neck and slow caresses on her thighs and stomach. Quickly she became the one who grew impatient as her breasts longed for his touch. She plunged her tongue into his mouth boldly and pressed his head close and knew a special exhilaration when he kissed her harder.

She felt a glorious freedom as the dizzying sensations took control of her. They were wonderful and marvelous when there was no worry, no guilt, no shame. He skimmed up the skirt of her gown, and then that tantalizing stroke was one of skin on skin. Something inside her sang with euphoria and relief. Her body came alive in an unearthly way, as if it possessed a separate consciousness that awoke beneath the intimacy of the strong hand on her body. She emerged breathless from his kisses, her arms tight around his neck, and looked into knowing eyes that absorbed her into him.

She touched that sensual mouth, caressing the lips with her fingertips. She kissed them softly, bit delicately, imitating him, trying to give him the sweet pleasure he had given her. His jaw tightened and his arms tensed and he accepted her small seduction for a while. Then something broke loose in him and he leaned her back into a dominating kiss of primitive possession.

Never breaking or loosening the bond, he eased them

both to their feet and cupped her bottom with his hands and pulled her up against the length of his body. Stretched and bowed into his support, her yearning breasts pressed against his chest, and her womanhood throbbed with a hollow ache.

How did he manage sanity when she knew only mindlessness? How could he separate when their heartbeats, their breath, and every inch of them both yelled for continuation, for completion? When he eased her away she almost cursed him, but then she felt his fingers working the lacing on her gown.

"You do not make it easy to go slowly, Reyna," he said, smiling his devastating smile while he slid the gown off her shoulders. He knelt on one knee to untie the garters at her knees and slip the hose off her legs.

"I am not afraid anymore," she said, looking down at him, stretching her fingers through his hair. "I don't want to go slowly."

He lifted each of her feet and swept the gown away. "But I do," he said. "I want to look at you while the pleasure builds. I want to watch your body tremble at my touch and beg for relief. I want to hear your cries when the madness makes you offer yourself to me." He rose and glanced down her body. "Remove your shift, Reyna."

His words sent a streak of lightning through her body, straight to that pulsing hollow. The shift slid down her arms, off her breasts, past her legs.

He reached for her breasts, caressing them lightly, and they swelled even more in that craving way. She soon knew what he meant about her body trembling at his touch and begging for relief.

"You are so beautiful. Perfect." His thumbs grazed the tight peaks. She lowered her eyes to the tanned hands holding her, teasing her, arousing incredible sensations.

She did not doubt that in the end it would be as he said, but she would not have it all one way. She began unfastening the closures to his pourpoint.

Her boldness pleased him. He continued caressing her, pulling her closer, moving his hands over her nakedness while she undressed him. That inflaming touch distracted her so it was slow, clumsy going, but finally she had his shirt off. He pulled her up against him, and she reveled in the heady intimacy of embracing his naked back and chest.

He lifted her up and laid her on the bed, and then sat to pull off his boots and lower garments. She watched the muscles of his back and shoulders move, and could not look away when he rose and slid the clothing down his hard hips. He turned, magnificently naked. She examined his sculpted chest and torso and phallus, astonished by the new heat that the sight of him brought.

He came down beside her. Resting on his forearm, he traced her lips with his finger and watched the path with a thoughtful expression.

"You have had little choice in this," he said. "I would know your will now. Do you want this?"

The question stunned her. Surely he could tell that she already almost cried for him as he had said she would.

He read her expression and shook his head. "I do not mean that. I have known from the first that I could make your body want me."

He was asking a harder question. She was surprised that he sought this knowledge, astounded that it even mattered to him. "Aye. I want this."

"With me?" The two words spoke volumes that included all of her references to his brigandry and dishonor, all of her curses. But her mind did not settle on those defensive denials now. Instead she remembered his swift justice for the poor tenant farmer, the strong arm saving her from the blackness at the motte, and his decision to continue a marriage that was her only chance for a decent future.

"With you."

He leaned down and kissed her so gently that she thought her heart would break. "Then let us see what is possible between us, Reyna." He pulled her against him until he molded her to his flesh, every inch of her skin connected to his.

He made love to her as if his own control were limitless. The kisses and caresses alone left her breathless and sightless, and her body stretched into his while her fingers explored the taut skin and muscles on his back and shoulders. He played at her breasts, creating a delicious anguish, brushing with a light touch and teasing with his tongue until she gasped again and again and arched her back, begging for more.

He gave it to her after a long while, sucking on her harder while his tongue continued its devastating torment, sending her into a frenzy. His thigh came between hers and she pressed down on its hardness, trying to relieve the need becoming the source and destination of all of the exquisite pleasure. All the while his hands explored, excited, and found unexpected spots of bliss.

His leg moved, and he eased her flat on her back. He palmed up between her thighs and she arched off the bed. He spread her legs and she arched again and cried out when he stroked gently. The finger touching her probed. She felt an invasive stretching, shocking but oddly welcome, at the site of her distracting need.

It hurt. He sucked her breasts and it hurt a little less. He withdrew his hand and caressed her thighs. "You are very small, Reyna." He carefully untangled himself from her arms and rolled away.

He pushed back, sitting up against the headboard, then lifted her, turning her toward him. "Sit here," he said, moving her knees to straddle his hips. "It will make it easier for you."

Blinking away the blurring passion, she settled herself, facing him close, her warm moisture sliding over his prodding hardness. The sensation was incredibly erotic, and she squirmed a little, making his whole body tense. He leaned her forward into a kiss while his hands took her breasts.

She went completely mad. He could caress her freely in this position, and she could touch and kiss him too. She reveled in his sighs when she moved her mouth over his chest, and in the scorching kiss he gave her when she drew her hands down his length from his shoulder to his hips. Deliberately now, while his hands moved over her body, grasping her bottom at times to lift her so her breasts reached his mouth, he pushed her farther and farther out of control. Low yearning sounds echoed around them, coming from her as the pleasure became increasingly desperate.

"Up," he said, raising her again, sliding his hand high between her thighs, stroking and touching her, provoking a series of mindless cries. Enthralling, demanding streaks shot through her loins. It was glorious, wonderful, exhilarating. She felt her body reaching for the flood of sensation she had felt by the river, and nothing else but that impending release mattered.

He moved her knees farther apart. Grasping her hips, he eased her down.

Pain split through her madness. Her breath caught sharply. She opened her eyes and saw the stern expression of his strained control.

"Do you want me to stop?"

"Nay," she whispered, lowering her forehead to his tense shoulder, digging her fingers into his arms.

He did anyway, briefly, caressing her until the initial shock passed and the pain dulled a little and pleasure reemerged. His hand drifted to where they were joined, and she jolted when he found a spot of intense sensation. He rubbed gently and her delirium returned, pitching higher and higher, making her want this joining despite the pain, forcing begging cries that mingled with her gasps of shock when he penetrated further. The heaven of sensation peaked and broke and spread, splitting her essence, and she screamed from its power. She was dimly aware of an agony submerged under the euphoria.

She collapsed into his tight embrace against his chest, feeling limp and raw, his fullness connecting them. He lifted her chin and gave her a tender kiss.

Carefully he slid down and rolled until he hovered on his arms above her. He gently withdrew and entered her again. It hurt, but it hurt less the next time, and soon she didn't care about that. Something like that climb to heaven began again, only the sensation was broader and richer this time, and centered where they were joined. Ian's slow rhythm teased at it, and she grabbed at him desperately, raising her hips to meet him.

He paused. "You are going to make me hurt you more if you do that, Reyna."

She looked into his dark, absorbing eyes. That beckoning sensation made her shake her head.

He moved again. The quivering intensified, and she saw him sense it, recognize it, know its meaning more surely than she. Gaze locked on hers, reading her reactions to her reborn passion, he brought her along with him, until the pleasure became one emotion shared by two and their mutual awareness created a connection that astonished her. He kept them linked in the unity a long time, leaving her overwhelmed, stripped of will and thought, floating in a place where his size and power and desire dominated her own. Only at the shattering end did she close her eyes.

She still grasped him tightly long after her tremors had passed. His deep breaths filled her ear. Her soul felt exposed, and her body boneless. He seemed disinclined to move or speak, and she was grateful for that. She wanted to hold on to him a little longer in the silence. His weight was comforting and protective, a barrier against the world that would soon tilt back into reality.

He rose up. "I am crushing you."

She began to protest, but he eased them to their sides, limbs still entwined and bodies still joined, and pulled her against him. She was grateful for the proof that he did not want to end this sweet mood either. The prize taken or the gift given? It had been both of those things.

A sharp burst broke through the spell, startling her.

"It is just thunder," Ian said. "A storm has come up."

She hadn't noticed. She listened to the downpour and watched the lightning make dim highlights on his face. His eyes, inches from hers, were closed.

"Is it always like that?" she asked.

"I will not hurt you again."

She glanced away. She hadn't meant that.

His hand touched her face and she looked over to find him watching her. "Nay, it is not always like that, but sometimes it is. It depends on you and me." He untangled her legs from his hips so she could be more comfortable, and pulled her into an embracing sleep.

Hours later Ian found himself awake and looking at her again. The storm's wind had blown out the night candles, and only the dimmest moonlight outlined her form. She looked very small and vulnerable, with her slender body nestled against his. He wanted her again, but he made no move to wake her.

As if sensing his gaze, she stirred in her sleep. Her eyes opened. She went suddenly rigid, and he realized that the darkness had assaulted her.

"I am here, Reyna. There is no need to be frightened."

She turned to him, and her body relaxed. He pulled her close and soothed her with caresses until she stretched drowsily.

"What now, Ian?" she mumbled sleepily.

"What now?"

"Aye. What now, with this reckless marriage that you kept because you wanted to bed me? You have had me. What now?"

He heard the assumptions that her question contained, and the fears it revealed. He couldn't blame her. She couldn't know that his feelings for her were more complex and confusing than simple lust, or that what had happened this night did not happen very often at all. Her opinion of his constancy, of his value as a husband, had every right to be low.

"Now we give each other pleasure in this bed, and have children, and if fortune wills it, we grow old together. That is the way with marriage, is it not?" he said.

And the rest depends on you and me, he silently added. He thought about her openness and giving this night. *Mostly me.*

chapter
FIFTEEN

Lips on her cheek nudged Reyna to consciousness.
"We must rise, wife. Morvan will be leaving soon."
Wife. Her lids fluttered open. She responded to
his kiss a little feebly, feeling awkward at finding herself
in his arms. She sought some casual remark that would
hide her disconcerting shyness. What did one say to a
man with whom one had done such things?

He threw off the sheet and swung to his feet. His
glance fell to the bedclothes. "Are there clean ones here?
We should remove these."

She saw the bloodstains. He was right, they would not
want the servants seeing that. She pulled on her shift
and fetched new linens from a chest. She tucked them
around the mattress while Ian washed and dressed.

Performing these routine tasks together possessed an
intimacy almost as heady as their lovemaking. It empha-
sized the reality that her life had changed forever in ways
yet to be learned, and that this man dominating the
chamber now owned her.

She wasn't sorry when Ian left to send a servant to her. She had the woman heat some water and comb out her hair, but made her leave before she scrubbed off the evidence of her virginity.

Wife. Not darling or love or some other endearment, but then, she hadn't expected any. She understood his reasons for making and keeping this marriage. He had made that clear in the garden, and then again last night when she asked him. He wanted the convenience of a woman whom he desired when he craved pleasure, and eventually children.

It was what most men sought, and she should be grateful that he had wanted her enough to go through with it. Ian had saved her from Duncan and Aymer, and would protect her from injustice in Robert's death. She had learned last night that what he expected in return would hardly be onerous to give. And yet she felt sad while she washed herself, as if their lovemaking had exposed a hidden corner of her heart that ached for something it knew she would never have.

She arrived in the hall just as Morvan and David prepared to depart. Her heart lurched while she observed their leave-taking from their wives. The expressions on the faces of both couples displayed unmistakable emotions—complete trust, eternal desire, and blissful contentment.

She suddenly understood her nagging melancholy. Deep friendship and exalted passion were combined into one powerful love in the unions standing in front of her. She herself had known the first with Robert, and had finally tasted the latter with Ian. But she would never know them both with one man. She should not be jealous, but the ache ripped rawly and she had to look away.

Reyna began reclaiming her position as the mistress of

the household at once. Her marriage to Ian had hardly laid to rest the suspicions about her, and the firm expressions worn by most of the servants suggested it had only made things worse. She knew that to them this marriage must appear very convenient indeed, and not in ways envisioned by Morvan. No one dared challenge her, but they obeyed in a stiff, silent way that made their opinions known.

After the midday meal, she retreated to the solar for some time alone. She looked for the *Summa* by Aquinas that she had been rereading and found it on the desk, not on the shelf where she had left it. On top of it was a metal box that she did not recognize. It had been there last night, she remembered.

She curiously opened it. Documents lay in a folded stack inside. She idly lifted the top one and read it. It was her marriage contract to Robert, and it described the dower lands that he had reassured her about.

The next document described Robert's entitlement from Maccus Armstrong, and below it lay a large, thickly folded sheet. She opened it and saw Robert's testament.

She read it with amazement. Lacking an heir, he had left everything to *her*.

That was what Ian had meant that morning when he spoke about the lands she would inherit. She also understood his reference in the garden to how this marriage would secure the land to him more completely. If Morvan failed at Harclow, Ian could claim Black Lyne Keep through her.

That bleak ache ripped again. This was the real reason Ian had kept the marriage, not desire for her.

She suppressed her disappointment and gazed at the parchment in puzzlement. Where had Ian found these documents? Who knew about this testament? She exam-

ined the signatures of the witnesses. One was the priest
in Bewton; the other she did not recognize. Not retainers
or castle folk, then.

She had just replaced the parchments in their box
when Ian strode into the solar.

"The day is getting warm, Reyna. We will go to the
river and bathe."

They mounted the horses waiting in the yard, and
trotted to the secluded place where the women went to
launder in a placid pool formed by some rocks near the
bank.

Ian untied a bundle from his saddle. Reyna recognized
the sheets that she had removed from their bed. He
weighted them with rocks, and then hurled the cloths
into the center of the river. She watched the water swallow the evidence of Robert's secret, realizing that Ian's
generosity on that score had not been nearly so selfless as
she had thought. If the world discovered that she and
Robert had not had a true marriage, the value of that testament and marriage contract might diminish to naught.

Ian sat on the trampled high grass and began pulling
off his boots. "I have decided that you will teach me to
swim. You were right. It is a useful skill for a soldier to
have."

Reyna undressed. She felt exposed and awkward walking into the pool naked beside Ian, and was grateful
when they reached water deep enough to cover most of
her body.

She debated how to teach someone to swim. She
couldn't remember learning herself. It had simply happened while she played in the lakes as a child. "You can
not swim unless you learn to let your body float," she explained. "I will hold you up at first. Everything is lighter
in the water. Now stretch out." She slipped her arms

under his back and hips, a little too mindful of the skin and muscles over her hands and the magnificent beauty of the body which she supported.

She stepped away. He submerged a few inches, but no more.

"It is a pleasant sensation," he said. "A little unworldly."

Reyna looked at his length shimmering beneath the water's ripples. Floating thus *was* a pleasant, unworldly experience. For a brief while one felt unbound by the earth. Just like Ian, with his strong awareness of his senses, to recognize and name the small joy for what it was.

Within an hour, Ian became a passable swimmer. He discovered that he could swim underwater and began sneaking up to lift her high and throw her forward in a confusion of limbs and splashes. They played like children, and their laughter banished the awkwardness she had been feeling with him all day. Finally, tired and sated, he took her hand and led her to the bank.

The warm sun and light breeze quickly dried them. Ian lay with his eyes closed, a river god lounging by his domain. He made no move to dress, but Reyna slipped on her shift.

Her movement made him open one eye a slit. "It is a little late for modesty, Reyna. Besides, if I were of a mind to take you again I would have done so already, in the water." He pulled her down beside him. "Rest with me. The sun and breeze are delicious."

They *were* delicious, creating cool fingers that fluttered over heated skin. Reyna closed her eyes and savored the sensation, concentrating on it. Her limbs grew languid under nature's light caress.

"You keep moving my book," she said. "The Aquinas. When I look for it, it is never where I left it."

"It is overlarge and in the way."

"Perhaps I should take it to my chamber, then."

"I will keep the books in the solar. If you insist on reading philosophy, you can do so there."

Insist? "You do not approve of my reading philosophy?"

"I do not approve or disapprove, but I think you are too young for it. Philosophy has no meaning without the wisdom of experience. How can you agree or disagree if you know nothing of life yet?"

"Rational thought can lead to truth, separate from experience, Ian."

"I do not dismiss philosophy, Reyna. I just decided long ago that it has limitations. And I have no patience at all with the philosophers and theologians who turn away from the world." He spoke lazily, as if his conclusions had been so self-evident as to require little thought.

She rose up on her arms. "They do not turn away from the world, but warn that it is a distraction."

He plucked a wildflower from the grass. "Smell that," he said, holding it to her nose. He stroked the bud against her cheek so she could feel its velvet caress. "How does that make you feel, Reyna? Distracted from the true path? The ancients never thought so. It was left for our Christian philosophers to reject the world as corrupting and take refuge in their rational theses."

She took the flower and sniffed. "Have you no respect for their lessons, Ian?"

He laughed. "I have great respect for them, as far as they go."

She nestled near his side again. While she lulled off to sleep, it occurred to her that she had just had a philosophical discussion with Ian of Guilford.

She awoke to find him lying on his stomach, propped on his arms, playing with some wood. She glanced down his naked length, tight and hard with sculpted muscles, the firm buttocks and thighs paler than the rest of his sun-bronzed body. A scurrying heat flushed her. She turned over and examined the little toy he had made.

"What is that?" she asked, her face hovering near his shoulder. She fought the urge to lick its taut skin.

"A gun," he said, pointing to the top twig. "They are very clumsy. If they could be made more mobile it would go a long way in their effectiveness."

She suddenly understood. Ian was playing with ways to mount the gonne on a cart. He tilted the stubby log back and forth on its wheels.

"Ian, about the books. Surely it would be better if I took the one I am using back to my chamber."

"Why so?"

"You will no doubt require your privacy some evenings. I would not like to disturb you."

The little cart stopped abruptly.

"If I ever do not want your company in the evening, I will tell you, Reyna."

He pulled her down, turning her on her back. He leaned over her and ran his fingers along her cheek. His touch warmed and tingled her skin much like the sun and breeze had, only the sensations sank into her body and spread through her blood.

"I think it will be a long while before I tire of you, Reyna." His gaze lowered, and he traced the bones of her neck and collar. "I plan to teach you all that I know of pleasure. Once you have healed from last night, we will begin your lessons."

The sight and scent of him filled her senses. Her heart began that pulsing, primitive pounding. Her misgivings about him suddenly no longer existed, but then neither did any rational thought.

"I do not feel any need to heal," she whispered.

He gently bit her lower lip. "I was hoping you would say that."

He kissed her slowly, savoring her taste with his lips and tongue. Her whole body floated in the rising tide of passion he created. Low waves of need began lapping through her. It was different from last night's feverish hunger, but exquisitely so.

"Remove your shift, Reyna."

She sat and slipped the garment up, aware of the quivering thrill that command always summoned, wondering at his repeated demand that she do this herself. As the light linen floated to the ground beside her, she realized that this gesture was one of willing submission, a symbol that she offered herself to him, but at his demand. The prize taken or the gift given?

He eased her to her side and settled close, facing her. "Touch and kiss me, Reyna. Use your hands and mouth as I do."

He led her through a long, luscious lesson, showing her how to give him pleasure by giving it to her first. He kissed and probed at her ear until she giggled and then did the same to him. She tried to imitate the way he explored her neck with his lips and teeth. When he caressed and licked at her breast, it took her a moment to realize he wanted that too.

Step by step, he guided her explorations of his body through example. A peaceful, languid sensuality submerged her that permitted no shame, and she followed his lead, caressing hips, buttocks, and thighs. When he gently stroked the soft flesh of her womanhood, she had no trouble translating the request and she carefully ran her fingers up the length of his phallus, looking down to watch, wondering at the softness of the skin stretched over the power, surprised that he had not hurt her more than he had last night.

She traced around its tip in circles, curious to know if she could create concentrated sensations similar to those he was drawing from her. A deep sigh said that she could. Soon he eased her on her back, pushed her legs apart with his knees, and entered her slowly.

She had not healed completely, but the tight fullness acted more like a salve than an irritant, and soon she lost awareness of everything except the exhilarating connection. Her body stretched to accept him, absorb him, bind him to her briefly and totally. She didn't understand the emotion that saturated her, but it echoed with that poignant yearning that had colored her soul all day.

It was so different here, in the sun, with the smell of grass and the sounds of birds and water nearby. No shadows obscured the body moving over and in her, no candlelight abstracted the tight desire in his face. She knew long before it ended that the strangeness would be gone forever after this.

He withdrew and rejoined carefully again and again, as if he cherished the sensation as much as she did. Hooking her legs over his hips so the connection became deeper, he angled his head to lick and suck her breast.

A deluge of pleasure filled her belly, swept through her limbs, and touched her soul, slowly spiraling all of her senses toward a central core. When release came, it did not obliterate her perceptions as it had last night, but crested wonderfully and subsided beautifully, enhancing her alertness to the man in her arms. And so she sensed the tension claim him, felt his muscles harden beneath her hands, accepted with joy the tremor of his fulfillment.

He pressed his lips to her brow. "It is good with you, wife."

Awhile later they went back in the river and washed, then dried in the sun before dressing and heading back to the keep.

"How do you know about philosophy?" Reyna asked while their horses crossed the moss.

"English knights receive some education. We are not complete barbarians bred solely to subjugate the Scots."

"Receiving a knight's education and knowing enough about philosophy to reject it are two different things. You spoke as if you had read these things."

"As a youth, I read them. My father had an excellent tutor for me. He intended that I become a priest."

He glanced over slyly and caught her shocked reaction. Their gazes locked, and they both burst out laughing.

"It is common enough. A younger son becomes a cleric, and serves a great noble as either priest or administrator," he said. "There is power to be had for a family in it. It became clear to me by the time I was twelve that I was not suited, however. I wanted to be a knight, and began training secretly. I liked women far too much, and began training there too. Eventually my father saw the futility of it, and sent me into service with a neighboring lord to be made into a knight. At the time, I considered it a great triumph."

"You do not now? Surely you could never have lived a priest's life."

"Nay, I could not have. But every change begets consequences, and the ride to that nearby estate wrought changes neither my father nor I could anticipate."

He said it thoughtfully, as if distracted by memories. She waited for him to continue and explain, but he only rode silently with a faint frown on his brow.

"Who do you think poisoned him?" he asked, startling her with the change of subject. He had not been contemplating his own past, but hers.

"I can think of no one who would have wanted Robert dead."

"If he was killed, it was to someone's advantage. Who *could* have done it? Had the chance to do it?"

"Anyone. Suppose he was drinking some wine in his solar. Any servant or knight or guard might ask to speak with him and manage to put something in the wine."

"What do you think was fed to him?"

She shrugged. "I do not know about these things, Ian. I never sought to learn, although there are always old wives in any town who claim to know about such things."

"Have you no books which describe such potions?"

"I have an herbal which mentioned some plants with such properties, but the writer refrained from explaining the recipes and only warned against confusing the plants with others."

"Where is the herbal?"

"I haven't consulted it in several years because I have it memorized, even the pictures. I assume it is on the shelf with the others." His examination was making her uncomfortable. "Why do you pursue this, Ian? Do you still think that I—"

"Of course not. But Morvan was right; it is best if this matter is settled. You will be living here with these people. No matter what happens, they will always wonder and suspect. I do not want you enduring that. Nor do we want a murderer in our household. We should try to learn the truth for everyone's sake."

"And what if the truth points to me?"

"Then we will know that it is not the truth at all."

She wasn't entirely reassured by his response. In Ian's

mind, her virginity had destroyed the motive everyone ascribed to her crime, but other motives could always be surmised by an intelligent man analyzing evidence.

He was right. She should try to find out what had happened to Robert, and why. For everyone's sake, especially hers.

I an descended to the kitchen that evening, and was glad to find that Reyna was not helping Alice. Servants at the hearth were lifting the soup cauldron from its hook, and he waited while they hoisted it between them to begin the careful journey to the hall. Alice placidly cut cheese onto wooden planks, only glancing once to where he idled by the wall.

"I am told that you came with Reyna from Duncan's household. Tell me about Reyna's mother," he said when they were finally alone.

Alice smirked. "I was wondering what you wanted. That is a subject best left alone."

"You were in the household. You must know what happened."

"I know. I be wondering why you need to, though."

He had no good answer to that. He had merely decided that the most sensible way to find out about Robert's death was to fill in all of the blanks in the various stories he had heard.

"I would know for my own reasons," he said, deciding that being the lord should count for something with a servant.

Alice shot him a look that said she had never been much intimidated by lords, and he would be no exception. "Duncan put Reyna's mother away, in a convent north of his land. Endowed the place, too, so's the abbess would be beholden to him and see she was kept there. Reyna was only four years old at the time."

"Did he annul the marriage?"

"Nay, not that I know," Alice said. "Jordana was his second wife, a beautiful girl from the Eliot clan. His first wife had died birthing Aymer, and he waited six years to remarry. Jordana tried to give that household some grace and manners, but Duncan is a hard man, and he was not a kind husband."

More servants arrived to collect the cheese and bread to be set on the tables. Ian waited while they scurried about and hustled out. "Why did he put her away?" he finally asked.

Alice studied him sharply, as if she debated his worth. "I'll tell you, but you're not to speak of it to Reyna. It's in the past for her, and best it stay there." She licked her lips. "They'd been married six years, about. Reyna was born, but no others. Things was going badly between them even before Reyna came. We always know, of course."

Ian knew that by "we" she meant the servants.

"Jordana was a good mother, and warm to Reyna. In fair weather she would take the girl out in the hills, to get her away from that place. One day they went out, and did not return for a long time. Finally, ten of Duncan's men came back with Reyna, but not Jordana."

"What had happened?"

Alice's round face fell into sad folds. "Duncan had been suspicious of her. This day, he'd left before her with some men and then waited and followed her. Found her with her lover, trying to leave for good, they say. She had her valuables with her, and extra things for herself and the girl. He caught up with them near the border, by the old motte." She shook her head. "She was with an

Armstrong. Maccus's son, James. He'd been her lover for about a year, some said."

She paused while Ian absorbed the startling story.

"Duncan hung James Armstrong, then and there," Alice said. "At the old donjon on the motte. Then he took Jordana to the convent at once, and we never saw her again."

"The blood feud ended by Reyna's first marriage," Ian said. "That was how it started?"

"Aye. The first few years it was like a war between kings, so many died. Slowed down after that, but reprisals kept happening on both sides. The region grew weary."

"And she knows about this? Why her mother left for good?"

"With Duncan calling her mother a whore for the next eight years, she learned the reason for the convent, and probably the rest." Filmy memories glazed her old eyes. "Afterward, Reyna was treated no better than a servant. She looked like Jordana, and Duncan couldn't bear the sight of her. Everyone knew there would be no punishment if she were hit or abused. She learned to stay quiet and invisible, the way a mistreated dog does. I tried to be a mother to her, but I had no authority to protect her. Still, in the kitchen I was queen, and she was safe with me there."

And then the marriage alliance ended the feud, and Robert of Kelso was given lands to separate the two clans, and he became Reyna's savior, Ian concluded. Duncan's lack of affection certainly made more sense now.

"I thank you for the love and care that you showed my wife during those years," he said, turning to the doorway.

"I would kill anyone who tried to harm her," Alice said sharply.

He glanced back at her, and knew that he had just

been warned by an old woman with every opportunity to carry out her threat. While he mounted the stairs to the hall, he wondered if Alice had heard rumors about Robert's letter to the bishop, and had worried enough about Reyna's fate to take action.

Andrew Armstrong glided into step beside him while he crossed the hall. A steward was another person with ample opportunity to use poison, but Ian could think of no motive.

"I have good tidings," Andrew said. "The water has returned to the well. I check periodically, and today, after dinner, I went down and all was as before."

"A miracle," Ian said.

"It would seem. Perhaps last night helped. The rain and all."

"In that case we can only hope that it keeps raining."

Reyna entered the hall then. She looked lovely as a spring sky in her blue gown, with her silver-blond hair shimmering like sunlight.

Memories of her by the river, her body slicked with water, made his body tighten. Considering the condition she never failed to put him in, it would rain more than enough for a good long while.

chapter

SIXTEEN

Robert of Kelso managed these lands well."
Reyna glanced up from the table where she read her Aquinas by candlelight. Ian sat on a stool by the hearth with the estate ledger propped open on his lap.

"Most of the income derives from sheep, and the English dealers are always glad for more wool," he continued. "There is a second mill far to the west, which makes sense, considering the breadth of the lands."

"He built that one. He had seen an old man who had traveled two days to bring his grain here, and decided it was uncharitable to expect that of the weak," Reyna explained.

"Is it also because of his charity that most of the farmers are free tenants and not villeins?"

"If a family asked to buy its freedom, Robert always agreed. He said that any man industrious enough to save the coin would surely make a good tenant."

Ian nodded and became reabsorbed in the pages. Reyna

returned to her philosophy, but periodically glanced over to watch the way the firelight flickered over his handsome face. His arrival this evening had surprised her. Most of their time together during this first week of marriage had occurred at meals or in bed. At the former they were lord and lady, and in the latter husband and wife. This evening, however, reminded her of similar hours with Robert, and of the comfort of friendship that they had shared.

Was it even possible to have that with a man who was a true husband? The emotions and intimacies that she felt when she and Ian made love were very different from those she had known with Robert. More intense and consuming, and also more dangerous, in ways she could not explain. Although potent during their passion, they seemed fleeting, insubstantial things that struggled to survive the daylight.

She tried to concentrate on her reading. Once again, the book had not been here where she left it last night, but on the shelf. In its place she had found the tattered treatise by Bernard of Clairveaux. She wondered if Ian had been reading that.

She swallowed the impulse to ask him his opinion of Bernard's ideas. More likely he was checking the library against the ledger to see if he could find entries that indicated its value. Besides, he had said he did not care for philosophy.

Her mind drifted to the conversation that day by the river, and his startling revelation that he had been tutored for the priesthood as a youth. It had been a rare reference to his life's history. He never spoke of his family or events from his past.

She had been thinking about him a lot these last few

days, observing him while she came to terms with this marriage. He was a restless man, always pursuing new projects and ideas, already planning improvements to the keep. His long spurts of activity would occasionally break at the least likely moment, however, while he sought silence and reflection, usually in the garden. She wondered what he thought about then.

She had gradually noticed, too, that he didn't have any close friends in his company. He enjoyed a familiar camaraderie with the men, knights and foot soldiers alike, but there was no man who was his special companion. He was usually with a group, or with her, or alone. That struck her as odd for a man with such an easy manner.

The candle flickered as the dead wick grew overlong. She picked up the little knife lying nearby and stretched to cut the burnt end. Ian glanced up at her movement before returning to his ledger.

"Is your father who sought to make you a priest still alive?" she asked.

She hadn't planned the question. It just emerged, a product of her thoughts.

He reacted as if it were an intrusive impertinence. She saw the subtle tensing, the lowered lids, the shift of his eyes that indicated he had ceased to read. But he did not even acknowledge her query.

The question hung in the air between them. She went very still, shocked by his blatant rebuff.

The silence grew thick with unspoken words. She made a show of returning to her book. The pleasant evening had been ruined.

She wished that she could believe that she read too much into what might only be a small claim of privacy, but the brittle mood in the chamber said otherwise.

His silence was a statement regarding the limits of what they would have. It was a pointed rejection by a man choosing to restrict her knowledge of his deeper self. It stunned her how deeply it wounded her. During their lovemaking, she thought she had felt ties forming. This silence revealed that he did not want them.

A sick feeling spread in her heart while she gazed at her page. She sadly admitted that the novelty of passion had obscured the facts about this marriage. Her rational mind had recognized them when she discovered the testament, but her heart, caught up in the false intimacy of the last week, and in the happy day at the river, had urged her to ignore them.

She had thought . . . she didn't want to name what she had thought. That would only add humiliation to the sad resignation filling her heart.

She heard Ian rise and walk over to her. She felt him behind her. His hands come to rest on her shoulders.

A stranger's hands. And he would forever remain one.

"Come to bed, Reyna."

In her disappointment, she stiffened slightly and hesitated. His hands slid along her chest and one dropped to caress her breast. With flawless skill he obliterated her brief resistance until she raised her face and arms to him with a yielding that belied her confusion.

But it was not the same. The melancholy that she had known the morning after their first night throbbed poignantly at the center of her desire. Although her body responded as it always had, her spirit resisted the flow of the passion. Her release came as a private journey.

She emerged from the ecstasy to discover Ian had finished too, although she had no memory of it. He fell asleep, leaving her to reckon with the sad lesson she had learned this night.

E arly the next morning, scouts tore through the gate to report that an Armstrong force was gathering near the northern border of Black Lyne Keep's lands. Men had been seen trailing out of villages and farms, heading toward it. The scouts judged the army to be three hundred strong and still growing.

"It sounds like Thomas Armstrong is calling up every able-bodied man on the Clivedale estate," Ian said to the men who gathered to hear the report.

Reyna sat beside him, breaking her fast. Things had been cool between them since they woke. They had been treating each other in the stilted, careful way people do after they have had a cutting argument.

"You'd think he would have them muster far to the west, or at least nearer to the road to Harclow," one of the knights said.

"I do not think he goes to Harclow. I think he comes here. It is a clever strategy. I did not give Thomas enough credit."

To Reyna that made no sense. She spoke, even though it was not her place to do so. "Maccus requires relief at Harclow. What can Thomas achieve by engaging with you?"

"Anna de Leon is here. By now, Margery has described Morvan's love for his wife. Perhaps Thomas expects Morvan to break off a section of the siege army and come here when he learns she is in danger. More equal numbers, and probably Morvan will lead them. The plan is risky, but the best chance that Thomas has. If he can defeat Morvan at Black Lyne Keep, the whole situation at Harclow changes."

"Sitting tight makes sense, then," she said. "If Morvan has to come, he will bring men enough to deal with Thomas. Their plan will fail."

"Probably, but I find that I have no taste for sitting here. Besides, there are spoils waiting on the border, and this company has been patient long enough. After a summer of indolence, we could all use some action." He turned to his men. "Spread the word that we move in an hour."

While the soldiers rushed off to prepare, Reyna glared at Ian. "The scouts said that over three hundred wait at the border. It is foolish to face such odds when it is not necessary."

"Whether Thomas intends to besiege us or continue on and attack Morvan, it is my duty to stop him."

"It is not logical to meet such a force on the field. Morvan could never have intended you to do so."

"Do not preach logic to me now."

"No doubt you think this some grand chivalrous gesture, but it is akin to suicide."

His expression hardened. "I did not know that your low opinion of me extended to my skills in warfare, Reyna."

"Do not confuse concern with insult, Ian. The bravest warrior is vulnerable against such odds."

He gave her a scrutinizing look. "You fear for your pretty neck if I fall on the field? Even if I die, Thomas will never take this keep, and Morvan will never let the Armstrongs have you. Do not worry."

But she did worry, horribly, and spent the next hours alternating between fury and despair. She realized that this was yet another way in which her second marriage differed from her first. Robert had last donned his armor ten years ago. She had been a child then, and when she watched him ride through the gate, it had never occurred to her that he might not return.

She was overwhelmed with mental images of Ian struck down, dying painfully, his blood leaking away into the soil of the hills.

She tried to distract her mind with dinner preparations, but she knew instinctively when the moment of departure had arrived. Wiping her hands, she ran up to the hall and out to the stairs.

Ian stood in the center of the yard, his armor looking like gray water in the silver light of the overcast day. Castle folk lingered around to watch the knights and horses being readied.

As Reyna walked down the stairs, a servant girl named Eva approached Ian. They spoke, standing close, with Ian looking down as he smiled his devastating smile. Finally, to Reyna's dismay, he reached out and stroked Eva's jaw and chin in the same affectionate gesture he had used so often with her.

Reyna bore down on the intimate conversation taking place in front of the whole household. Eva saw her coming, said something quickly, and melted away.

"Where have you been?" Ian asked, not at all embarrassed at having his new wife see him charming his slut.

"I did not want to be in the way. I am not well schooled in how a wife behaves at these times. If I was supposed to attend on you, I apologize for my neglect." Her eye caught Eva by the wall, speaking to a young archer. A pretty young woman, with large breasts that stretched her gown. Not at all puny and scrawny.

"You need never attend on me if you do not choose to," Ian said. Reyna heard an allusion to more than just preparations for battle. Nay, obviously she need not. One woman was as useful as another to the Lord of a Thousand Nights.

She forced an expression of indifference onto her face. It had been an evening and morning full of disheartening discoveries, but she was gentle-born and knew how to act with dignity.

Knights mounted and began pacing through the gate with their squires. She stretched up and kissed Ian's cheek. "God go with you."

He looked down with an especially brooding expression, and then turned away. Halfway to his horse, he pivoted abruptly and strode back. He pulled her into a savage embrace, pressing her to his steel, claiming her mouth with a furious kiss. "Be waiting for my return as a wife should," he ordered roughly.

I an led his men toward the border, trying to ignore the strange ill ease that pricked his spirit. He tried to blame Reyna for having unsettled him with her arguments and cold behavior. He knew, however, that the cause did not lie with her. He suspected what this sensation really was, for he had felt something similar long ago, but he refused to name it.

Half of his mind kept busy reexamining the strategy they would execute when they engaged Thomas's army. The other half, however, was full of Reyna, as it had been since he first met her. It annoyed him that possessing her had not resolved the way she intruded in his head. That was something else that he had only felt once before, long ago—with dire consequences.

She had considered denying him last night. He had known her hesitation for what it was, but had not allowed her to contemplate it long. In the end, however, her withdrawal might as well have been physical, so clearly had an invisible wall appeared between them. Although her body had joined his with a heightened abandon, the essential part of her had remained aloof.

For the first time with Reyna it had been as it had always been for him over the years, two people exploiting passion and relief for their own sakes. The passing of Reyna's innocence, which had permitted joyful sharing without counting the cost, had wounded him more than he expected.

It had been inevitable, he supposed. She was not some silly girl. The day had to come when she would begin examining what lay within the pleasurable haze. And then she would weigh the value of what she had been giving, and judge the worth of the man to whom she offered it.

His final attempt to forestall that reckoning last night had been in vain, and, he suspected, had only hastened the opening of her eyes.

Does your father who sought to make you a priest still live? It had been such a simple question. Perhaps a simple answer would have sufficed, but he doubted it. This question would lead to others, as was the way with such things. He had not emerged into the world with their meeting, and eventually she would seek the story of the years that had brought him here.

Little could she know that the dishonor of the past four, the part that she already knew, had been the least and last of it.

He had considered answering that question, but had found that he could not risk it. He did not dare test the delicate ties that had been forming between them, because his isolated soul relished those tenuous connections more than he thought possible. But in the tense silence of his re-buff and then later in bed, he had felt some break just the same, as surely as if she had snipped them with a pair of shears.

T wilight was gathering when the troop straggled down the road to Black Lyne Keep. They made slow progress, what with the carts loaded with the spoils of armor and the trailing line of Armstrong horses.

It had been a brief battle, following a surprise attack, and had ended sooner than it might have, when Ian challenged Thomas Armstrong to individual combat. Defeating the man had been easy enough, and Ian had spared Thomas's life in return for an oath to keep the Armstrongs at Clivedale, north of the border with Black Lyne Keep and far from the siege at Harclow.

The mood in the company was high-spirited. On their own the common soldiers decided to share the spoils with their members who had missed the fun by be-ing sent to Harclow. Ian traded jests, and soaked in the familiarity and friendship. Most of these comrades would depart from his life soon, he realized. In six months the company would be back in France, laying siege to some exhausted town. The majority were brigands at heart and could know no other life.

He stayed in the camp outside the wall for many hours, sharing the ale and food brought out the gate by some servants. He listened to the old stories of past cam-paigns and adventures, letting the good cheer flow around him. A fine drizzle had been falling for some time when he finally rose and drifted away.

He had removed his armor, and wore only a long cloak and tunic and soft low boots. He approached the gate looking like a mendicant, and had to call out before the guard recognized him in the torchlight.

The portcullis rose. He paused and glanced back to the fires. Then he walked through, into the deserted yard. With a loud thud the iron gate bit the ground behind him, cutting off the sounds of his company.

He approached the keep. A single torch sputtered in the drizzle by the door, and in its dying light he saw a huddled form in the middle of the wooden stairway. He slowly mounted the steps toward it. Reyna's pale face peered out from a cloak swaddled around her seated body.

He had forgotten that he had ordered her to wait for him.

"You could have stayed in the hall. It is damp and cold here."

"I am warm and dry enough. I have little experience in greeting a man after battle, but I met Robert here when he came home from a journey. There are those within who remember that. I would not have it thought that I honored you less."

He accepted the statement of duty without comment. He could not see her expression, but her tone had been soft and careful. How does one end an argument that never started? No words had been spoken that could be retracted, no insults hurled for which to apologize. She had merely asked for a small thing, but still it was more of himself than he dared to give. And yet he knew, to the core of his soul, that she had resigned herself to never ask for anything again.

"You may have little experience in greeting a man after battle, Reyna, but you have many more years as a wife than I have as a husband."

She cocked her head thoughtfully, and when she

spoke again her voice sounded more natural. "Aye. And the wife is going to scold you now, for waiting so long to walk through that gate. I heard about your combat with Thomas, and you have wounds that should be cleaned. There is warm water heating by the fire in the solar, and I will use some salves on your cuts."

The idea of Reyna's fussing over his cuts pleased him. He opened his cloak with one arm to take her small body next to him. She was neither warm nor dry as she claimed, but he would take care of that very soon. He wanted her, and would accept whatever she gave, and perhaps with time it would again be as it had been before last night.

"They say that you let Thomas live," she said.

"There was no profit in killing him. If I thought that his death would end the accusations against you—"

"Nay, nay . . . I am glad you did not. People would say it was because . . ." Her voice trailed off.

Because I desired Thomas's wife, and sought to have Margery free of her husband. He did not care what other people thought, but he would not have Reyna wondering about that. This at least he could give her.

"There was never anything between me and Margery," he said. "Now come out of the rain."

With his cloak floating around them both, he guided her into their home.

chapter SEVENTEEN

I an looked out over the moss from his position on the southeastern curve of the wall walk. Below him spread the wildflowers and heather, and further off snaked the line cut into the land by the river. Beside him stood Giles, his most experienced sapper.

Ian pointed to the land due south. "Andrew Armstrong says the river once flowed closer to the keep, years ago, and ran more broadly, covering that wetland there."

Giles nodded. "I've seen such before. A river's flow moves or thins sometimes."

"I am wondering if it can be moved again. Why couldn't one excavate and bring the river close to the wall?"

"It is how moats are cut, of course."

"Not just divert part of the river for a moat, but move the whole thing. I want to know how many men, and how long?"

"Let us say a hundred men from the farms. Can not use them during planting and harvesting, so it is only the growing months and a few before winter. If you do not find rock, and if it is easy going, maybe three seasons."

Two months ago, if anyone had proposed a project taking so long, Ian would have laughed at the suggestion. Now, three years seemed a small investment in a lifetime.

Ian gave Giles orders to draw up plans for the project, then strolled along the wall toward the stairs. As he descended to the yard, he saw Reyna walking by. She wore her hair in a thick plait wound around her head, but he knew that she would arrive at dinner with it flowing freely the way he preferred. She did that to please him, despite the inconvenience.

He watched her amble to the garden with a basket over her arm, going to pick the flowers and herbs with which to flavor the food. She helped Alice at every dinner now, because he preferred her cooking. At the meal she would chat about his plans for the keep and the news of the siege at Harclow. In the evening she would retire to read or write her philosophy, and at night her arms and body would welcome him. Those intimacies throbbed with pleasure, but were always marked in silent ways by boundaries that she did not let herself cross anymore.

She was beautiful. Not a perfect face or body, but beautiful to him just the same. Dutiful and cheerful and compliant and lovely. More than he had ever expected.

So why did he find himself gritting his teeth over her courteous banter, and longing for the days when she cursed him as a bastard and a whoreson? At least her earlier conflict with the despicable Ian of Guilford had possessed blood and life, and a peculiar friendship. In contrast, this polite wifely duty promised to stagnate into boring routine very quickly.

He began mounting the steps to enter the keep.

Movement and noise at the gate stopped him. A guard announced that a lone knight approached.

The portcullis rose and a horse passed through the gate in the wall. Its rider turned and studied the white-and-green pennants flying from the towers, then cast his gaze over the yard. He sat on his steed straight and proud, in full armor, with a long black cloak thrown back from his shoulders.

The man was maybe thirty years old, with golden hair waving around his head and neck. He turned his narrow, delicately sculpted face toward the keep, and his liquid blue eyes lit upon Ian. As he swung off the stallion, his black cloak fell forward and unfurled.

Ian took in the white cross on the cloak's shoulder, and knew at once who had arrived. Edmund the Hospitaller. He stood there like the embodiment of an archangel, as perfect and clean as if he had stepped out of a colored glass window in a cathedral.

A squeal erupted from the garden gate. Ian watched Reyna drop her basket and run like a doe into the outstretched arms of the smiling blond knight. She gave Edmund a kiss of greeting and smiled up with a delighted, trusting expression.

Forcing a smile of welcome that he hardly felt, Ian approached the knightly monk. Reyna stepped back, turning in the arm resting around her shoulders. "Ian, this is Edmund, whom I told you about."

"Welcome, Edmund. We are honored to have a knight of Saint John visit us."

"Some business for the preceptor brought me to the area. I thank you for the welcome, since I have heard during the last few days that there have been many changes here."

Aye, Edmund would have heard the news about the

siege of Harclow and the fall of Black Lyne Keep while he rode through those hills. How much else, though? Ian decided to clarify the situation. "Our hospitality is always open to my wife's friends."

The man was good, Ian had to give him that. His expression barely changed at all. Just a blink of vague surprise.

Edmund's arm fell away from Reyna. Ian could tell that the knight had many questions for the lady, and that Reyna felt some need for explanation, but of course they couldn't hold that conversation now. Eventually they would find time alone to do so, and Ian imagined Reyna's half of that discourse and not much liking what he heard her say.

"I have met your brother, Reginald, of course," Ian said.

"I heard that you hold him."

"He said he swore to Robert to protect me, Edmund, but before taking me to you he was going to force a marriage," Reyna explained sorrowfully. "He was like a different man. I did not understand it."

"He was wounded, but he heals well," Ian added.

"I would like to see him, if you will permit it."

"Of course. I will take you to him now. Have the servants prepare a chamber for our guest, wife, while I bring Edmund to his brother."

"I know my duties, Ian," she said. "We will talk at dinner, Edmund. It is so good to see you again, dear friend."

"My brother is not the smartest of men," Edmund said quietly while Reyna walked away.

"I disagree. He forged a brilliant plan, and would have gained both the lady and her lands if it had worked."

"I know nothing of her lands, and if Reginald offered marriage it was only to protect her."

"You may be avowed to chastity, but your brother is

not. Surely more drove the man than chivalry, and it is a strange offer that does not permit refusal."

Edmund's face colored. "Since she is bound to you now, it is clear that you know all about offers accepted under duress."

"At the least, we can assume that I offered more courteously than Reginald did."

"Or more violently."

"Or more persuasively."

Ian led the way down to the cellar chamber where Reginald languished. He unlocked the heavy door and stood aside.

Seeing the two men together, Ian could note their resemblance. Edmund was a smaller, finer version of his older brother. He possessed a more handsome face and, he knew from Reyna, a much sharper mind. Still, their relationship was obvious.

"I will leave you together for a short while." He closed the door and locked them both in. The temptation to leave Edmund there for good, to ensure that Reyna never again saw this friend, played in his mind.

The short passageway was only dimly lit from light seeping down from atop the steps, and so he didn't notice the other door until he rested against it.

He turned and felt along the heavy planks, finding the iron hinges and finally the rough handle. The door swung smoothly, and light flooded to his eyes from a tiny high window. A confusion of complex aromas filled his head.

His gaze took in a crude table covered with terra-cotta bowls and a variety of flora hanging in bunches from the low ceiling. He dipped a finger into the crushed, dried contents of some of the containers.

Herbs.

Pacing around the chamber, he told himself that Reyna had not deliberately kept the location of this chamber hidden from him. It had been unlocked, and the whole castle must know of its existence.

He remembered a tour of the building that he had demanded of Andrew Armstrong the day after the keep fell. The steward had merely gestured down the stairs and said the prison cells were there, and Ian had not doubted their predictable location. If there had been any deliberate deception, it had been Andrew's.

Through the forest of brittle leaves, Ian spied a wide plank resting on its side against the window wall. He ducked over and examined its thin, flat shape. Scanning the right wall that did not connect with Reginald's chamber, he saw a slight gap an armspan wide between some stones.

Crouching down, he fitted the plank into the open slit and pushed. The plank worked its way through the wall and then slid smoothly until it hit a solid barrier. He guessed that if he didn't pull it out again, the keep would be without well water once more.

The postern tunnel and the escape stairs, and now this opportunity for sabotage if the keep fell. Robert of Kelso had been a very clever man.

He removed the plank and left it near the slit, so Reyna would know that he had discovered it.

Returning to the prison chamber, he pulled the door open. Edmund wore a sour expression, and Reginald looked as abashed as a child who had just been whipped. Without a word of farewell to his brother, Edmund joined Ian in the passage.

"I must apologize for him to the lady," he muttered while they mounted the steps. "My brother can be hardheaded in his simple way. He interprets his duty and then goes forward, and none can stop him. Useful in battle, but otherwise . . ."

Ian accompanied him to the hall, where Andrew supervised the laying out of the keep's silver plates on the high table. It appeared that Reyna had decided to honor her friend with the trappings of a feast. Ian told himself he shouldn't mind, since he would derive the benefits of the food, at least. Also, the preparations would occupy Reyna and ensure no private chats with her pure knight for a few hours. Very abruptly Ian decided that a long hunt to entertain his guest in the afternoon seemed like a very good idea.

"Is it your intention to keep Reginald imprisoned?" Edmund asked.

"Until the events at Harclow are settled and there are terms with the Armstrongs, I don't see any choice."

"He was Robert's liege man, but if you have set a ransom, I will see if the Armstrongs will pay it. If not, I will try to raise it myself. If you could see your way to be generous on this, I would take him back with me, far from here. He would swear not to return."

"He forswore one oath already."

"He did not think he did so, but if you prefer, *I* will swear an oath, and promise to keep him with me."

"I will consider it," Ian said. "Now, the steward will show you to your chamber. You have been on a horse many days, and I am sure you would like to refresh yourself."

The dinner was almost as elaborate as their wedding feast, and Ian tried to quell the prickling resentment he felt whenever he pictured Reyna fussing with excitement while she cooked the meal. She kept up an animated conversation with her friend across his body, but Ian could sense the strain with which both avoided the subjects that they most wanted to discuss. Robert's death. Her attempted escape. Reyna's forced marriage to the conspicuously unsaintly Ian of Guilford.

He finally succumbed to a devilish urge to prick the self-satisfied perfection of this archangel.

"Do you normally work at the hospital at Edinburgh, Edmund?"

"I did, as all do, during my training. Caring for the sick is one of the missions of the order."

"Aye, and liberating Jerusalem is your other great mission, is it not? Have you spent time in the Holy Land?"

Edmund's lips pursed. "The order has not campaigned there during my time, I'm sorry to say."

"In fact, the holy knights have not fought in the East since the Templars were disbanded, I think," Ian said.

"There has been talk of a new crusade."

"Well, there is always *talk*. Tell me, what does a Hospitaller do who neither tends the sick nor fights for God? What are these assignments that bring you south?"

"I am a clerk for the preceptor, and help to attend to the order's properties."

"Ah. So you travel to collect rents and such? Like a bailiff?"

The insult was subtle, but Edmund did not miss it. "My duties are a little more involved than that."

"How so?" Reyna asked curiously.

She had never asked Edmund about his life, Ian suddenly realized. Never wondered. He was a saintly monk who talked philosophy with her and who had become Robert's friend, and that was all she needed to know.

"We are pursuing the matter of certain properties granted to us by the Holy Father years ago, but which we never received. I am trained in canon and civil law, and have been looking into this."

Reyna's inquisitive mind had been stimulated. "Properties held by others? But if your claims are upheld, you will displace families."

"Those families knew when they procured the properties that they had no right to them, that the Holy Father had given them to my order."

"You speak of Templar lands, do you not?" Ian asked, delighted for the opportunity to raise another subject sure to make the Hospitaller uncomfortable.

Edmund shot him a quelling look.

"The Templars were disbanded by the pope over forty years ago," Ian explained to Reyna. "Their property was to be transferred to the Hospitallers, but in England the King gave much of it to friends instead. Parliament finally passed laws to see it went to the Order of Saint John, but there were many petitions as the families fought the transference. I assume the same happened in Scotland, Edmund?"

"Aye."

"Why were they disbanded?" Reyna asked.

Edmund grimaced. "They were accused of blasphemy and demonic practices, my lady, and other crimes which are not fit for your ears."

"And the pope and kings took their gold, and the Hospitallers their lands," Ian added.

Reyna lifted one eyebrow, showing that she had not missed the possibilities for unjust prosecution there. Ian took some satisfaction in having tarnished Edmund's halo a little.

Reyna and Edmund launched into a discussion of some philosopher. While Ian vaguely listened, he leaned forward and observed his other guests. Anna de Leon was quizzing Andrew about the stable, deciding which horse she would request for the afternoon's hunt.

Ian decided that he would arrange to have Edmund hunt with Anna. He had heard that she could outride most men and had a bow eye few could match. He smiled at the image of Anna outdistancing her escort and bringing down more game than the perfect, pure knight. He would let Morvan's wife take this Hospitaller in hand, and put him in his place.

chapter

EIGHTEEN

T hat is the message as it was given?"

"Word for word. Sir Morvan said I am to wait and bring back your answer."

Ian repeated the message in his head. Not an order, but a request. That had been an acknowledgment on Morvan's part that Ian held Black Lyne Keep through Reyna now, and had not sworn fealty to any man yet.

"Tell him that I will come tomorrow. Now go and get some food, and tell Gregory to see to a fresh horse for you."

The man left, and Ian paced to the solar's windows. A cool night breeze flowed through them. He wished Reyna were here so he could tell her at once about this.

He had known that the call might come. He had even been resentful when it did not immediately after Black Lyne Keep fell. It had been as if Morvan's refusal of his help at Harclow had been a silent reflection of his opinion of the value of the brigand who had saved his life.

Now, however, the situation at Harclow had become

critical, and every sword was needed. Morvan had been mounting aggressive assaults for some time, and the next fortnight would most likely decide things. Maccus Armstrong showed no inclination to surrender, and the fortress would have to be taken through sheer force.

He wished Reyna were here. Tomorrow they would be separated indefinitely, perhaps forever. He had no illusions that he was invulnerable. Scaling walls and fighting on siege towers was very different from meeting on the open field, and better men than he had fallen during the ensuing carnage. The strange ill ease that he had experienced when riding to face Thomas Armstrong prickled again, and he experienced a soulful need to hold onto Reyna's warmth throughout the hours before they parted.

He wished she were here, but she was not, and he knew where she was instead. Reyna had pointedly invited Edmund to visit Robert's grave with her when the evening meal drew to a close. Ian had watched them depart from the hall together, barely resisting the urge to forbid it. They had left before the messenger from Harclow arrived.

Turning abruptly from the window, he went down to the hall and out to the yard. He mounted the steps to the wall walk and circled to the southern curve that looked out over the small graveyard at the foot of the hill.

What did it matter if she spent time with this man who, of all men, should present no threat? Did he seriously think a seduction was occurring, that the pious knight would try to take her on that consecrated ground? Did he believe Reyna would permit it? His rational mind said nay, he did not, but mental images of their joining invaded his head all the same, feeding the resentment and jealousy that had been growing an ugly, angry edge all day.

He gazed in the direction of the graveyard, barely making out the shadows of crosses over its low wooden wall, thinking he saw two forms sitting in the moonlight beside the central grave.

Edmund the Hospitaller. Noble and learned and chaste. No blemishes on his body or soul, no insurmountable hungers, no damning sins to hide. He was, for all intents and purposes, a younger version of Robert of Kelso. No wonder Reyna had been drawn to him from the first.

He was also, in many ways, the direct opposite of Ian of Guilford. She would not miss the stark contrast. First King Alfred and now Saint Edmund. It had been one thing to compete with the memory of a dead man. This one lived and breathed.

She is not lying with him, but she is giving him parts of herself that she withholds from me.

He stood on the wall, waiting for movement from the graveyard, resisting the urge to go and fetch her. Time passed, and with every moment his irrational reactions grew and his sensible thoughts receded. Tomorrow he would leave her for God knew how long, and she dallied away the last of their time together down there with that man. That she did so unknowingly ceased to weigh much in his anger.

When it seemed an eternity had passed and still he did not see them emerge through the graveyard gate, he turned and strode back to the solar.

R eyna finished her prayers and sat back on her heels, looking at the folded hands and closed eyes of the knight who knelt across the grave. He appeared a little mysterious in the breezy night.

"It is good to visit here," she said, trailing her fingers through the soil of the long mound of dirt. Her heart felt full of Robert's memory, and she sensed the comfort of his love and care reaching through eternity to her. "It is good to be here with someone who knew him as I did."

Edmund shifted and sat on the ground with the grave still between them, a connection more than a separation. "I brought you a manuscript. A copy of one of Plato's *Dialogues*, in the original Greek. It reads differently from the translations, and I do not think you have it."

"Did you? Oh, Edmund, thank you. Nay, we have no Plato. You must let me pay you for it."

"It cost me nothing. The preceptor had it in his library, and one of the brothers copied it for me. Besides, I do not think your new husband would want to spend coin thus."

Reyna knew that Edmund was politely moving the conversation in the direction of her marriage, but she didn't want to discuss that just yet. "It will be a joy to have something new to read."

He took the hint and they talked about the books he had read and the scholars he had met since his last visit. She envied him the variety of experiences made possible through his man's life near a city. Ian had enjoyed such a life, too, and she wondered how he could ever be content immured in the isolation of Black Lyne Keep.

"I am glad to hear that you still pursue your studies," Edmund said. "At dinner I could tell that you did, for your ideas were provocative. I hadn't realized when I visited last year how much your mind had grown."

"I was a girl when we met. Five years is a long time in a young life. I am a girl no longer."

"Nay, you are not." His head bowed. "Tell me about his death, Reyna. I have heard . . ."

"I know well what you have heard. How far has that story traveled? Not to Edinburgh, I hope."

"Not to Edinburgh."

She described Robert's abrupt illness and quick death, her voice catching when she related his suffering.

"Could it have been a natural passing, Reyna? The human body is complex, and he was old."

"It could have been, but it did not look so. No one will believe it was now, anyway."

"Is there no indication of who did this? No evidence besides that which suggests it was you?"

"Ian always asks questions about it. He wants to find out, so there will not be suspicion about me forever. I have been trying to learn the truth too."

"And what have you learned?"

"Nothing. I have searched the chambers of those who lived in the keep at the time, not even knowing what I sought. In the end, it was all in vain."

"And your husband? Has he learned nothing?"

"I do not think so. He has promised to fight for me in trial by combat if necessary. I trust it will not come to that."

"You believe he will do this?"

She heard the skepticism in his voice. "He has promised that he will."

A low sigh flowed across the grave. "Reyna, such a man lives only for himself and his gain. If you put your trust in him, I worry that you will be horribly disappointed."

"You do not know him. He is not as you say."

"You truly believe that he will protect you? That he will risk his own life to save a wife who can be easily replaced, and whose value has already been secured to him?"

"I had no value to him. Morvan is giving him these lands anyway."

"Morvan may fail at Harclow. It can go either way."

She did not need Edmund reminding her of the ways in which this marriage had been convenient for Ian. A week ago, she had looked the facts in the face and accepted them as realities with which she must simply live.

"Are you sure that he truly seeks to prove your innocence, Reyna?" His voice came slowly and carefully.

"What do you mean?"

"Why hasn't he sent you away from here? Why not see to your safety until it has been settled? Then, if he did not succeed in the combat, you would still be protected."

"If there is a judgment, I must be here to speak for myself."

"Very neat, and assuming that Morvan holds these lands perhaps all will turn out well, but what if he does not? If Harclow does not fall, Morvan and his army will leave this region, and Black Lyne Keep alone can not hold off the Armstrongs for long. Perhaps that is why Sir Ian needs you here. His loyalty is to himself, I think, and he would serve the highest bidder, even old Maccus, if it meant getting what he wants. Relinquishing a wife who has served her purpose would be a small cost to retain what you have brought him."

His suggestion contained a ruthlessly practical possibility which her mind could not ignore, but her spirit rebelled against the accusations. "You do him a disservice, my friend. I would never have married him if I thought him capable of what you describe."

"I think that you had little choice."

"You are wrong there too. I most definitely had a

choice. Several, in fact. I could have returned to my father. I could have agreed to go with Reginald."

"The choice of Reginald came before that of Ian, and
you made each decision independently of the other. Are
you saying that if they had been presented together, to
either go to Edinburgh as Reginald's wife or stay here as
Ian's, you would have chosen the latter, with all of the
dangers it holds?"

It was a devastating question, in ways he could not begin to guess. She had indeed been making her choices as
they arrived, one at a time. She had told herself it had
been either Ian or Duncan, and the choice had been inevitable once Ian had agreed to keep Robert's secret.

Now Edmund forced her to face a new reality. His
presentation of a choice which had never existed revealed her emotions with stunning clarity. Safety with
Reginald would have been the sensible, logical course.

But it would never have been the one that she took.

Edmund misunderstood her stunned silence. "Ian ma-
nipulated your situation to coerce you. A marriage made
under such duress need not stand."

"No one forced my hand to sign the contract,
Edmund. I was neither drugged nor beaten into this."

"A woman need not be beaten in order to break her.
Your danger created coercion just the same. This marriage can be set aside." He took her hand in his. A cool,
dry hand, she noted, and not nearly as rough as Ian's.
More like Robert's had been. The hand of a good man,
but with less life and blood flowing through it than the
palm and fingers of Ian of Guilford. "I am known by the
bishop in Edinburgh, Reyna. When he hears how this
came about, he will surely dissolve the vows."

"And then what, Edmund? Do you now offer me the
choice between Ian and Reginald that I never had?"

"My brother is out of this. I offer you freedom and safety, and my protection, which was there for you from the first. Now that the defenses of this keep have relaxed, it will not be hard to get you away. You will come with me, Reyna, and will never be in fear again."

She gazed at the mound of soil. His last sentence summoned distinct memories of the first time she had seen Robert, and the first words he had spoken to her. He had arrived at Duncan's home for their wedding a day earlier than expected. She had not been in the yard to greet him because Aymer, angry at some perceived disobedience on her part, had dragged her to the crypt and locked her in to fight the terror and darkness.

Demanding to meet her, Robert had been brought there. For an instant, while she peered at the grave, she was that twelve-year-old child again, huddled against the crypt wall, fighting for her sanity. And then, suddenly, footsteps sounded on the stone stairs, and the flare of a torch broke the black eternity, and a hand reached through the glow toward her. *You will come with me, child, and you will never be frightened like this again.*

The memory fell away and she was staring down at her clasped hand. She felt Robert's presence suddenly, in an astonishingly vivid way, as if he stood beside her, no longer dead. She closed her eyes and reveled in the poignant awareness of his essence, and sensed his spirit trying to speak to her.

Perhaps the souls in heaven knew the future. Was Edmund's offer, spoken in words so similar to Robert's promise, meant to be a sign? Was Robert's spirit urging her to accept their friend and the safety he afforded? Did he know that, if she did not, it would be as Edmund predicted, and Ian would forsake her?

The image from her nightmares, of her face blue and

her neck stretched, assaulted her. Ian was a brigand and an opportunist, and she could definitely be replaced without difficulty by the handsome, exciting man known as the Lord of a Thousand Nights.

"I will arrange it, and I do not misunderstand my duty like my brother. You will be long gone before your husband knows," Edmund urged in a whisper.

She knew that she had to make a decision now, for they might never get the chance to speak alone again. She wavered with a heart full of confused emotions. Panic gripped her, and her mind clouded with doubts and fear.

Then the breeze rose and caressed her hair, much as Robert's hand had stroked her tresses when he departed on a journey. Her eyes teared while his memory and presence totally invaded her, bringing her comfort, quelling the confusion. She sighed at the relief he afforded, and dwelled in that invisible security, pulling her wits about her.

When she had calmed, she felt his presence recede, reining in all the confusion and pulling it with him as he left, moving aside the obscuring shadows in her heart so that she could see what lay within more clearly.

With sorrowful reluctance, she let his spirit ease away, then turned her inner eye on what he had uncovered. Another emotion glowed in her heart, frightened and tentative, but giving off a strong, compelling heat. She acknowledged its existence, and her acceptance acted like a fuel that made it flame.

But it is not like the love I had for you, Robert, she silently argued. *There might be much pain and little contentment in it.*

Again the breeze stroked her hair in that familiar, comforting way. Then the retreating memories and essence were swallowed by the night.

She carefully withdrew her hand from Edmund's. All of the logic in the world, all of the analyses of her danger and potential disappointment, had no strength against what she had acknowledged just now. She would not doubt Ian, and if he ultimately forsook her, so be it.

"He is my husband, Edmund. I have accepted him as such in my heart, and no bishop's decree can undo that."

She saw his body tense and straighten, and felt his eyes peering at her through the darkness. "Reginald said it was thus, but I could not believe him."

"I do not know what Reginald said, but—"

"He said this knight had played on your grief and loneliness. Seduced you. A more insidious form of coercion, but if the woman is vulnerable it is much more persuasive than violence."

Perhaps he was right, but it did not change anything. Her decision derived from her own emotions and motives, not Ian's. "He did not seduce me. I did not lie with him until our wedding. However, there was a peculiar affection between us, and I will not pretend there was not."

"Reyna, what you interpret as affection is no more than lust. Such hungers of the flesh pass, especially with men, most especially with men like him."

"You do not know my husband, and yet you speak of his character and intentions with such certainty."

"I asked about him this morning. The servants know me, and were willing to talk."

Aye, they would fill his ears, Reyna had no doubt of that. "It may well be only lust between us, but he is my husband now, accepted by me willingly. I will not lie to a bishop in order to have that undone. Do you think me so undeserving of affection that it is impossible for a man to feel it for me, Edmund?"

"You know that is nonsense. Robert had boundless affection and deep love for you. It awed any who saw it."

Robert loved me as a daughter, she wanted to say.

"I will leave on the morrow, Reyna. If you change your mind you must send word to my chamber tonight. Is there someone here whom you can trust?"

"Alice, but I will not change my mind. Must you leave so soon?"

"I must attend to the preceptor's work, and despite Ian's hospitality, he does not like my presence."

While they walked toward the keep, Reyna could feel a new distance growing between her and Edmund. He was so much like Robert that it wrenched her heart to know that he was reevaluating his judgment of her, and not for the better.

They paused outside the gate. "Have I lost you as a friend now, as I lost Reginald?" she asked quietly.

He took her hands and kissed them. "Nay, my lady, I am always here for you. Still, I think it unlikely that we will meet again for a long while. Ian does not care for our friendship."

"He will not deny me my friends."

He gazed down at her in the torchlight. "If it suits his purposes, he will deny you everything. I fear, if he is forced to a choice, that he will deny you even your life."

An echoing silence shrouded the keep. It was very late as if everyone slept, Reyna realized. She and Edmund had talked longer than she thought.

She climbed to the fifth level and paused in the passageway. A torch lit the space, and she guessed that Ian had ordered it left burning for her. He probably slept already, but she looked forward to lying beside him. She needed the reassurance of his strength warming her right now.

As she approached the solar door, it eased open and a skirted figure slipped out. A kerchiefed head turned with a bright smile that wiped away when it faced Reyna. Eva flushed deeply, ducked away, and scurried down the stairs.

Reyna stared at the solar door. Numbness splashed her limbs down to her fingers and toes, as if someone had dumped a bucket of icy water over her body.

The *bastard*.

Seething with hurt and fury, she strode to her own chamber. In the moonlight cast from the windows she groped for a rush at the hearth. Bumping into the table and bed, she made her way back out and took a flame from the passageway's torch, then returned to make some light for herself.

She prepared for bed with a head full of curses heaped on the black soul of Ian of Guilford. While she pulled off her blue cote-hardie, her gaze fell on the parchments stacked on her writing table. The letter to Lady Hildegard had not progressed very far. Too many days she had sat here quill in hand, trying to form her Latin phrases, only to find the hours had passed in daydreams dwelling on the man who consumed her thoughts.

A mistake there, that was obvious. The *whoreson*. She wished suddenly that she were as big and strong as Lady Anna. She wished that if she used her fists on a man he would feel it. She might not be able to touch this brigand's heart, but if he insulted her like this, it would be very gratifying to at least bruise his body.

With jerky movements she stripped off her hose and shift and threw back the bedclothes. She pounded the pillow and twisted to find some comfort in the narrow,

cold bed. Maybe she should go to Edmund and tell him
she had changed her mind. They might even manage to
leave tonight. God knew that Ian had ample cause to
sleep soundly through it all.

Her newly acknowledged love flickered through her
outrage, telling her that of course she would do no such
thing. She faced the emotion as though it were an invasive body that had intruded on her spirit. *You will not
control me*, she warned it dangerously. *I will not let you do
so. You are a form of torture, and I will continue to deny
your fire any fuel because if fed you will grow into the inferno
of hell itself.*

She wondered if Anna were awake still. Anna didn't
like Ian either, and they could find some wine and get
besotted and tear him to shreds with insults . . .

"What the hell are you doing in here?" The harsh low
voice came from the doorway. Reyna twisted her head to
see Ian. She had been so distracted by her furious
thoughts that she hadn't heard the door open.

"Sleeping. It was rude to awaken me."

"You were not asleep. I heard you come in."

He strode into the chamber and glared down at her.
She sat up against the wall and glared back, taking in the
tautness of his body and the deep lights in his eyes. He
looked as angry as she felt. She thought that took a lot of
gall on his part.

"You were up half the night with that man," he said
crisply.

"He is a friend whom I rarely see, and we had much to
discuss."

"I'll wager that you did. Did you debate philosophy all
these hours, Reyna?"

His insinuation made her blood pulse hard. He
had just bedded buxom Eva, and he dared to throw

accusations at *her*. The strain to control her fury pained her, and her head split from the effort. Deciding that speaking would undo her, she just looked at him, meeting his query with the same cold silence he had once given one of hers.

With an abrupt movement he turned on the writing table, grabbed its edge, jerked his arms upright, and threw it violently against the wall. One board split from the force of the impact. Parchments and quills flew out in all directions and fluttered to the floor like the debris of an autumn storm.

Her fragile control broke with the table. Pulling the bedsheet around her body, she bolted to her feet. "You despicable son of the devil. By what right do you—"

"You are my *wife*. If I ask what you have been doing half the night with a man, *you will answer me*."

"We spent most of the time cursing you!"

"And the rest of the time?"

Complex, ominous emotions streaked out of him, un-settling the air in the room like lightning, but she didn't give a damn. "Is that what this is about? Is that the rea-son for this display of outrage now? You still cling to the notion that Edmund and I share that kind of love? You *madman*. He is a celibate knight. Do not judge all men by your base standards, you English whoreson."

"My standards may be base, but I can spot a man who wants something when I see him. What did Saint Edmund want of you, wife?"

A dangerous, cold peace swept away the heat of her fury. She hadn't really calmed, but merely found the cen-ter of her storm. They faced each other a mere armspan away, two tense bodies locked over space by unwavering eyes.

"He wanted to take me away," she said. "He doesn't

trust you to protect me if you find it does not benefit you. Like a fool, I refused him, but no sooner did I climb those stairs than I regretted that decision."

His jaw clenched. "And so you came here to your philosopher's study to reconsider? To subject that dutiful decision to cold logic and weigh your options?"

"I came here because your *slut* was leaving your bed when I passed the solar door."

He didn't reply to her accusation, but then, what could he say? The winds of fury began rising in her again. "Did you intend me to find you together, Ian, or would you have been satisfied if I just learned about it from the servants' gossip tomorrow? Tell me, you rutting knave, did you call for her because I was not there to satisfy a passing hunger, or did you plan this as revenge and punishment because I dared delay with my friend and not attend on you as was customary?"

His eyes got hotter, but she didn't back down. She felt too hurt and angry to know any fear. A horrible tension arced between them. She almost hoped that he would hit her so that she could strike a few blows of her own, if only to relieve the tightness racking her.

He turned away, hands on hips. "If it had been as you say, it would have been no more than you deserved. You should have been here, and not with him."

"*Damn you.* Edmund is a friend who loves me as you never will. Like a fool, I chose against all logic to trust you more than him, and like a spiteful child, you lash out because for one evening you have not had all the attention."

He swung back to face her with a startled expression, but his face quickly retreated into its hard planes. "It is neither childish nor spiteful for a man to want his wife with him the night before he rides off to war, Reyna."

A physical blow could not have shocked her more. The impact of his words knocked the anger out of her completely.

She felt the full onslaught of the emotions thundering out of him. The anger and desire she recognized, but there were other currents there, too, unfamiliar ones. Gusts of needs and yearnings that did not have names seemed to be feeding the storm of his mood.

"When did you learn this?" she asked.

"The messenger came just after you left the hall. I will leave in the morning." His voice carried a bitter edge.

"Why didn't you come and tell me, or send word?"

"It was clear that you longed to talk with your knight and discuss your misfortune. I sensed that he wanted something from you, but I did not think him so bold as to violate my hospitality by trying to steal my wife."

"That implies . . . it was not . . ." She let the explanations die. She did not want to talk about Edmund anymore. Worry and fear had replaced her anger. Edmund's warnings, Eva's smile, even this wounding argument, had become instantly insignificant.

In a few hours Ian was leaving. Going away, and not to a quick battle on the border, but to a dangerous siege where men died every day while they scaled walls on which the enemy waited with arrows and fire.

They still faced each other stiffly, like stone statues decorating a building buffeted by a soundless gale.

"How long will you be gone?"

"Two weeks. A month. Until it ends."

Two weeks. A month. *Forever.* "Do you go alone?"

"I will bring most of the company with me. Your Hospitaller will have to leave in the morning, because the gate will close when we depart and none will enter without my sign." He was not looking at her directly, but

she could see the steely lights glowing in the depths of
his eyes.

She ached to bridge the space between them, but his
stance and face said the few feet of wooden floor might
as well have been a mile of cliffs. She took one step anyway, and raised a tentative hand as if to touch him. It
hovered there, not completing its path, a helpless, frail
command for the whirlwind to calm. "So we will live as
in siege until your return?"

"You will not. Morvan has ordered that his wife and
sister be sent to Carlisle. You are going with them."

Going to Carlisle sounded so permanent, as if he were
sending her to the other side of the world. "This is my
home, Ian. I do not understand."

"You will be safe there."

"I will be safe here."

"Not if Morvan fails and I die."

A soul-tearing anguish full of fear and regret and love
had been building inside her, and it overwhelmed her
now so badly that her throat clenched and her eyes
burned. Groping for composure, she took refuge in prac-
ticalities. "You are right. I should have been here. You
expected me to see to preparations, and your departure
will be delayed now. I will wake the servants in a few
hours, and—"

"I do not give a damn about preparations." He
reached out and grabbed her and pulled her across the
divide, into his turbulence. The violent movement so
startled her that she cried out. Iron fingers gripped her
upper arms, practically lifting her feet from the floor, and
he looked at her with dark, intense eyes. "For a widow
married twelve years, there is much you don't know
about being a wife."

The danger in his eyes and the brutal grip of his hands

should have frightened her, but they didn't. She did not understand much about this mood, but she recognized some of it.

"Then it is for you to guide me," she whispered.

With a hard movement, he pulled her into an urgent kiss and a rough embrace. Cruel fingers imprisoned her head so she could not avoid the mouth bruising her lips, devouring her misgivings, demanding its rights. Arms of steel bowed her body against his so tightly that her hands holding the sheet became small rocks gouging into the flesh and bone pressing against them. There was no request for willing submission in his savage assault. Her body responded with a staggering wave of heat, and her love blazed at the evidence that, whatever drove him, he clearly needed and wanted her.

He lifted his head and the blood flowed back to her ravished mouth, prickling her tender skin. Through filmy eyes she saw his uncompromising expression. He grasped her cocooned body tighter, with one hand splayed over her bottom so that the hard ridge of his arousal cleaved her belly and stomach. "Aye, this is what the thought of our parting does to me," he muttered hoarsely, examining her face as if he sought to memorize it. "If I am less than gentle, blame yourself for giving me too much time to dwell on it."

"I do not think to blame anyone."

"You may think differently before this night ends." He kissed her again, only slightly less violently. "I will see that you do not quickly forget that you are mine. If another man looks at you, it will be my eyes that you see on his face, and at night in your dreams it will not be some specter who takes you but me. If your holy knight dares to follow you to Carlisle, you will feel this devil's hands on your body while he lures you, and this brigand's breath in your ear while he persuades you."

She barely heard him. The storm had absorbed her, and she spun in its center with her body molded to his, dangling against it weightlessly, his strength the only solid connection with the world.

He lifted her in his arms, and his hot kisses scorched her mouth and neck while the chamber and passageway and solar blurred by. He dropped her on their bed and yanked aside the sheet which she still grasped to her body. Fully dressed, he came down on top of her, pushing her legs apart, settling on her. One rough hand stroked firmly up her thigh in a path that ended at the moisture coating that secret center.

His arm circled her shoulder and his hand entwined her hair, holding her head so that she faced him directly. She saw his triumph when he discovered her own arousal, but she didn't care. She ached painfully for the fullness of him, and groaned with relief when he thrust inside her with one hard move.

It was far from gentle. In primitive possession, his body slammed into her again and again while his rage of passion whirled around them. He bent up her legs so he could penetrate more deeply, and his violent thrusts lifted her hips with their strength. He watched her reaction to this bruising claim of rights, and lightning flashed in those dark pools when her response broke loose and their mutual frenzies clashed in battle. She became powerless against a spiritual invasion as the ecstasy began tightening and building and pulling her into him.

"Aye, Reyna," he said lowly as the taste of fulfillment quivered and licked through her. "Robert may still hold your heart, and your monk may inspire your mind, but in this you are wholly mine. You will deny me nothing tonight."

She knew that he did not just speak of physical things, but she found no will to summon resistance. Acknowledging her love had undermined the fragile walls with which she fearfully protected her heart. Now they wobbled and cracked and fell beneath the on-slaught of his intensity.

In the fevered heat of that larger unity, the aggressive taking became a soul-scorching sharing. She reached to absorb him with all of herself while the turbulent plea-sure rose to its frenzied peak. They came to each other in a long ferocious release full of bites and cries and clawing holds, merging in a violent rapture.

They lay entwined together in exhaustion, bodies sealed with sweat and embraces. She slowly grew aware of the breath in her ear with which he had promised to mark her memory. The sound reminded her of their im-minent parting. She closed her eyes and listened to its rhythm, and tried to suppress the sadness that wanted to intrude on the perfection of holding him.

chapter

NINETEEN

She caressed his back, and he felt her touch grow alert to the cloth of his tunic. She moved her hand beyond the sheet bunched beneath them and stroked the coverlet.

Ian rose on his forearms to look down at her. He saw her calculating that he was still clothed, and that the bed had not been used before he flung her on it.

He experienced a renewed annoyance that she hadn't asked about Eva before accusing him. Most of his wounded anger had been absorbed by their passion, but not all of it. "Maybe I took her on the floor or against the wall."

She glanced away with a dismayed expression, and he felt guilty for deliberately hurting her, especially now, after this.

"That was churlish of me," he whispered, nuzzling her ear. "I did not call her. She came on her own, to finish the request she had begun in the yard last week. There is a young archer in my company who has befriended her, but he wouldn't touch her because of me."

"She asked you for permission to bed another man?"

"Something like that. I doubt that Eva is concerned with such formalities, but the man thought it prudent. He wants to marry her. Her father has no sons, and they would go to his farm."

"She wants to leave?"

"I said that I had to ask you if you could manage without her."

She puckered her brow thoughtfully. "I don't know if I can. She is an excellent needlewoman. And if my husband decided to brutalize a woman on a regular basis, it might be useful to have her here."

He looked down at the evidence of his hard use. Finger marks showed where he had gripped her shoulders, and a love bite glowed red on her neck, where it would be visible to the world tomorrow. He gently kissed the spot, knowing that if he could make it permanent, like a brand, he would do so. "I would say that I am sorry, except that I am not."

"Nor am I."

He lay still a moment, grateful that she neither regretted nor resented what he had forced.

He slid off the bed and stripped off his clothes, then went to the hearth where a bucket of water warmed for morning washing. Wetting a rag, he returned and eased next to her, pressing the cloth to the marks he had made.

He moved lower to bring the warm compress between her thighs. In his mind he heard the echo of Morvan's words, spoken in this room: *Hell, Ian, didn't Elizabeth teach you anything?*

Aye, she had taught him much, but while he waited for Reyna tonight, those lessons and his years perfecting them had been forgotten. He had become a callow youth again, consumed by desperate needs and raw hurts, and all of them had become centered on Reyna. The notion that he shared any part of her with another man had maddened him. He had entered her chamber full of furious, mindless emotions, and her own anger and passion had pushed him over the edge.

Then, seeing what was in him, she had simply opened herself to absorb it.

He stroked the cloth over her body, watching the skin below his hand, burning the memories into his head. Unnameable things still churned inside him, quelled but not killed by their passion, unsettling him with their power. The idea of leaving her saddened him in a surprising way, shading his heart with the foreboding and pain a child might feel when separated from his mother. Perhaps it would have been better to have avoided her tonight and never demanded that she cross those boundaries. The cost might be very high, especially if she ever withdrew again.

He turned his head and their gazes met. Her face looked very young and sweet, but her eyes carried a woman's knowing.

"Is your father who sought to make you a priest still alive?" She asked the question as if she had never spoken it before, but her gaze contained a challenge.

Aye, it would have its cost. This was Reyna. She would never be so stupid as to have the giving go only one way.

"He is not alive."

He braced himself for the next question, and the next, and began to taste the loss of her after they had all been asked and answered. And so he almost groaned with relief when she chose to follow a connected path instead of the main one.

"Did he die when you were still a youth?"

"He died when I was nineteen, just after I was dubbed, right before I went to court. He had arranged to send me to a kinsman there." It was the truth, although incomplete.

"Your kinsman served the king?"

"He was a minor functionary. He took me into his household." None of it lies, not really.

"You lived with him the whole time there?"

Aye, one question would lead to another, and he saw where these were going. She merely followed her thoughts while she constructed forms of substance inside the deep but indefinable knowledge that they had of each other.

He couldn't deny her without losing what he had just fought to regain, but he sickened a little at the judgment awaiting. "The plague came not long after I arrived. My kinsman was away, and died of it. The household moved to one of his wife's manors in Sussex until the death passed."

He paused, wondering if he could leave it there. Probably not. Alone with Christiana in Carlisle, she might learn about this lesser sin. "I stayed with his wife for two years, living off tournament winnings mostly."

"And then you left for France?"

"I lived alone for a year after that before seeking my fortune in France."

She immediately found the gaps. "Why? Did you fall out with your kinswoman?" When he didn't answer, her eyebrows rose and he watched the pieces fall into place. "The woman you told me about that day . . . the trade with Morvan . . . it was your kinsman's wife?"

"Aye." He was relieved that she didn't look more shocked.

"She must have been much older than either you or Morvan."

"She was my kinsman's second wife, and much younger than he. Still, almost old enough to be my mother."

"Did you love her?"

She wanted him to say that he had been mad with love. Elizabeth had not been blood kin, but she had been related through marriage. While such liaisons were not unheard of, they were not acceptable. Claiming he had been besotted would make this more palatable, but he found that he could not lie to her.

"I loved her much as I could, which wasn't much. Less than I should. More than she wanted."

"Why did it end?"

Because I ceased being faithful, which was all that she ever demanded of her lovers. Because I knew she loved someone else and I resented it, even though I would never have known what to do with that love if it came to me. Because we had healed each other's worst pain, and it was time to live the lives left to us.

"Elizabeth had much of the mother about her, and it was tempting to stay forever at the comfort of her breast. But as with a mother, there also came a time to leave."

"I think that I can understand that. It was something like that with Robert and me."

Of all the reactions he had expected, the last had been this calm understanding. She surprised him yet more when she added, "I am glad she was there if you needed her friendship."

She reached up for the edge of the bed coverings and pushed them down and then drew them back over their bodies. "What with the hunt and all, you must be very tired. You have a long ride facing you. Sleep, Ian. I will wake you at dawn."

"You should be tired too."

"I find that I am not. In a few hours I must rouse the servants to prepare for our departure. I do not think I will sleep."

"Nor will I, then. I learned long ago how to take my rest in a saddle. I do not plan to waste these hours with dreams when the best dream lies beside me." He pushed the bedclothes back down, exposing her body, and rose up on his arm to look at her. "Besides, who knows when I will have the chance to give you another lesson?"

He kissed her, memorizing the softness of her lips and the sharp edge of her teeth and the velvet depths of her mouth. Gathering her hands, he pressed them above her head so she was stretched out completely vulnerable to him. He did not want her embracing him or doing anything to speed his own response. He would make her mad and desperate and begging, and maybe the sound of her cries would sustain him for the next days and weeks.

He caressed her slowly, watching his tan hand move around the swells of her small feminine form, doing nothing to arouse her beyond a languid pleasure. Her breasts filled and nipples hardened anyway. He smiled at her quick response, but he would not be distracted.

"You are so lovely, Reyna. There is always this faint blush on your skin, and it is soft and moist, as if it is covered with invisible dew." Her breath caught when he lowered his head and first kissed and then licked the valley between her beckoning breasts.

She arched invitingly, but he rose away so he could caress and memorize the shapely lines of her legs. Her creamy thighs quivered and tensed when he moved higher to the scent and moisture already waiting at their top. He touched gently, testing to see if she was too bruised for more, glad for the evidence she was not when her body trembled elegantly in response.

She frowned when he drew his hand away.

"Not yet, Reyna. This is punishment for calling me a whoreson and bastard again. I warned you not to do that." Actually, that passionate invective had been music to his ears. He ran his finger over her lower lip, drawing the moisture from her quick breaths, studying the filmy desire in her eyes. He felt an inexplicable flattery that this woman wanted him at all, let alone so badly and so quickly.

He drew a line down her chin to her chest and then circled, circled, circled up the rise of one pretty breast. She squirmed and groaned, and he flattened his palm to gently graze her tight nipple. "Is this what you want, Reyna?"

She tried to wrench her hands free of his hold.

"Is it?"

"Aye, damn you."

"Another curse? This could take until dawn." He teased her with his fingertips, lightly rubbing the pink tip, and she jerked at her arms again.

"Let me go, you whoreson, and we'll see who cries enough first."

"Keep that up and we may not depart until noon." He lowered his lips to her other tip. "You are so soft, like velvet. The first time I kissed you, I almost forgot all sense of duty." He licked and sucked slowly, lost in the delicious taste and feel of her, wonderfully alert to the abandoned cries and moves that his tongue and hand drew out of her.

Her hips rocked slowly while he made love to her breasts, and he let their rhythm of desire tantalize his own tight hunger. He savored each impassioned reaction, storing away its memory like a precious possession.

He released her hands and eased her over on her stomach. Hovering above her he slowly kissed down her spine,
then turned to watch her body while he caressed the back
of her legs and thighs. She half buried her face in her arms
to smother her surprised gasps. When his gaze and hand
moved higher, the soft hills of her buttocks tightened to
his touch and her back arched in reaction. She looked incredibly erotic like this, and he bent to kiss the small of
her back while his fingers followed the shadowed cleft.

Her muffled cry almost undid him. The storm, quelled
but not sated, erupted again. She parted her legs for more,
and her hips rose when his finger found the tight passage
and stroked its hot depths. She lifted her head and looked
back at him with wary eyes. "Are you going to . . ."

He pictured her hips rising to him and a piercing heat
shook him. But he doubted he could maintain much
control if he took her that way, and anything less than
gentleness would be unforgivable this time.

He turned her on her back. "Another time, Reyna,
and you will like it, I promise you. But tonight I want
your face against mine and your arms around me."

She made to embrace him, but he slipped from her
arms and trailed hot kisses down her silken length. One
other memory and possession he would not deny himself.
He lifted her legs over his shoulders and kissed her inner
thighs. A new fever entered her eyes. Her body seemed to
know what he was going to do, even if her mind did not.

He caressed her intimately, finding the spots that
drove her mad, and she moved in responses out of her
control. He turned his kisses higher, seeking her passion's
center. She cried his name and he glanced up at her wild,
shocked expression.

"I am going to do it, Reyna. If you do not like it, I will
stop."

She stiffened like a board when his mouth replaced his fingers, but the pleasure immediately demolished her resistance. "Aye," she whispered, and then the affirmation became a cry repeated over and over, and the sound of her breathless chant and the throes of her passion pushed him into a glowing oblivion.

When he rose up over her, she grabbed at him, pulling him to her, lifting her legs in an embrace, trying to bind their desperation together. "What do you want, Reyna?" He barely possessed sense anymore, but he wanted to hear her say it. Needed to hear her say it.

Her fingers clawed at his shoulders. She looked up and blinked away the obscuring passion.

"What do you want?" he repeated.

A fierce light flashed in her eyes. "You. All of you. Deep inside me and all through me."

Searing hunger streaked through him with a dangerous force. If he followed his blood, it would be like before. Rolling over in their embrace, he brought her above him. "Then take what you want. As much or as little as you need."

She moved to absorb him deeply, bending to caress and kiss his chest, drawing his spirit to her as surely as he had forced hers to him. She made love beautifully and hungrily, and his chaotic emotions swirled beneath her urgent aggression. Her cries started again, and she began to demand more. He grasped her hips and responded with his own thrusts, impatient now for the completion that he had delayed, trying to contain the complex needs so they wouldn't overwhelm him this time.

She groaned at his movement and buried her face in his neck. "Harder," she whispered shakily. "Deep inside me and all through me."

"I will hurt you. You are sore."

"Nay, my love. If we must separate I want to feel you for days. Weeks. Forever."

Her muffled voice contained a tremor. Caressing her face, he felt a tear. An astonishing tenderness washed him, full of awe that she cared enough to feel such sorrow about their parting and his danger.

Suddenly he wanted nothing from her at all, but only to give whatever she sought. Submerged with her in a soulful harmony laden with pleasure and joy and sorrow, he embraced her closer. Pressing her to his bursting heart, he whispered lies of reassurance while he drove into her.

chapter

TWENTY

I an looked down on the precise drawing that David had made in the dirt floor of the tent. It showed a detailed image of Harclow as seen from the eye of a flying bird. There was the square keep with its four corner towers, and the inner wall surrounding it. Some distance away ran the thick line of the outer wall. Along two sides floated the lake, and David had even indicated the placement of the siege camps on the surrounding terrain. Ian had never seen anything quite like it, with all objects seen from the top and everything in scale. Most maps were not drawn this way.

"Have I forgotten anything?" David asked Morvan, who also studied the image.

Morvan shook his head. "It is astonishingly accurate."

"Good. Now I only ask that you hear me out. This rain looks likely to last many days, so there is time to do it now, if you agree."

Ian walked over to the tent's opening and gazed into the steady drizzle that had halted assaults for two days.

Behind him, David began explaining the elaborate plan that they had concocted.

Restlessness gnawed at him, and he stepped out into the rain and strolled through the camp to where he could see the wall of Harclow. Dotted along its length were the soldiers keeping watch, fewer than normal because of the rain. The mud and wet only made dangerous work more perilous, and Morvan's army needed the rest anyway.

For weeks the assaults had continued, the siege towers had rolled forward, the machines had hurled their missiles. The men within Harclow kept falling, just like Morvan's own, and their numbers must be much diminished, but old Maccus would not yield.

Ian himself had commanded one of the siege towers every day since he arrived. It was a great honor, and the assignment had surprised him. But it was not honor that he had felt while he waited atop, sword ready, as the high wooden construction was rolled to the wall. Something else prickled in his blood then, so forcefully that its name could no longer hide.

Fear. Its pervasive power astonished him, and he had no experience dealing with it. But he knew what it was, had known in his soul since he rode to meet Thomas Armstrong that day.

When he was eighteen, he had known such fear once and had succumbed to it completely, but then it had died in him, and his skill in warfare had been enhanced by his freedom from it. Others might lie awake before battle anticipating the death that awaited, but not Ian of Guilford. Others might debate the cost of rushing to the aid of a stranger outnumbered at the Battle of Poitiers, but he had never reckoned with such accounts.

Until now. All around him were battle-hardened men

who had long ago learned to control fear, but suddenly he was a green youth again, bloodied for the first time, calculating risks he had never noticed before, relying on instincts that he no longer trusted.

He circled toward the lake, passing the path that led to the periphery of the camp. He peered toward the tents that held the merchants and washerwomen and whores who formed the little town that had sprung up to serve the soldiers. Normally, on an empty day like this, he would go there and pass some woman a coin to break the monotony. Today, the notion of following that path struck him as somehow obscene.

Because of Reyna.

Reyna. She was at the heart of it all. She was in his head worse than ever, and the fear was hooked firmly to those images and thoughts. He did not admit this to himself with any rancor or blame. He simply recognized the truth while he walked through the mud to the lake's edge.

Across the expanse of water, he could see the break in Harclow's outer wall that David had made with his gonnes. It had taken many tries to find the angle that would hurl the round stones across the lake, but then David had fired a day's worth of balls until the wall had cracked and fallen. It had been an experiment more than anything else, to see if the repeated impact could effect such a thing from such a distance. But today, while they lay on their cots in the tent that they shared, he and David had come up with a way to make the achievement more meaningful.

Images of Reyna claimed his thoughts again in their insistent way. He wondered what she was doing right then in Carlisle. Did her thoughts turn to their last hours together as often as his did?

My *love*. It had sounded so right when she said it, just one more strand in the seamless intimacy they had shared that night. Perhaps he should not put too much weight on a simple endearment, but that night another emotion had also demanded its name, and the fearful, hopeful youth resurrected inside him badly wanted to believe that they were together in this.

They had been her words, not his. Why hadn't *he* spoken them to *her*, if not that night, then the next day before they parted? Had he left it unsaid to reassure himself that he would survive to speak of it later? Was the fear so entwined with the love?

Fear. It kept coming back to that. The love and fear were two sides of a transparent coin—impossible to see one without the underlying side of the other affecting the view. What did he fear? Dying, that was certain. Losing her, to be sure, either through death or disillusionment. Loving her?

He retraced his steps back through the camp. A small fire burned outside his tent under a high canvas awning, and he settled himself on a log near it. Morvan emerged and walked over to join him.

"Do you think we should try this plan, Ian?"

"It is no more dangerous for the men than any other assault. The walls on the lake are barely manned. If the surprise comes fast enough, it might work."

"We will prepare for it, then, and if the opportunity comes, we will do it. I will want you with David on it, though."

Ian shot him a sharp glance. Morvan had not missed the fear, it seemed. He sought a discreet way to remove Ian from the tower.

Morvan caught the look. "It is not that," he said, acknowledging both Ian's suspicion and the fear itself. "You are clever in matters of construction and strategy, and as the plan unfolds there may have to be sudden changes made. Between David and yourself, if something goes wrong, it might still be salvaged."

They had never developed an easy friendship, and so it surprised him when Morvan spoke again. "As to the other, I think no less of you. All knights must face it sooner or later, except the ones lacking in wits or imagination. You used to fight like a man with nothing to live for. Now you fight like a man with everything to lose. Of the two, I would rather have the latter by my side." He walked away into the camp before Ian could respond, but then there was nothing to say.

Ian returned to the tent. He found David sitting on his cot, making calculations in the dirt with his pointed stick. "Twenty rafts, I would say, each large enough to hold ten men. Better a good number of smaller size, so there is a chance of more making it across."

Ian flung himself down on his own bed. "If the rains continue, the rafts will be wet enough that flaming arrows may not ignite them. Still, some are bound to go down, so you are right." He studied the map etched into the ground. "This will only get us inside the first wall, of course."

"How often have you seen strongholds stand after the enemy has breached the wall?"

Never, Ian had to admit. But old Maccus was turning out to be a tenacious foe.

He tried to give himself over to rest, but it would not come. With exasperation he swung up and walked to the opening again. Perhaps he would gather some men and begin work on those rafts.

"Does she know?" David's quiet voice asked.

Ian turned in surprise. He assumed that David referred

to his feelings for Reyna. No doubt he smelled of that, just like the fear. "Nay."

David calmly continued his calculations. "She is bound to hear of it. The story is better known than you think. The men in your company, for example, are aware of most of the details. If they have never indicated so, it is because they fear your reaction and your sword."

Ian felt his blood run a little slower. In his cool, impassive way, David had just broached a subject about which Ian never spoke. Perhaps he had always suspected that the company knew. Maybe that was why he avoided close friendships with any of those men. Inevitably the questions, then. Ultimately the judgment. One could remain indifferent to the opinions of people who didn't really matter.

"Christiana. Would she speak of this to Reyna?" Ian asked.

"Nay, if only because she herself is ignorant. We were not in London when the rumors spread."

"But you heard the rumors all the same."

"I knew before that. When I saw Elizabeth's interest, I made it my business to learn about you. All kinds of information passes among merchants."

Ian felt a chilling resentment. "And you told Elizabeth?"

"Only enough so that she would know the truth when the story followed you to court, as it eventually had to."

"You think that *you* know the truth?"

"I know that you were a boy who didn't want to die. I know that your father should have put aside pride and anger." He paused. "I know that a bad woman played an elaborate and dangerous game, and won. Such a woman at any age is more formidable than most men. When they are young, they do not even comprehend the destruction they will cause with their schemes." He tapped the stick against his boot. "She has a child, I'm sure you know. A boy nine years old."

"Not *my* son."

"Nay, not your son. He is the image of his father."

"His father was ignorant and innocent."

"If you say so. I had drawn no conclusions from any of this."

"I'm sure that you are the only one who hasn't. The typical conclusions are sordid and damning."

"I smelled the truth upon first hearing the tale. No doubt others did too."

"You have knowledge of the world. You have experience with what people can be."

"And you think that your wife does not? Perhaps you underestimate her. I am continually amazed at the capacity of women to be understanding where their men are concerned." He turned back to his calculations. "I think that we will need five men working on each raft. Since you show evidence of driving me mad with your pacing, perhaps you should go out and choose them."

Ian thought that an excellent idea. He turned to leave, only to find the opening filled with Morvan's looming form. The big man pushed past, hauling a soldier by the scruff of the neck. With a sweeping movement he threw the man down on the ground. "Look who I found lurking around your company's tents, Ian."

The man cringed at Morvan's feet. It was Paul, a member of his company sent to Carlisle to guard the women.

"What the hell are you doing here?" Ian demanded.

"I just came to see the lads for a bit, didn't I? No great harm, as I see it."

"You are supposed to be in Carlisle."

"I was getting bored."

"*Bored.*" Morvan roared. "By God, if anything has happened to my wife or sister because of your negligence—"

"If it has, it ain't my fault." Paul raised an arm to ward off the blow promised by Morvan's anger. "I couldn't stop 'em from going, not with them all determined-like, and that big one, well, show me the man who wants to try telling *her* what to do. And they did take Gregory with 'em at least, and insisted it wouldn't be for long. And I did suggest that maybe I should come and let Sir Ian know at least, but Lady Reyna was most insistent that I shouldn't bother no one over such a small thing, and the dark one agreed, and the big one, well, when they left she practically threatened me, just stared at me dangerous-like and felt her dagger hilt and told me to obey their orders and all would be well."

Morvan's expression got darker. "Are you saying that the ladies have left Carlisle?"

"Aye, that's what I be trying to explain. Got on a boat and ordered me to stay at the house, but it got very boring just sitting there in that empty place with only that old hag of a servant. So I decided that a quick visit here would do no harm."

"This is Lady Anna's doing," Ian said. "She did not want to go to Carlisle, and she all but cursed me when I gave her your instructions, Morvan."

"Do not accuse my wife of starting this, Ian."

"Are you suggesting that Reyna forced Anna into leaving? Hell's teeth, Morvan, your wife could pick her up with one arm."

"Perhaps we should find out where they all went," David interrupted. He lifted Paul to his feet and solicitously gave his garment a few dusting swipes. "Do you know where they were headed?"

"Seems to me I think I heard talk of Glasgow. A quick journey by way of the sea mostly, they assured me."

Two husbands looked to Ian with annoyance. Only Reyna would have interest or cause to go to Glasgow.

"No doubt Anna joined in for the fun, and Christiana went along to keep an eye on them both," David said dryly.

"I will go after them," Ian said. "You can not leave, Morvan, nor will you need me for some days with this rain."

Morvan nodded. "Take extra horses with you, Ian, and at least two men. When you find them, send a man back to me in haste with word of their safety."

"I will come with you," David said.

"Nay, David, you will stay here," Morvan said. "You convinced me of this plan of yours, and now I have warmed to it. You will need to supervise the preparations. Ian, when you find Anna, tell her for me that I am most displeased and that she is to return with you at once. As for Lady Reyna, I leave her to you."

Grabbing Paul by the shoulder of his garment, Ian dragged him out to the fire. "When did they leave from Carlisle?"

"Seven days ago."

Seven days. Since they went north by boat, they would be in Glasgow soon. It would take too long to follow by way of Carlisle and the sea. He would have to cross Armstrong lands. With hard riding he might get to Glasgow before they left.

"Gregory was to be with them the whole way?"

"Aye. And Lady Anna took a bow and sword. Dressed like a man, too, but then she always does that, which is odd for a woman, not that she looks all that peculiar, for some reason—"

"Why the hell didn't you come at once and tell me of this, Paul? While I do not think ill has befallen them, if it has I can not protect you from Morvan."

Paul glanced over his shoulder cautiously. "I would have explained inside the tent, but he was fit to kill, wasn't he, and it wouldn't do to throw oil on the fire."

"Speak sense, man."

"Well, I assumed that you already knew they had gone to Glasgow. I sent word about it back with your man, didn't I? No reason for me to come at once and tell you, if he was going to."

A chill danced down Ian's spine. "My man? What man?"

"The one who came five days ago with a message from you to Lady Reyna. Not from our company, but I figured Morvan had given him to you. He came asking for her, said he had a message and gift for her from you."

"I sent no man, Paul."

"Nay? Then who—"

"What did you tell him?"

"Just as I told you now, where they had gone and when."

Ian's head almost burst as fear and love joined and transformed into one ripping fury.

"Describe this man."

"Light-haired, medium height, and stocky is all I remember. Scot, I would guess from his speech, but the burr was not strong so I figured he was from the border lands here and one of Sir Morvan's men."

Perhaps it had been Edmund, following Reyna to Carlisle to cajole her further, but neither Edmund nor Reginald, whom Ian had released before their departure, fit Paul's description. Nor was Thomas Armstrong light-haired. But either Thomas or Edmund might have had someone else deliver a message that would draw Reyna into their hands.

The realization that Reyna might be in real danger almost scrambled his thoughts, but he forced himself to think it through carefully. He should probably tell Morvan about this, but if he did, Morvan would lead this army on Glasgow. Things here would crumble and all hell would let loose on the border. Nor would he tell David. The stranger had shown up in Carlisle asking for Reyna because it was Reyna whom he sought. Edmund pursuing his case? Or Thomas looking for revenge in Robert's death?

He strode off to where his company camped. He would take more than two men, and plenty of horses and weapons. If they rode hard they might get to Glasgow before whoever was following Reyna found her.

chapter

TWENTY-ONE

R eyna waited on a stool in the anteroom of the bishop's study with an unsettling foreboding plucking at her. The decision to come to Glasgow had seemed very sensible when she made it. Sitting in Carlisle had grown tedious, and important facts regarding Robert's last months could be learned here. Still, now that her meeting was imminent, she wondered if pursuing Robert's private intentions was wise.

A side door opened and a young cleric entered. Stiffly straight in flowing robes, he had dark hair, and brown eyes dulled by a forbearing expression. "I am Anselm, one of the bishop's clerks, madam. Father Rupert said that you insisted you had urgent business."

Reyna had never realized how hard it was to see a bishop, and her entreaties to the various officials had gotten a little exaggerated over the last hour. "It is urgent to me, since I can not remain in Glasgow long."

"Then I am sorry to disappoint you. As you have been told, the bishop is not in residence, but up north, where we expect him to remain on church affairs for some time."

"Father Rupert thought that maybe you could aid me. It is information that I seek, not a bishop's dispensation or judgment."

Anselm lowered himself into a nearby chair and regarded her while he smoothed his robes with fastidious fingers. "I will hear you, but most of the bishop's affairs are confidential."

"I hope that this is not. My name is Reyna Graham. My husband was Robert of Kelso, who held the border lands of Black Lyne Keep through Maccus Armstrong. My husband died several months ago. Shortly after his death, a letter came from the bishop." Reyna described the letter, and its reference to Robert's request for guidance.

"I remember it well, since I wrote it for His Excellency," Anselm said.

"No one knows to what it referred," Reyna explained. "If my husband had some desire or wish before his death, I would like to know of it so that I can see that his will is done."

Anselm ignored her during a protracted period of contemplation. Reyna began to feel anxious. Perhaps the secretary hesitated because Robert's inquiry had indeed concerned her. Was it possible that she had known her husband's mind and heart so little?

"It is likely that I can explain this, Lady Reyna, but I have one question first. How does your husband's testament dispose of his property?"

"The lands were left to me, although it is questionable whether his liege lord will permit that to stand," she said, deciding that tangents into the fall of the keep and her marriage to Ian would serve no purpose.

"Not the lands. His personal property."

"That also came to me."

"In that case, there can be no objection to my speaking with you." He settled more comfortably in his chair, if a man with such rigid posture could ever be said to find comfort. "Your husband wrote a letter that we received five months ago. In it he explained that he possessed some property that was not rightfully his, and which he sought to dispose of in an honorable way before his death so that it would not become entangled in the estate. He wanted to give this property to a monastery engaged in educating the young. The bishop intended to speak with the blackfriars here in Glasgow and make the arrangements, but other business called him away."

"Did my husband describe this property?"

"Nay, but it was clear that it was not land. He referred to 'them' at several points in the letter. He felt that it would ease his conscience to have the matter settled with death so near at his advanced age."

Them. Not land, but objects. "Did he indicate the value of this property?"

"His letter indicated several thousand pounds. Three or four."

Objects. Useful in education.

Books.

She knew that the library was valuable, but not *that* valuable.

"Did my husband mention how he came to possess these objects?"

"Nay, but the request was not unusual. Men gain wisdom and piety as they age. They seek to make amends for youthful transgressions."

Reyna met his gaze. "You think that this property was stolen, don't you?"

"More likely it was procured after a siege or battle. Few knights or soldiers settle for the small coin their lords pay, and often that pay never comes because the lord assumes they will enrich themselves thus at no cost to him. Indeed, most barons claim one third of such spoils."

"All the same, you are saying that my husband was a thief. Little better than a brigand," she countered hotly.

"What is theft in one circumstance are the wages of war in another," Anselm said. "The Church urges men to forgo it, but it is a small sin if the war is just. Even the Crusaders . . . And your husband, unlike most, sought to make restitution. It would be impossible to return this property to its owners after so many years, so he wanted to give it to the Church for her work."

"I did not realize that the Church had decided that sin was conditional upon circumstances. I shall have to remember that in the future. No doubt it will prove convenient."

Anselm sighed. "I only seek to relieve you of your obvious distress."

Distress didn't begin to describe her reaction. Robert, dear, good, honest Robert, had lived a very different life before he arrived on the Scottish border and taken service with Maccus Armstrong. It had occurred a lifetime before she met him, and he had put it behind him, except for the evidence with which he could not part, the books that he loved so dearly.

Stolen books. What had he thought while he studied the moral imperatives that they contained, even while his possession of them defied those truths?

Anselm's excuses might have served him. They might now serve her too, if she could be convinced that those books had been looted during a just war. But the possibility loomed that Robert had indeed been a thief or brigand as a young man. Just like Ian of Guilford, or even worse. She grimaced at the irony. She had been comparing Ian with an old man who, in his own youth, had been just as reckless.

"I think that I know the property to which my husband referred. If it was Robert's desire that these items be given to the Church, I will endeavor to make it so." She rose to leave. "Would you give me a letter explaining this? It would be easier to effect this donation if his request could be clarified."

"If you inherited . . ."

"I have recently remarried."

His dark eyebrows rose in understanding. He went over to the table. "If you have remarried, the property is no longer yours," he said while he wrote. "For whatever good it may do, here it is. Do not let this become a point of strife in your marriage, however. It is a rare man who would part with the wealth that came to him through his wife."

Reyna clutched the parchment that proved Robert had never sought to put her aside. As to Anselm's last comment, she had no idea how Ian would react to fulfilling Robert's last wish. Probably he would refuse, once he learned the value of the books.

Then again, perhaps one brigand would have a special sympathy for another brigand's quest for salvation.

G od is punishing us for disobeying our husbands and leaving Carlisle," Christiana muttered as she peered out the bedchamber window. "This rain has gone on for days, and it looks to last forever." She caught Reyna's attention. "When Anna comes back we must tell her that we leave in the morning. Enough is enough."

Reyna flipped over on her bed and stared at the ceiling. This journey had occurred only because Anna, seeking a respite of activity and adventure, had supported her decision to make it. Under the circumstances, it had seemed only fair to grant Anna one extra day in Glasgow.

Reyna herself would have gladly departed yesterday, once she returned from the bishop's house. Her mission accomplished, she itched to return to Carlisle. Perhaps she could send a letter to Ian and tell him what she had learned. Maybe, if this rain had stopped the action at Harclow, he would come and see her. The notion that he might have already tried to do so, only to arrive at a house empty of everyone but Paul and the serving woman, saddened her, and she was already feeling low because of the new discovery about Robert.

He had never deceived her, she reminded herself again. She had never asked about that ancient history, and he had told her no lies. Perhaps only a girl who trusted a man as she would a father could have accepted the presence of all those beautiful books without question, but so it had been.

"Here they come," Christiana said. "They look like two drowned dogs, and Gregory's face is black with annoyance, but Anna looks radiant. You must stand firm with me. If we don't corral her now, she will be leading us into the Highlands by week's end."

Corralling a rebellious Anna proved anything but easy. She reminded Reyna that they should get full value out of the trouble awaiting with their husbands, and indeed proposed a journey up to Argyle. Christiana scolded and cajoled, but it was Reyna's suggestion that the rain might make a visit from their husbands possible that won the argument. They spent the evening making preparations to return to the coast.

The next day they rode out of the city of Glasgow, with Anna looking as much like a guard as Gregory, dressed in tunic and hood with her sword strapped to her saddle. The rain had stopped, but heavy clouds promised more. Christiana kept up a bantering conversation, lightening the mood which threatened to sink under the discomfort of damp and mud.

Five miles out of the city their talk lulled, and in the sudden silence a distant thunder mumbled. Anna jerked her horse still and listened with alert attention. The thunder grew closer much too quickly, and Anna pivoted her horse, called a warning to Gregory, and unsheathed her sword. Reyna looked over her shoulder to see a company of men galloping toward them.

"To the side of the road," Anna ordered, resting her sword across her saddle. "Let them pass."

Unfortunately, the company did not gallop through them. The men paused, then moved forward at a trot. When they were a hundred paces away, Reyna recognized the man in their lead and her breath caught in surprise.

He rode forward and stopped a horse length away. "Well, now, little sister. What are you doing so far from your husband's protection?"

"Visiting Glasgow. And you, Aymer? This is an odd place to unexpectedly meet you."

"I have been looking for you. I sought you out in Carlisle and learned you had made this journey, and worried for your safety."

"How brotherly."

Aymer's twelve men clustered in, making escape impossible. Anna held her weapon firmly. Out of the corner of her eye, Reyna saw Gregory measuring their situation and not liking what he saw.

One of Aymer's knights pushed up beside Anna, squinting at her. The point of her sword followed the movement.

"By God, it is a woman," he exclaimed, pulling at her hood. Blond curls tumbled down her body. "Have you ever seen one so big? Pretty enough in an odd way, though, eh?"

The other men laughed. "Aye, enough woman for all of us, maybe," one of them snickered.

"Enough woman to cut off the manhood of anyone who touches us," Christiana said coolly.

"Stop this at once, brother," Reyna said. "If any harm befalls either of them, Morvan will lead that army into the hills—and my father's stronghold is no Harclow."

Anna had thrust the point of her sword against the knight's neck, staring at him down its length.

"There are too many of us, bitch," he snarled, his head and neck angling back from the threatening weapon.

"Perhaps. But *you* will move away or *you* will surely die," she replied.

A sudden flurry saw Gregory pushing toward them, sword raised, expression determined. One of the knights thrust his horse in the way, and with a sweeping movement he brought the flat of his own weapon down on Gregory's temple. The guard slumped on his saddle and then fell in a heap to the ground.

The attack made Aymer decide to end the little drama. "Countess, I have business with my sister requiring she come with me. You and Lady Anna are free to continue on your way."

"If she comes, so shall we," Christiana said. "We complete this journey as we began it, together."

"This is a family matter, my lady, and none of your concern. If you insist in this nonsense, I will have you both tied to a tree."

"And left to thieves or animals? Either Reyna continues with us, or we follow with you. And you would be wise to take the greatest care with our persons and health. My brother has two thousand at Harclow, and if he comes for you there will be no mercy. As for my husband, his methods are more subtle. You will not even know that he is there until you feel his boot on your neck." The icy tone crystallizing these quiet words was all the more effective coming from such a delicate, courtly figure.

Reyna was impressed. Aymer was too. He stared flush-faced at Christiana, then turned his horse furiously. "Bring them all," he ordered. "Leave the man."

Reyna and Anna fell in next to Christiana. "That was very brave, my friend, but this is unnecessary," Reyna said. "He will not harm me."

"He will certainly think twice now if he had planned to," Anna muttered. "Do you think that fool of a guard Paul actually kept our secret about leaving?"

Christiana rolled her eyes. "Since you all but threatened to slit his throat . . ."

"Still, a messenger might have come."

"Even if our husbands find out we left Carlisle, they will not know where we have gone now. Nay, sister, we could be on our own here."

"Turn back," Reyna urged.

Christiana shook her head. "I do not trust this brother of yours. You will be safer with us present. It would be useful to know where we are going and why he wants you, though."

Reyna kicked her horse to a trot and moved through the small company to Aymer's side.

"Do we return to Glasgow?" she asked.

"Nay, but we will go west and then head south. I am taking you home."

"To Black Lyne Keep?"

"*Home*. You do not belong among Armstrongs and Fitzwaryns, Reyna. You will return to your own people."

"My father misses me so much?"

"Duncan is an old man. Already a sickness eats at his gut. He has no will to do what must be done, so it is left to me."

"And what is that, Aymer? What is this about?"

"Land, little Reyna. Isn't it always about land? The devil must have possessed Duncan to give what he did as your dowry. For years I have waited for old Robert to die so that it would return to you as dower lands, and through you to us."

She sighed at Aymer's predictability. "How impatient were you, Aymer? Did you find a way to hasten his passing?"

"Would that I had possessed the means to do so. Interesting that you ask, though, Reyna. I have assumed all along that you killed him."

"I had no reason to do so."

"Didn't you?" Aymer asked slyly. "He was old when you married him, and older when you grew to womanhood. Your mother was a whore, and such is probably your nature too. Did those cold hands content you? I think not, if you so quickly found your way to that knight's bed."

His tone and look made her very uncomfortable. "It is well that you mention Ian, since the dower lands that you think to control through me belong to him now."

"Not if he is dead."

She twisted in her saddle. "You have not . . ."

"Not yet. I count on his coming for you, though. Let him bring his whole company, or even half of that army Fitzwaryn has raised, so long as he comes himself." He leaned over and stroked her cheek. She pulled back in revulsion. "You have a whore's blood, Reyna. I count on your having pleased him enough so that he indeed comes for you."

"You are disgusting to speak thus of your sister."

The hand stayed on her cheek and stroked again. "Perhaps. But then, you are not really my sister."

chapter

TWENTY-TWO

C old. Damp cold and eternal darkness
    Voices murmuring in the stones, and hands reaching for her, prodding her. Quiet laughter, lower now, close by, and other hands not prodding but caressing, raising a new terror that she did not understand. A new voice, not the ethereal one of a ghost but a living one, chuckling with pleasure at her fear. *You are not really my sister.*

She pressed against the stones, feeling it all, hearing it all, but it was different this time. Her soul experienced none of the terror. A tiny part of her remained rational this time, watching the old fear unfold around her, within her, as if she observed a pageant.

Legs pressed against hers and hands held hers. Real legs and real hands, anchoring her to a time and place, preventing her senses from spinning away from her control.

"He can not keep us here forever," a voice intruded. A real voice. Whose? Ah, Anna's. "Not even a candle. What is the point?"

"He holds me here until Ian comes," Reyna heard herself say. Surely she had explained this before, the first night when they camped and slept together with Anna's sword lying amongst them. An eternity ago, before their ride brought them here one night and Aymer had imprisoned them all. Food had been brought, she seemed to remember, but Aymer had not returned.

"He could still give us candles. This crypt unsettles me."

Aye, the crypt. That was where they were, huddled on the stone floor against the cold wall. If the place unsettled even the brave Anna, perhaps she need not feel so childish herself.

Christiana's hand gripped hers tighter. "You are doing fine, Reyna," she reassured.

The voices in the stones answered with their inaudible mumbles. High laughter pierced her ears. She clung to Christiana's delicate hand and vaguely remembered it slapping her again and again while someone's screams filled the small chamber.

She gathered her courage, what little there was, and her soul listened for the voices. There had been something familiar about them the last time, something human. She urged them to assault her again, and pressed her legs against her friends. *Come on, damn you.*

And they came, the stones echoing their mumbles, the sound summoning memories long fragmented beneath the terror.

She was in a dark place, and teasing prods poked at her again and again. A finger moved invisibly around her body, and a boyish laugh took pleasure in her fear. The stones themselves grew hands and arms, and whenever she turned they were behind her, jabbing her into a terrified frenzy. Her own voice cried lowly for help, and then that youthful voice spoke, bored suddenly. *You stay here now, or the demons will get you. I'm going out to watch.*

But she didn't stay. She was running through the blackness, following the sound of retreating steps. . . .

"How long do you think we have been here?" Anna asked.

Forever, maybe. There was no time here. An hour could be a week, a week no more than an hour. The darkness swallowed time.

"From the meals, several days, but I sleep in fits and can not tell if it is night or day," Christiana answered.

Reyna listened to the soft voices of her companions. They both still clasped her hands, and those smooth grasps felt very real now.

Space and time had righted itself. The pageant had ended, but she had seen the source and cause of that horror. Maybe it had been just a child's game to Aymer at first, but the taste of fear had fed his cruelty over the years. No wonder her soul shrank from his very presence.

Still, she knew that there was more. Something nudged at her mind, tempting her like a sore tooth that one prods despite the pain. *I will be done with this today,* she decided savagely. *I will see it all and it will no longer rule me.*

She stared into the blackness and urged it forward. Releasing the hands holding hers, she blanked her mind to her companions' presence.

At first the darkness greeted her benignly, an empty void, but then slowly, subtly, it came alive. The voices emerged again, low and distant and not so threatening. Even the screams that sounded like her own were far away. She was running, running, toward the sounds, following the scruff of boot steps.

Suddenly the fear was new and fresh, and the heart

that she felt inside her was not a woman's heart but a child's. She was streaking with relief toward some light in the distance.

She gasped as the sun almost blinded her eyes and the horrible image filled her mind. For a split instant the picture of herself, limp and dead, hands dangling by her side and face twisted and blue, flashed in front of her. *Not here. That is the other nightmare, not this one.*

Hands reached for her, pulling her away, back into the blackness. They shook her roughly, and grabbed her face. "We are here. We are here," a firm voice soothed.

Anna was embracing her tightly, and Christiana was speaking gently in her ear. She stayed thus for a few moments, and then pressed to disentangle herself. "I am all right. It is over. It will not happen again."

"We must get her out of here," Christiana said.

"Aye, you must get me out of here, but not because of this," Reyna said. "Perhaps Aymer sought to drive me mad. Easy to lock away and forget, then, and who would care? But it has not worked, nor will it. It is over, I tell you."

"Since that is more than you have said since they threw us in here, I am inclined to believe you," Anna said.

"But we must get out all the same," Reyna repeated. "He means to kill Ian. It will be a challenge to individual combat, most likely, but he will have a plan to assure his victory, and it will not be a fair fight." She contemplated their plight. "This crypt is below the chapel, and that is outside the wall and close to the forest. I wonder if Duncan even knows what Aymer is doing."

"It does not matter. If we get out, we run," Anna said. "Do you remember these hills, Reyna? Can you lead us west?"

"I think so. It has been a long while, but the paths can not have changed much."

"How do we get out?" Christiana asked. "You tried the door after they put us here, Anna, and found it locked. No doubt there is at least one guard outside, and they took your sword."

"Let us hope that there is indeed a guard," Anna said. "Not more than one if we are lucky, though. If we can get him to open the door . . . This is a crypt. There must be something to hit him with. A crucifix, a stone plaque, something . . ."

She rose and began stumbling around the small chamber. "Here is something. A stone cross." She grunted from strain, and then cursed. "It is too heavy for me. I hate to say it, but we could use a strong man right now."

"Since we neglected to bring one, it looks as though we are stuck here," Christiana said.

"Nay. We will rush him all at once. But we need the door open. You are the one to do that, Christiana. Offer him a kiss or something. The chance of having a comtesse should make him forget his duty."

"Oh, saints help me," Christiana muttered. "You had best overpower this guard before it comes to a kiss, let alone *or something*."

They clustered together and stumbled their way up the stairs. Christiana took her position, and Reyna and Anna pressed against the wall beside the stairway.

Christiana rapped on the door. "Please open the door for just a moment, kind sir. I am feeling most unwell. My companions are already unconscious, and I fear we will all die if some fresh air is not permitted in at once."

The oak door opened a crack, and dim light leaked down the stairs. The guard's head blocked some of it.

"Could you open it just a little more? I am sure that

they will revive with a bit more air. If you are kind in this, I will be grateful."

"I am sorry, Comtesse, but my orders were—"

"I will be *most* grateful."

"Well . . . if the ladies are as bad as that," the guard muttered. "It was not the intention for you to be harmed."

The sliver of his form disappeared from the crack. Moments later the door opened wide, and his dark shape filled the threshold.

They lunged.

chapter TWENTY-THREE

They had him flat on his back, buried under a tangle of soft bodies, immersed in a chaos of grips and squirms and whispered feminine excitement.

"Get his sword arm . . . nay, that's mine, grab *his*."

"Someone sit on his chest."

"Damn, this whoreson is big."

"Ladies . . ."

"I've got his sword . . ."

"*Ladies*."

The whirlwind froze in mid-gale. Three moonlit heads jerked around in surprise.

"Ian?"

Ian sorted out the various women sprawled on him. "The small one holding my arm is my wife, and the big one holding my sword to my throat must be Anna. That means that the rump crushing my chest belongs to the Comtesse de Senlis. Perhaps, Comtesse, you would be so good as to . . ."

The rump quickly moved off. The gripping hands fell away. They all scrambled to their feet.

Anna handed back his sword, and pale light reflected off its length.

Unfortunately, that brought his men rushing to his rescue.

"Stand back!" Ian whispered sharply to them while he reached toward Reyna and pulled her up against the shield of his body.

Reyna immediately melted into the sanctuary of his body, holding him tightly, burying her face against his chest. He wrapped her with his arms and cherished the feel of her small frame and woman's warmth. She was here, very alive and real, and his joyful relief matched her own.

He kissed her head again and again as he led the group out of the chapel and into the cover of the trees.

"I thank you for distracting the guard, Reyna. I was debating whether to engage him and see if you were imprisoned in that crypt, or to just march into the keep and demand your release. In either case I would have had all of the Grahams on me."

"How did you find us?"

"I learned from Paul that you had gone to Glasgow and that someone had followed. When I arrived there I found Gregory, and he told me the rest."

"Gregory is well?"

"He made it back to Glasgow. Since I didn't know what inn you used, I decided to track you by looking for him at the taverns and whatnot. I found him at the second brothel I tried, laid up in bed like a prince, with the whores enjoying the chance to play mother and nurse."

Anna moved in closer. "I don't suppose that you

brought extra horses? Since we were hardly silent back there, they may be looking for us soon."

"I did, but left them along our route. We rode non-stop, and switched to the fresher mounts when our own could go no farther. You ladies will have to double up with us. The horses are not far away."

"It is not Duncan doing this, but only Aymer, I am almost sure," Reyna said. "If he comes, he may have only the men he brought to Glasgow, and not those still loyal to my father."

"Duncan must have known that you were there, surely."

"Aymer never brought us inside the wall, but put us immediately in the crypt. Duncan may be unaware."

His grip on her shoulder tightened. He had been concerned about physical abuse, but days in the crypt could have harmed her in ways that rods and fists never could. "Were you . . . did you . . ."

"I don't remember much, but Anna and Christiana helped me. In the end, I could face it. So much has become clear. I have much to tell you."

"And I have much to say to you, wife." He tasted again the worry that had owned him while he tore through the hills, careless of safety or prudence as he rode the last miles across Armstrong lands to save time. "You were told to stay in Carlisle."

She pressed against him in a snuggling way that made his spike of anger very small and brief. "It was foolish, Ian, I will not deny that. And yet I have learned so much. I think that I know who killed Robert."

"Aymer?"

She nodded. "I asked him, and he didn't really deny it. He admitted that if he had had the means, he would have done so. For enough coin, one of the servants or guards might have used the poison for him. He meant to kill you when you came for me, too, so that the dower lands would be his to control."

"It makes sense. Land, and strategic land at that. The simplest explanation, and the oldest one in the world."

When they reached the horses, Ian gave instructions for two of the men to take the other ladies up behind them.

"It will be quickest if we head west, toward Black Lyne Keep," he said as he lifted Reyna onto his own mount. "I sent word to Morvan from Glasgow, and if help is coming it will arrive that way. Do you know these paths well enough to guide us?"

"I recognize where we are. I think that I can do it."

He swung up behind her. Across the clearing, Christiana was thanking her soldier for his generosity in sharing his horse, and Anna was criticizing hers for the way he sat in his saddle.

Ian took the reins and slid his arm around Reyna. He grasped her tightly and pressed his lips to her neck. "I have much to say to you, wife, and not all is scolding," he muttered. "I will forever be in the ladies' debt for staying with you. I thank God for delivering you safely."

She turned to accept the kiss waiting. "You call me that a lot. Wife. I have always wondered why."

"You are my wife."

"I assumed it was because you needed to get accustomed to the idea."

He laughed. "That, too, but I found that I like the sound of it. And it is something I have never called any woman before. But if you prefer I will use other endearments." He kissed her cheek. "Darling." He pressed his lips to her temple. "Sweetling." His mouth found her ear. "My love."

She leaned into him with a contented sigh. "Aye, but wife will do, Ian, especially since it is mine alone."

"Let us go, Reyna. We will take it slowly, so you are sure. We don't want to get lost in these hills."

They traveled all night without stopping for rest. Ian could tell that Reyna made her choices of the paths relying more on instinct than decision, trusting her childhood rides to have emblazoned the route on her memory. In the utter stillness that heralded dawn, they finally heard the sounds of horses following, and pushed harder in an effort to reach Black Lyne Keep before Aymer caught them.

It might have worked if the paths led directly to the waste beyond the keep, but instead their route gave out farther south, near the old motte-and-bailey fortress. Suddenly they were tearing down the waste with reckless haste, running from the company thundering up behind. Their horses scrambled down the old bailey ditch and made it up the hill just as Aymer's red head appeared at the crest of the waste's rise.

Ian peered at the men following Aymer down the cliffs. No more than a dozen. Reyna had been right, and Aymer was doing this on his own.

He jumped off his horse, brought Reyna down, and called for the men to position themselves around the circumference of the motte's hilltop with their bows.

Black Lyne Keep loomed in the distance. There was no possibility of help from there. Only a few men remained inside that sealed fortress, with strict orders to remain there.

Down below, Aymer was also deploying his men around the old castle hill. He had more with him, but he also had a much bigger circle to cover.

"If you tell one of your men to give me his bow, I will try to even the odds some," Anna said.

"They are longbows, and too much for a woman."

"I have been using a longbow for some years now, Ian. From this distance I should hit my mark three times out of five. A few bad arms and legs will make Aymer think twice about attacking."

He looked at the lady, with her snarl of curls flying wildly around her head and body. If she said she could make her mark three times out of five, he believed her. Calling to the nearest man, he ordered him to relinquish his bow.

Reyna snuggled in close to him behind a large stone that served as protection from similar assaults from be-low. Aymer and his men spanned the periphery of the bailey ditch, thinking that they were out of range. Anna tested the bow's tension, then fitted an arrow to it. Stepping quickly around the stones to the edge of the hilltop, she drew the string back to her ear. A second later, a crying curse echoed through the haze of dawn.

"She is really magnificent, isn't she?" Reyna said with admiration as Anna carried her bow to the other side of the motte. "You should have seen the reaction Aymer's men had to her. She was a challenge they itched to meet. I can understand why they . . . why you . . ."

"You present a much more interesting challenge than she ever did. She was a means to an end for me, and not a very noble end at that. But she and I have something in common, I think. She was born for one man, and she found him. I was born for one woman, and by God's grace I found her."

Utter stillness greeted this statement. He pulled his gaze away from his surveillance of Aymer's men and saw her startled expression. He smiled and ran his finger

along her jaw. "Well, it was either God's grace or the
devil's doing, but if it was the devil, he did not count on
you stealing my heart, so his plans to ensure my damnation were foiled."

She wrapped her arms around him and he pressed her
closer. Such a strange time and place to be saying this to
her, but it felt right and natural.

"I think that my body could float and my heart could
burst right now," she said. "I love you so much, Ian."

"And I love you. You have swallowed my ragged soul
into the beauty of your own, but it is an enlivening place to
be held prisoner. From the start you have dared me to be
better than I am. No other woman would have cursed me as
you did, and forced me to see what I had become, and then
offered the love and friendship needed to pull me back."

"Nay, Ian, do not . . . I only sought safety in those
words . . . you are not . . ."

"True words, Reyna." Truer than she knew. Would her
love survive knowing all of it? *Not now. Another time.
Maybe.* "I was fast on my way to becoming the worst of
men, and you had known the best. I should warn you,
though, that no matter what my resolve, I will never be a
Robert of Kelso."

She looked up sheepishly. "Well, Ian, as it turns out,
even Robert of Kelso was not always a Robert of Kelso."
She told him about her meeting with Anselm, and the
reason for Robert's letter. "It was the books, Ian. They
are stolen."

"You are sure?"

"It can be nothing else."

"Do not judge him too harshly. Looting is customary
after battles and sieges. No one considers it theft."

"But these are not silks or jewels or silver. They are
books. Who would own such things, except clerics? Nay, I

will not fool myself. Robert took them from the Church, which is a serious sin even in war, and sought to return them to expiate his offense."

He frowned. "David said they were very valuable. I wonder how valuable."

"From what I learned in Glasgow, at least three or four thousand pounds."

Four thousand pounds. No wonder David had been hesitant to acknowledge Reyna's right to any of them.

It changed everything. The future they could have and the security they could know. Learning this was like uncovering a hidden treasure. They would not sell the ones Reyna loved, of course, unless misfortune demanded it, but even having that protection against ill fate would affect many other choices.

He gazed down at her with joy.

She looked back with wide, innocent eyes.

He guessed the meaning of her hopeful, earnest expression, and really, truly hoped he was wrong. "You want to send them to the bishop after all, don't you?"

She bit her lower lip and nodded.

He sighed, and the brief dream of wealth flew away on his breath. "Hell, you do not make being good easy, Reyna. *Four thousand pounds.* Damn."

M orvan arrived two days later, when the sun shown high in the sky. Those on the top of the motte saw his company pouring into the distant horizon first, but the sound quickly reached Aymer down below.

Peering around the big stone, Reyna saw her brother strain to see the thunder's source, and then stiffen comically when the moss filled with men and armor and horses.

Aymer shouted to his men, and they hurriedly claimed their horses and mounted the wounded and themselves. The little group by the donjon shouted jeers while the red head tore away in the direction it had come. Then Ian strode to the edge of the motte and hailed the arriving army. He sent a man down on the fastest horse to tell them that the ladies were safe.

The messenger reached the army and it halted.

"Morvan is there. I can see him. And David too," Christiana said. "Oh, dear."

"They may be just a little angry," Anna conceded.

"A little? Because of your willfulness they have disrupted the siege, brought half the army, and now it turns out we don't need much saving after all, and you think they may be a *little* angry?"

"My willfulness? You—"

Ian interrupted with a devilish smile. "Ah, now that I think of it, Anna, Morvan gave me a message for you. In the excitement I forgot about it."

"What message?"

"I was to tell you that he was most displeased about your leaving Carlisle. He was furious with your disobedience. Stomping around with that black look he gets, threatening to lock you away, swearing he would see to it that you didn't sit comfortably for a month . . ."

Several of the men brought up horses. In the distance, two tall men dismounted and walked forward from the army. Morvan crossed his arms over his chest and David set his hands on his hips and both waited, their stances eloquently speaking their annoyance.

"It really does not look good, sister," Christiana muttered while Ian helped her into the saddle. "It will take a very artful ploy to get out of this."

Anna swung up on her horse. "It wasn't really willfulness,

if you think about it, but chivalry. Reyna proposed the trip. We could hardly let her go alone."

"Oh, they already know that, but it didn't appease Morvan at all," Ian said. "He thought you should have stopped her. Besides, as is appropriate, he left *her* punishment to *me*."

He gave Reyna a glance that she didn't much like. Just her luck that, once the relief at finding her safe had begun to wear off, these husbands seeking an accounting would show up to remind him that he had his own ledger to balance.

Once settled on her horse, she paced over to Christiana. "What artful ploy do you intend to use?" she whispered.

"Well, I do not plan to cook David a meal or read him philosophy, Reyna. I may have to use that Saracen game that I described to you the night in Carlisle when we all got besotted on wine."

They made their way to where the army waited. The ladies pulled up their horses fifty yards away.

Morvan strode forward. "I see that you found them all well, Ian."

"Aye. A very small adventure, as it turned out, although your arrival has simplified the last part. I might have had to kill Aymer otherwise, and we would all like to avoid that." Ian strove for lightness but to no avail. Morvan's sparkling eyes had not cooled one whit.

Morvan shot his sister a sharp glance of dismissal. "Your husband is waiting."

Christiana looked apologetically at Anna before turning her horse away, but Anna didn't see her. Her own gaze had locked on her husband's with a challenge.

Morvan walked over until he stood beside her. "Have you been enjoying yourself?"

"I am completely unharmed, and I thank you for asking. Not the slightest discomfort."

His expression silently responded *not yet*. "I trust that you left Duncan's stronghold standing. Or did you raze it to the ground?"

"We were able to escape without doing so. More's the pity."

Reyna rolled her eyes. Of all the ploys that she could imagine, goading an angry husband did not strike her as the smartest.

"Are we to head back to Carlisle immediately?" Anna asked. "I hope that you are not planning to wait until morning at Black Lyne Keep, Morvan. The excitement of this ordeal has had the most surprising effect on me, and I find myself very restless. A good ride seems just the thing."

He didn't move and his expression didn't change, but a different light entered his eyes. "You will all come with us, but not back to Carlisle. We ride straight to Harclow, where work awaits that can not be delayed." He rested a hand on her knee. "The long ride should take care of your restlessness."

Anna's hand smoothed over her husband's. "I doubt that."

Reyna and Ian turned their horses away just as Morvan reached up to pull Anna over to his kiss. Near the army, Christiana was enclosed in David's arms, speaking earnestly up at him. The naked love in the comte's blue eyes suggested that he would accept whatever his wife told him.

Reyna and Ian's approach broke their embrace. Christiana remounted, and a squire brought David's horse forward.

"Morvan says we go straight back to Harclow," Ian said.

"Aye. We would have arrived sooner, but your man came right in the middle of an action yesterday morning," David explained. "We are inside the first wall, Ian."

"How—"

"Used our plan is how. I'm sorry we couldn't wait for you, but the opportunity was too good to miss. A huge storm broke a few hours before daybreak. The wall was barely manned, and we were almost across the lake on the rafts before they realized what was happening. The first men used their axes to cut through the wooden barrier placed over the hole the guns had made, while those on the rafts used their bows to protect them. Once inside, we fought our way to the gate before too many fell on us."

"Will Maccus yield?"

"He wants to negotiate, and has sent us terms. Morvan decided to let him stew while we dealt with this other problem."

Morvan and Anna joined them, and they all rode to the rear of the army. "David has told you, Ian?" Morvan asked.

"Aye. He said that Maccus has terms, however."

"The predictable ones. The safety of the knights and soldiers and such as that. I have refused to consider them until he yields, and for the most part he will set them aside and open the gate."

Reyna rode two horses away. She stretched forward on her horse until she could see him. "Morvan, might I speak with Maccus Armstrong once he surrenders? I have some questions that developed during this journey, and he may be able to answer them."

Morvan looked to the western horizon. "Your request is very interesting, Reyna. Because one of Maccus Armstrong's terms was not at all predictable, and I sensed it is the only point on which he will not move." He turned his gaze on her. "Old Maccus will not yield until we hand him the widow of Robert of Kelso."

chapter
TWENTY-FOUR

Reyna stood on the wall walk behind Ian's armored body. David also formed part of her human shield, and Anna stood nearby with her bow in hand, to answer any movement that threatened from the opposing wall. Other archers were deployed for the same purpose, but her friend had insisted on standing by her side, and Morvan had warned the Armstrongs that any errant bolt finding his wife would mean the death of every man in the keep.

Maccus had demanded that Reyna Graham be given into his custody for her safety, but Morvan had refused. Reyna considered that very chivalrous, since this one point was all that kept him from reclaiming his family's honor. Since Maccus had referred to her safety, Morvan had offered to let him see for himself that she was present and unharmed, even though no one believed Reyna's safety had been Maccus's goal at all.

"There he is," Ian said. Reyna peered over his shoulder to the far gate. Atop one of the towers, a white-haired man appeared. "I will step aside, Reyna, but keep yourself behind David's and my shields."

He moved over, holding his shield next to David's so they formed a steel wall. Reyna pressed up against it and faced the distant scrutiny of Robert's friend and lord. The white head looked her way and a silence fell over the castle. Down below, Morvan Fitzwaryn stood alone in the outer bailey, protected only by his armor.

Maccus Armstrong raised his arm in a sweeping gesture. Bodies began leaving the battlements around him. Soon, not a single Armstrong soldier or archer could be seen. Maccus waited until the last had gone, and then his head disappeared.

Anna ran for the wall steps. Reyna and the men followed and joined the expectant crowd forming in the yard. Slowly, the portcullis rose.

Ian kept his hand on her shoulder while they waited among the circle surrounding Morvan. Reyna's throat burned, and she knew her emotions were evidence of her divided loyalties. She felt elation for Christiana and Morvan, who had been driven from their home so long ago, but also anguish for Maccus himself, who had been Robert's trusted friend and an instrument in all that had been good in her life.

Suddenly, a lone figure appeared in the yard beyond the gate. Maccus strode forward without hesitation. The crowd parted for him, and he crossed to Morvan and silently unsheathed and handed over his sword.

Maccus was a hearty man, and still a powerful figure despite his sixty-plus years. He looked Morvan right in the face, studying him shrewdly. "You have your mother's eyes and color, but you fight like Hugh sure enough."

"I wouldn't know. He died when I was still a boy."

"He did at that, and we both know 'twas one of my archers who brought him down. But such is the way with war."

Morvan nodded. "The way with war. Better for you in the long run if you had killed the son as well."

"I do not kill children. Besides, you were a brave figure of a lad. Would have been a waste." He glanced around and smiled with chagrin. "Although, under the circumstances . . ."

Something like a smile softened Morvan's expression. "Since you were generous in victory, I can do no less. Any man who swears to stay north of the borders of our lands can leave at once to be escorted to Clivedale. You will remain here until a ransom that I set is paid."

"And Lady Reyna?"

Morvan shook his head. "You worried for her safety. She will be safe with us."

"There have been accusations about her."

"We are aware of them."

Reyna felt her face redden as glances in the crowd shot her way.

"They aren't true, those stories about her killing Robert," Maccus snapped.

"Your nephew Thomas thinks otherwise."

"Thomas is an ass. Nonsense, all of it. Anyone who knew him and her knows that. I was on my way to put an end to it when you caught me here. I have been worried that Thomas would do something stupid while I was pinned down. All the same, best if you keep her until my ransom is paid. Then I will bring her to Clivedale and clear all this up for her."

Reyna stared dumbfounded at this public announcement of her innocence, coming from the man she had been sure intended to send her to her death.

"She will not be going to Clivedale," Morvan said.

"If you don't give her to me, you had better swear to her safety, Fitzwaryn. I will not have you judging her and listening to people spin their tales, remembering things that never happened and whatnot. She's a Graham, you know, and there are old feelings about that."

"Everyone's interest in the lady has perplexed me from the start, Maccus. What is the reason for yours?"

"I owe it to Robert."

"A good man, Robert of Kelso. But her new husband is a good man too. He will swear to her safety, and if you swear to her innocence, I have no inclination to hold her in judgment."

Maccus looked as stunned by this announcement as Reyna had been feeling about his. He scanned the crowd until he found her. Turning abruptly, he strode over and peered down, then studied Ian. "I would speak with you," he said brusquely.

Ian nodded. "Somehow I thought so. And Reyna would speak with you."

Some knights took Maccus away then. Morvan strode toward the inner gate, and a new hush fell over the crowd. Pausing, he looked back and gestured for Anna and Christiana to join him.

With his wife and sister beside him, he walked back into Harclow.

Reyna turned to Ian while the crowd followed through the gate. "That was very surprising, Maccus defending me like that."

"Was it?"

"Perhaps not," she conceded. She met his serious gaze. "How long have you known?"

"I have not known at all. But I have wondered for some time."

"You are quicker than I. I spent a lifetime before I wondered."

"Perhaps you should leave it at wondering. Are you certain that you want to know for sure? All of it?"

"It is the all of it that I need to know, and I think that only Maccus can tell me the truth."

"Then let us go and speak with him, Reyna."

They found Maccus in a small chamber. He had sworn his parole, and no guard stood at the unbolted door.

He stood near the cold hearth in a thoughtful pose, hands clasped behind him, staring at flames that did not exist. Over the years Reyna had come to know him fairly well, but he had always been a little remote in his dealings with her. He had been different with Robert, and often she had heard their laughter behind the solar door.

He turned at their entry and scrutinized her. "Didn't take you long, girl. Robert be barely cold."

"Well, she did not have much choice, Maccus. It was me or return to Duncan," Ian said.

"Hell of a choice, that's for sure," Maccus groused. "Learned a bit about you from the knights that brought me here. You took Black Lyne Keep, they say, and it is to be yours now. Not a bad summer's work, Ian of Guilford. Still, if it's done it's done. I had planned to give her to another man, but if she is content I'll accept it. An English knight no less. Hell."

"I am more than contented," Reyna said. "And it is well that I am, for you would not have found me willing to be given to any man at your bidding should this summer have unfolded differently. At four-and-twenty, I am tired of being moved like a chess piece and kept in ignorance."

Maccus showed surprise, then smiled. "Robert always said that you had more spirit than I ever saw. Well, you have cast your lot with these English and this man, so I hope it will suit you. If it does, I will accommodate my-self to the notion."

"It will suit me. But I would know some things now. I am a grown woman, and have a right to know them, I think." She chose her words carefully. "Aymer Graham has said that I am not really his sister. I do not think that he just referred to our half-blood connection, not with how he said it." She squared her shoulders and looked Maccus in the eyes. "Who was my father?"

His face fell, and he suddenly looked very old.

"Was it Robert?" she whispered.

"Robert! Hell, girl, what did you take the man for? Robert would never marry his own daughter."

"Who, then? Was it really Duncan?"

"Duncan Graham should pray that he could get such as you by any woman. Nay, not Duncan. And no knight of his, no matter what they say about your mother in that place. 'Twas Jamie. My boy James was your father. Duncan always suspected but never was sure, but your mother knew, and so did Jamie."

"James Armstrong? I knew that they said he had been her lover later, but—"

"A long time, almost since she first came to these parts. They met early on. The families were not enemies then." He turned away, his gaze seeking the empty hearth again. "I warned him off. Told him naught but bad could come of it. Well, he was young . . . still, it might have gone on like it was, except she saw how things were going to be for you. For herself she didn't mind, but you . . . Jamie decided to take you both away. Duncan found out, caught up with them just past the waste, near the old motte. Hung my boy like a thief right there, and left him. Robert found his body."

Memories from the crypt suddenly assaulted her, insinuating into her awareness. Cold. Damp cold and fear. Fingers prodding, and a boy's laugh. *Stay here or the demons will get you. I'm going out to watch.*

"We retaliated, and then they did, and it grew, as such things do. Robert would speak to me sometimes, urge me to make peace, tell me how the people suffered, but I wouldn't hear him. An eye for an eye, the old book says, and I was waiting for Aymer to come of age and earn his spurs. I do not kill children, but when he grew I planned to even things with Duncan the only way it could finally be evened."

Running. Running. Toward the voices and screams rumbling down the black space and rocks, following the retreating steps.

"Then word came of how things were for you. I had never seen you, but you were Jamie's child. So I started listening to Robert, and we started thinking of ways to get you out of there."

Light just ahead. Slower now, approaching cautiously.

"Duncan agreed only because of Aymer. He knew I was waiting for the boy to grow. He began negotiating in earnest when Aymer turned eighteen. I made him give those dower lands because he wasn't really giving a daughter. He agreed because it would be Robert who held them, and he knew him to be honorable. And so we found some peace and got you free of him."

The image of herself, hanging . . .

She faced Maccus dazedly, scrambled images and emotions blurring her sight. "And my mother? Where is she?"

"He put her away, in an abbey."

"Nay, I do not think so. Robert would have taken me there when I asked if he had."

She walked over to Maccus. "Do you think that a child forgets such things forever? That if a hand covers her eyes she has not seen? That if a world remains silent she never remembers?" She clenched her fists until her nails bit into her skin. "All of my life, my soul has remembered. These last months, whenever someone spoke of my own judgment, I would see myself hanging, limp. I thought it was a premonition of my own death, but it was not. That is not me hanging there in that nightmare at all. He killed her, too, didn't he? Didn't he?"

She didn't realize that she had begun to yell until she felt Ian's presence behind her and his arm around her waist. "Calm yourself, love," he said quietly.

Maccus's expression crumbled. "We did not know for sure. Robert found only Jamie, but he saw evidence that perhaps another . . . And she is not in that abbey, not living, anyway, because I went there to see if I could help her. I think Duncan regretted it as soon as he did it. In the old days an unfaithful wife might be punished thus, but it is considered murder now. Even his own people were told he had put her away."

Her strength left her. She turned into Ian's supporting embrace and vaguely heard him whispering soothing words in her ear.

"You are Jamie's girl, Reyna," Maccus said. "My granddaughter. If you ever have need of me, you know where to find me."

A note in his voice penetrated her exhaustion. She turned and saw the flickering hope in his old eyes. She went over and embraced him. "You did your best for me, Grandfather, and it was better than even you knew."

His hands cradled her head. "Well, now, girl, it is good to be able to acknowledge you." He took her hands and kissed them. "Leave us now, if you will. I need to warn this English knight to take care of you if he doesn't want to battle the whole Armstrong clan."

She kissed him, then went to the door. "I will find John for you, Ian, and procure a chamber so that you can remove your armor."

Maccus watched her go, and faced the door for a few moments longer. When he finally turned to Ian, a mischievous spark lit his eyes. "Well, Ian of Guilford, this marriage is an interesting surprise for me, and this conversation a more interesting one for you, I'll warrant."

"Not too surprising. It is rare for men to treat their own blood the way Duncan treated her, and I had learned the story of your son's death. But since you are her grandfather, it is useful that you accept our marriage."

"Oh, I accept it. What choice do I have?" He gestured around the chamber with a laugh. "But if I were you, I would not repeat this to anyone. When Fitzwaryn offered you Black Lyne Keep, he wasn't counting on a marriage alliance with the Armstrongs for you, was he?"

"Nay. Still, I will tell Morvan about this. Marriage to an Armstrong or not, I am his man. He may warm to the idea and lower your ransom as a result. What are the chances that you will try to attack Harclow if you must first take the keep in which your granddaughter lives?"

Maccus chuckled. "Who knows, twenty years from now . . ."

"In twenty years you will be dead and Duncan will be dead and the Armstrongs and Fitzwaryns will be watching their backs every day for Aymer Graham. This marriage alliance may prove very useful in the future. Until then, Black Lyne Keep will remain as it was under Robert of Kelso, lands separating three families, held by a man sworn to one and married to the daughter of another. It worked before. Let it work again."

Maccus considered that and nodded. Then he glanced to the door and frowned. "Speaking of Robert . . . where do you think she got the unnatural notion that he might be her father?"

"Not so unnatural, since she was still a virgin when he died."

"The hell you say. No wonder . . . Well, Robert never did have much doings with women. A good friend, but not one of the ones who went whoring and such when we were young. . . . Damnation. Those dower lands. If he never . . ."

"Very few know about it, and we all have our reasons for keeping silent," Ian said. "I would like you to let your relationship to Reyna be known. She will not be judged in Robert's death, but many still suspect her. It is also un-likely that the real killer will ever face justice. If it is known that she is your granddaughter, those whispers will cease."

He took his leave of Maccus and went in search of Reyna. He found her and John in a chamber, dumping the straw from the mattress into the hearth.

"There have been no women or servants here for over a month," Reyna said. "The keep is filthy, the straw bug-ridden."

"Get this armor off, John. I have lived in it for days."

Reyna had found a broom, and she began sweeping while mail and plate clanked to the floor. Ian observed her small body move to her industry, bending and stretching while she continued to mutter about men who would live under such conditions. Her gown was dirty from her ordeal and her hair unbound and snarled, but he thought that she looked absolutely beautiful.

"Is Morvan looking for me, John?"

"Nay. He is organizing the soldiers and Sir David is

bartering with the merchants for provisions like a steward. Maccus's knights had to leave their horses and armor and our company got some of it, so they are
contented, though Morvan is planning to pay them off
soon. Don't need two thousand to hold a keep once it's
fallen."

Ian reminded himself to speak with certain members
of the company to see if they wanted to remain at Black
Lyne Keep, but his gaze never left Reyna. "Are there any
servants about, John?"

"Some, not many," the squire said as he inspected a
piece of plate that he had just removed. Ian wished he
would speed up and remove certain other sections that
had suddenly become very uncomfortable.

John glanced over to Reyna. "She wants *me* to find
clean straw for the mattress. As if I am some common—"

"I think that is an excellent idea. But first find some
men and bring a bath."

"A bath! There's feasting and drinking planned, and a
whole castle to be explored, and you want me to—"

"A bath. And then the mattress, John."

John's scowl darkened, then suddenly disappeared. He
glanced at Reyna and flushed. "*Oh.*" His fingers began
working the straps and buckles more quickly. He finished
just as Reyna was pushing the dust and dirt into the
hearth. "I'll go see about that bath now," he mumbled,
darting out and closing the door.

Ian went to Reyna and took the broom and set it
aside. "How are you faring? It must be strange to spend
your whole life thinking that you are one person, and
then suddenly learn that you are another."

She pursed her lips thoughtfully. He fought the urge
to nip them. "It is strange, but in a peaceful way. Like a
shadow has received light. I am feeling oddly free, in

fact. Duncan never loved me, nor I him, and it is good to know the reason. And my mother . . . in a way it is good to know that too. I do not feel at all like a different person, just that I know better the one who I have always been." She rested a hand on his chest. His heart rose to his throat. "Do you think that people will tell me about him if I ask? About James?"

"Aye," he managed to say, bending to kiss her puckered brow. The small taste of her undid him. He pulled her into an embrace, pressing fevered lips to her cheek, her neck, her breast, and he knew that he could not wait for the bath and the mattress. "You have been in my head every moment, Reyna, day and night." He pressed and lifted her body to his, wanting to connect with every inch of her. "You are the light illuminating my shadows, love, and the need I feel for you astonishes me again and again."

She sighed a little gasp when his hands moved in a long, savoring caress, and he couldn't have said another word after that if his life hung in the balance. Delicious desire swept him like a flood, drowning all thought until only his senses existed, hungry and alive, stimulated by her scent and sounds and hands.

He pressed her to the wall, lifting her skirt, anxious for the dewy feel of her skin, desperate to touch her body but immediately devastated by the warmth when he did, knowing at once that he could not even wait for that. Mindless now, he lifted her legs around his hips and took her there, his head buried in her breast, his hands grasping her bottom, listening to the music of her soft groans, grateful for her quick passion because he could have known no restraint.

She arched against him with a little cry just as his own finish came, and then her head collapsed against his shoulder. Consciousness returned, and with it awareness of what he had just done.

"I am sorry, Reyna," he muttered, holding her tightly, cursing himself, and worrying that the stones had bruised her back. "I did not mean to . . . when I spoke of my need for you, it was not . . . but it has been a very long . . ."

Her hand found his lips and silenced him. "What wife would not be flattered? And if it has been so long, I am honored."

He eased her down and managed to right their clothing without releasing her. "Honored? Should I feel honored if you are faithful to me, Reyna? It is what I expect. If you went to another man, I would think that you loved him and that the best part of my life had died."

"Aye, but . . . I thought . . ."

"I know what you thought and had good cause to think." Her surprised, hopeful expression pained him to his core. "Could I be content with some whore after you? Settle for base pleasure? It is different with us, it has been from the start. Even when I act like some callous boy, as I just did now. Nay, wife, you are mine and I am yours, and there will be no others so long as our love lives."

"But that will be forever, Ian," she said, as if the eternity of her love could not be doubted. God, but he prayed it would ever be so. She did not really know the man to whom she offered her love so innocently. It seemed such a fragile thing, too, this precious euphoria that saturated his whole being. He dared not risk its destruction, and yet it also made him want to pour out his heart to her, and have her grace absolve the worst of his sins. *Not now. Not yet. Let it last.*

"Aye," he said. "The Lord of a Thousand Nights removed forever from the field. There goes my chance at immortal fame."

They embraced until the bath arrived. He took her in with him, cradling her on his lap while he washed her, his gaze and kisses giving substance to the memories that had sustained and plagued him. When they emerged, he found the fresh mattress waiting outside the chamber and he took her to bed. He made love to her the way he had planned, loving and praising every part of her, still caressing and covering her long after their passion was spent.

C an you be content here in Scotland, Ian? It will be very dull after the life you have had," she said while her small fingers played through his hair.

"Blissfully dull, I hope. I will never be able to see warfare as a sport again. Besides, we will go down to London sometimes, as soon as we can in fact, when Christiana is in residence. She made me promise to bring you." He paused. "You can stay with her while I return to Guilford. I think I will go back." He rolled to his side. "I can not take you with me until I visit my brother and his wife first, and see how I am received."

"Would his wife not welcome her husband's brother?"

"She certainly will not, but it is my brother whose feelings I must learn."

He looked so serious, contemplating that meeting. Christiana had said that he could not return home.

"What stands between you and your brother?"

He turned his eyes on her, and his gaze deepened with an intensity that looked like anger. *I have done it again*, she thought sickly, looking away.

His hand turned her face back to him. "Can you love me without hearing about it? Love the man whom you know and forget about the rest?"

"My love does not start with one part of you and end

at another, Ian. Whatever this is that you have buried inside yourself, I still love you. Do not speak of it if you choose, but not because you fear that it will kill how I feel. There are no conditions on my love. It is yours, as is my friendship."

His lips parted as if he would speak. When he didn't, she admitted disappointment that he did not trust her to understand. Well, she would accept however much he could give, and if he never spoke of this past which he hid, so be it.

He rested his head on her breast so the embrace was more hers than his, and she sensed his conflicted mood easing away while he nestled contentedly there. He had not rested much the last week, and she knew that he would sleep deeply.

Before he drifted off, he lazily kissed her cheek. "I feel that I have forgotten something. Ah, now I remember. I was supposed to punish you for your disobedience."

Consciousness emerged slowly, barely breaking through the delicious peace. Subtle sounds came to him, and then the awareness that Reyna was not by his side. He began to reach for her, only to find that his arm would not move.

With a rough jerk he burst into wakefulness and glared at the recalcitrant arm. A rope bound it to the bedboard. He turned in shock to find the other hand tied the same way, and looked down to see his ankles restrained as well. He was trussed spread-eagled and naked like some human sacrifice.

He jerked all his limbs in violent defiance. The bed creaked and thudded from the force.

"They are bound securely," a quiet voice said. "They will not come loose."

He turned in fury. Reyna stood several paces from the bed, wearing a long, oversized robe that billowed from her shoulders. Something she had found in one of the other chambers, he guessed.

"Untie me. This is very annoying."

"Nay, not yet. Not for quite a while, I think."

"Reyna . . ."

"It is only what you have done to me, Ian. I thought you might like to experience it yourself. How do you feel, my love? Helpless? At my mercy?"

That was exactly how he felt, damn it. "Reyna, I command you to untie these ropes. Why have you done this, anyway?"

"You spoke of punishing me."

"Saints, Reyna, I was only jesting."

"I am relieved to hear it, but a little disappointed too. This was to be such a good ploy. To distract you from that idea."

"You have no need of a ploy. I would never—"

"Still, the ploy suddenly has its own appeal. Perhaps I should see it through."

"Untie these ropes, damn it, or you will surely need a ploy to distract me when I get free." He jerked at the bonds again.

She smiled sweetly while the bed crashed and groaned. "I had hours to work on them, and they will not come loose." She drifted closer and looked down on him. "You really have a magnificent body." She ran a languid finger down the center of his chest.

He ceased his struggle and looked into her eyes. His whole body reacted to what he saw there. He smiled his best smile. "Untie the ropes and come lie with me, love."

She gathered her billowing robe and stepped up on the bed, her feet straddling his hips. "I do not think so. I find that I like you this way." She began plucking at the lacing down the center of the robe. "I am surprised at how thrilling this is. I mean, you are so big, and I am so small."

Ever so slowly, she slid the garment off her shoulders and eased it down her body. The fabric fluttered around her feet, rasping his skin like a caress when she kicked it away. She glanced down and smiled. "You seem to like it too."

He liked it enough that his jaw was clenching. She "was not naked beneath the gown, but wore a leather jerkin, a boy's garment a bit too small for her woman's form. It laced up the front as well, the sides separating and half covering breasts that peeked through the crossing thongs. The bottom edge just barely covered her hips. The effect was unbelievably erotic.

"It was a wonderful ploy, darling. Really, I am totally distracted."

"But I have just begun, Ian." She stepped forward, one small foot on each side until he was looking up her length, seeing the suggestive shadows beneath the edge of the jerkin. She plucked a pheasant feather out from under the garment. "It is supposed to be a peacock feather, but of course there are none here. You will just have to imagine."

She bent and began stroking his body. "Oh, you really seem to like this, Ian." She turned the feather's ministrations to the clear evidence of that.

The exquisite torture teased every inch of his skin.

Furious passion made him jerk at the ropes again. "I want you to untie me *now*."

"Heavens, you sound angry. I think it would be best if I continued. It seems that I need this ploy, after all." She scooted down and knelt between his feet. "Besides, what you want is not important just yet. It is what I want."

"And what is that?"

Her hands stroked up and down his legs while she examined him. "I want to see you while the pleasure builds. I want to watch your body tremble while it begs for relief. I want to hear your cries of need."

He couldn't believe the forceful desire her words and expression produced. He thought his body would split apart. Still, she had things unrealistically reversed. After all, those were *his* words.

"Do your worst, woman, but remember that eventually you must release me, and then I plan to rebalance the scales."

"I certainly hope so. Now, lie back and submit, Ian. This could take awhile. I have completed only the first two steps." She bent and began caressing him with her lips and tongue the way the feather had, slowly working up his legs. Very slowly.

He looked down at her leisurely progress while his body both screamed for completion and relished the delay. Her kisses and tongue reached his knees. Her raised bottom peeked out behind the leather jerkin. "Just how many steps are there?"

"Six," she muttered, moving upward, upward. She was going to kill him. "Actually, eight when done the Saracen way, but David refused to tell Christiana about the last two."

He barely heard her. Her mouth was on his thighs

now, and every fiber of him waited and hoped and urged. She rose up on one arm and her curtain of hair blocked his view, but he tightened like a coil when her finger stroked up his phallus and circled. "Is this what you want, love?" she asked. "Is it?"

"Nay."

"Ah. Then maybe this." She swung her leg and straddled him on her hands and knees, facing away, her woman's scent inches from his face.

"Move back," he instructed.

Her breath brushed him, creating an agony of anticipation. "Not yet. Tell me what else you want, Ian."

His muscles tensed in final rebellion before collapsing helplessly to the pleasure and control. A strangled request tore out of him and her lips replaced her fingers.

All resistance and thought blurred then, except a vague curiosity at what could possibly constitute the later steps.

chapter
TWENTY-FIVE

L ate blooms filled the garden with a riot of colors and smells. The chaotic beauty drenched Ian's senses. Beside him on the stone bench lay a basket. Two roses peeked over the rim, the petals intended for some delicacy that Reyna planned to cook for the midday meal.

He wondered how long she would be gone on the pilgrimage she had made today. He had agreed to let her visit the old ruins alone, but not without misgivings. He understood her need to confront the memories buried in the dark stones of the old donjon, but he had wanted to go with her in case the terror had not been conquered as thoroughly as she hoped.

He would wait for the sun to move a bit more before following her. Most likely they would meet on her way back, but if she had succumbed to the darkness he would find her before it got too bad.

He tried again to distract himself from his concern by reviewing his plans for Black Lyne Keep. Reyna's confrontation with Aymer implied that the Grahams would be a lance forever poking at the western border of these lands. The notion of meeting Aymer on the field did not concern Ian. He looked forward to the day he would mete some justice for Reyna's and Robert's sakes. But he wanted his family and people safe when that private war came, and he intended to improve the fortifications over the next few years.

His family and people. Still an odd-sounding phrase, but a pleasant one. He looked forward to that family. The sons he would raise to be strong and true knights. The daughters . . . He laughed to himself. The daughters he would probably lock away to protect them from men like Ian of Guilford.

He smoothed out the dirt with his boot and considered the decision he had made last night. A second wall for the keep needed to be built at the base of its hill.

He tried to envision the completed fortifications, and how moving the river would affect them. He poked the stick into the ground. He would draw it the way David had drawn Harclow and see if that gave the images substance. The stick scratched. Here the river, there the square keep on its round hill. The jagged waste over here, the old motte and donjon down below. Now, to move the river . . .

He abruptly stopped scratching. Standing, he stepped over so that his feet were below the circles of the old fortress. He peered intently at the drawing of square and circles and curving lines.

It almost exactly duplicated the little one on the scrap of parchment that he had seen in Reyna's Book of Hours.

Something was missing, but he couldn't remember what it was. He strode from the garden, wondering why someone had drawn a map of Black Lyne Keep and its lands as seen from the eye of a flying bird.

He found the little Book of Hours on the solar shelf. Flipping through the pages of devotions and images, he found the scrap of parchment. It still looked like something drawn by an astrologer.

He realized what his own map had not included. Two straight lines bisected the old motte and donjon, forming a cross.

He examined the frail and ragged quality of the lines. A Book of Hours was the sort of book one would keep near the dying, reading familiar prayers to comfort them. If Robert of Kelso had drawn this, what was so important that he would use his last strength to do so?

He replaced the book on the shelf, but tucked the little map into his sleeve. It was one more mystery left by the good Robert, and as unlikely to be solved as the others.

He left the keep and climbed to the battlements, then circled around to the south where he could see the old motte in the distance. He narrowed his eyes and peered in vain for signs of Reyna returning. He would wait only a little longer, and then go looking for her.

His gaze fell to the cemetery, and the central cross marking Robert's grave. He remembered standing here, his fury building while he imagined Reyna with Edmund. That jealousy seemed distant and foolish and he knew he would never feel anything like it again. He would never doubt her thus, not if a hundred Edmunds passed this way to talk philosophy.

Nor would he ever again resent her memories of the man buried under that cross. Robert had become a friend of sorts. Hadn't they both arrived here the same way, cut off from family and past, only to stay and build new lives? He was no Robert of Kelso to be sure, but oddly enough he found himself following that man's steps. He smiled at the irony, because it had been Edmund's more obvious similarity to Robert that had fed his torment that night.

He began to walk away and then paused, frozen for a soundless moment. A scattering of notions poked at his mind in unison, arrows from numerous quivers of memories sighting in on him all at once. He stared down at the cross while he absorbed their onslaught, astonished and annoyed that he had missed such obvious explanations.

He walked slowly to the stairs, mulling what had just occurred to him. Surely he was right, and he thought he knew how to be certain. He would find the proof, and then go and tell Reyna what he had learned. It was not a big mystery, but she would be glad to know the truth, especially on this day when she had garnered her courage to face what she called "all of it."

Alice's grandsons played in the yard and he called to them. "Come with me. I need small strong bodies, and you look just right."

Adam and Peter hopped and skipped beside him into the tower. He took a torch from the hall and they marched up to the solar.

He handed Adam the torch and bent down to press the stones that opened the wall to the hidden stairway. He should have done this a month ago, but he just assumed . . . well, he had just assumed that it was exactly what it was. "Go and stand down two steps to give us light," he instructed his torchbearer.

The light ducked and disappeared into the wall and Ian followed, bringing Peter. He turned the small boy toward the niche. "I am going to hoist you up and I want you to crawl in and see what is there. I should warn you that there may be huge spiders."

The idea of confronting huge spiders enthralled Peter. Ian lifted him onto the edge of the deep niche, then took the torch to raise the light. Peter's rump and legs began crawling away. Soon only one small foot was within reach.

"What is back there?"

"Lots of cobwebs and squishy bugs. Wish you had let me bring a sack. Seems unfair that Adam should miss all the fun."

"Besides bugs. In the back, isn't there armor and cloth?"

"Aye."

"Can you get the cloth out without tearing it overmuch?"

"It's falling apart. Stinks bad too. What do you want this old thing for?"

"Just hand it to me." The rump inched backward, and a hand shot out with the tattered cloth. Ian took it and gave the torch back to Adam, then helped a very dirty Peter out of the niche.

Back in the solar, the boys waited expectantly to see the nature of the hidden treasure. Ian didn't have the heart to send them away, and so they flanked him while he carefully unfolded the filthy cloth and spread it over the chair.

"It is only an old surcoat for armor," Adam said with disappointment.

Ian mentally cleaned the dust and rot off the garment and filled in the sections lost to time. This rag explained much.

Peter traced the horizontal and vertical lines where dark fabric met light in the center. "Looks like part of a cross. And this could be red, and this white. It's a crusader's surcoat."

"Something like that," a new voice said.

Ian turned to see Andrew Armstrong standing near the door.

"No doubt a Fitzwaryn long ago left that there," Andrew added.

The boys began imagining that ancient warrior, speculating on the battles he had fought against the Saracens.

Ian smiled, expecting that the siege of Antioch would fill the yard for the next few days. "Go now, and see if your grandmother or the grooms need you for any chores," he said.

They ran off, filling the passageway with war cries. Ian and Andrew faced each other in silence.

"You knew," Ian said.

"I was his squire when he first came. Not a very good squire, but he understood it was not my nature, and saw to it the others did not mock me too much. We both knew I would never earn my spurs, and so he convinced Maccus that my worth lay elsewhere. Eventually I became steward here, and then later he was given the lands and I served him again."

"How did you know?"

Andrew gestured to the surcoat. "I found it by mistake. One day while I squired for him I decided to clean up the old armor he kept in some sacks, even though he would never use it again. That was with it. I recognized it. Anyone back then would have. I asked him about it. He was a good man, and I swore never to speak of it. By then I knew something about secrets which some men need to keep. He knew mine and I knew his, and we neither of us judged."

Ian fingered the tattered red-and-white cloth. "Red cross on white field, in reverse of a crusader's livery. A Templar's surcoat. Scottish?"

"Nay, I do not think so. He had been in the East when

he was a boy. Scottish by birth, I'm sure, but he hadn't lived here for many years and was still young when he returned." He glanced to where Ian's fingers lay. "His French was impeccable."

Ian did some calculations. "One of the last to be dubbed, I would guess. Perhaps the last to die."

"There is no need for anyone to ever know."

"He is dead. There is no danger now."

"Still . . ."

"Reyna needs to know. Other than her, perhaps not. If he chose to keep this secret while he lived, we can let it be buried with him."

Andrew nodded gratefully. He turned to leave, but paused. "His first years here, I always had the sense that he was waiting for something. He kept a subtle distance from the others, and formed no close friendships. Even with Maccus, he held something back."

"It might have just been the secret itself. Hiding a past has a way of isolating a man," Ian said, realizing that he and Robert had even more in common than he had thought.

"Perhaps. And yet, as the years passed, he changed, as if he knew it would never come, whatever it was. Knew he was here to stay." He shrugged and walked to the door. "Not such a bad secret. No sin in it. I always thought that he should tell Reyna, at least. He once said that he would, that she would need to know."

Ian carefully refolded the surcoat. He stored it in one of his own trunks, then walked over to the books to investigate yet another arrow point that had pricked at his memory.

A short while later he had made two stacks, one high with the Gospels and Aquinas and Bernard, the other

much smaller and poorer, with the herbal and a few secu-
lar treatises.

He turned to leave, but halted. Lifting the little Book
of Hours from atop the tall stack, he opened it and tore
out its first page, then placed it on the stack with the
herbal.

chapter

TWENTY-SIX

Reyna sat on the ground against the stone she and Ian had shared the day she escaped from Aymer, feeling its warmth against her back, thinking that she really should finish this or Ian would begin to worry and come for her.

She gazed again at the lintel spanning the ancient entry to the donjon's foundations. Aye, it had happened there. She was sure of it now. Still, it looked different and not very threatening, possibly because she saw it from this angle, and not as one leaving the blackness.

The memories and images had come clearly, almost too clearly, once she knew what she sought. Not lined up in a composed tale, but as flashes of sight and sound and emotion.

Two bodies, not one, but she had barely seen the second after the horror of the first. Duncan cursing loudly, and yelling for someone to get her away. Strong arms grabbing her, dragging her back into the blackness. A hand covering her eyes when she was brought out again and carried down the motte.

Had she forgotten at once? When had she started believing that her mother lived in that abbey? Her whole childhood had become a blur, except during those nightmares and terrors. Otherwise her life might as well have started the day Robert found her in the crypt.

She rose and dusted off her gown. She had already said her prayers for that poor woman whose unhappiness had ended here. Had Duncan forced her to watch her lover die first? The distant screams in her terror suggested that he had.

She approached the lintel. A knot twisted in her stomach. The dark had not frightened her during the two weeks since returning from Harclow, but then Ian was usually reassuringly nearby. This would be different. And this was not a passageway or a chamber or even the crypt, but the place where it had all begun.

She entered the old foundations and marched bravely forward, until she lost the last of the light and only blackness faced her. Sweat slicked her palms and her heart beat rapidly, but the unhinging fear stayed away. Groping her way along the stone wall, she proceeded forward until she found a slight turn and the entry behind her disappeared.

And then she halted in horror.

Voices mumbled toward her, off the stones, through the blackness . . . A low laugh . . . The stone beneath her hand felt the sounds as surely as her spirit heard them echoing quietly all around her.

Nay, she cried silently, dropping her hand and turning in circles to confront them. *It is over. No more!*

She turned to run, but the shock had disoriented her. She reached out blindly, seeking the wall, but her hand found only blackness. Stumbling forward, with panic rising, she struggled for breath and prayed that she headed toward the entrance. Then suddenly she was sprawled on the ground, her face against the stone floor, her body bent in an unnatural pose.

The impact cleared her head. She groped around and realized that she had fallen into a hole half a body deep. Her hand hit a pile of dirt and a stack of stones.

The rocks still spoke to her. Nay, not the rocks. The sound did not come from them. The whispering mumbles were up ahead, louder now than before. Relief broke in her. Ian must have come, and brought someone with him.

She crawled out of the hole and began walking toward the voices. Her foot hit another pile of dirt. She moved to her left until she found the stone wall. Flat against it she eased forward.

After a while she could see the dimmest light. That made no sense. If she was retracing her way to the entrance, how could she have missed all these obstacles on her way in?

The passage angled a little, and suddenly the light grew stronger. A huge shadow moved up ahead, and she caught her breath in shock.

Another shadow moved and took human form and looked right in her direction. It stiffened and swung out an arm. "Get her."

It sounded like a threat, even though that would make no sense. Still, she turned on her heel and began to run.

Pounding steps came up behind her. Large arms grabbed and lifted her and carried her toward the light. Finally, she found herself set down on a large stone between two torches.

The passage spread wider here, and she looked around in confusion. Stone slabs had been moved and more shallow pits dug. The handles of picks and shovels crossed each other on the floor. Rolled blankets and leather sacks rested against a wall.

She looked up at the broad naked chest hovering over her, and then into Reginald's worried, rugged face.

"What are you doing here, Reyna? Robert said that you feared the dark," a soft voice said. Edmund stepped around Reginald. The torchlight turned his hair into a halo of fire. Edmund had also stripped to the waist, and sweat sheened his body.

"What are *you* doing here? Why are you digging? How long have you been here?"

Edmund eased down beside her on the rock. "Too long. It is getting annoying and tedious, but we should be done soon." He looked at her curiously. "Perhaps it is good that you came. Robert was trying to tell you at the end. Reginald heard him speaking one night, not aware that you weren't beside him. Heard enough before he stopped so we know it is here. Why don't you tell us the rest, Reyna, and spare everyone further trouble. At this point I am even willing to share."

"You speak in riddles," she said with exasperation, getting to her feet. "You had best leave at once, Edmund. You swore to take Reginald away, and if Ian finds—"

He pulled her back down with a hard yank. "Is he with you? Did your English knight come too?"

She didn't like his dangerous tone. His fingers gouged her arm. "Nay, he is not here." But he would come. He had not wanted her to do this alone, and would not wait long for her to return.

Edmund looked at Reginald and jerked his head

toward the passageway. Lifting a battle-ax from its place against a stone, Reginald lumbered off into the darkness.

"What is he going to do?" Reyna asked.

"He will make sure that you speak the truth, and get rid of Ian if you do not." He released her arm and looked away, his eyes squinting thoughtfully, his mouth a red slash. The flaming light shadowed his cheeks and eyes. He appeared very different from the way she remembered him, and not just because of the light.

"What are you digging for here?"

He smiled in that gentle but superior way he had. "Treasure. Why else would men live like beasts for weeks on end inside the belly of this donjon? Robert put it here. Hid it when he returned from France, and then moved it to this place after he wed you. He told you about it, didn't he? When he was ill, before he died. Wanted you to take it to the bishop, as he had planned to do. Reginald read Robert's letter to Glasgow, you see, so we know about that part."

"Oh, saints have mercy, Edmund. It is not here. The books are where they have always been, in the solar. That is what he sought to give the bishop. Those are the valuable objects he brought back from France."

Edmund's shocked expression held a moment, and then his face cracked into a mocking smile. "Books? *Books?* You think that this is about those books?" He grasped her face. "What is buried here far surpasses those few books. It is gold, lots of it, and jewels. Enough to buy hundreds of books."

He examined her, his eyes holding a hot expression, his fingers squeezing her cheeks. "Tell me what he said, Reyna."

"He never spoke of this place to me, not even while

he was dying. He was barely conscious most of those days."

His hand fell away. "Then you are of no use to me at all anymore." His flat tone made the skin on her neck prickle and her blood pulse frantically. "Whatever brought you here, it was the devil's doing."

"What do you mean?" she asked, but a sick feeling spread through her.

He ignored her. "Such a damn good plan too," he muttered. "If Robert could have just died in his sleep like most old men, and taken this secret to his grave . . . if he had just let things lie here as they were, I would have gladly waited. Then you would have come north and this land would have been yours and we could have looked at our leisure after that. But he had to write that damn letter, and your knight had to go and marry you . . . well, there is nothing for it now."

He clamped his hand down on his knee and patted her cheek with the other. His utterly casual attitude chilled her.

"I will find a way that doesn't pain you, except it will need to look like an accident, or someone else's doing. Aymer perhaps. Aye, that would work. Reginald and I watched that little siege here from the waste above. Good thing that we had left to get supplies, but then none of you came inside, anyway. Perhaps we can make it appear that the Grahams punished you for marrying that English—"

"Nay." a voice boomed.

Reginald loomed at the light's edge. "You'll not harm her. You said if I did this you would give her to me."

Edmund rose to his feet with a sigh of exasperation. "I have explained this again and again. We can not do it the way we set out to, can we? Not with Fitzwaryn taking the lands, and her married to Ian."

"All the same, I swore to Robert to protect her."

"Hell, you poisoned the man. In comparison, for-swearing the oath you made to him is a small thing."

Reyna gasped. Reginald? Not Aymer, but Robert's trusted man?

"You made me do it," Reginald said.

"I made you do *nothing*. You wanted her and the gold, and you told yourself that he was old and would die any-way. Then you didn't even follow my instructions with the potion correctly, and so everyone knew he had been poisoned." Edmund turned apologetically to Reyna. "It was supposed to be quick, I promise you. It should have looked like a natural death." He shot a scathing glance at his brother. "At least the idiot had the sense to hide the herbal when people began suspecting you."

Outrage vanquished her nauseating fear. "You did this thing?" she said to Reginald. "Murdered your liege lord and friend? A man who trusted you without question?"

"He was old and would have died soon anyway," Reginald said defensively. "But you are not old, and I'll not let this happen."

Edmund threw up his arms. "Should we let her leave and tell her husband what she has learned?"

"She will stay with us and—"

"And he will bring a hundred looking for her. When he does, let him find her, but not able to speak. If you want to take her before we do it, I will not object."

Reginald hesitated and looked over at her, and Reyna felt her stomach heave. He turned back toward his brother, and the grip on his battle-ax tightened. "Nay."

A deep sigh issued from Edmund. "I suppose I've known for some time it might come to this." He stepped away, into the shadows, and emerged sword in hand. "Put the ax down, brother. Go up to the waste where the horses are sheltered, and take one and ride. You are out of this now, and I will deal with it."

"I can not."

"Nay, with the way you see the world, I suppose that you can not," Edmund said regretfully.

He lunged with his sword upraised.

It was a small space, and their battle moved near Reyna while they thrust and swung and paced around the pits obstructing their path. She balled herself up and cringed against the wall, forcing herself to watch so that she might avoid a swinging weapon that came too near. The chill of the stones matched that in her limbs, but she dreaded the end of this contest because whoever won, she would not be safe.

In the end, Edmund's willingness to kill a brother surpassed Reginald's. She watched in horror as the thrusting sword finally brought the bigger man down, the blade piercing the muscular chest. Reginald looked at his brother in shock as his body sagged and fell.

"You did not have to kill him," Reyna said, breaking the icy silence that followed.

"It is your fault. For coming here. You should have stayed in your knight's bed today. I had convinced Reginald that he could not have you now, not after he had grown impatient and ruined the chance to get you away. In Edinburgh there would have been time to convince you of the logic of it, but once you wed Ian . . . If you had not come today . . ." He looked down on Reginald. "I always warned him that his sense of duty would be the death of him."

His lack of grief terrified her. She clasped her knees to turn her body into a ball of sanctuary. Edmund walked toward her and she shrank back against the wall.

He smiled reassuringly. "Nay, not yet. Not here. Out

by the big stones, I think, so that your knight finds you easily. I don't want him coming in here to search."

"Perhaps he will not search at all. He was forced into our marriage."

"He will search for you. Forced marriage or not, he is quite taken with his virgin bride."

Her eyes widened.

He laughed at her reaction. "But of course I knew, little Reyna."

"Robert said he told no one."

"He did not tell me, but I knew. On that first visit I guessed what he was. Who he was. I knew for certain when I saw the books."

"The books? You said that you seek treasure, and not the books. If I am to die, at least explain this to me. What treasure? What gold?"

"Templar gold," Ian's voice said.

Reyna's heart leapt with relief. Ian emerged from the shadows of the passage, and the dim light illuminated the hard expression on his face. "Templar gold, from the Paris temple."

Edmund stepped to the center of the space between two pits, his grip whitening on his sword hilt.

"Be careful, Ian. He just killed Reginald, and he killed Robert too."

"I did not. Reginald—"

"By your instructions, and as surely as if you had thrust a dagger into his neck."

Ian unsheathed his sword. "Well, Edmund, I have never fought a monk before, but I do not mind the prospect at all. You are a very clever man if the books alone told you Robert's secret."

"I suspected long before. His time in the East and in France. His sudden appearance here with no history. The books only confirmed it. All the preceptors have a description of the property never recovered from the Paris temple. The gold and the library."

"So when you saw those rich volumes marked with the device J.M., you knew for sure. The library of Jacques Molay, the Grand Master of the Templars. Why didn't you just confront Robert and claim the property for the Hospitallers?"

Edmund laughed. "And give it to my order if he relinquished it? The monks of Saint John are rich enough. I was meant to have it. It was fated on the day those Templars sent it here with their young knight."

"They did not send it here for you or for the Hospitallers, and Robert knew that. It is not hard to see what occurred all those years ago. He was sent away to sit out the purge and wait for the order to renew itself. But it never happened, and Robert of Kelso found himself with a treasure that did not belong to anyone. Did he suspect that you knew who he was?"

"Nay, I was careful, and so was he. Too careful, which only piqued my curiosity. He never spoke of the Templars to me, or asked questions. Everyone else does, just as you did. That was how I knew that you had not guessed, despite your wife's virginity and Robert's vague history."

"Why would I guess? That order is long gone. If it were not for his similarity to you, I would have never wondered." Ian gestured to the passageway. "Leave now. If you move quickly you can be on the sea before I tell your crimes to the bishop and your preceptor. I give you the chance to walk away with your life."

The blond head angled back, and Edmund studied Ian with hooded eyes. Reyna's spirit recoiled from the cool evil emanating from the smaller man.

"You know where it is," Edmund said.

"I think that you are wrong about the gold, and Robert never had it. He would have considered the books treasure enough to protect," Ian said.

"You lie. You plan to take it for yourself. Do not expect me to let you do so. I told Reyna that I am willing to share. Let us put up our swords and become partners in this. Half for each."

Ian looked down to Reginald's inert shape. "I see how you deal with your partners."

"My brother needed to claim honor long after he had abandoned it, but you are not a man who indulges in self-deceit. We will work well together, Ian. With the other sins on our souls, the theft of this gold is a small thing."

His insinuations infuriated Reyna. "Do not presume to compare yourself with him, Edmund. You are a cold-blooded murderer, and—"

"You have not told her," Edmund interrupted with amazement. "Did you think to hide her up here and hope she never found out?"

Ian's eyes burned. Edmund grinned. "Should I tell her? I would never betray a partner, but . . ." he let the offer hang there.

"There is nothing that you could tell me that would make any difference," Reyna said, catching Ian's attention, trying to tell him that whatever decisions he made about Edmund, they should not be because of this.

"Is there not?" Edmund raised one eyebrow at Ian. "*Is there not?*"

Ian didn't move or speak, but his jaw clenched like a man expecting a blow. He glared at Edmund, but his silence spoke his response.

Edmund shook his head. "You moved from heaven to

hell in your choice of husbands, little Reyna. I learned about this one from one of his own men, a knight who worried that my interest in you was lustful, and sought to warn me off by explaining just how dangerous his captain could be." A wicked sneer distorted his face. "You damn me because of Robert and Reginald? Then what will you say to a man who killed his own father and bedded his own mother?"

She gasped in shock. She turned to Ian for his denial. An anguished expression flickered over his face, and he refused to meet her gaze.

"At least I committed my sins for a worthwhile goal," Edmund said.

"A goal worth dying for, I hope," Ian said. "Leave us, Reyna."

Edmund took a battle stance. "She stays. If she moves, I will cut her down."

Ian's eyes flashed. "Then let us be done with it, monk."

Reyna screamed when they engaged, and her eyes followed each swing of the swords while horror pinned her against the stone. Her mind chanted a reassurance that Ian was strong and skilled, but Edmund's wild determination appeared to double his danger.

Ian fought at a disadvantage, not accustomed to the placement of the pits, and he endeavored to keep the contest away from the wall where she cowered. Then Edmund drew first blood. A curse hissed from Ian as a streak of red blurred into his tunic. His fighting instantly transformed as he unleashed his full warrior's force.

She had never seen him fight before, had never seen the mastery those keen senses and sharp mind and lithe body gave him. Methodically, ruthlessly, he blocked every blow that the fevered Edmund offered. When

Edmund tried to move the battle toward her wall, a singing swipe from Ian's weapon grazed his upper arm, shearing off a patch of skin. "Go near her and I will cut you to pieces before you die," Ian growled.

Ian had several opportunities to end it, but he drew back each time, declining the thrust that would kill his opponent. Finally, two quick swipes incapacitated Edmund's sword arm and one leg. Edmund fell beside one of the pits, pressing hands against the wounds as blood oozed through his fingers.

Ian stood above him, the torchlight making him look like an angel of vengeance facing the damned in the flaming pit of hell. His sword hovered high, ready to take Edmund's head.

Reyna stared, her skin clammy from the hell of fear she had just lived. She watched the decision play out on Ian's furious expression.

If you do it, do it for Robert, and not because of what he told me, she urged with her heart.

With a curse, Ian kicked Edmund's sword aside and lowered his own.

Striding over to her, he grabbed the hem of her skirt and ripped. With the strips of cloth, he returned to bind Edmund's two wounds. Then he found some rope and tied the man's hands and feet.

He looked down at the surprised monk. "The temptation to kill and bury you here is strong, but I will let the bishop deal with you. I'll not be explaining the disappearance of a Hospitaller in these parts." He reached down and lifted a shovel. "And, aye, I do know where it is. Let your failure to find it be your hell."

Reyna's mouth gaped. Ian came and took her arm. "Watch the pits," he instructed while he guided her into the passageway.

"How did you know, Ian?" she asked as they stumbled along. "Robert a Templar—it is too fantastic."

"It all fits. A vow of celibacy that he kept secret. His arrival here about five years after Jacques Molay was executed and a few years after the order was disbanded. I suspect that he went to other temples for sanctuary first, but the pope's command eventually closed them all. And so he came here and waited to turn over what he had saved, but the day came when he knew it would never happen, and then that treasure became a burden."

"Why not just give it to the Hospitallers?"

"Most likely Robert did not want the Order of Saint John to have it. The Templars suspected that the Hospitallers had encouraged their suppression in order to enrich themselves."

They emerged into the sunlight. Reyna blinked up at the stone lintel. No ghost hung there.

"Is it true? You know where it is?"

He did not look at her. "I think so. We will find out soon if I am right." He propped the shovel against a stone, and withdrew a scrap of parchment from his sleeve. "It was in your Book of Hours. I think that Robert had some moments of lucidity before he died, and drew it. He planned to tell you what it meant. But the day he tried you were not there, and Reginald heard instead."

She looked at the lines and circles. "What is it?"

"A map. Not how they are usually drawn, but more accurate in its own way. David makes them thus. Look, here is the motte where we stand, and the square is the Black Lyne Keep." Holding the scrap he moved until Black Lyne Keep was positioned to them as it was to the motte in the map. "He would have needed some markers to know himself where it was later. This large stone perhaps."

He stood in front of the stone, then walked to the edge of the motte and peered down. "There," he pointed. "The depression in the ditch. These bisecting lines may either mean it is where they join in the ruins, or where they cross the circle of the ditch. Edmund has disproven the first possibility."

Taking the shovel, he walked directly down the slope of the motte, and Reyna hurried after him. Checking his position against the stone and the keep, he began to dig.

The hole had deepened considerably before the shovel met resistance. Ian excavated a rotting sack, and hauled it up. A faint glint showed through its worm holes. Reyna helped him pick at its tie, and her pulse quickened as the sack fell away. Her hands shook as she placed the contents on the ground.

Objects. Precious objects. A gold chalice embedded with blue stones, and two heavy gold candle holders. A treasure to be sure.

"From their chapel," Ian muttered.

The gold flamed in the sunlight. "Oh, Ian, they are beautiful."

"Aye. And very, very valuable." He thoughtfully paced away, hands on hips. He looked up at the donjon, where Edmund lay bound. "Hell."

"No one knows it is here but him and us," she said. "But if you want to keep it, you will have to give him some, or he will say that he came here to reclaim it for his order and you concocted the tale of his murdering Robert."

"He will claim nothing if he is dead."

"You did not kill him in the heat of battle. Would you return and do so now?"

"Why not?" he said harshly. "You heard what he said. A man with my sins is capable of anything. Especially for a prize such as this."

He looked at her for the first time since they had left the donjon. A blatant challenge burned in his eyes, daring her to react and argue. Daring her to condemn.

"I do not believe him," she said.

"You should. It is the truth."

"There is much I don't know about you, Ian, but the man I love never did such things, and it was not as he said."

"Close enough."

She had promised not to ask about his past. If he had not brought it up himself, she would have pretended Edmund had never spoken and just trusted her love in the Ian she now knew. But beneath its stony defiance, his expression held a pain that wrenched her heart.

"How close?"

He strode over to a candle holder and kicked it furiously. It flew and fell and skidded along the ditch. She calmly retrieved it. When she returned he was standing with the chalice at his feet, bitter resignation written on his face.

"I am going to tell you, but you are not going to like what you hear."

"Do you doubt my love so soon, Ian? Are you so sure what I will think?"

"I am sure, but I will tell you anyway, because it was not as he said, and when I lose you, let it at least be over the truth."

He looked toward the waste, as if organizing his memories and forcing them to his lips. "I told you once that I went to a neighboring lord to squire. He had a young daughter. She had hair like fire and skin like snow, and I worshipped her. All those years we rarely spoke and never met alone, because she was kept close with the women and protected. And so, I didn't really know her, but I loved her with a burning pain anyway. When I got older I would take others, serving girls and whores, and pretend I was with her, and then loathe myself for having dishonored her in my mind. By the time I expected to earn my spurs, she had reached marriageable age, but I knew that was impossible. I was a younger son, and she was not for me."

He had not said her name, Reyna thought. Nor would he.

"That last year, my father and older brother came to visit on their way back from Windsor. The estates were not far apart, but they had not seen the beauty she had grown into before that. My mother was dead, and my father not yet forty. He offered for her the first night."

"Oh, Ian."

"Aye, a moment of pure hell when I heard. Her family was delighted with the match. I swallowed it, but the notion of having the girl I loved as a new mother, the idea of her sharing my father's bed, made me sick."

"But you did nothing wrong. We can not be blamed for what our hearts feel."

"Jesus, but you are such an innocent, Reyna. If that were all . . ." His words were barely audible. "My father stayed. A betrothal was planned for a week later. I feigned joy for him, but it was an agony. For one thing, the girl who had never spoken to me was speaking a lot, suddenly. The eyes that rarely noticed me seemed always to meet mine. Finally, one day, while our fathers were out hawking, she sent me a message asking to meet me in the garden behind the keep."

"You went?"

"My legs took me there even while my head told me to stay away. I don't know what I expected, but I know what my heart secretly prayed for, and those prayers were answered, but by the devil. She kissed me, and I had no sense after that."

He glanced at her, and his look said it all. She did not have to ask what had happened.

"We were found there. The men returned while the hall was in an uproar and her mother was crying. My beloved was frightened and shocked into silence." His lids lowered. "Even when I was accused of rape, she didn't say a word."

"How could she remain silent when you were accused? I do not care how frightened she was, she should have spoken. Her great shock makes no sense."

"It will." Bitterness dripped in his voice. "My father had a quick temper, and it flared like an oiled torch when he heard. Then and there, in front of the whole household, he challenged me. I pled what innocence I could claim, but within an hour of holding that girl in my arms I found myself in the yard facing my own father with a sword in my hand."

A horrible thickness lodged in the pit of Reyna's stomach. She guessed how this tale would end, and almost urged him to silence to spare him the pain of telling it.

"She watched. They all watched. I had never experienced such fear and confusion in my life. This was *my father*, and he came at me with fury, and I was sure that I was going to die. But I was young and skilled, and we were more evenly matched than I expected. I do not know how long we fought, but finally he stepped back for a moment. In that pause, I looked over at her, and from her expression I knew that she had planned it, that she did not want the marriage, that she sought him maimed or dead and herself free of him, and that she had used me for that end."

"Why you? Why not one of the others there?"

"Perhaps she knew that he would be more rash with his own blood. Maybe she had heard that of the squires my sword arm was the best. Most likely she just recognized a fool when she saw one. I turned back and saw my father also looking at her. When his eyes met mine again, I knew that he had seen what I had. And I also saw that we had both been fools, that he had fallen in love with her too. Something went out of him then. You could practically see it fly away. I urged him to end it, but he did not. Perhaps it was pride, but I think it was despair. I hoped I could bring it to a draw. But we were both tiring, and our blows were getting careless. His guard fell, and he all but turned into my blade."

His jaw flexed and eyes narrowed. Reyna ached to say something to soothe him and ease the guilt written on his face.

"He did not die right away. I stayed with him, and we never spoke of her the whole time. He forgave me and made my brother do so too, and bid my lord come and dub me in his presence. Then he gave me some coin and told me to go to my mother's people, far away from the whispers that were already saying that I had lusted after my new mother and killed my father in order to have her."

"But it was not so. She was not yet tied to him."

"A small point, Reyna."

"An important one. You would have never . . . if the betrothal had been made . . ."

He turned smoldering eyes on her. "You are so sure? I confess I am not."

"I am. Nor did you seek to kill your father. How could people speak such slander?"

"People only know what they saw. This tale might

sound very different coming from another mouth," he said harshly, but the anger was not for her. "I made excuses for her at first. Tried to convince myself she had sought my death, not his. Perhaps she was not a maid, and my rape would provide an explanation for that. I found it impossible to accept that one so young could be so evil. But while I was in London, I heard that she had married my brother. The old lord or the second son would not do for her, but the young heir—that was different. I think that she wanted him from the start, and was dismayed to learn that the offer came not from the son but the father. So she needed my father gone before the betrothal, or the true prize would forever be out of reach. A son can not marry his dead father's wife."

"Does your brother know?"

"I wondered for a while if he had been a partner in it, but I can not believe it of him. But when I go to Guilford I will find out. And I will let her know that I know she killed my father as surely as I did."

"You did not really—"

"I did, Reyna. I accepted the truth of it long ago. I am grateful that you try to defend me, though. I thought that you would damn me for this."

He looked tired, as though the telling of this story had taken most of his strength. She embraced him and hoped he could feel her love. "How could I damn you? You were unjustly accused. Should you have offered your neck to your father's sword?"

"He gave me life. Most would say it was his right to take it away. I was not blameless, and patricide under any condition is unforgivable."

"Nothing is unforgivable," she said. "However, I think that you never forgave yourself. I think that you believed the deed had revealed and determined your nature and you let your soul drift without reflecting on where it went. But in truth your nature is warm and good, Ian. I could never have loved you if I did not sense that."

"Nay, love, not so good. You make me better than I am." He turned into her embrace and buried his face against her neck, as if he took succor from her warmth. "I should have shown more strength, and calculated what she wanted from me. It was a hard lesson, but I have been thinking that I learned it too well."

He finally set her away and lifted the chalice. "There is more, I think. Four lines cross the circle of the ditch. This is just part of it. I thought it would be a few hundred pounds' worth of gold. Nothing like this."

"I do not care what you decide to do. It belongs to no one."

"If I hand Edmund over to the church, he will probably never see justice. The ecclesiastical courts take care of their own, and they never execute their clerics. He will claim self-defense with his brother, and there is no proof with Robert. He will spin a tale that they will be glad to believe rather than condemn a Hospitaller."

"Easier then to give him some gold and send him away. He will leave Scotland if you demand it."

"It was you he wronged, Reyna. Your husband and friend whom he killed. Your life he endangered. Will this gold satisfy you that you have been compensated?"

Would it? The yellow metal glittered, offering to bury all pain in luxury never imagined. It worked its seductive magic on her in an insidious way, and excuses and rationales seemed to literally flow to her with its glow. If it had this effect on her, what did it do to Ian, who had pursued booty and plunder for years?

"You decide, Ian. I can not. You discovered it."

He ran his finger along her jaw and tilted her chin up. "It would secure our children's futures."

"Aye, that is so. You are right."

"Make this humble keep strong and safe, and buy a house in York or even London."

"Robert would have wanted us safe."

He gazed at the gold he held. "Then why do I feel this would be a worse theft than any ransom that I ever asked a town to pay? Keeping it, especially if it means giving some to his murderer—no justice at all for Robert, and not what he planned for this treasure."

She sensed the battle in him. It mattered not to her love which course he chose, but she wondered if it mattered to him in ways she could only guess. "So, what do we do, Ian?"

He ran his thumb over a blue stone. "Sapphires, I think." He sighed, shook his head, and smiled ruefully. "Ten years from now, if you are impoverished, I am going to curse myself."

Little wings of joy fluttered in her chest. "There will be enough for me here. Will there be enough for you?"

He turned his gaze and looked right in her eyes. The gold in his hand ceased to exist. "I love you with all my heart, Reyna. There will always be enough for me if you are mine."

He placed the chalice and candle holders back in the sack. "We will take these to the keep. Later, after I have sent some men to fetch Edmund, I will come back and dig up the rest. We will send Edmund and the gold and books to Glasgow. We will tell the bishop that the books are for an abbey school, but the gold is to be used to aid the poor and those displaced by war. If I make this sacrifice, I want to expiate a few of my past sins."

They walked up the motte to their horses. "I will miss the books more than the gold, I think," Reyna admitted.

"We will send only the ones with Jacques Molay's initials, so it is not all of them."

She grimaced. "That is all the philosophy."

"You know it by heart. You can spend the winters explaining it all to me, and I will argue against the logic. The debate should keep your memory fresh."

"My Book of Hours will have to go. I know that by heart too, but I will miss it."

"That one stays, I think."

"It bears the initials, I am sure."

"I looked before I came here. I saw no initials."

"On the first page—"

"I think not." He lifted her onto her saddle.

"Ian," she said, eyeing him suspiciously.

He looked up with a smile.

Dear saints, what a smile.

"There is such a thing as being *too* good, Reyna."

chapter

TWENTY-SEVEN

I will miss this," Reyna said lazily. She stretched her naked body against Ian's, and the flowers that he had entwined in her hair streamed amidst her tresses over her face and his chest. The late summer sun shimmered her skin with warmth. She soaked in the sensation, knowing that it might be months before they lay near the river like this again. Already some days held winter's chill, and the nights had cooled the water enough that she and Ian had ventured only a brief swim.

"Winter has its own pleasures," Ian said. "Furs by the hearth fire. Warm spiced wine. Very long nights."

"And I will get to wear my new gowns. It was kind of David to bring the cloth from Carlisle."

"They are lovely, although I wasn't picturing you by the hearth in one just now."

She giggled and propped herself above his chest. "Just as well you got rid of those books on philosophy, Ian. I remember there being sections warning against carnal pleasure. I never paid much attention to those parts, not having had experience in such things, but now . . . and those penitentials! Did you know that one of them forbade coupling on Mondays and Thursdays as well as Sundays, not to mention Advent and Lent and dozens of holy days?"

"I am fortunate that you never were swayed by such misplaced logic."

"Well, I was never very logical where you were concerned. You have a talent for making philosophy the last thing on a woman's mind."

He pulled her into an embrace, laying her along his length so that her toes tickled his shins and her breasts pressed against the firm warmth of his chest. With kisses and caresses he lured her back to the sensual dream they had recently left.

Abruptly, his hands stopped and his expression turned alert and concentrated. "A horse. Someone comes." He slid her away and knelt. "Cover yourself, Reyna. We have a visitor."

She had just pulled on her shift when the horse approached. She smoothed the garment down and blushed up at the smiling face of the Comte de Senlis.

"I have intruded," David said while Ian pulled on the old cut chausses. "I apologize, Reyna. They said at the keep I would find Ian here, and I am only passing by."

"I am the one you should apologize to, but it is good to see you. And this is an odd place to pass by, David, since we are on the route to nowhere," Ian said.

David swung off his horse, and Ian glanced pointedly at Reyna's gown. She bent and snatched it up.

David made a casual gesture. "Do not bother, my lady. I'll only stop a moment, and then you two can return to

your play." He settled himself down on the grass beside
Ian. "I am on my way to Harclow and then Carlisle.
Christiana and I will sail to London soon, and from there
to France. On my way back from Glasgow I sidetracked
to see Duncan. I just came from there. It was a pleasant
visit. I informed him of how things stand between
Morvan and the Armstrongs, and slipped in some words
about Aymer's kidnapping the ladies. Duncan knew
nothing about it, and I thought his fury at his son would
bring the hall beams down on us." He smiled. "I do not
think that you will have trouble from that side for a few
years, as long as Duncan lives."

"You went there from Glasgow? It is done then?"
Reyna asked.

"Very done. The bishop received the books and gold,
and gladly accepted your instructions as to their use. He
appears a good man, and I think none of that gold will
find its way to paying for his own comfort, which is always a danger with bishops."

She knew that if he had sensed otherwise he might
not have delivered the treasure to that particular bishop
at all. Nor would she and Ian have objected. In en-
trusting him with that duty, they had accepted his judgment.

"And Edmund?" Ian asked.

"Ah. Well, there was a little trouble there. Edmund is
dead." He looked at Ian directly, his expression inscrutable. "It happened on the way north. Because of the
gold, we took less-traveled routes, high roads mostly. On
one particularly treacherous path, his horse lost its foot-
ing. The fall was steep." He paused. "A tragedy. Under
the circumstances, however, it hardly seemed worthwhile to mention any of his crimes to the bishop, so the

whole story of Robert and the Templars and the source of the gold never was explained. I think that the bishop will be grateful for that. It would have been difficult to battle the Hospitallers over their claim to that property, if Edmund had decided to tell all and bargain for his life."

Reyna looked at Ian, who carefully studied their guest.

"We must thank you for your aid in this, David," Ian said. "It has delayed your return to London by several weeks, and dragged you all over southern Scotland."

"Merchants are accustomed to travel." He turned to Reyna. "Christiana charged me to remind you that we will return to London in the spring. She expects to see you there. And Lady Anna insisted I add that unless a birth is imminent, you are not to let Ian stop you from coming if you are with child."

Ian groaned. "That woman. I swear it is her quest to subvert all men."

"Nay. She just knows her strength and her worth, as your nymph knows hers. I doubt that Reyna needs any instruction from Anna."

Reyna blushed at this peculiar compliment. David rose and brushed off his garments. "I must go. Morvan and Anna will stay at Harclow at least another month before they sail for Brittany. I'm sure he will visit before he leaves. He has arranged for one of his knights to stay as seneschal, but he will rely on you to keep an eye on things, Ian."

They accompanied him back to his horse, where he opened one of the saddlebags. "This had been packed on a separate horse from the others, and I forgot about it while I was in Glasgow. You will have to keep it until someone goes north again." He pulled out the thick *Summa* by Aquinas and placed it in Reyna's arms.

Startled, she stared down at the huge tome cradled against her breasts. "We should really—"

"It is the one work the abbey school is sure to already own, my lady. It will not be missed." He swung up on his saddle and bent to clasp Ian's hand. "Until the spring, then."

They watched him trot toward the men and banners waiting in the distance. "I wonder if it was really an accident. About Edmund, I mean," Reyna said.

Ian's gaze had not left the group turning now toward the moss. "I'm sure it was an accident."

"Fortuitous, then."

"Some justice at least." He looked down at the book. "It may be a long while before I travel to Glasgow. Years."

"Something else to do on long winter nights."

"Aye, we can discuss philosophy part of the night and make love the rest. I might have never given it up if such a reward had waited in my youth. I shall have to finish rereading it, though, if I am to hold my own with you."

He led her back to their bed of grass. She sat cross-legged and opened the tome on her lap.

"Half the time for the mind, and half for the passions. That sounds like a fair division, Ian."

"I said part, not half. I have no intention of being fair. Especially not right now, since I think it is time to rebalance the scales that you tipped at Harclow."

He stood by her shoulder. She glanced up. From beneath those feathered lashes, the Lord of a Thousand Nights looked at her. His expression made her tingle with anticipation. Nay, he was not going to be fair at all.

He removed the book from her arms and set it aside on the ground. Taking her hand, he pulled her back up on her feet. He stepped to where he could see all of her.

"Remove your shift, Reyna."

ABOUT THE AUTHOR

MADELINE HUNTER has worked as a grocery clerk, office employee, art dealer, and freelance writer. She holds a Ph.D. in art history, which she currently teaches at an eastern university. She lives in Pennsylvania with her husband, her two teenage sons, a chubby, adorable mutt, and a black cat with a major attitude. She can be contacted through her Website, www.MadelineHunter.com, where readers can also find more information regarding the historical events and characters used in this novel.

Read on for a preview of
Madeline Hunter's
next historical romance
STEALING HEAVEN
on sale in August 2002

Marcus smoothed his palms over the stone wall's surface. Cleanly worked and neatly mortared, its facing and joints offered no toe-holds for in-truders who might seek to scale it. That didn't surprise him, since this thick curtain of rock protected one of crown's properties.

However, it also served as a barrier to some of Marcus's property, and scale it he would. It had been many years since he had played the thief, not since the hell of his youth, but one never forgets such skills. This wall would not keep him out.

He moved through the night, over to where the wall curved around a corner of the garden it enclosed. Here the flat stones could not be laid in straight courses and their corners would protrude. The best masons would finish the surface to be as smooth as on the straight sec-tions of wall, but most builders were not that fastidious. That was something else that he knew a thing or two about from the dark years of his youth.

His fingers swept the joints, and he found what he needed. The jutting edges were shallow, but deep enough for a body practiced in such things. Groping his way in the silence, he climbed upward until he sat straddling the wall. A convenient fruit tree grew near the corner, its branches like silhouettes in the full moon's light. He jumped over to it, his soft boots barely making a sound. With the stealth of a cat, he lowered himself into the early autumn smells that filled the garden.

He studied the bulk of the house, guessing how its chambers were arranged. Would she be in the large one on the second level, the one on the left indicated by two windows rather than one?

The vaguest sound interrupted his inspection of the building. He slid toward it along the wall until he could see a section of the garden not shadowed by trees. The bright moon displayed a little pool, its glittering surface dotted with fallen leaves. A woman strolled along the path surrounding it, pausing every now and then at bushes to touch one of the late blooming roses.

Her unbound hair, darker than the night, fell around her body, swaying with her step. She wore a straight, pale flowing robe with long broad sleeves. It was the sort of thing a woman might put on when she first rose from bed. He could barely see dark patterns on it indicating rich embroidery. The night was cool, but she did not seem to notice that the thin fabric offered little warmth.

She moved toward him, close enough that he could see her moonlit face. Pale of skin, and large in eyes and mouth, it appeared mysterious, and matched the descriptions he had been given. One of the knights who had brought her from Wales had called her a moon goddess, and the praise had been apt. Her subtle glow cast a spell on the garden. And on him.

She paused in her stroll, not more than ten paces from where he lurked in the shadows. "I know you are there. Go back the way you came, and no one needs to know that you dared such a thing."

Her voice was quiet and melodic, steady and unfrightened. But then the princely blood that flowed in her veins would neither quicken nor slow easily, for any man or any danger.

"I know that you are there," she said again. "I can smell that more than plants are in this garden."

He could smell her too. Something freshly earthy, a memory of spring, floated on the small breeze along with the scents of dying leaves and flowers.

He stepped away from the wall. She heard him, and turned.

"Who are you? Not a thief, despite your furtive arrival, if you make yourself known."

"Nay, not a thief."

"Whoever you are, it will go badly for you if you are discovered here."

"For any man but me, maybe so. But something that is mine is here. I am Marcus of Anglesmore."

She reacted. Barely, but it was there, a vague stiffening. She gave him an encompassing glance, from head to toes. "What is here is not yours."

"Nay, not yet. Soon, however, since the illness that has confined you these last weeks is clearly over." There had been no illness, of course. Only a long lie. He had always suspected as much, and her barely clothed presence in this chilled garden proved it.

She cocked her head, and regarded him as if she could see him very clearly in the dim light. "It took you long enough to decide to find out how serious this illness was. Perhaps you do not welcome this either, and prayed the malady was fatal."

Her perception surprised him, although he had never prayed for her death. He simply had allowed the ruse to continue until the insult it implied had conquered his reticence.

He did not know why he had reacted so strongly

against the offer of this girl. After all, the marriage promised power, and the favor of the King, and a chance to prove Anglesmore's loyalty beyond any doubt. His response had come from deep inside his soul, perhaps a rebellion by the part of him that knew how to scale garden walls in the night. It had made no sense, but still an inexplicable resentment had seethed in him ever since hearing King Edward's plan.

Until now.

He had hoped that seeing her would soothe that rebellion, and it did. She was not childish, as he had feared. She possessed a poise and confidence far beyond her young years. She had not screamed for guards or her women on discovering his intrusion.

She was not running away now, even knowing who he was. That was a good sign.

Perhaps a very good sign.

He walked over to her. She took one step back, but no more. He lifted a strand of her silky hair, and then pushed all the tresses back over her shoulders so he could see her face better. The moon's light did not illuminate her much and the subtle details were invisible, but he could tell that his first impression, that she was beautiful, had been correct.

"I find myself thinking that I should thank my king," he said.

"You can barely see me."

"I can see enough to know you are lovely."

"And that alone reassures you? You are a man easily appeased, if a woman's beauty is enough to satisfy you."

"I see more than beauty, and I find myself pleased, not appeased, that is all."

"Aye, the true prize is the land and wealth that go with this marriage. A bride's beauty is merely a sweetmeat added to a full meal. It is the way with such things, I know. But the favor of a king always has its cost. Do you understand the price of this banquet?"

He understood. But, oddly enough, that was not the part that he had resented. "The duty that Edward gives me is a small cost, and his to demand of me even without the prize."

"With that duty goes danger."

"That is also the way with such things." He stepped closer, and deeply inhaled her spring scent. Rich. Full of sensual fertility and the delicate odors of flowers. It reminded him of carefree days as a child, when the warmth of May promised freedom and play and joy. "It is very sweet of you to warn me, though." He touched her face, and slowly skimmed his fingertips down the curving line of her heart-shaped face.

Very little space separated them. He could decipher the patterns on her robe now, and their intertwining Celtic lines. She did not retreat from his touch, but merely looked into his eyes. Hers were dark pools glimmering like the pond at their feet. He felt a subtle tremor beneath his fingers, but still she did not pull away.

Something invisible and wordless passed between them. A mutual sharpening of awareness. A recognition, and acceptance, of what was to come. Images of that possession entered his head, and the garden shrank to a very small space fully occupied by a stark intimacy.

"I remind you of the danger for your own sake," she said. Her words came low and halting, as if she knew that what filled the air made everything else irrelevant. "It would be a pity if the knight standing in front of me died soon."

He smiled at her warning. Then again, perhaps it was meant as a threat. Right now he didn't care which it had been. His thoughts were on other things. He rested his entire hand against the warmth of her face. She did not pull away, and a heavy silence beat between them.

His thumb wandered to her lips, and brushed their full, velvet swells. "Why do you dislike that notion? Does the knight please you just as you please him?"

"You appear handsome enough, and not as brutish as I expected."

"Not brutish at all with you, I promise. Here, I will show you." He bent and kissed her alluring mouth.

She did not react with shock or surprise. Just a small hesitation stiffened her. Then a subtle yielding seemed to sneak out before she could catch it. She might have lost a debate before arguing very far.

He had intended it to be a small kiss, a gentle first step to reassure her. Her acceptance served to fuel his simmering blood, however, and the small kiss became a long one. He took her face in both his hands and gently tasted and nipped until a barely audible sigh breathed out of her and into him.

He gazed at the face he held. Her expression, heavy lidded and bright eyed, appeared unbearably sensual in the moonlight. Desire began a fierce pounding through his head and body and the same primitive excitement pulsed in her. He felt it. He almost *heard* it. It flowed around them and between them and in them, luxurious, tantalizing, and seductive.

He should leave. He should woo her slowly the way a good man does his intended. He should not take advantage of her ignorance, and her vulnerability after her first kiss.

He knew full well how a chivalrous knight should behave. Instead he pulled her into his arms.

Shock this time. Confusion. "I do not think . . ."

He silenced her with another kiss, and caressed down her back. She was naked beneath the thin gown, and the feel of her feminine softness and warmth, of her full, invisible curves, inflamed him. Her body moved in reaction to his touch, both retreating and encouraging all at once. He pressed her closer, enclosing her in his arms, and turned his kisses to her neck. She gasped quick breaths, a series of tiny, astonished announcements of delight.

And then, with a pliant stretch, she surrendered and impulsively embraced him back.

She intoxicated him. Her scent, her body, the kiss she returned, maddened him. In his mind he was already on the ground with her, sliding the robe off, warming her with his hands and mouth, covering her with his body. Kissing her still, he lifted her in his arms and carried her to a bench near the wall.

He settled her on his lap, swearing he would only dally a bit more and then take his leave. But the feel of her on his thighs and the new closeness of her body, so available beneath the thin robe, defeated that moment of good sense. Nor did she resist. The kisses turned mutual and hot and savage. Passion made her wild and her abandon became audible. For an instant, no more, she hesitated one last time when he slid his tongue into the moist warmth of her mouth.

He wanted more. Everything. Now. He caressed to her stomach, then higher to the swell of her full breast.

A startled, muffled cry escaped her. She broke the kiss, gasping for breath, and leaned away as she shook her head. It looked less like a denial than that she sought to clear her thoughts.

"This is wrong. A mistake," she whispered.

He eased her closer again while he smoothed his

fingers over her breast's tip. Its erotic peak hardened more at his touch. "It is permitted. We will marry soon."

"Nay, we will not."

She disentangled from his embrace, jumped from his lap, and began to run away. He grabbed for her, but caught only a thick strand of trailing hair. Still, it stopped her. She froze, her back to him, her shoulders still trembling from the passion they had shared.

"Come back to me. You know that you want to."

"What I want is a small thing in this. In *all* of this."

"Not to me. Making you want me, and then fulfilling your desire, will give me great pleasure when we are wed."

"You and I will never wed."

"We will. Very soon. I will not permit more delay now that I know what is waiting."

She glanced over her shoulder. "It must have been the full moon. It makes some women mad."

"Nay, it was the pleasure. That too makes some women mad, and you are one of them. If Edward had not given you to me, I would fight to claim you now anyway."

She walked away. It made her hair yank in his hand, and he released it.

She gave him one last look. "Now the moon is making *you* mad. The King's man should not be swayed so easily by a kiss in a garden."

Nesta rose from her bed, sleepless again. Naked, she walked to the window and peered down at the spot where she had recently behaved very stupidly.

She should stay away from moonlit gardens. They kept getting her into trouble.

Marcus would return in the morning. She did not

doubt that. He would come, and demand entry, and no tale of illness would work this time. He would come to speak of the betrothal, or just to woo his lady, but he would be here all the same.

That was going to complicate things.

A muffled sound distracted her, and she turned to the bed. A dark head rose and darker eyes blinked away sleep. "Are you awake still?"

"Aye. Go back to sleep," Nesta said.

"You should put on a robe, or wrap yourself in a blanket."

"I do not feel the cold as most others do. You know that."

"Still, you might take ill. That would be a fine thing, and hard to explain a real illness after this long false one. And it might keep us here."

"Nothing will keep us here."

The head sank back into its pillow. "I have been told that he is very handsome."

"Not handsome enough. No English knight would be."

A deep yawn filled the chamber. Nesta turned back to the window. In her mind's eye she saw a man standing near the pool, tall and strong and young, with a stimulating vitality in his aura. Aye, very handsome, and exciting enough to take her breath away and turn her knees to water. But still, not handsome enough.

It had been her own fault, what had happened down there. She should have screamed when she heard the stranger in the garden. But the punishment for such a trespass would be severe, and she did not like the thought of bringing it on some poor soul who might only seek to steal a few apples to ease his hunger.

Only it had been no poor soul, and a very different hunger that she had confronted.

Her fingers drifted to her mouth, and the memory of those kisses filled her mind and body. Titillating sensations crawled deeply in her again. A mistake to permit that, but who ever expected him to be so bold? Or so compelling as he approached her with command and confidence, the moon finding lights in his dark blond hair and the depths of his dark eyes captivating her.

Nay, it had been the moon's fault too, not just hers. And the garden, and the night. There was danger in the beauty of such places. They seemed removed from the world, and full of a magic that made people do unthinkable things.

He would come in the morning, eager to see her in the light of day. And he *would* see her, because she did not have time to escape by then.

She imagined that meeting.

Perhaps she had not been so stupid after all. He had said that he would not delay any longer with this marriage, but tomorrow would change his mind. After he saw her, *really* saw her, it would take a few days at least for him to accommodate himself to this marriage again.

And before he had done so, she would be gone.